THAT ONE
CIGARETTE

A novel

by Stu Krieger

Harvard Square Editions
New York
2017

ISBN 978-1-941861-44-8
Printed in the United States of America

Published in the United States by
Harvard Square Editions
www.harvardsquareeditions.org

For Hillary, Gus and Rosie

The lights in my life's lantern

"Some men see things as they are and say 'why'? I dream things that never were and say 'why not'?"

—*Robert F. Kennedy, inspired by George Bernard Shaw*

1963

— 1 —

IT WAS HIS PRIZED POSSESSION, the very first thing he owned that made him feel like a card-carrying adult: a 1960 Philco Predicta with a blonde wood cabinet and hi-fi speakers, flanking a gleaming twenty-one inch picture tube. "The Townhouse model," the salesman down at Beckman Brothers called it. Ed Callahan loved that TV. It was tangible proof that, in the league of life, he might not finish in the cellar after all.

Ed's cue to start his morning ritual was the sound of his wife Bonnie clicking that television awake as she made her way to the kitchen to fix breakfast for their two kids. The calming voice of the *Today* show anchorman Hugh Downs told Ed it was time to get his backside in gear.

Facing the sagging plaid couch they'd inherited from Bonnie's mother, the Philco was the focal point of the couple's living room. Its proximity to the kitchen allowed Bonnie to listen to Hugh and newsman Frank Blair as she slapped together peanut butter and jelly sandwiches and poured bowls of sugary cereal.

Already behind schedule because his bum knee begged him to remain in bed five minutes longer, Ed quickly buttoned his short-sleeve white shirt and grabbed a fresh pack of unfiltered Camels off his dresser. Ripping open the cellophane, he pulled out a cigarette, sparked it with his favorite lighter, and hustled out buckling the skinny black belt that held up his pressed khaki slacks.

Sailing into the kitchen Ed found Bonnie setting a plate of toast, glistening with melting butter, in front of their kids. Seven-year-old Kenny, with his hair slicked back and an orange and white striped shirt tucked into cream-colored slacks, gazed into his cereal bowl mesmerized.

"Look, Daddy, my Trix turned the milk all pink. Ain't that neat-o?"

"*Isn't*, honey," Bonnie corrected, "the proper word is isn't."

Ed nodded to acknowledge his son, snatched a wedge of toast from the pile and exhaled a long plume of smoke.

"Oh my stars, Ed, must you smoke at the breakfast table? You know it's not good for you; I been tellin' you that for ages, now it says so right here in *Time* magazine."

Before Ed could respond, Bonnie plucked the latest issue, folded to a specific page, off the counter and moved toward him. The article had one paragraph neatly underlined in red ink. Ever the thwarted schoolteacher, if Bonnie had a point to make, she was going to come at you armed with indisputable facts. "Meeting at the National Library of Medicine on the campus of the National Institute of Health in Bethesda, Maryland, Surgeon General Luther L. Perry and his committee have been compiling evidence since late last year to support recent findings that there is an indisputable link between chronic cigarette smoking and an alarming increase in lung cancer-related deaths," Bonnie read.

"Are you gonna die, Daddy?" asked ten year old Libby with a tremor of terror.

Bonnie jumped in. "No, sugar cube, Daddy is not going to die because he's going to stop smoking right this very day. Aren'tcha, Ed?"

"Sure thing. Or at least very soon." Ed took the percolator off the stove, grabbed a mug from the cabinet above the sink and filled it with steaming coffee.

"I'm serious," Bonnie said.

"Me, too. Tell you what," Ed said patting the pack of Camels in his shirt pocket, "I'll finish this pack and when it's gone, I'm done. For good."

With a sunburst of gratitude Bonnie threw her arms around Ed's neck and asked if he really meant it.

"What's the point of all this if I won't be around to see my grandbabies?"

Bonnie gave Ed a passionate kiss that made Libby blush; Kenny crinkled his nose and snorted. "Ew, don't kiss! It's sick'ning!"

Breaking their embrace, Bonnie looked at Kenny and giggled. "You should be glad we love each other. It'll only make life easier on you."

Ed downed his coffee while Bonnie cleared the dishes, prodding the children to collect books and jackets. On the television in the background, Frank Blair was reporting on an erupting dispute between the Congo and the Soviet Union. Hardly paying attention, one thought skipped across Ed's mind: what the heck is "the Congo?"

Bonnie handed her husband the sack lunch she'd grabbed from the refrigerator, gave him a peck on the cheek, and escorted the kids out the door. While Kenny struggled into his cardigan, having trouble finding the second sleeve drooping off his shoulder, he excitedly reminded Ed he'd promised they could work on Kenny's Pinewood Derby car that evening. Ed grinned. "It's a deal."

Reveling in the solitude, Ed took a last luxurious drag on his cigarette before grinding it out in the Alamo ashtray beside the toaster.

"Morning, Oak!"

He glanced up to see Marsha, his mother-in-law, shuffling into the kitchen in her pink-and-white checked housecoat. The large pink rollers in her salt-and-pepper hair and the puffiness under her eyes told Ed she'd just woken up. "Oak" was the nickname she'd given him when he and Bonnie started dating in Ed's last year of high school. Bonnie off-handedly told her mother that what she loved most about Ed was his solid dependability and Marsha quipped, "Like having your very own oak tree."

"Can you believe Thanksgiving's but a week away? If time flew any faster, I'd swear the world had sprouted wings. You wait and see, we'll blink and it'll be 1964."

One thing Ed learned in the five years since the then-newly-widowed Marsha moved in with them was that, once she was off and running, he didn't need to respond. Marsha would blithely carry the conversation all by herself. She grabbed a mug, filled it with coffee and continued: "Big surprise: Louis and family are too busy to come down. I talked to him last night. Long distance. He says he's swamped at work and Ellen has something with her Ladies Auxiliary – although, what those ladies actually do is beyond me. Plus, apparently, Billy has a football game. Can that be right? Who plays high school football Thanksgiving weekend?"

Ed remarked that many schools did; Marsha espoused her disapproval. "Well, in any case, I thank the Good Lord I have y'all to be with or I'd be out on the street like some hobo woman. Heaven forbid."

Ed set his mug in the sink, grabbed his car keys off the pegboard, and told Marsha to have a good day. Lost in thought, she drifted to the Formica table and settled into one of the chrome chairs with its candy apple red plastic seat.

Backing out of the driveway, Ed stared at the flaking paint on their two-bedroom ranch house on Jimmydee Drive. The lawn needed mowing and the flowerbeds needed weeding but there were never enough hours in a day. He rolled down his window as he turned onto South Story Road; the distinct autumnal smell in the air carried Ed back to when he used to walk a similar route to school.

Growing up seven or eight miles away in suburban Dallas, he'd planned on being a fireman. Until he got tackled by a sophomore grizzly bear from Waco during his senior year Homecoming game, completely shattering his kneecap. The damn thing never did heal right despite three surgeries his parents could ill afford. The army didn't want him and the fire academy couldn't take him because he lacked the necessary stamina. During one test, he had to drop fifteen yards of heavy hose when his knee buckled near the top of a twelve-foot ladder. And that was the end of his dream.

His father didn't earn enough managing their local Piggly Wiggly to send Ed to college and, besides, he had no idea what he would have studied. He and school never had been a great fit. He was much more focused on girls and football than civics and mathematics. The only kind of social studies Ed cared about was learning how to convince Bonnie Lee Bismark to date him.

After high school, Ed worked as a delivery boy at his uncle's pizza parlor quickly getting promoted to manager. He somehow saved enough to buy Bonnie a tiny diamond ring and asked her to marry him on his twenty-first birthday. Five weeks after their small wedding at his father's Elks Lodge, Bonnie told Ed she was pregnant. Libby was born in early '53 and Kenny came along three years later. They knew they couldn't stay in their tiny one bedroom apartment, but, even with Bonnie working the evening shift at Skillern's Drug Store four nights a week, they couldn't foresee any way they'd ever be able to afford a house. Ed was working for a company that filled book orders for schools statewide. After eighteen months, he'd worked his way up to Assistant Warehouse Manager but he was still only making $2.75 an hour.

And then Bonnie's father dropped dead. The poor bastard was only fifty-one years old when a massive heart attack knocked him to the showroom floor at Patio World, just as he was about to close a sale on a six-piece white wicker ensemble with cobalt cushions.

Marsha dove into a spiraling panic. She had no marketable skills, had never worked outside the home and Lloyd somehow forgot to keep up with his life insurance payments. The only thing Marsha owned was her compact house on Bowman Street but she was terrified of living there alone.

That was how the Callahans came to buy their house. Marsha sold her place, gave a healthy chunk of cash to Bonnie and Ed as their down payment, and took up residence with them. It meant she'd share a bedroom with her grandkids, but Marsha didn't mind. She felt she could handle almost anything as long as she didn't have to navigate life alone. Despite repeated declarations that she was ruining their lives, Ed and

Bonnie did all they could to reassure Marsha she was a welcome and helpful presence in their home.

Now they'd been in the house nearly five years. Kenny was a Cub Scout. Libby took tap dancing lessons at the community center. One of the kids' most beloved rituals was to be bathed and in their pajamas by 8:00 p.m. on Thursdays to watch *The Flintstones* before Marsha hustled them off to bed while Bonnie was at work.

Ed still felt an electric twinge in his crotch when he thought about Bonnie. They'd been together since high school, married for eleven years, but he felt great pride, not to mention a modicum of awe, in the fact that she was his wife. Sometimes during a quiet night at home, he'd look up to find her mending the kids' socks or cutting coupons from the *Times-Herald*, her dirty-blonde ponytail fastened by her favorite plastic Scotty dog hairclip, and he'd wonder what it was she saw in him. Reflecting on his "radar-dish ears and slightly bucked front teeth," Ed thought she definitely could have done better for herself; he only hoped she never figured that out.

When the guys at work would gripe about their wives' spending or whine about how they practically had to beg for sex, Ed felt nothing but gratitude. Bonnie truly was his best friend but he didn't dare say that out loud. The last thing he needed was his Book Depository buddies razzing him, calling him a big homo.

Back at the house, Bonnie and Marsha sat at the kitchen table having one last cup of coffee before they had to get moving. Bonnie was due at Skillern's by 2:00 p.m. and would work until 8:00. Marsha would greet the kids' school bus and make dinner. When she got home, Bonnie would grab a plate of leftovers, always back in time to kiss her children goodnight.

Before getting ready for work, Bonnie had several loads of laundry to do. Marsha was meeting a girlfriend for lunch. She'd stop by the market on her way home and pick up a fresh head of lettuce for a salad to accompany the pot roast defrosting in the Pyrex on the countertop.

"Talked to your brother last night," Marsha said.

"Let me guess: they're not coming down for Thanksgiving."

"Bingo." Marsha touched her index finger to the tip of her nose. "He makes three bucks more than God, has banked more vacation days than Queen Elizabeth, but heaven forbid we should ever be his priority. And forget Christmas. They're goin' to her folks. After they get back from Aruba. Must be nice, I tell ya, must be nice."

"We'll have a wonderful Thanksgiving, in any case. Ed's folks are coming, plus we invited Nate and Lucy."

Marsha asked if Nate was still planning on marrying "that woman"; Bonnie said it was happening on New Year's Eve. Ed was the best man.

"If Ed truly is his best buddy, he'll warn poor Nate that that gal will bring him nothing but heartache. Don't he see the way she's on him every minute?"

"Mother, Nate needs a girl like that."

"Honey, trust me: nobody needs a girl like that. She's got more opinions than a gypsy fortune teller and never knows when to keep them to herself. Yes, she's awful pretty, bless her heart, but pretty only gets you so far."

Filling the sink with hot water, Bonnie busied herself doing the breakfast dishes as Marsha glanced at the newspaper. "President's coming to town tomorrow," she said. "Jackie, too. Talk about pretty! That gal has more style than Grace Kelly and Oleg Cassini combined."

Gliding along the freeway in his '56 Ford Fairlane, Ed pulled a Camel from his shirt pocket, punched the dashboard lighter and waited for the cylinder to heat up. Sticking the cigarette between his lips, he heard the lighter's familiar pop and plucked it out. With its neat concentric circles glowing a deep orange, Ed pressed the filament to the end of what Bonnie sneeringly referred to as his 'coffin nail;' he reveled in a deep inhale. The instant he sucked the smoke down into his lungs, he felt that euphoric rush the nicotine never failed to deliver. He knew it was a filthy habit, but quitting wasn't going to be easy. He'd been smoking since he was sixteen and loved the ritual, the comfort. Taking that last drag and grinding the butt out on his boot heel made him feel like a man.

Ed recalled his first cigarette, with Nate when they were fourteen; Christmas break, sophomore year. Nate stole a pair of Marlboros from the cigarette box on his parents' living room end table. The night was unusually cold for Dallas. They were in the woods up behind Nate's house, wearing identical denim jackets from the downtown J.C. Penny's, every button buttoned, collars upturned. Nate was taller than Ed and always about ten pounds heavier, but most folks took them for brothers. Ed had pilfered two cans of Budweiser from his parents' refrigerator and he and Nate were going to drink the beers, smoke the cigarettes and swear like a couple of bad-asses while they fantasized about groping Francie Yerman's huge tits.

Of course, they choked on the smoke and grimaced drinking the beer, but when they reminisced later, they called it one of the coolest nights of their lives. From then on, they were eternally bonded: two East Dallas rebels searching for a cause.

Now Nate was finally getting married. His fiancé Lucy Wallace was a true southern belle. Born in Memphis, raised in Louisville, she moved to Dallas to work as a buyer at Dillard's and met Nate at a "Ladies Drink Free" night at Rusty's Saloon. Ed and Bonnie agreed Lucy was a bit rigid, often acting more like Nate's mother than his girlfriend, but they also believed no one but a take-charge woman could get Nate Stokesberry to the altar.

What made Ed most uneasy about Nate marrying Lucy was her huge collection of porcelain dolls. There was something about their painted faces and yellowed frilly gowns that made Ed sweat every time he entered Lucy's apartment. They literally gave him nightmares: he'd be alone at her place and the dolls would come alive, cackling hideously as they turned their evil eyes on him. He'd wake up with his heart about to pop like an over-inflated balloon.

Ed sucked vigorously on his cigarette and exhaled the curl of smoke; he swiped uncomfortably at his armpits to combat the prickly sting of perspiration that erupted whenever he thought of Lucy's creepy collectibles. Realizing he was about to miss his off-ramp, he swerved across two lanes to exit the freeway. Heading for the book depository parking lot, hearing an unsettling scraping behind him, he knew it was the tailpipe dragging. The wire he'd rigged to hold it up must have broken when he veered to catch the ramp. Checking his watch, Ed saw it was 7:56. No time to deal with the tailpipe now; he couldn't afford to be late. His boss Roy Truly was a decent guy who seemed to like Ed but with nineteen warehouse men to manage, Roy liked to keep things running shipshape.

Pulling into his regular parking spot parallel to the chain link fence, Ed saw his coworker Junior Jarman arriving in his Chevy station wagon. Ed snatched his sack lunch off the passenger seat and hopped out. "Morning, Junior. How they hangin'?"

"Tight and to the right, just the way I like 'em."

Both men chuckled. Junior was clutching a black metal lunch bucket with a union decal on the butt end. That thing had more miles on it than a '51 Dodge.

Junior had been working at the book depository on and off for years. For a while he left and went to work at Parkland Hospital; Ed wasn't sure what sent Junior back to the warehouse. They never socialized outside the job but were friendly enough at work. They ate together once or twice a week in the second floor lunchroom or met in the domino room to play a quick game of bones as they gobbled their sandwiches and guzzled Dr. Peppers.

Leaving the parking lot, the two men crossed several sets of railroad tracks. Ed made a point to stop and look around the boxcars to ensure no oncoming train mowed them down.

"See the morning paper?" Junior asked. "President's motorcade's gonna pass right on by just after noon tomorrow. If we time it right, we're like to get a look at him on lunch break. Course, I ain't been too crazy about the man since he nearly got us into World War III over that showdown with the Rooskeys —"

"The Cuban Missile thing? Heck, Junior, he did what needed to be done. Otherwise that maniac Khrushchev would've bombed us to Kingdom Come."

"Looks to be one helluva procession: Johnson, Governor Connally, Mrs. Kennedy, too, I believe. Going by us heading to some fancy VIP luncheon at the Trade Mart. Must be nice, flying around on private jets, riding in limousines, having folks cheer ya just for showing up."

"It all looks like a giant pain in the butt to me. Can't belch without it turning into front page news."

Minutes later, Ed and Junior moved past the loading dock and slipped through the rear door of the Texas School Book Depository. Heading for the basement stairs, Ed spied Roy Truly hustling across the plywood planks lining the first floor. Ed offered a 'good morning' and a chipper wave. Spying Ed and Junior, Roy grinned and nodded.

Ed stuck his lunch in his basement locker and hung up his corduroy jacket. Junior was at his own cupboard a few feet down. Closing his locker door, Ed turned and nearly collided with a skinny, pale fellow he knew as Lee. Seven or eight years younger than Ed, he'd only been working at the depository about a month. He always seemed to move without making a sound.

"Sorry," Ed said as he sidestepped the newcomer.

Lee nodded, remaining silent. Ed could see the yellow stains in the armpits of Lee's once-white T-shirt that was now the color of an exhausted Brillo pad. Lee swiftly moved up the steps and disappeared. Turning toward Junior, Ed shook his head and chuckled.

"Jeez, even on our crummy salary, you'd think the kid could spring for a clean T-shirt."

2

BRIAN SCOTT STEPPED OUTSIDE to check the weather before dressing for his classes at Saint John Fisher College. Grumbling to himself about the only town he'd ever called home he knew he sounded exactly like his father. Why was Rochester often baking in the morning and then freezing by early afternoon? There had been plenty of Halloweens here in Upstate New York when Brian went trick-or-treating in his shirtsleeves one year but then the next had to cram a bulky winter parka under his Mighty Mouse costume, fretting about ruining the whole effect.

On this particular late November Thursday, Brian left his parents' house not knowing if the black clouds overhead meant rain or snow. He wore his yellow slicker but threw a heavier coat onto the back seat of his '59 Renault Dauphin.

After Brian's three-hour class, the sun was shining so he slung his raincoat over his shoulder. Absently rubbing the dimple in his chin he looked to the classmate beside him. "I don't know, this whole college thing? Not convinced it's for me. Sure it's only been three months, but seriously, I'm dying. I hit my classes, go home, bug the crap out of my little brother, and that's about it. Pretty sad."

His buddy suggested Brian might enjoy things more if he lived on campus.

"My old man says it's a waste of dough. We only live six miles from here. I mean, he's got the cash if I pushed it…"

As Brian let the thought drift off, his compatriot hustled away to his next class.

From the time he was ten years old, Brian wanted to be a doctor but it required so much school. Everybody told him he was smart enough, but lacked focus and discipline. He'd skated through high school exerting very little effort but still managed to graduate near the top of his class. He had the fortunate ability to retain nearly everything he read but had never applied that skill to a particular passion. The appeal of a career in medicine was the lure of big money and the respect that came with it. His Uncle Nelson was a cardiac surgeon; he had a bigger house and took nicer vacations than anybody Brian knew.

Halfway to his car, Brian had an epiphany: maybe he should join the army. He recalled seeing a recruitment table near the student union. The guy in camouflage fatigues with a fire-hydrant neck was talking to an eager senior about this golden opportunity to see the world. That might be exactly what Brian needed – some perspective, adventure, the chance to get his head on straight. Pivoting, he headed up the hill toward the quad.

The guy at the table decorated with red-white-and-blue bunting was a different fellow than the one Brian had seen previously. If that first recruiter was a former all-star tackle, this one was a quarterback. Tall, lean and all muscle, he looked like he could snap Brian in half with very little efffort. The soldier introduced himself and launched into his pitch before he finished shaking Brian's hand.

"You've seen the posters, Uncle Sam pointing his finger? I want you! It's true; we do. And you know the great thing about enlisting? You don't make friends, you meet your brothers."

Brian was completely taken in. Sergeant Bowers talked at him for nearly a half-hour and answered every question with vigor; he wouldn't let Brian leave without taking his card.

"Just so you know, brother, I don't go after everybody this hard. That's the truth. But you're the kind of kid we need. I see it in your baby blues. Bet they drive the ladies crazy, right? You're a thinker, Brian. A leader. I got more sheep than I can handle; what I need is a few more shepherds. Are you ready for the adventure of a lifetime?"

Brian pulled his red Renault into the driveway on Woodside Lane and parked behind his mother's Studebaker. He sat contemplating, running his fingers through his wavy chocolate hair. Heading into his two-story white clapboard home, the sergeant's sales pitch rang in Brian's head.

Opening the back door into the kitchen, he heard his mother's lilting alto. He recognized the song immediately: "Till There Was You" from *The Music Man*. The Broadway show had recently become a hit movie. It was his mom's second favorite soundtrack behind *The Sound of Music*. She loved to sing along to both original cast recordings, especially when she was baking.

Brian found his mom at the cutting board, rolling pin in hand, working the pleats out of a homemade piecrust. A dish of sliced cinnamon-coated peaches waited on the counter nearby. Nancy looked up at her oldest son with a blazing smile. "Here's my best guy! Home from the sawmill. How was Biology?"

"Biological," Brian said.

Why give a straight answer when you can be a smart aleck?

"Your brother's at soccer practice, dinner's at six. Unless he gets stuck in some awful staff meeting, Dad should be home by 5:45."

"And that's the up-to-the-minute news, Nancy Scott reporting."

Pulling the pie plate closer, Nancy lifted her delicate crust and folded it into the tin; she pressed it into place, scoring the edges with a fork. She offered to fix Brian a snack, but he said he'd just grab an orange and get started on his homework.

Rolling out the second crust to top the pie, Nancy glanced to her sky-blue hi-fi and picked up the song where she left off. "There were bells, all around, but I never heard them ringing... 'til there was you."

Peeling the fruit he'd snatched from the refrigerator, Brian grabbed his book bag and headed for his bedroom. Both sides of the plywood-paneled hall were lined with framed photos of him and his younger brother Johnny from infancy to last summer. Brian was convinced that because his father worked for Eastman Kodak, his mother felt it was her duty to take enough pictures to single-handedly keep the company afloat.

Brian locked his bedroom door, threw his books on the floor and collapsed onto the bed to devour his orange. As he finished, licking the sticky juice from his fingers, his mind began to replay its most frequent mental slideshow: images of Karen Peterman. She was the girl Brian had been madly in love with since sophomore year of high school; even if he didn't have her as his girlfriend, he did possess a pair of her panties.

Pushing off the bed, already half-aroused, Brian moved into his closet to part the row of shirts hanging on the back bar. He tugged an old Boy Scout backpack off a recessed shelf. Pulling out a crinkled manila envelope that once held his Pony League All-Star certificate, he opened its fragile clasp and extracted its prize: a lemon-colored pair of silk underwear.

Falling backward onto his bed, Brian dropped the inside-out panties onto his face and took a deep inhale. Although he was no longer sure if their scent was real, or simply a sense-memory embedded in his brain, he unzipped his pants, dug into his underwear and pulled out his thickening dick.

He'd replayed the moment so many times, by now it was like a scene from his favorite movie. It was October, right before Homecoming junior year. Karen was hosting a flower-making party to work on their class float. Folding Kleenexes, stapling them in the center and fanning them out into tissue-paper flowers to adorn their float was a ritual that went on at different kids' homes for weeks before the parade. The girls did most of the work while the guys goaded each other, wrestled and drank smuggled-in beer. Karen was dating a football goon who would appear every five minutes to give her a possessive mauling kiss that made Brian crazy.

The class president and the math genius were at the kitchen table tweaking the float's blueprint. Brian couldn't believe his eyes. All the miniscule details and endless hours those guys put in for a stupid homecoming float? Who would even care?

Feeling restless, wondering why some gorilla was kissing the girl that should be his, Brian wandered down the hall; almost by accident he came upon Karen's bedroom. On impulse, he ducked in and closed the door, guilty and excited to be in her private space. Its smells enveloped him: perfume, cherry lip balm and teenage girl. He pushed open the sliding closet door and discovered a laundry basket with the lemon panties on top.

Back in Karen's living room, Brian kept one hand shoved deep into the pocket of his dungarees, convinced that if he didn't, the purloined contraband would rocket out on its own to reveal itself to his friends and classmates.

Arriving home that night, he went straight to his room, turned the underwear inside out and inhaled for hours. It was the first time he'd smelled those intoxicating female odors and when he came, it was the most convulsive orgasm of his young life.

Two years later, the panties still held him in their thrall. They symbolized danger, a touch of forbidden excitement. As he grabbed a wad of Kleenex to catch the explosion of milky lava, Karen's underwear on his face like a cockeyed burglar mask, Brian heard his mother sail past his door: "There was love, all around, but I never heard it singing…'til there was you."

What Brian didn't know was that a short time later, Nancy was locked in her walk-in closet upstairs doing all she could to muffle her heaving sobs. It was a secret rite she engaged in three times a week. She'd be working in the kitchen or vacuuming one of the boys' rooms when a crushing sadness would rise inside her like a tidal wave. She feared if she didn't give into it, she might simply disintegrate.

When the sobbing subsided, Nancy had a second part of the ritual. She'd slink into her bathroom, lock the door and press a cold, damp washcloth to her eyes to reduce the redness. She'd reapply eyeliner, pucker up for a fresh slash of lipstick and return to her domestic duties. Five minutes later, she'd be singing again.

Moving to his desk to crack his *American History (1492-1700)* textbook, Brian became fixated on a sound bleeding into his consciousness. It was a repetitive thump…thump… thump. Like the hyper-magnified drips from the leaky faucet keeping Donald Duck wide awake in one of Brian's favorite cartoons.

Springing from his chair, he bolted into the hall. As he sailed into the kitchen, the thumps grew louder, coming from right outside the kitchen door. Brian barreled out like an enraged bull and found exactly what he was expecting: his fifteen-year-old brother. Wearing a Spaulding fielder's glove, Johnny was repetitively throwing a tennis ball against the closed garage door calling the play-by-play.

"It's a high pop-fly to centerfield, but, don't worry: the dependable Johnny Scott is under it. He makes the grab ending the inning!"

"Hey, moron, did'ja ever think some people might be trying to study?"

Johnny heaved the ball and jockeyed to grab it out of the air. "Who's stopping ya?"

"You and that noise. It's like a sledgehammer to my brain."

"Maybe you need to take a Midol and relax."

Brian zoomed down the back stairs with such fury that Johnny froze, holding his gloved hand out in surrender. "Okay, I'll stop."

Brian hit the brakes. "You'd better. Or I'll give you a

wedgie that'll turn your balls bluer than your Yankees cap."

Pulling into the driveway in his prized 1962 Buick Electra coupe, John Scott groaned. He was convinced his across-the-street neighbor, Marsh Ditlow, stood at his front window waiting for John's approach before going out to get the day's mail. Climbing out of the car, John fumbled with his briefcase doing his best to look preoccupied, knowing his charade was for naught.

"Hey, neighbor! How's every little thing in your Kodachrome world?"

"Fine, Marsh," came John's lifeless response.

"Got a second?"

John knew if he tried to demure Marsh would only persist; it was easier to surrender.

Minutes later, they were standing in Marsh's spotless garage as he showed off his latest purchase. "It's a Lawnboy. D'you love it? Snow gets sucked in here, blown out there and – presto – you've got a spanking-clean driveway without breaking your back. They call it the Snow Thrower. Fantastic, am I right? I can't wait for the first blizzard to try it out. You should get one, sport. You can afford it."

"I've already got two Snow Throwers: Brian and Johnny."

"Well, if you're content living in the Stone Age, my friend, suit yourself."

When John came into the kitchen, Nancy was at the stove basting a roast beef.

"I don't know why I let that guy get under my skin."

"Marsh again? I've told you, honey, you simply need to avoid him."

"I try! He's like a fungus. No matter what you do, it appears. And it's, it's that thing he does; I talk to him for two lousy minutes and end up feeling like everything I'm doing with my life is wrong."

Nancy took his briefcase and gave him a kiss. "If it's any consolation, he and Louise never have sex."

"How in the world do you know that?"

"She told me. Flat out. We weren't even drinking wine. One minute we're talking about artichokes at Wegman's and the next she's in tears wondering when she got so undesirable and old. Apparently, he goes months without touching her. I'll bet that pompous windbag is keeping a little something on the side."

While John passed the mashed potatoes and Nancy sliced the beef, Johnny helped himself to creamed corn. Brian announced he was thinking of joining the army. Nancy stopped mid-slice. "What? You just started college. Why in heaven's name are you considering the military?"

"Why not? Seriously, I can see the world, do something good for my country, and when I get out they'll pay for school."

"You wouldn't last four days in the army," Johnny said.

Brian whirled to slam a fist into his brother's arm. Johnny cried out, "Dad, did you see that? He hit me! For no reason."

"That's enough," Nancy snapped. "Both of you." She returned her attention to Brian. "You really need to think about this, honey. The military's no day at the beach."

"What're you going to do when they send you to Vietnam?" John asked.

"What? Where's that?"

"In Southeast Asia. In case you're not aware, there's a good chance we'll soon be engaged in a full-blown war over there."

"The recruiter guy didn't say anything about a war."

"I'm sure not. Look, even if it hasn't been officially declared, that's hardly any comfort to the families whose boys are already coming home in body bags."

Later, settled on the family room couch to watch *Perry*

Mason, Nancy looked to John. "Do you think he's serious about this?"

"Hard to say. You know how he is. He gets an idea in his head and off he goes."

"But what you said at dinner, about a war, you were just trying to scare him, right?"

"Oh no, it's very real. They're claiming the only folks there are 'military advisors' but what does that mean? Our presence is supposed to stop the spread of Communism, but what if they don't back down? Kennedy already called Krushchev's bluff once; maybe the second time won't be the charm."

"Then we just have to tell Brian he can't enlist. I'm not going to have my son sent off to some god-forsaken part of the world to die."

At his bedroom desk, Brian rolled his neck and glanced at his watch: 9:00 p.m. After reading about mitochondrion and lysosome cells for the past forty-five minutes he was beginning to feel like he was going insane. He closed the biology book, capped his yellow highlighter, and dropped to the floor. He started doing push-ups like he was back at a Pittsford High baseball workout. He was panting, his arms burned, but he didn't stop. Thirty. Forty. Fifty. He collapsed on the rug, working to get his heavy breathing under control. And then with the same frenzy, he flipped over, hooked his feet under his bedframe and began a vigorous set of sit-ups. When he was done, his abs were taut and tender; he felt much calmer.

Hopping up, Brian yanked open his closet door and gazed into the full-length mirror. He sucked in his gut and threw back his shoulders. He tried to snap off a crisp salute like Kirk Douglas in *Town Without Pity* but knew his first attempt was pathetic. He tried again, holding his shoulders tighter. He saluted once more.

This time, he really liked the image staring back at him.

3

THE THING DAVID GOLDMAN HATED most was waking up to realize he had no idea where he was.

Coming back to awareness, battling through the fog enveloping his throbbing head, the first thing he heard was the sound of a television coming from another room; the *Today* show with Hugh Downs. David cracked one eye to scan the small, cramped bedroom. Nothing looked familiar. Staring at the gold swirls on the wallpaper he momentarily felt like he was having a stroke. He sat up and opened his other eye. Scanning the room, he was relieved to find his clothes folded into an unsettlingly neat pile on the seat of a straight-back chair. Glancing at his watch, David's heart started to race. It was 8:32 a.m.

Mentally reviewing his day, David remembered he had a graduate student due at his office at 10:00. Without knowing exactly where he was, it was impossible to calculate how long he'd need to get to campus. He craved a shower and food to settle his stomach but wasn't about to do any of that at the home of his unknown host. Wondering what he was thinking the previous night, the answer was painfully clear: he wasn't thinking at all.

David pulled up his slacks, tucked in his wrinkled pinstriped white shirt, and fastened his belt. He dropped onto the edge of the bed, tugged up his socks and tied his wing tips while trying to conjure a picture of the person who'd greet him when he emerged from the bedroom. He was drawing a total blank.

He'd been at Corky's Tavern across from *The Herald-Examiner* to grab a quick drink after his evening class. David liked that bar; it was dark and anonymous, filled with alcoholic newsman and ink-stained editors who cared about nothing more than getting drunk in peace.

"Well, good morning."

David's head snapped up. The stocky guy standing in the doorway had a thick dark moustache. His belly hung over his boxer shorts and he was wearing black socks pulled up to his calves. David felt his face turn scarlet. Staring at the carpet, he responded with a curt, "Hello."

"Somebody slept well." The man chuckled.

David nodded. A suffocating silence nested between them.

"Can I, uh, may I fix you something to eat?"

"No. No, thank you. I, I need to get going. Work." David snatched his tie and black sport coat off the back of the chair and moved forward with an awkward smile. "So, uh…anyhow…." Looking down, he moved past his host into the hallway. "I'll…you know, thanks." He started off to his left. The man chuckled again, seeming to revel in David's discomfort.

"If you're looking for the door, it's that way."

David reversed course and barreled into the living room.

"By the way, it's Nolan, David. My name's Nolan."

Gripping the doorknob, David pivoted just enough to give Nolan a nod and then yanked the door open and sailed outside. Struggling to get his bearings, David spied the intersecting corner streets: Cochran Avenue and Edgewood Place. Was that Wilshire up ahead?

He dug into his pocket, thankful to find his keys. Now all he needed was his car. He walked along Cochran past several apartment buildings and modest homes. At last, he spotted his Plymouth. He glanced at his watch. 8:46 a.m. The best thing he could do was get acclimated, get to USC and make a beeline for any spot on campus selling a muffin and a huge cup of coffee.

The street he thought was Wilshire turned out to be Olympic. He knew he could use that to head east to Hoover and still get to school in time to grab a quick bite and settle

into his office before the scheduled grad student showed up
with his usual endless litany of questions.

Exhuming the rest of his day's agenda buried in his foggy
brain, David realized he was slated to have dinner at his sister
Lisa's house. He was glad he kept a clean shirt at the office. If
he showed up in the wrinkled, stained shirt he currently had
on, Lisa would be all over him, badgering him about settling
down instead of living like a rebellious teenager. "You're thirty-
three years old, David. You need a wife; you need to start a
family. You're a college professor who should be focused on
teaching, writing and molding young minds which you could
do with more diligence if you had a bride."

He knew she meant well, but he already had a Jewish
mother in New Jersey. He'd moved three thousand miles away
to escape her, only to have his little sister follow him to the
West Coast, carrying the maternal mantle on her delicate
shoulders. Still, he was willing to put up with every moment of
Lisa's nagging if it meant he got to spend time with baby Gina.

At only three months old, Gina Rose Kaufman was already
the light of David's life. He swore they bonded the first time
he held her in Queen of Angels hospital. Her eyes focused on
his and held there without wavering. Then she fell sound
asleep in his arms making precious cooing noises. David loved
everything about her, the way her soft skin felt, the way she
smelled – she was a gift from God. "Good gravy," David said
out loud, "now I'm crying."

As the tears slid down his cheeks, he fought to keep focus
on the road while searching the glove compartment for a
tissue. He couldn't help wondering why he was such a mess. A
vision of Nolan in his underwear and black socks jumped into
David's head. He relived the sex, urgent and sweaty. Finished
in minutes. A searing wave of shame threatened to drag him
down into the dark mental muck.

By noon, David walked into the lecture hall feeling back in control. He'd downed several cups of black coffee, changed his shirt, had his meeting with the inquisitive grad student, and was now ready to pontificate on the root causes of the First World War. It was part of his current undergraduate class, *World History of the Twentieth Century.*

David was an engaging and popular professor. His classes were peppered with visual aides and entertaining anecdotes; he did his best to try to connect the past with corollaries relevant to his students' contemporary lives. He was also well regarded among his colleagues and on the path to tenure. He was working on a book about the Jewish American immigrant experience in turn-of-the-century New York. The project grew out of an interview he'd done with his grandfather a few years earlier, looking to capture that bit of family lore before the old man passed. The majority of David's research was done, he had a firm outline and a clear sense of where he wanted the book to go; all he had to do now was write the darn thing. If only he could find twenty extra hours each week.

When the class ended, the students departed locked in animated conversations. It was their unrestrained enthusiasm for the most mundane details of their lives that David found so touching; they practically percolated with unfettered optimism. Too bad they have no idea life is lurking around the corner waiting to kick them in the teeth.

As he packed up his notes, David spied a reticent student hovering in his peripheral vision. "May I help you?"

She giggled and twisted her big toe into the linoleum. She wanted to know if she could write about General Franco for their paper on the rise of Fascism even though they hadn't yet covered him in class.

"Since I'm certain the majority of your classmates will write about Adolph Hitler, it would be a welcome relief to have you focus on Franco."

The student thanked him, then blurted, "Okay, I know this is out of line, but if I worked up a detailed outline before I start the essay, is there any way you'd look it over and give me notes?" David informed her that that was his teaching assistant's job.

"The thing is, I really need to get an A this semester because forever I've wanted to do my graduate work at Harvard and that won't happen unless I do amazingly well here."

"Okay, yes. I'll review your outline. Drop it by my office when it's finished."

The girl gushed with thanks, then vanished before he changed his mind. Buckling his briefcase clasp, David heard his colleague Charlie Yamamoto's voice in his head. "The reason you get approached for this kind of malarkey is because you're too nice, David. You let them take advantage of you. Doesn't happen with me; they enter my office like they're taking their final steps to the electric chair. And that's how I prefer it. You need to learn to say no."

David heard variations on this rant every time he and Charlie were together. David knew he was a soft touch. So what? He wanted his students to like him; he got into this field to see them succeed. He also knew that if he stayed busy, he was less likely to wake up in a stranger's bed.

Lisa Kaufman darted into the first-floor powder room at her home in Sherman Oaks finding it hard to believe that having a few moments alone to pee had become the highlight of her day.

As soon as her intense-but-relatively-brief four-hour labor was over, Lisa knew Gina was going to be her easy baby. Gina's older sister Debbie had inflicted twenty-four hours of nonstop, searing contractions before making her debut. Even her first child Michael's delivery took thirteen hours. Gina was a calm observer from the get-go. As long as she was being held, all was right with the world.

Sitting on the couch giving Gina a bottle of formula as *The Guiding Light* flickered on the TV, Lisa knew she needed to revel in this rare peaceful moment. Soon, four-year-old Debbie would be up from her nap, they'd hurry out to meet Michael's school bus and it would be chaos until bedtime. Her husband Martin was a wonderful man, a great provider, and a loving dad, but not much help on the domestic front. He made the money, tended to the yard and during baseball season took Michael to a half-dozen Dodger games. What more could a man be expected to do?

Standing with the perky saleswoman in a boutique on Ventura Boulevard, David held a set of plastic stacking rings in one hand and a jack-in-the-box in the other. The clerk asked to be reminded of David's niece's age. "Three months tonight. That's what we're celebrating."

"Frankly, I'd take the rings. The jack-in-the-box is a classic but tends to scare the dickens out of children. Parents crank the handle, "Pop Goes the Weasel" tinkles, then that clown springs up and the tykes get hysterical. I mean, honestly, is it a toy or a certified instrument of torture?"

David chuckled. "I'll go with the rings."

As the saleswoman wrapped the gift in bright yellow paper dotted with buoyant red balloons, David raked his fingers through his gnarled curls, worked to press his short sideburns into place; he smoothed the front of his pale blue shirt. After having survived the day on little sleep and a backbreaking load of Jewish guilt, the last thing he needed was an inquisition from his baby sister. He hoped she wouldn't notice his prickly stubble.

Driving to Lisa's two-story white-shingled home on Vista del Monte, David's mind wandered to the book he was currently reading, *From Russia With Love* by Ian Fleming. The main character was a dashing undercover spy, James Bond. David knew the novel had recently been turned into a film but he had no intention of seeing it. He preferred to hang onto the Bond that lived in his head.

David's fascination with spy novels started when he was a teenager. Because he was a college professor, often calling himself an "alleged intellectual," these books were a cherished respite from the more scholarly tomes he read for work. *The Thirty-Nine Steps* by John Buchan was another favorite but David hadn't seen that film either. He didn't care that the supposed master Alfred Hitchcock directed it; he was convinced it would let him down.

David was well aware of why he loved these formidable secret agents with their cool demeanor and multiple identities; each possessed qualities he'd never have: they were unflaggingly brave, cocksure, and determined to seduce any woman they encountered.

Lisa was in the kitchen adding a splash of olive oil to the kettle of boiling water when the doorbell rang. She heard the thundering footsteps of Debbie and Michael racing for the staircase.

Moving into the living room, Lisa snatched Gina out of the playpen. Debbie and Michael were right behind, squealing out guesses about who might be at the door.

"Uncle David!" Debbie and Michael shouted as they wrapped themselves around his legs. David handed the gift to Lisa and reached for baby Gina. "Come on, give her up. I need to hug that little bundle this instant."

Eying the present, Michael piped up. "Is that for me?"

David cradled Gina in the crook of one arm and reached into his pocket with his free hand. "Afraid not, champ." He opened his hand to reveal two quarters. "But I do have…twenty-five cents for you and the same for Debs!"

Michael grabbed the quarters, doling one out to his sister declaring they were rich. Lisa told them to run upstairs and put the coins into their piggy banks before they got lost. The kids eagerly obliged. As soon as they were gone, Lisa waved the gift at David. "You know, you can show up without a present."

David hoisted Gina into the air and lowered her to his face until their noses touched. She emitted a tiny giggle so pure and sweet it broke David's heart.

Pacing the kitchen floor holding Gina to his chest, David watched Lisa slice a loaf of French bread. She asked how it was possible that Thanksgiving was only a week away. David reminded her she still hadn't told him what he could bring.

"Grab two pies from Marie Callendar's, apple and pumpkin. I'm sure you heard the folks are driving to Aunt Ruby's. Mom's told me forty times already – between boundless whining about how you and I moved across the country to ruin her life."

David looked over the top of the baby's head. "Is she asleep?"

Lisa nodded. Gina looked completely at peace in her uncle's arms. David asked who else would be joining them for Thanksgiving.

"Ken and Marilyn and their two kids…Martin's parents, of course – oh, and did I tell you? I invited my friend Joanne." Seeing David's blank look, Lisa went on. "You know, Joanne from my painting class. I've told you about her: she's smart, funny, really pretty. She works at Yamashiro as the evening hostess." Lisa raised an eyebrow. "And she's single."

Feeling his face flush, David turned away.

"Honestly, David, you need to find a bride. And, you know, you really should shave before work. What kind of an example are you setting for your students?"

Later, after a delicious dinner with homemade strawberry tarts for dessert, David sat with his brother-in-law in the den. Lisa was upstairs putting the other kids to bed as David gave Gina a bottle of formula. *Dr. Kildare* was on in the background. David asked Martin about work.

"All of a sudden everybody's listening to Dinah Shore, wanting to see the USA in a Chevrolet. And ya know what? Whatever it takes to bring them in is okay by me."

Martin was partnered in a Chevy dealership in downtown Burbank with Teddy Winslow, his UCLA roommate. When they set out to name their business six years earlier, they'd tried to come up with a catchy hybrid of their names but Martin feared any variation on Kaufman sounded too Jewish. "Not that I'm ashamed," he said, "but why shove it in people's faces? We're in Burbank. If we were in Encino it'd be a whole different ballgame."

In the end, they simply called it Winslow Chevrolet.

As Martin prattled on about the latest fancy features on his favorite new models, David's attention drifted to the television. He got lost in thoughts of playing doctor with Kildare.

When Lisa rejoined them, it was time to get Gina up to her cradle in the master bedroom. Martin was anxious to move the baby into the antique oak crib waiting in her own room, but Lisa wasn't ready to let her go. "She's our last baby, Mart; please let me spoil her a bit longer."

As Lisa lifted the sleeping infant from the warmth of David's arms, Gina woke up. Her heavy lids blinked a few times and then snapped wide open. Fixing on Lisa's enamored face, Gina broke into an ear-to-ear grin. David was ecstatic. "Oh my God! Did you see that? It was a purposeful smile for her momma, her first true smile. And I was here to witness it!"

Driving home through Beverly Glen Canyon, David was on the steep incline that peaked at Mulholland before taking a sharp downward grade to Sunset. It wasn't the quickest way back to his Silver Lake bungalow but, on this particular night, it was the route he felt the need to take.

Approaching the top of the mountain, his mind was whirling. He thought about lectures to prepare and letters of recommendation to write. He worried that the Yamashiro hostess Lisa invited to Thanksgiving would assume he was a prospective husband. He envisioned Nolan in his black socks before recalling a young man with haunting green eyes he'd picked up late one night on Santa Monica Boulevard. And what about that Midas Muffler Man? A two-fer: brake job and a blowjob. David doubted if that kid was even eighteen.

Stomping on the gas pedal, he was getting closer to the hairpin turn where he'd have a light-dappled view of the San Fernando Valley in his rearview mirror while the open, empty canyon appeared in front of him. All he'd have to do was drive over that rim and it would all be over. The shame. The guilt. The self-loathing. He'd never have to admit anything to anyone.

He'd sail into the air, finally free.

HOLDING HER INFANT daughter's sweaty head against her shoulder, Rima Kashat was trying to suppress the baby's screams. Overhead, a rickety metal fan pushed around hot, stale air without offering a modicum of relief. Rima paced and swayed; she was humming, cajoling, and pleading. Nothing she did calmed seven-month-old Adiba who'd been bawling since the sun had risen over Baghdad five hours earlier.

Across the room, Rima's three-year-old, Shemma, looked up from where she was exuberantly scribbling purple shapes. "Make it stop! It is too loud."

Fighting her own urge to cry, Rima assured Shemma she was doing her best. Receiving a dubious sneer in response, Rima glided down the hall to her bedroom and closed the door. Adiba continued to scream, her tiny tomato face flush with despair.

Rima felt totally incompetent. She had no idea what she was doing wrong. She silently asked *Allah* why she had been burdened with such a wretched child.

Although she was only twenty years old, Rima had been married for four years. Her husband Hadi was fifteen years her senior, the son of her mother's cousin. He owned a small tailoring shop in downtown Baghdad, inherited from his father. Rima had been promised to Hadi two years shy of her high school graduation and was commanded to drop out before finishing. The farthest she had ever traveled was to visit relatives in neighboring Kuwait. Now she was a mother of two, trapped in her sweltering bedroom with an infant who refused to be consoled.

In his one room shop off Rashid Street, Hadi was measuring a neighbor for a new suit. As the men chatted, Hadi scrawled measurements on his notepad with exacting care. Trying to sound nonchalant, the neighbor inquired about Hadi's brother Emad, wondering if the family had any updates on his whereabouts.

"The consequences of my brother's actions affect us all yet Emad does not seem to grasp this," Hadi said. "He is gone, leaving me to look out for not one family but two."

In early February, Prime Minister Abdul Karim Qasim had been overthrown in a violent coup spearheaded by the Ba'athist party. Qasim had taken refuge in the Ministry of Defense where the fighting was brutal. Simultaneously, hordes of Communist sympathizers took to the streets to resist the coup. The clashes caused heavy casualties. A day after the overthrow, Qasim was executed despite his pleas for safe passage out of the country. He received a swift mock trial and was immediately put to death. Coup leaders displayed his body on national television.

It was reported that more than 5,000 Iraqis were killed in the three days of fighting. Members of the National Council of the Revolutionary Command conducted house-to-house searches attempting to ferret out any Communists who had fought against them. Emad was one of those joining Qasim loyalists in the street skirmishes. Realizing he was a marked man, he abandoned his family to take refuge in a remote mountain village. His wife had not heard from him in nine months.

Already responsible for a wife and two daughters, and now expected to also care for his older brother's brood, Hadi seethed with resentment. "His rash choices," he said as he knelt to measure his neighbor's inseam, "burden me with undue stress amplified by an infant who wails around the clock like a tormented rooster."

Unable to quiet Adiba, afraid she might be driven to some

unspeakable act of violence, Rima dressed her younger daughter and brusquely jammed her into the rusting stroller inherited from her sister-in-law. Pushing the infant into the living room, Rima barked at Shemma who was still on the floor with her stubby Crayolas, telling her they were going to visit *Jiddo* and *BB*. Shemma pranced across the rug to grab her stuffed dog, announcing that her grandfather was sure to have sweets for her.

As the trio walked the three blocks to Rima's parents' home, Adiba continued to howl. Passing neighbors shook their heads in sympathy. Seeing the pained look on Rima's face and the exhaustion in her eyes, one neighbor clucked her tongue, remarking that only a child with evil in her soul could cry with such vehemence. Reaching her parents' walkway, Rima spied her mother out on the front porch awaiting them. "I could hear you a mile away. No other baby has the lungs of my Adiba."

Rima pushed the wailing cargo to her mother. "Please do not act as if this is a blessing."

Nazik gave her daughter's arm an empathetic pat, then stooped to embrace Shemma. "How is *BB*'s angel?"

"Where's *Jadda*?" Shemma asked. When told her grandfather was at the park playing chess, she slumped. "Then who will give me sweets?"

Glaring at his apprentice, Hadi slammed the deficient bolt of gray wool onto his workbench. "I tell you to get me fifteen meters, you bring me ten?"

"That is all they had," the young man replied.

"Should I tell Mister al-Hussaini I could make his coat but not trousers? I can make him a suit with only short pants like an English schoolboy? I have promised him his order tomorrow afternoon; if a man cannot stand by his word, his business will evaporate like a mirage!"

With a ferocious bang of his fist, Hadi ordered his assistant to go out and find another fabric seller who did have fifteen meters of gray wool, forbidding him from returning until the task was completed. Despite having no idea where to go, the boy exited and hustled up the street.

The instant the apprentice was gone, Hadi locked his front door, scooted to the cabinet below his sewing machine and extracted a buried treasure from beneath a pile of cloth: a book he had acquired from a black market boutique. It was filled with secrets Hadi longed to learn: *The Art of the Female Orgasm*.

Rima sat at her mother's table having tea with fresh mint from Nazik's garden. Cross-legged on the floor, Shemma sat with a weighty book of Arabic art open in her tiny lap; although she was only three, something about its colorful images captivated her. Knowing the expensive book was a treasured gift from her grandmother's wealthy older brother, Shemma turned each page with delicate precision. Rima was amused to see her daughter take in the pictures like a credentialed art historian. Mesmerized, Shemma gawked at a portrait of a mysterious dark-eyed woman in crimson robes and a blood red veil covering her mouth; it was labeled with a single word Shemma could not yet read: *Death*.

Much to Rima's relief, her mother had finally gotten Adiba quiet. Singing softly, Nazik gently rubbed the sleeping baby's belly. Recalling the ancient lullaby from her own childhood, sadness swelled in Rima's chest. She wondered why she would never be as capable and strong as her *Mama*. As if she knew what her daughter was thinking, Nazik said, "She cannot help but absorb tension through your touch. If you relax, she relaxes. It is no more complex than that."

Rima wished she believed it was that simple.

Gently easing the sleeping Adiba from the couch to a blanket on the floor, Nazik stood to face Rima and Shemma.

"Come now, my loves. It is time to offer afternoon prayers."

As Nazik knelt on her mat in quiet supplication, Rima and little Shemma were behind her on their mats following along. With covered heads and open hearts, they praised all that was good and holy in their lives.

Gazing at her sleeping baby, an evil thought put a stitch in Rima's heart: she is so beautiful when she sleeps; why can she not stay asleep forever? Nazik's voice cut through Rima's fog. "Did you not hear me? I asked if you and the children might stay for lunch."

Rima replied that she had to get home; Hadi would be there soon and insisted on having his midday meal waiting, and the children already fed, when he arrived so he could dine in peace.

Reaching for the art book her grandmother had put up on the shelf, Shemma lost her tentative grip on it. The heavy volume hit the floor with a firecracker slap. Instantly, Adiba was bawling again. Rima unleashed her fury on Shemma. "Look what you have done!"

Shemma burst into tears. Overcome by a cresting wave of frustration, Rima also began to bawl. Nazik looked from her crying daughter to her hysterical grandchildren. She brought the baby from the blanket to her shoulder, patting Adiba's heaving back. As the trio of wailers continued their discordant song, Nazik swayed and danced with the baby until she found herself facing the doorway. Frozen like a crystal figurine, her husband was gawking at the melee in his home, his face filled with bewildered distaste. "What is the meaning of this?" Faraj barked.

"I am afraid, my love, it is the price you pay for siring a lineage of females."

Closing up his business early, Hadi paid a visit to his parents on the way home. His father Omar, the founder of the tailoring shop, had expected to pass it on to his elder son.

Emad rejected the family trade to embark on a career in the oil fields. Although Emad's refusal to come to work with him had been a blow to Omar's pride, he and his wife knew Emad was too restless and hot tempered to ever make his living seated behind a sewing machine. He was a large, burly man with thick fingers and a brusque manner ill suited to customer service. Hadi was much more his father's son: creative, blessed with an innate sense of style.

After several years in partnership with Hadi, Omar retired a year earlier at the age of sixty-nine. Two months later, he suffered a devastating stroke. He was now confined to a wheelchair, barely able to speak; the few words he could muster were unintelligible. The true tragedy was that it was evident Omar's mind was still very much alive. When conversations swirled around him, his eyes would flash, his mouth would twitch; muted grunts that no one was able to comprehend would escape from his dry lips. He'd occasionally try to write his thoughts but, born a southpaw, his left side was severely impaired. Writing with his right hand left him so frustrated hot tears would glide down his leathery cheeks.

Being unable to help the man who had given him life tormented Hadi. His father seemed like a miner imprisoned in the collapsed cave of his body; Hadi couldn't imagine a more horrible fate. Sitting with Omar under an orange tree in his parents' backyard, he relayed random tales of his day. Without realizing his monologue had veered from the mundane, Hadi found himself voicing his deepest fears to his mute *baba*.

He told of a recurring nightmare about the government minions who were hunting his brother. In the dreams, faceless soldiers dragged Hadi from his bed. They would punch his face, accusing him of being feminine and weak, mocking him for being a tailor. Hadi would race downtown to find his shop engulfed in flames. He would see his wife and daughters inside, banging on the window as tongues of fire swallowed them.

He'd grab a nearby bench and attempt to shatter the unbreakable glass while strangers jeered and taunted him. Watching the flames inhale his family, Hadi would awaken with their screams in his ears.

He raised his eyes and found his father gaping at him. Omar's jaw was perpetually slack since the stroke yet there was something in his gaze, a glimmer of understanding, an affinity, that made Hadi believe the old man related to his torment. He wondered why he felt more connected to his impaired father now than he ever had when Omar was well. Perhaps it is because when *Baba* did possess the ability to speak to me, more often than not he chose silence.

That evening Adiba was bawling relentlessly once more. After nursing vigorously for forty-five minutes, she at last surrendered. Rima gently lowered the baby into her crib. Shemma was already asleep, following a fairy story read by her father.

Slipping under the muslin sheet in their airless bedroom, Rima was disheartened to feel Hadi reach out to clamp a sweaty hand onto her thigh. "Please not tonight. I am exhausted."

Hadi hushed her and moved closer to kiss her shoulder. Rima closed her eyes to will away a rising sadness. She took comfort in the fact that sex with Hadi usually finished quickly.

Turning onto his side, he gently unbuttoned Rima's nightgown and assisted her in pulling it over her head. He was already naked, the way he slept every night; his dark hairy body glistened with sweat. Still, something about the way he moved on this night was different. He was usually frantic when they made love; now he executed each move with care. He tenderly kneaded her breasts avoiding the chafed nipples she warned him were raw from Adiba's aggressive feeding. He rolled her onto her stomach and climbed onto her exposed buttocks, leaning forward to massage her shoulders while he gyrated, stimulating them both. He leaned forward, easing her lush, dark hair aside so he could kiss the back of her neck.

All of these sensations were unfamiliar to Rima. He was the only man she had been with and throughout their four years together she often felt like an invisible partner in his sexual samba. This attention, this loving care, was new. Rima could not deny that, despite her reluctance, she was enjoying it.

Hadi slid down her back, kissing each vertebra, then probed her buttocks with his tongue. Rima emitted a simultaneous gasp and a giggle; he drove his tongue deeper. Part of her wanted to tell him to stop; this felt wrong and wicked but it also felt rather wonderful. He eased a hand under her and slowly turned her over. She gasped again as he used his extended tongue to explore her vagina. A short time later when he entered her, Rima's mind was a pinwheel of kaleidoscopic colors. Grounded but floating, she was welded to her husband as if they had become a single form.

And then something terrible happened. Her insides ignited; rolling waves rocked her body like an internal earthquake. She was quivering and on fire, overheated but chilled, wanting to scream yet needing to cry. She gripped Hadi's shoulders, digging her fingernails into his flesh, fearing she was about to die. But she didn't.

She dropped back to Earth realizing her husband was having his own orgasm, ramming into her, snorting, growling before finally going still. It was only moments before his weight felt like an entire building toppled onto her chest. She pushed on his shoulders to signal her distress.

Hadi rolled off with a prolonged moan. Rima tried to move but couldn't. The damp area between her legs felt charged with high-voltage electricity, numb but tingling. She wanted to laugh but was afraid she might never stop.

In a crowded outdoor market, Rima concluded that only an octopus could be an effective mother.

Two hands were simply not enough. She was trying to select ripe tomatoes while rocking the stroller where Adiba was wailing like a banshee; at the same time, Rima also needed to keep track of Shemma who tended to wander off when surrounded by so many delectable treats.

Handing tomatoes and a bulb of garlic to the vegetable seller, Rima heard a neighbor's voice. "She is a crier, this one. We hear her night and day, all the way down the block."

Since Rima considered this woman an acquaintance not a friend, she found her snide opinions galling. She nodded curtly; the lady went on: "I have medicine my physician prescribed when my son had severe chest congestion. It was helpful for that but also made him sleep many hours nightly. I have a nearly-full bottle if you wish to take it."

Rima said Adiba's chest was clear but was told she missed the point. "If she is sleeping, she is not crying. Peace for her, peace for you and, if you do not think me rude for saying so, peace for the entire neighborhood."

Well, Rima thought, I do find you rude but I'm desperate enough to try anything.

Dinner was done and the dishes were washed. Hadi was reading the newspaper; Shemma was building a tower with colorful blocks gifted by her grandparents. Rima walked the floor trying to quiet Adiba. She asked her husband to take a turn but Hadi refused.

"I have worked all day. I am tired. If you were a better mother, Adiba would not be so constantly upset."

Humiliated, toting her bawling infant, Rima slipped out to visit her neighbor.

Later, nursing Adiba, Rima stared at the medicine bottle nearby. The label showed a feverish toddler with bloodshot eyes. The neighbor woman had instructed Rima to add one teaspoon of the medicine at bedtime. "That should knock her out long enough to give you and your husband a restful night."

Gazing at the purple decongestant, an exhausted Rima had a thought: if one teaspoon calms an even-tempered child, I am certain it will take three or four times that much to quiet my demon Adiba.

WHEN ED CALLAHAN RETURNED home from work that November night, Kenny was waiting at the door clutching a rectangular block of pine. "Can we work on my car now, Daddy? Please?"

Ed eased Kenny back so he could step inside. "Isn't it almost dinnertime?"

Marsha appeared toting a glass of red wine. "I been telling him all afternoon he'd have to wait 'til after dinner, but he wasn't about to listen." Setting her glass down, Marsha moved to the oven and prodded the pot roast with a fork. She turned to Ed. "Five more minutes, Oak. How was your day?"

Ed tugged off his corduroy jacket. "Same old same old. Bon's at work?"

"'Til eight. Libby's upstairs doing homework."

"But right after can we do my car?" Kenny asked.

"Sure, pal. But you do know the race isn't until March?"

Kenny didn't care; he wanted an early start so his car would be the very best.

After dinner, doing dishes wearing the yellow Playtex gloves she and Bonnie shared, Marsha looked over a stack of homemade flashcards on the counter. "Oregon."

Seated at the kitchen table, Libby contemplated. "Give me a hint, please."

"Ahhh…if you had a bunch of wooden ships, you'd want to…"

Libby scrunched her face, narrowed her eyes and shouted "Salem!" From there they moved on to Georgia. Libby knew that capital: Atlanta.

In the adjacent living room, Ed and Kenny sat on the carpet with a protective layer of newspaper around them. Ed clutched the prized block of wood as he slowly whittled away bits of pine with a pocketknife. Pencil marks along the side of the block outlined the form of the car.

Kenny incessantly begged for his chance to give it a try.

"Gotta be careful. This knife is real sharp and your mother will have my hide if she gets home to find you missing a thumb." Ed turned the knife so the blade faced him and passed the handle to his son. "Hold it tight. And remember whittling's most important rule: always move the blade away, not toward ya." Ed pantomimed the action. "Up and away, you got it?"

Kenny nodded, wriggling his impatient fingers at his dad to hand over the wood.

Following Kenny's deliberate movements as he dragged the blade along the pine, eying each curly shaving falling to the newspaper, Ed felt a rush of pride. Kenny was concentrating so intently his dark brow was creased to a perfect V. All prior impatience had been supplanted by his desire to do a first-rate job; he's just like his mother, Ed thought.

From the kitchen, he could hear Marsha continuing to drill Libby on her state capitals. Libby was a bright, serious, and creative student. For any school project, her most valued ally was a deluxe box of sixty-four Crayola crayons with the built-in sharpener.

Sighing, Kenny set down the wood and stretched his cramping hand. A moment later, Ed was surprised to hear his pal Nate in the kitchen. "Must be my lucky night. Came looking for Ed, found two beautiful ladies instead."

Libby giggled. Marsha announced that Nate's night was about to get even luckier; she had leftover pot roast.

As Nate sat on the couch, sporting his signature Ken doll crew cut that made you want to rub his head for good luck, he devoured the plate of reheated meat and whipped potatoes. Appearing with Libby in tow, Marsha told Kenny to stop whittling: it was time for bed.

"Ten more minutes? Pretty please?"

"It's ten 'til eight; your mama wants you in bed at eight-sharp. Tomorrow's Friday; you can stay up 'til nine."

"I don't think ten more minutes will hurt," Ed said. "Why don't you get Libby started? I'll send this guy along soon, Scout's Honor. He needs to finish a little whittling." Then he laughed. "Little whittling; that's not easy to say."

"Hey, be thankful you ain't been knocking back a case'a Bud," Nate said.

"Don't say 'ain't', Uncle Nate," Kenny chided. "The proper word is isn't."

Marsha shook her head. "You're impossible – all y'all. Let's get a move on, Libby-Bibby. We'll leave these men to their…whatever."

As Libby and Marsha left, Kenny's chest inflated. He was being allowed to stay up later than his older sister *and* getting to use a real knife. What a glorious day.

Lost in a heated discussion with Nate on the merits of Tom Landry's defensive strategy in the Cowboy's 27-20 victory over the Eagles the previous Sunday, Ed failed to notice Kenny was still with them, carving away, a half hour later. The revelry ended the instant Bonnie returned from work. Unbuttoning her blue Skillern's Drugs smock with her name stitched above the pocket, Bonnie asked why Kenny was still awake. "He's not. I mean, he is, but he's heading to bed right now." Ed redirected his sharp gaze at his son. "*Right* now."

Kenny jumped to his feet waving the shaved hunk of pine. "Look, Momma. I whittled it all by myself!"

"That's great," Bonnie said flatly, "now go get into your jammies or you'll never be able to get up for school tomorrow. I'll be right there to tuck you in."

"After you yell at Daddy?" Kenny asked.

Bonnie nodded.

Settling into bed, Bonnie told Ed he let Kenny get away with murder.

"It was a half-hour, Bon. I doubt if the world will end. Now why don't'cha c'mere and give me a kiss?"

Moving closer, Bonnie pulled back. "You smell like smoke. I thought you quit?"

"When the pack's done, remember? Three more 'coffin nails' and that's it."

He gave her a passionate kiss before Bonnie settled into her pillows.

"Good thing you weren't around to hear Nate tonight," Ed said. "Not that we should be surprised, but I think our boy's gettin' cold feet."

"Did you mention that at this point if he doesn't marry Lucy, she'd kill him? I mean, literally; she will hunt him down and cut his heart out."

Driving into work the next morning, Ed was surprised by the heavier-than-usual traffic until it hit him: the president. It was over four hours until the motorcade would pass through downtown but Ed was sure all the extra cars were heading to stake out a prime vantage point. Noticing the many extra policemen visible on this drizzly Friday, Ed was glad he'd taken time to wire his tailpipe back up. The last thing he could afford was a ticket.

Entering the Book Depository off Houston Street, Ed instantly felt the buzz of excitement as his coworkers chattered about the presidential visit. Through the front windows he saw folks gathering on the sidewalk. It was only 8:00 a.m.; how crowded would it be by noon?

Ninety minutes later, working at the long table on the first floor filling an order for sixth grade history books, Ed heard Junior Jarman and that spooky guy Lee chatting near the windows.

Lee asked what everybody was gathering for. "Didn't ya hear?" Junior replied. "The president's passing by soon."

"Know which way he'll be coming?"

"Paper says they'll go down Main, turn on Houston, then go right onto Elm."

Nodding, Lee disappeared between two tall bins.

Gazing at the box he was loading, Ed chuckled to himself. He couldn't begin to guess how many books he'd put into identical boxes with the same words on the side but he still didn't have the slightest clue what the slogan meant: *Building for today, pioneering for tomorrow.* Ed figured if he'd paid more attention to these books when he was *in* school, maybe he'd be smart enough to understand the motto now.

A minute before 10:00 a.m., Junior passed behind Ed startling him with a clap on the shoulder. "Break time, buddy. Smoke 'em if you've got 'em. I'm heading out to grab a sandwich off the carrying truck. Get you anything?"

"No thanks. Bonnie packed pot roast-on-rye."

Rolling his neck and rubbing his temples, Ed realized he had a screaming headache. Figuring it might help to grab a few quiet minutes alone, he hurried down to his locker, got two aspirin and made his way to the second floor lounge. There he bought a Dr. Pepper to wash the pills down. Riding the rickety freight elevator, Ed got off at the sixth floor for some craved isolation. Most of the space up there was used for storage. A renovation of the oil-soaked floorboards was in progress leaving the area in disarray. Stock had been shifted to the east wall; the stacks of brown cartons in between were piled unusually high.

Clutching his soda, Ed used his free hand to tap his shirt pocket, relieved to find the final pack of Camels. Distracted, he pulled out a cigarette and stuck it between his lips. Aching for fresh air, he maneuvered between the rows of boxes to a corner where the raised windows overlooked both Elm and

Houston Streets.

Fishing his silver lighter from his pants pocket, Ed flicked the wheel to ignite the flame.

As soon as he took a luxurious drag, he felt the pain in his skull start to ebb. Gazing down at the folks in view along the parade route, Ed absently set his lighter on a box by the window. He drank his soda and took deep gulps of crisp air; the morning drizzle had given way to crystal sunshine. Maybe the president wouldn't need to keep the top up on his car after all.

Ed's headache abated and the rest of the morning passed in a blink. Meeting his buddies in the second floor lounge at noon, Ed sat with Junior and another fellow, Harold Norman. All their chatter was about whether or not they should finish their meal and get outside to catch a glimpse of the motorcade. "Be something to tell the grandkids," Harold said. "I mean, heck, how often do us Regular Joes get to see a president?"

Ed devoured the sandwich and apple Bonnie had packed and tossed the paper sack in the trashcan by the pay phone. Then, he, Junior and Howard hustled downstairs. Several coworkers were stacked like choirboys on the staircase hoping to see the parade from there. Ed and his crew opted to go outside. Both sides of the street were lined with people as far as they could see. Ed pulled out his last cigarette knowing that keeping his promise to quit wasn't going to be easy.

Digging in his pants pocket, he was perplexed when he couldn't find his lighter. He checked his other pockets, then extracted the Camel pack and patted his breast pocket. No luck. Harold asked if everything was okay. Dangling the cigarette between his lips, Ed confessed he'd lost his lighter. Harold offered a pack of matches from a place called The Carousel Club; Ed waved him off. "Thanks but I really gotta find my lighter. Birthday present from my folks, engraved with my initials."

Reviewing the morning, Ed recalled that the last time he'd had a smoke was during his break on the sixth floor. He must've left the lighter up there.

The elevator stopped with a jolt. Ed raised the wooden gate, stepped out and lowered the barrier in case someone needed to use the lift before he returned. Moving between the columns of stacked boxes, he heard the elevator gears whir as the car was summoned back down.

Winding among the cartons, Ed navigated the maze-like path to the far corner. It seemed as if several boxes had been shifted since he was up there only hours earlier. Although no one was in view, he began to hear an odd sound, wondering if it was steam or someone murmuring. A prickly shudder raised his neck hairs but Ed forced himself forward. The low mumbling gelled into words: "Stay calm. Steady. Focus."

Fighting the urge to flee, Ed felt an inexplicable compulsion to discover the growl's source: "Steady. Nearly here."

Approaching the southeast corner windows, what Ed saw took a dizzying moment for his brain to accept. Everything devolved into slow motion. Someone was crouched at a window facing Elm Street with a hunched, rigid pose that told Ed the man wasn't simply there to watch the motorcade. Wait, is that Lee?

Ed's advancing footfalls caused the apparition to turn. It was Lee. Holding something against the windowsill. A pipe? No, Ed realized in utter shock, it's a rifle!

A rush of adrenaline shot Ed forward. Charging for the window, he cried out. "Lee! What the hell?" He dove at the younger man, calling up every long-forgotten move from his days of high school football. He wrapped both arms around the skinny man's chest and tugged him to the right, slamming him against the floor. In the melee, the rifle discharged sending down a rain of plaster. The air was filled with beastly grunts and strangled yelps. At last, Ed was able to yank the firearm from Lee's grip and fling it away while Lee fought to escape Ed's bear hug.

Then, totally disoriented, Ed heard his own desperate yell echoing off the walls. "Help! I need help up here!"

With one vigorous tug, Ed flipped Lee onto his back and sprang up to straddle him. He sat on Lee's chest pinning his arms to the plywood. Footsteps thundered up the stairs. Junior Jarman galloped into Ed's sightline, gasping as he spied Ed looking like a wild man sitting on top of Lee Oswald. "What in the hell's goin' on?"

From outside, the sounds of roaring motorcycles and cheering spectators filled the air making it hard for Ed to hear his own voice. "This maniac was going to shoot the president."

Lee Oswald was being dragged toward the waiting elevator, hands tightly cuffed behind his back. Police officers and coworkers surrounded Ed. The headache that plagued him earlier was back with a blood-pounding vengeance. A Dallas police officer was in Ed's face, barking questions while his partner collected and tagged the rifle. Both men had been accompanying the presidential parade on their motorcycles stationed behind the press vehicles when they heard a single shot from the Book Depository; instantly, they dropped their bikes and ran to investigate. Before they reached the building, a frantic Harold Norman intercepted them, imploring them to follow him inside. He explained that he and a buddy had gone up to the fifth floor to get a better view of the parade when they'd heard screaming from the floor above.

"How'd you find Oswald? What brought you up here?" the cop asked Ed as the initial interrogation continued.

"Came looking for my lighter."

"You just happened to come upon this guy seconds before he pulled the trigger?"

"Looks like."

Ed heard Roy Truly call him a hero and caught wind of Junior Jarman joking that he hoped Ed would share any reward money he got. As the enormity of what had happened washed over him, Ed felt his bum knee buckle. He reached out to grip the officer's arm. "Could I sit down a second, sir? I'm not feeling so hot."

Ed feared he might throw up. He wondered what would have happened if Oswald had swung around and shot him. He knew Bonnie would be furious when she heard what he'd done. She'd demand to know why he'd been so reckless. The hardest thing for Ed to grasp was why Lee Oswald would want to kill the president.

It was nearly midnight when the Dallas Police Department decided they'd gotten everything they needed from Ed, at least for now. It seemed as if he'd told his story no less than three dozen times to an endless stream of police officers and detectives who all looked oddly alike: square heads bearing crew cuts above broad shoulders encased in dark suits with skinny black ties.

The only guy who stood out among Ed's interrogators was robbery-homicide captain Will Fritz. He was older than the others, weighted down by decades of dealing with lowlifes. At one point late in this interminable day, Fritz expressed gratitude to Ed with a glint of moisture in his weary eyes. "Thanks for stopping that nut job, Mr. Callahan. It would'a been a crying shame for this country to lose such a fine young leader. And a Catholic boy, to boot."

Spying Bonnie in the station's foyer, Ed couldn't remember ever being happier to see her. He'd spoken to her briefly from the pay phone when he first arrived at the police station so she'd know where he was and what was happening, but it felt like that was days ago. Wrapping his wife in his arms, Ed hoped he wouldn't fall completely apart.

"You're all over television," Bonnie gushed. "They even talked about you on Walter Cronkite. Your mother called three times; she really needs to hear your voice."

As they made their way outside, blinding flashbulbs ignited. Bonnie sheepishly said she should've warned him. There were at least two-dozen reporters and cameramen bellowing overlapping questions. Ed waved them off and kept moving. "Not tonight, boys. No more tonight."

The reporters stayed on them, nearly stepping on Ed's heels as they reached the car. Bonnie offered to drive and Ed didn't balk; he was exhausted. When they were locked safely in the Fairlane, she looked at him. "I know you must be sick to death of talking about it, but was that boy Oswald honestly going to murder our President?"

"Seems like. I mean, I knew he was strange, but...Jesus...who'da guessed he'd go and pull a stunt like that?"

Reaching into his shirt pocket, Ed tugged out the pack of Camels. He fished in the corners of the crumpled cellophane and found that one cigarette he'd never gotten to smoke. He worked to straighten it out before lighting it. "Last one," he said.

Bonnie looked to her husband, hit by a sudden realization. "Oh my stars, Ed, just think where we'd be tonight if you'd gone and finished that pack this morning."

1965

— 1 —

FLOPPING ONTO HIS BED, chemistry book in hand, Johnny Scott yanked off his horn rimmed glasses, dismayed to see the screw securing the temple arm to the frame go flying across the room. He pushed off the mattress, got down on all fours and foraged through the gray pile of his bedroom carpet. He knew he had to find that screw; his father would not be happy if Johnny needed to get his glasses fixed again.

Relieved to find it a minute later, he headed to his parents' bedroom to get the jeweler's screwdriver his dad kept on his nightstand. Entering their room, Johnny was struck by how seldom he was in there. It had been years since Rochester's explosive summer thundershowers would compel him and Brian to dive into the protection of the parental bed. Now, he couldn't help but feel like a trespasser. Moving to the nightstand, Johnny was halted by a muffled sob coming from inside the closet. The hair on the back of his neck jumped up. His voice was tight and high. "Mom?"

Silence. Followed by another stifled sob. Unable to stop himself, Johnny slowly pulled open the closet door. There sat his mother, upright yet somehow fetal. She grabbed the yellowed news clipping at her feet attempting to hide it behind her. Johnny froze. "What's…ah… what's going on?"

Nancy snatched the article from the floor and sprang to her feet. "Nothing. I'm…I'm fine, honey. I promise." She stepped out of the closet and closed the door behind her. "Did you, were you looking for me?"

"No, ah, I needed to borrow dad's little screwdriver to fix my glasses. No big deal." A clumsy silence lingered. "Was that newspaper thing about Pamela Moss?"

She gaped at Johnny who'd recently turned seventeen. "How do you know about her?"

"I remember. I mean, it was only a few years ago. This kid at school said the killer used to be their gardener; how creepy is that?"

Nancy stared at the dust dancing in the afternoon sunlight. "The whole incident was just …so incredibly sad."

"But you didn't know her, right?" Nancy shook her head. "Then how come you care so much?"

"Johnny, if I don't cry for her, who will?"

Wishing to be anywhere but there, Johnny thought even being in the Washington state army barracks with Brian would beat being trapped in this awkward exchange with his mom.

Feeling emotionally exposed, Nancy launched into a breathless defense. "She was fourteen years old, just a year older than you were then. Walking home from school, minding her own business, only to be raped and killed. Why? I think about her poor parents…and those people who found her alone and half-naked, under a pile of leaves on Panorama Trail…"

Nancy was crying again. Johnny wanted to comfort her but didn't know how. *His* mother was supposed to be gliding around the kitchen singing Broadway show tunes. This woman in front of him was a stranger. Sniffing back her tears, Nancy forced a laugh and wiped her eyes.

"I know I must sound crazy to you. I'm sorry. How could you possibly understand?"

Staring at the ceiling of his city block-sized barracks at Fort Lewis, Brian was convinced dawn would never come. He'd been awake for hours. Around him his fellow soldiers slept, snoring, grinding their teeth. Brian feared he'd never sleep again. How could he with the untenable sense of dread gnawing at the inside of his skull? Each time he started to doze, that image was there again. Of his pal Eric Leyman back from Vietnam. On crutches, missing most of his right leg.

Eric, the company clown, was from Massapequa with the Long Island accent to prove it. He had a nickname for everybody, calling Brian 'Butt Chin' due to his pronounced dimple. Remarkably, he never seemed down. Even during those first grueling weeks of basic training, with sergeants kicking their butts nonstop, Eric ended every day with a six-pack and a wisecrack. "Ya know what, Butt Chin? Life is a grab in the ass; if ya can't get that, you'll be dead in no time."

The guy was a crack marksman and natural leader, which is what got him singled out for the NCO Candidate course. He was swiftly assigned to a more seasoned platoon and was shipped out while Brian and the rest of his unit were still doing their Advanced Individual Training in Washington State. Four months later, Eric came home without his leg.

He was still doling out smart remarks, calling everybody Twinkle Toes or Wonder Bread, but it was different. You could see he was working to be light; the smile required more effort. There was no escaping the haunted look clouding his eyes.

Now rumors were swirling that Brian's company would be shipped out any day. Things were heating up in Vietnam. Combat was growing more intense. The moment of truth was rushing closer.

Brian had only felt this kind of terror one other time; the first night his parents let him baby-sit Johnny. He was twelve. John was eight. His folks were going to dinner and a movie and figured the boys could handle the three hours alone. Brian was saving up for a new baseball glove; his dad promised him a dollar if he kept things under control and got Johnny ready for bed by 9:00 p.m.

He and Johnny were in the family room watching *People Are Funny*. The host Art Linkletter was putting a Topeka salesman through some silly memory test when Brian heard a noise at the back door. Someone was rattling the knob. A moment later there was a clattering crash. Brian's throat went dry; his heart pounded. He jumped off the couch and dragged Johnny into the closet across the room. "Somebody's breaking in. I'll bet they watched Mom and Dad leave and now they're gonna rob and kill us."

The brothers wedged themselves behind two big suitcases in the dark stuffy closet and sat there holding their breath. Eventually, they both fell asleep. Returning home, their parents found the boys in their hidden nest. Hearing Brian's story, his father looked outside and concluded a raccoon must have invaded the trash, knocking the cans into the back door. As he finally calmed down enough to fall asleep that night, Brian hoped he'd never again feel fear that intense.

But now, as he lay on his cot in the barracks, the panic was back. Brian didn't want to go to war. He didn't want to lose a leg. He didn't want to die a virgin.

When he returned to see the recruiter on campus that Monday in November sixteen months earlier, Brian was convinced that signing the enlistment contract was the answer to all his woes. Coming home in his dress uniform would definitely impress Karen Peterman. Training as an army medic would be the perfect bridge to medical school. If he served with distinction, his benevolent Uncle Sam would pay for his education.

Planning to break the news to his parents that evening, Brian found them glued to the television. Walter Cronkite was reporting on a story out of Dallas. Some lunatic had attempted to shoot President Kennedy but a coworker of the would-be assassin had stopped him, averting a national tragedy. That was what finally made up Brian's mind: he wanted to be *that* kind of a hero. He wanted the opportunity to make his family and country proud.

Nancy cried all weekend. Why didn't Brian realize he had a beautiful individual spirit the army would pulverize? No matter how much John, Brian and Johnny tried to console her, Nancy couldn't stop sobbing. She didn't even have tears left for Pamela Moss.

Brian was ordered to report for induction on a Monday in mid-January. His father took the day off from Kodak; much to Brian's chagrin, both parents insisted on accompanying him to the federal building downtown.

Driving there, Brian thought it was ridiculous that the city center was only nine miles from home but seemed as exotic as Egypt. Except for bus rides to rival high schools when he was on the baseball team, most of Brian's life had been lived within a four-mile radius: school, friends, his grandparents and paper route were all right there in Pittsford. Now he was about to embark on an experience that could send him anywhere in the world. As his dad parked, Brian's head was throbbing.

The second they stepped into the Selective Service office everything happened at a dizzying speed. Brian assumed he'd be inducted on the spot but that wasn't the case. A huge man barked at him to say his goodbyes and get on the bus. What bus?

"Let's go, let's go!" bellowed the guy in olive fatigues. Brian kissed his mother's tear-stained cheek, gave his father a firm handshake and was shoved out a back door. Eighteen other guys were already on the beat-up bus; three were black, one was Puerto Rican. To Brian's eyes, they all looked unbearably young. Just like him.

A few of the recruits were horsing around but the majority looked completely shell-shocked. Brian dropped into a seat. A ferocious drill sergeant was at the front of the bus yelling at the boys to make sure they enjoyed their last seventy minutes of freedom. Once they entered the Armory in downtown Buffalo, their lives would cease to be their own. For the next three years they would be the property of the US government.

The ride to Buffalo was a blur. Brian thought he recognized one guy sitting a few rows in front of him but couldn't quite place him. Anyway, he was too off-balance to make small talk. He just stared out the window wondering if he'd ever again inhale the sweet fading scent of Karen Peterman's panties.

Standing in the Buffalo Armory in his underwear, Brian was freezing. The hair on his arms and legs was standing straight up. The guys surrounding him looked like they were using every bit of self-control to keep from screaming out for their clothes. Glancing down, Brian was shaken by a new horror: a dime-sized neon yellow pee stain was visible in the middle of his briefs. Staring ahead, he lowered his hands in front of his crotch hoping to hide the stain.

One guy started sneezing with such fury that half the recruits began to chuckle. A few titters turned into guffaws; pretty soon they were all howling.

"Shut…the fuck…up!" one of their superiors screamed.

That only made it worse. It was probably the pent up tension of feeling like shanghaied Eskimos, but no one could get control. The next thing Brian knew, they were on the frigid floor doing an infinite series of push-ups. His arms ached, his legs cramped, but the drill sergeant kept going.

Following their physicals, two guys were sent home. One had a cyst on his tailbone; Eric Leyman promptly nicknamed him TBA (Two Big Assholes). The other guy had a history of ulcers; the stress of the day had already taken its toll. As the pair got dressed and headed out, Eric whispered what the rest of them were thinking: "Lucky basta'ds."

Brian passed his physical, breezed through the eye exam

and wound up in a room packed with wooden school desks. There they completed a lengthy IQ test designed to ferret out hidden weaknesses. Many of the questions seemed absurd, but Brian pushed through. He'd already been up since 5:00 a.m. and had no idea when this day would end.

After the testing, they were herded into another hollow room and told to sit tight. The next step would be their official induction whenever the commanding officers were good and ready. In the meantime, their job was to stay put and shut the fuck up.

Once the newbies were left on their own, Brian moved over a few rows to sit next to the guy he thought he recognized on the bus. "Do we know each other?"

"Brian Scott, right? Pittsford Third baseman?" Brian nodded; the freckle-faced redhead stuck his hand out. "Kurt Bitkoff. Brighton, Class of '63. Centerfield."

"Wait, you're the fool who caught my deep pop fly that could've sent us to States my junior year."

Kurt nodded and grinned. "That's me, loser. Deal with it."

An hour later they were sworn in. Standing shoulder-to-shoulder, right hands raised, they pledged allegiance and obedience. Once the final words were spoken, they were soldiers in the United States Army. Kurt whispered to Brian, "Now what?"

The answer came quickly: another bus ride, this one to the Buffalo airport. Then a plane to Newark and onto another bus packed with guys who looked exactly like Brian: in over their heads and scared shitless.

Someone said they were going to Fort Dix. It was nearly midnight. Brian had been up for nineteen hours with no promise of sleep in sight. The thing that scared him most was that he was already having trouble pulling his father's face into focus in his mind's eye.

As they approached the road into the fort, lines of identical buses were ahead of and behind them filled with new recruits arriving for basic training. They faced a disorienting mix of blinding floodlights, inky darkness and the smell of diesel fuel. Men in green yelled overlapping orders. A banner read, "US Army Reception Station: Welcome Soldier – Stand Proud!"

Bodies crisscrossed like a jumbled zombie parade. More screaming. Humiliation. Intimidation. No matter what you're doing, you're doing it wrong. And you are a piece of shit for not knowing it! They wound up in a giant classroom. More paperwork. The eighteen recruits Brian started the day with had mushroomed into four hundred exhausted young men waiting to surrender their hair to malevolent sadists gripping electric clippers. After Brian's papers were filled out and his hair was history, it was 3:00 a.m. Still nobody was mentioning sleep.

They were marched back out into the night. Another huge building, another endless queue into an enormous supply hut. Waiting in that line, Brian saw the guy ahead of him turn to check him out. Brian offered a spent smile. "Whoa, Butt Chin, hope I don't fall into that dimple. And what's with them crazy blue cat eyes?"

That was how Brian officially met Eric Leyman, back when Eric had two legs.

Three hundred miles away, Nancy was also wide-awake, squirming to get comfortable without disturbing John. She couldn't stop thinking about an earlier conversation. Louise appeared at Nancy's back door asking some inane question about the town's annual Memorial Day parade still two months away. Nancy knew that wasn't the real reason Louise was there. She invited her in, poured them each a cup of Sanka and asked how the Ditlows' ten-year-old daughter Sarah was enjoying her tuba lessons. Embarrassed, Louise laughed. "I guess you hear her practicing."

"Don't worry, we get a kick out of it. The image of skinny

little Sarah with her mouth full of braces puffing away on a big tuba? It's priceless."

"It's ridiculous. But she seems to love it so who are we to discourage her?" Louise spaced out, staring into her cup. Suddenly, her head snapped up. "Marsh is having an affair with his secretary, could anything be more of a cliché? It's so humiliating. But if I didn't tell somebody, I was afraid I might burst."

"I'm so sorry, Louise. You're a wonderful wife and mother. You don't deserve this."

"Darn tootin' I don't. I've done nothing but cater to that man's needs for fifteen years. I put him through graduate school and this is how he repays me? But what can I do? I'm trapped. I have no skills; I need to be home for my girls...I have no way out. And you know how I found out about it? I called his office to ask him to pick up a few things at Super Duper. Glenda his secretary wasn't in; some temp gal answered and when I asked if I could speak to Marsh, she wondered why I didn't know he was taking the day off. Can you imagine how foolish I felt? Then because I'm a masochist, I called Glenda at home. When she picked up, I put on my best business voice asking to speak to Mr. Ditlow. Want to hear the height of nerve? She said, 'one moment please' – and passed Marsh the phone! In the middle of the day, at her home, in the middle of the workweek! Can you imagine? When I heard his voice, I said, calm as can be, 'Don't bother coming home, you despicable, disgusting pig,' and hung up."

"How did you keep from driving over there and killing them both?"

"Frankly, I don't think either one of them is worth the effort. He came home with candy, flowers, the whole bit. The girls were there so I had to act civil but what I really wanted to do was hurl the Fanny Farmer's at his stupid head. After I put the kids to bed, I found him in the den hiding behind his newspaper. I told him if he ever touched me again, I'd break off both his arms and use them to beat him to a pulp." Nancy gave a startled laugh. Louise went on, "You know what he said to that? Not a damn word. We haven't spoken in five days. My mother thought he was an egotistical jerk from the get-go. But, 'for better or worse,' that's what my vows said, so I'll simply carry on like the good English stock I come from."

Flipping over in bed, Nancy put a hand on her husband's elbow; he kept on snoring. She didn't care. She just needed to touch him. She had a good man and had every intention of hanging onto him, literally and figuratively.

The Washington night wouldn't end. Brian was still wide-awake. He'd arrived at Fort Dix only fourteen months earlier but it felt like a hundred years ago. He couldn't remember a time when he'd tasted decent food or worn a single article of clothing that wasn't hideous green.

One thing that was harder than he'd envisioned was contact with home: the letters and phone calls. Brian couldn't articulate it but each time he finished reading something from his family or hung up the barracks' pay phone, he'd feel great for a minute or two…and then those other feelings would seep in: a teeth-gnashing anger, a tamped-down sadness, an aching hole in his heart.

It really wasn't okay that life in Pittsford was flowing right along without him.

2

SITTING IN A PADDED LOUNGE CHAIR beside the circular pool at the Royal Hawaiian Hotel on Waikiki Beach, Mai tai in hand, David couldn't remember ever feeling happier. His fluffy terrycloth robe was closed to cover his sunburned chest, his hairy legs were slathered in Coppertone; a spotty film of sea air, pool water and grease coated his sunglasses. But in his alcohol-clouded head, David was absolutely convinced he looked like Cary Grant with dark curls.

Halfway through the first real vacation of his adult life, every day had been better than the one before. It was his sister Lisa who convinced him to go to Hawaii on his spring break from his professorial duties at USC. David knew he'd have to find the perfect island gift as a thank-you.

When he'd first mentioned this trip, his friends thought he was out of his mind. "You're a historian," his colleague Charlie Yamamoto reminded. "What do you care about sitting on a beach watching honeymooners frolic in the surf? Spend your meager academic salary going to Europe! Or at least visit Pearl Harbor."

David had no intention of going to the war memorial. So far a busy day took him from his bed to the pool, to lunch and back to the pool. Maybe if he felt truly ambitious, he'd wrap up with a sunset stroll along the beach.

Licking the rum-laced foam from the pineapple wedge in his drink, David recalled a night fifteen months earlier when he was driving home from dinner at Lisa and Martin's home in Sherman Oaks. Speeding toward the top of Mulholland Drive, he'd found himself consumed by a despondency overlaid with guilt and shame that came dangerously close to propelling him off the road. An instant before he gave the accelerator a final stomp, he heard his niece Gina's innocent giggle inside his head and slid his foot from the gas pedal to the brake.

The past year had been one of discipline and productivity. He'd finished his book on New York's turn-of-the-century Jewish immigrants and it was currently out to several publishers, one of whom seemed extremely interested. His classes were going well, several of his students had gotten into prestigious graduate programs and he was ever closer to tenure. He was drinking less and sleeping more. Only once in the past ten months had he woken up in a stranger's bed.

"Dinner, 7:00 p.m., you and me. The Ocean Terrace at the Sheraton."

David turned to the lounge next to him. "Sounds perfect."

The man perched there in red and black checked bathing trunks with a deep tan and sun-streaked blonde hair grinned at David. "How's your day going?"

"Sun, swimming, a Mai tai or two…it's hell. How was tennis?"

"Brutal. Hot. But I left some cocky kid from Cleveland begging for mercy."

Aaron Hausman was the reason David was having such an incredible vacation. It was on his second night in Oahu, sitting at the bar in his famous pink hotel with its renowned view of Diamond Head, that David first spotted Aaron chatting up a pair of locals about their favorite surfing spot. When he and David made eye contact, David's cheeks flushed to match the hotel walls; he quickly looked away. Aaron sauntered over to ask if it was okay to grab the empty stool beside David.

Aaron was a housepainter, working to save up to go back to school to earn a graduate degree in graphic design. He was in Hawaii to recover from an ugly break-up, unwilling to go into details. The thing that scared David most about that first night was that Aaron had invited him back to his room – and David declined. Even after three rum drinks mixed by a generous bartender, David showed restraint. He didn't want to seem too eager with this one. He exercised self-control and that scared the shit out of him.

Twirling linguini onto his fork, David watched Aaron ravenously saw into a slab of sirloin. "Isn't it odd we live three miles from each other but ended up meeting here?"

"It's fate, David. Who cares where we met as long as we did."

David asked Aaron how he managed to be so healthy and rational. Aaron laughed and asked what kind of psychos David usually dated. Prying open a clam nestled in the bed of linguini, working to pull it from its rubbery mooring, David felt his face grow hot. His eyes stayed fixed on his food. "Okay, the fact is…I don't date. I, ah…"

"Oh no. You're a virgin?" When David denied the charge, Aaron went on. "Wait, let me guess – you're a hit and run artist."

David gave a sheepish nod. "Because of my job, the university environment. Given how conservative it is, it's best my private life remains private."

"So you're a 'confirmed bachelor'?" Off David's nod, Aaron added, "Then I guess it's up to me to change all that."

The rest of the week went by quicker than the pop of a flashbulb. As David packed, Aaron sat on the bed scrutinizing his every move. "That's the third time you've folded that sweater, pal; I'm guessing it's as neat as it's gonna get."

David gave a nervous laugh. "Okay, I'll confess: I'm hoping if I don't finish packing, I won't have to leave."

Aaron said he wished they were on the same flight home but David told him to be glad he still had two more days in paradise. "Yeah, but none of it's gonna be much fun without you."

"Okay. Stop. Right now. I'm not going to let you make me cry."

Aaron stood up, pulled David into his arms. When they kissed, David melted the moment they touched. "This makes absolutely no sense. How can I feel like this? I don't even know you."

"Yeah you do. This is me. No hidden agenda, no secret identity. I just want to be happy, David, and I feel like you're the guy to make that happen. Wait, am I scaring you? I'll calm down. We can take this as slow as you need to go."

Loading her three kids into the Chevy station wagon, Lisa wondered why she hadn't thought ahead and booked a babysitter. Michael scrambled over the back seat to the rear compartment, declaring he wanted to ride "in the way back." Six-year-old Debbie demanded to know why she couldn't ride back there, too.

"I need you to hold the baby," an exasperated Lisa said.

"On my lap, the whole way? She's so wiggly and squirmy."

"That's why you have to hold her; otherwise she'll be trying to climb up front with me. It isn't safe."

With a pout and a stomp, Debbie scooted into the back seat, positioning herself in the middle. Lisa carefully passed off Gina who was clutching a stuffed rabbit by one ear. "Go to sissy," Lisa said, "she'll give you a bottle."

Michael chimed in that he was hungry, too. Lisa reminded him they were going to Ship's for dinner as soon as they picked up Uncle David.

"Unca David!" Gina echoed.

"That's right, pumpkin. He's coming home from Hawaii!"

Sitting across from each other in the red leather booth at Ship's Coffee Shop in Culver City, Lisa grinned at her tanned and relaxed brother. "Okay, enough chit-chat, when are you going to tell me about her?" Holding Gina on his lap, David furrowed his brow. "The girl you met. It's the only explanation for the way you're acting. You actually seem happy; I hardly recognize you."

"There's no girl, Lisa. I read, swam in the ocean, had great seafood and just enjoyed. But I can promise you, there's no girl."

"Then you won't mind me fixing you up with Kelly's sister. She's not Jewish, but she's adorable, a stewardess for United. We'll do a barbecue; Martin can make his famous ribs."

Over the next month, David and Aaron saw each other one or two nights a week and at least once every weekend. They hiked in Griffith Park, frequented a dark bar near Aaron's apartment and had sex at every opportunity. David found Aaron's tiny one-bedroom place on Franklin to be claustrophobic but never complained. At his airier house in Silver Lake he had to worry about what his neighbors might think seeing a handsome blonde athlete coming and going at all hours.

One Sunday morning as they lay in bed reading the *New York Times*, Aaron took the front section from David and set it aside. "Have you told your sister about us yet?" David insisted he hadn't had the chance but Aaron called bullshit. "You talk to her ten times a day. They have no clue you're a big homo, do they? I mean, I get keeping your private life quiet at work, but you and your sister are so close; why're you living a lie, even with her?"

"Oh…what…you told your family you're a queer and everybody was copacetic?"

"No," Aaron snapped. "Actually, I told my parents and they haven't spoken to me since. They're total shits about it, David. But at least I had the balls to tell them the truth."

A week later, sharing chips and salsa as they awaited their entrees in the family-run Mexican restaurant on Western, David had a proposal for Aaron. "Lisa and Martin are having a barbecue on Sunday with some friends and two stewardesses Lisa wants me to meet. Why don't you come with me…you know, so everybody can get acquainted, and we can feel things out from there."

"But I'll just be playing the part of your random heterosexual buddy?"

"Yes. For now. Please? We'll mingle with the stewardesses, you can talk baseball with Martin; we'll relax and have fun."

"Without mentioning that we can't wait to get home to have hot sex."

Aaron weighed the pros and cons before deciding David's willingness to bring him to the barbecue was progress. Even when dating a history professor, Rome wasn't built in a day.

Having grown up in Murray Hill, New Jersey, David never stopped appreciating eighty-degree days in March. Driving to Sherman Oaks with Aaron in the passenger seat, he was singing "Oh What a Beautiful Morning" in his deep, full baritone.

"Okay, pal," Aaron warned, "if we're trying to keep our secret today, you might want to quit with the show tunes."

Grilling chicken and ribs, Martin was enjoying watching David and Aaron at the picnic table laughing with the pair of attractive flight attendants. The guys chugged beers while the girls sipped white wine spritzers munching on potato chips and onion dip. Toddling outside dragging her ever-present stuffed bunny, Gina bee-lined to climb into David's lap. Awed by how adorable she was, the stewardesses gushed over Gina's obvious love for her uncle. Sucking her thumb Gina absently used her free hand to stroke David's cheek as she gazed off into space.

The next interaction Martin observed unsettled him as Lisa appeared at his side with the extra barbecue sauce he'd requested. Distracted, Martin managed only a grunt of thanks.

Getting ready for bed that night, Lisa was brushing her teeth when Martin joined her.

"Everybody asleep?" she asked.

"Finally. Debbie was so wound up I didn't think she'd ever go out."

"Maybe it's because of the entire box of chocolate donuts she ate."

"Um, do you…" Martin stammered, "…did you get the feeling David and Aaron are more than just friends?"

"What in the world are you talking about?"

"I'm thinking they might be…ya know…a couple."

"David and Aaron? Are you insane? David doesn't like men, Martin. Where is this coming from?"

"It was just…you didn't see it but…when they were together at the picnic table, Aaron reached over and wiped a crumb off David's chin."

"So? I honestly don't get where you're going here."

"Guys don't do stuff like that, Lisa. They don't touch each other that way; they just don't. There was something a little too intimate about it."

"So because his friend wiped a crumb off David's chin, you think my brother is a homosexual?"

"Yeah," Martin shrugged. "I kinda do."

When the alarm trilled the next morning, Lisa realized she'd hardly slept. She'd tossed and turned, wondering if Martin's suspicions were true. Working to convince herself David wasn't a queer, she didn't entirely succeed. Reviewing his entire romantic history, she realized the only women he'd dated since high school were the ones she'd fixed him up with.

David looked up to see his department chair Henry Rosenthal in his doorway. "Henry. Is everything all right?"

Henry stepped into the office and dropped into the straight-back chair. "Everything's splendid. And you?"

"Wonderful. Terrific. Classes are going well, the students are quite engaged…" David felt himself starting to chatter nervously as he was prone to do around authority figures; he stopped and exhaled. "What may I do for you, Henry?"

"I have a favor to ask, a favor I'm hoping you'll view as a bit of an honor. As you may have heard, we have an exciting guest speaker coming to campus next month: William Shirer."

David knew Shirer as the author of the incredibly successful *The Rise and Fall of the Third Reich*; it had been published five years earlier but continued to grace many bestseller lists. "Yes, yes. I can't wait to attend his talk."

When Henry said he wanted David to moderate the appearance, David was breathless.

"Don't be so shocked, my good man. You're one of our brightest and most popular professors. Shirer is a man in his sixties and…well, frankly, your involvement might serve to draw in more of our student body."

David told Henry he was flattered and hoped he could do the man justice.

Bouncing around Aaron's apartment that night, David was like the Home-Ec Club president invited to prom by the star quarterback. "I can't believe he picked me. William Shirer is a big deal. We have multiple tenured professors with major published works—"

"But none of them are as cute as you."

David blushed and went on. "The best part of this is that it's a huge vote of confidence from Henry. I'm rather stunned."

"Congrats, Professor. Now why don't you get naked and let me blow you stupid."

Standing in the linen department at Bullock's Wilshire, David watched Lisa study two sets of queen-size bed sheets, considering lemon versus sea foam. "Oh dear," she murmured, "I had no idea this would be so hard…" Turning to David, her face sagged. Tossing the sheets onto the shelf, Lisa blurted, "Is Aaron your boyfriend?"

All color drained from David's face. His throat was

suddenly drier than a charred bagel.

"Excuse me?"

Lisa was trying not to cry. "I'm sorry. This is all Martin's fault. He's... he said – it doesn't matter what he said; just tell me, David, is it true?"

David managed a guffaw of protest so genuine he almost convinced himself. "No, of course not. Where would Martin get a crazy idea like that?"

"He saw Aaron wipe your chin. I told him he was being silly but then I got all caught up and let my imagination run wild – I'm sorry. I'm, honestly, I'm mortified. I believe you, David, I do. I feel so stupid."

"Forget it! It was an innocent misunderstanding. Aaron's a very physical guy – with everybody, that's just how he is. I see why Martin might've gotten confused. But don't worry, sis, as soon as the right gal comes along I'll be marching down the aisle."

"I apologize, David, I do. I love you and I can't wait to come to watch you interview William Shirer."

Storming around David's living room that night, Aaron had no intention of keeping his voice down, no matter how intensely David begged. "What do you mean I can't be there? Are you prohibiting me? Banning me?"

"I'm just saying I don't think it's a good idea right now."

Aaron grabbed a pillow off the couch and began to beat it against his thigh. "Well, fuck you. Either I'm in your life or I'm not."

"Why are you doing this?" David wailed.

"Why am I doing it? Why am *I*? Maybe you need to ask yourself that question, David. Maybe you need to wonder why your sister gave you the perfect opening to get this whole thing out in the open and you punted it."

"You didn't see her face. You have no idea how she was

looking at me—"

"That's bullshit! It doesn't matter how she looks at you. What matters is how you look at yourself."

"Aaron, I care about you, I want to be with you, but if you're at William Shirer and Lisa and Martin are there, how will I focus? The night is very important to me."

"I get that. But I'm not gonna be treated like some whore you're ashamed to be seen with in public. Either you tell Lisa we're a couple or I'm walking out and never coming back."

A hurricane of emotion whirled in David's head. Finally he gave a heartbroken whisper: "I can't."

"Then aloha, David. We're done."

Over the next few weeks, David called Aaron several times a day but the instant Aaron heard his voice he'd coldly ask if David had come clean yet. When David couldn't say yes, Aaron hung up. David went by the tiny apartment on Franklin three nights in a row but Aaron wouldn't answer the door. Every single night for two weeks, Professor David Goldman cried himself to sleep. On the fifteenth day, picking up the phone Aaron had a new response: "Stop calling me, please. Leave me alone."

Inviting David into his office, Henry Rosenthal was taken aback by David's appearance.

"I've, ah, I've had a virulent flu and I'm hoping you can take over the Shirer interview for me. I feel dreadful letting you down, Henry, but I don't want to do something this important if I can't give it one hundred percent. I hope you understand."

On the Friday evening of the interview at USC, David was home with two-year-old Gina. When he called to tell Lisa he wasn't moderating the program, blaming a work overload, Lisa was disappointed but decided she and Martin would use the schedule opening to take their two older kids to see *The Sound of Music*. David offered to babysit Gina. He'd swing by after school on Friday and bring her to his place for a sleepover. "I'll take her to the zoo Saturday morning and have her home by naptime. What do you say?"

Digging through Gina's overnight bag, David ran a mental checklist before loading the baby into the car. "There's Flopsy, and her bottles; what about Blankie?" Lisa told him it was in the bottom of the bag along with plenty of diapers.

"Any problems, just jam her thumb in her mouth, she'll be fine."

All the lights were out in David's house except for the softly glowing reading lamp over the bed. Huddled under the quilt, David was propped up on a pair of pillows, holding a paperback novel with Gina wedged against his side. The lingering smell of cinnamon he'd added to Gina's apple juice gilded the air with serenity. The contented child had the fingers of her left hand wrapped around her bunny's creased ear.

Reading, David kept his voice low. *"What do you think spies are: priests, saints and martyrs? They're a squalid procession of vain fools, traitors too, yes; pansies, sadists and drunkards, people who play cowboys and Indians to brighten their rotten lives."*

David paused and glanced down. Gina's eyes closed, her bent arm dropped like a wind-blown pup tent; her bottle fell into the blanket. She was asleep but David didn't budge. The book he was reading, *The Spy Who Came in from the Cold*, had him deeply engaged. Its author, John le Carre, was a masterful writer and David was dying to know what was going to happen next to the novel's hero Alec Leamas.

Even though Gina was out, David kept reading aloud. Devouring a taut tale of espionage with his favorite niece pressed to his side, he was feeling inordinately at peace.

Even if he wasn't conscious of it in the moment, it was the first time in several weeks David had gone one full hour without pining for Aaron Housman.

3

L<small>IFTING THE RED CERAMIC BOWL</small> to pour batter into the hissing waffle iron, Bonnie Callahan wished her hands would quit shaking. It seemed as if they'd been trembling ever since she and Ed received an unexpected phone call two months earlier.

They were in the living room watching *The Adventures of Ozzie & Harriet* when the phone rang. Knowing Bonnie's mom was in the kitchen doing the morning's Jumble, they waited for Marsha to pick it up. Moments later, she stood before them, struggling to catch her breath. "I am not…making this up…that was the White House calling," Marsha panted.

"White House Liquor?" a befuddled Ed asked.

"No, Oak. I mean, *the White House* White House. Sixteen hundred Pennsylvania Avenue. They said President Kennedy wants to give you the Presidential Medal of Freedom."

Ed and Bonnie were shocked. It was only later, after several more official phone calls and a visit to the North Dallas Public Library, that the entire thing began to make sense.

Kennedy spent the final month of 1963 and the initial ten-months of 1964 running for reelection against New York governor Nelson Rockefeller. He'd been on the road making endless campaign appearances plus two overseas trips to address ongoing tension with the Soviet Union, leaving no time to focus on much else.

After his second inauguration in January he'd finally been able to deal with a number of domestic issues that had fallen by the wayside. One such bit of business involved a file of letters from across the country urging the president to award the Medal of Freedom to the courageous Dallas hero who saved his life.

On this Saturday morning in March, Bonnie was too preoccupied to notice the batter she was pouring was overflowing out of the waffle iron. Leaping up from her seat at the table, twelve-year-old Libby yelped. "Momma! What're you doing?"

"Sorry, sugar cube; I guess I'm just—"

"Worrying about what to wear to the White House again?"

Bonnie nodded. "It's, well, she's so beautiful and fancy and, oh my stars, there will be cameras and people from TV and I haven't gotten a new dress since Kenny's christening. Let's face it, no matter what, I'll look like an old washer woman standing beside Jacqueline Kennedy."

Libby suggested maybe Bonnie could borrow something from Nate's wife Lucy.

"If I lose a dozen pounds! Aunt Lucy's got a waist like your Barbie doll. Daddy's telling me buy something new but where would I ever wear a fancy dress again, to work at Skillern's?"

In the eighteen months since Ed had wrestled Lee Harvey Oswald to the Book Depository floor, Bonnie felt like life was racing by. For months after Ed's gallant deed was reported around the world, there wasn't a day when newspapermen or television anchors weren't camped on their lawn trying to capture the family's every move. They received cards and telegrams from folks as far away as Singapore thanking Ed for averting a disaster that would've rocked the globe.

One of the most amusing gifts Ed received was a lifetime pass to the Carousel Club in downtown Dallas. Although Ed had never been there, he knew it was a place where busty "exotic dancers" stripped down to their G-strings to entertain the clientele. Its owner Jack Ruby wrote that he was a tremendous admirer of President Kennedy and would be proud to serve a cocktail to the man who saved JFK's life.

In early '64, Ed was hired by the Beckman Brothers appliance store chain to be their "celebrity spokesperson."

After a few months of doing their radio and television ads, the owners were so pleased with the response Ed was generating, they hired him to manage their flagship store in Plano. He was making almost $5,000 more a year than at the Book Depository, but still every dollar was out the door at month's end. He remained friends with some former coworkers, occasionally grabbing a beer with Junior Jarman or meeting Harold Norman for a pick-up basketball game. A week earlier, he'd sold the Trulys a Frigidaire with an automatic icemaker. Still, it was Bonnie and the kids who consumed most of Ed's time and attention.

Gently setting her favorite sleeveless pink blouse into a suitcase on her bed, Marsha paused. Her nostrils filled with a sense-memory of cherry pipe tobacco as she thought about her boyfriend Miles Ludwig. They'd been seeing each other for more than a year. This coming weekend, she was driving down to meet him in Galveston for a beachside getaway.

Miles was a traveling salesman based in Oklahoma City who sold ladies handbags to high-end department stores across the southwest. He and Marsha met sitting next to each other at the counter at a downtown Denny's. Miles asked her to pass the ketchup, they started chatting and, an hour later, they were pulling their clothes back on in a motel on South Hampton Drive. It was the first time Marsha had had sex since her husband Lloyd dropped dead six years earlier. And Miles was only the second man in her fifty-seven years she'd gone to bed with.

Sensing her discomfort as they prepared to part, he gently kissed her cheek. "Sometimes you just have to shut off your brain and go where your body takes you."

Driving home that autumn afternoon, Marsha rolled down every window in the car convinced the smell of sex was clinging to her like a Saran Wrap ball gown. The last thing she wanted was to walk into the house and be confronted by her daughter.

Over the next several months, Marsha snuck away for an afternoon rendezvous with Miles whenever business brought him to town. It was on their second date that he took Marsha's hands and told her he had a confession to make. She feared he was a married man. And that was exactly what Miles admitted. But instead of getting upset, Marsha was relieved. Miles explained his wife and three kids were tucked away in Oklahoma City, he had no intention of abandoning them, but he needed more. His wife was a fine woman and a terrific mother, but sex for her was a dirty obligation. She would endure it because it was part of her sacred marital vows but was determined to never enjoy it. Her rapture was reserved for her Lord Jesus Christ. Miles told Marsha that what he loved most about being with her was her capacity to get lost in the moment; it made him feel alive to provide her with such pure pleasure.

There was part of Marsha that believed Miles might be completely full of shit, one of those men with a woman in every city, but she didn't care. She'd been married for thirty-three years, raised two kids, buried her husband; she didn't need to do any of it again. She adored being touched by a man who treated her with dignity and respect. Considering there wasn't a week that went by without someone commenting on her resemblance to Vivian Vance, ("you know, the gal who plays Ethel on the *Lucy* program,") which Marsha never particularly took as a compliment, she felt lucky to be seen on the arm of a man as handsome as Miles.

During the first six months of the relationship, Bonnie constantly nagged her mother about when she'd finally get to meet this "mystery man." Unable to put Bonnie off any longer, Marsha brought Miles to Libby's twelfth birthday party at the Irving roller rink. As ten giggling, gliding adolescent girls circled the wooden floor, Bonnie interrogated Miles with the grit of Sergeant Friday. Through it all, Miles remained cool and composed…and, to Marsha's relief, never dropped a hint about his marital status.

Later, scraping leftover birthday cake into the trash, Bonnie eyed her mother with a coy smile. "So…are you going to marry this fellow? He's quite lovely."

"Which is exactly why I see no reason to ruin a good thing."

That night at dinner, Libby and Kenny were shoveling in forkfuls of beefaroni, beseeching their parents to let them come along to meet President and Mrs. Kennedy.

"And John-John and Caroline, too," Libby wailed. "It's not fair."

"How many times do we have to explain this to you?" Ed asked. "You weren't invited. Neither was Granny. It would be nice if y'all could just be happy for your mother and I."

Kenny crossed his arms and slid down in his seat. "I still say it stinks."

Marsha made a proposal she thought might please everyone: since a limousine was coming to take Ed and Bonnie to the airport, maybe Marsha and the kids could ride along and then take a taxi back home. Kenny thought Granny's idea sounded swell. He and his sister jumped up, begging Ed to agree.

"We have to take lots of pictures," Libby said. "Maryanne Forbush would die if she saw me riding in a big ole fancy limousine. She's so goll-darn stuck-up and thinks, just because she's been to Paris – *France*, not Texas – she's better than the rest of us. I wanna show her I got to do something really cool, too."

"Okay, fine." Ed said, "You can get your ride and still be to school by noon. We might could even arrange for the limo to drop you at school. How would Maryanne Forbush like that?"

Bonnie was at the table helping Libby with her math

homework when Ed came in, his worn corduroy jacket slung over his shoulder. He and Nate were going out to grab a beer. Reminding him to lock up when he got home, Bonnie gave Ed a kiss.

Pulling into the driveway of Nate's canary-yellow ranch house, Ed tooted his horn hoping to save himself from having to go inside. No such luck. Lucy opened the door and waved Ed in.

When Nate and Lucy got married fourteen months earlier, Ed hoped she might get rid of the collection of antique porcelain dolls that terrified him. They were all over the living room: up on bookshelves, caged in a glass cabinet, sitting on the coffee table. In Ed's mind, they were just waiting to come alive to cut his heart out.

"Nate's finishing his…business," Lucy said, closing the door. "How's everything with you, stranger? How thrillin' y'all are off to Washington. Has Bonnie decided what to wear yet?"

"No.   And it's been the only topic of conversation for weeks."

Lucy gave Ed's arm a playful swat. "Well, of course it has, you silly man. You're gonna be photographed with Jacqueline Kennedy!"

As Lucy offered to lend Bonnie a string of cultured pearls she'd gotten from her parents as a Sweet Sixteen present, her words faded into an inaudible murmur. Ed's eyes locked onto one particular doll seated atop the entertainment cabinet. The paint on its ceramic face was flaking, one eyebrow was gone and its cheek bore a pronounced black blemish. Its glass eyes were fixed on Ed as its nasty little fingers with their chipped red polish rested in the lap of the yellowed dressing gown – poised to strangle Ed if he came closer. His heart thudded and blood whooshed in his ears.

Before Ed could respond to Lucy's unheard question, Nate appeared, buoyant as usual, to rescue his rattled buddy.

Following Nate out the door, Ed took one last look over his shoulder; he swore that wicked doll was still eying him.

Ed loved that he and Nate had been going to the Double Wide Bar & Grille since the day they were both of legal age. They knew the bartenders and most of the regulars; they had favorite stools away from the TVs blasting an endless parade of sports. Nate asked about work, Ed said all was well and turned the question back.

"Had to fire another damn busboy for stealing tips," Nate said.

For the past decade, he'd been the owner of the Wander Inn, a tube-shaped diner out on Route 30, open for breakfast and lunch six days a week, closed Mondays. Due to his gregarious personality and 'we-aim-to-please' style, Nate had a loyal customer base and a dependable staff of waitresses. The bane of his existence was the rotating pack of unscrupulous busboys. "Wasn't one of my beaners; they're fine. It's the damn greasy white kids from Arlington I can't trust." Draining his draught, Nate looked to Ed. "So…must be getting excited about goin' to meet Jack Kennedy?"

Ed stared into his beer glass. "Can I be honest? I'm kinda feeling like, do I really deserve this? I mean, a Medal of Freedom? That shit's for war heroes."

"Well, you did keep that nutcase Oswald from blowing the president's head off."

"Anybody would'a done it. It's not like I thought about it; I just reacted."

"Exactly! And I can think of a hundred other guys – me included – that might'a totally froze up. But you jumped on it, buddy. And that makes you a hero. Hey, tell you what: I bet nobody understands how you're feeling better than the President himself. Didn't ya hear what he said when they praised him for saving his men after the Japs blew up PT-109? Everybody was congratulating him for being such a hot-shot and JFK goes…" Nate cleared his throat to launch into the president's New England patter: "I had no choice. They sank my boat."

Ed laughed. "Wow, that's the worst JFK impression I've ever heard!"

"You're missing my point! You're as much a hero as anybody – so go to DC and enjoy the hell out of it." Nate waved the bartender over. "Jay, help us out. This chump is fixing to get the Presidential Medal of Freedom and—"

Slapping his dishtowel like a whip, Jay interrupted. "I heard! Way to go, buddy. How exciting is that?" He turned to the rest of the patrons. "Hey, everybody! In case all y'all don't know, this here is Ed Callahan and he's going up to Washington to get a Medal of Freedom from President Kennedy!"

Several guys crowded around slapping Ed's back, urging him to swipe as many White House ashtrays as he could. When the furor ebbed, Ed tipped his empty glass at Jay signaling the need for a refill. He looked to Nate with a smirk. "You're such an asshole." Ed slid off his bar stool. "I need a cigarette."

"Thought you quit?"

"Bonnie thinks so, too – so rat me out and I'll hurt you bad."

Dropping a dime into the machine behind the quarter he'd already inserted, Ed shook his head in disbelief at the tobacco companies' insane greed, charging him thirty-five cents for the privilege of slowly killing himself.

He yanked the knob under the white and gold Camel label and watched the soft pack drop into the slot below. Ripping open the cellophane, he could feel the electric eel of anticipation swimming through his veins. Sticking the cigarette between his lips, Ed pulled out his engraved lighter, flicked the flame to life and touched it to the Camel's tip. Heaven on Earth.

Stopped at a red light as he drove Nate home, Ed asked how married life was going. Nate blurted that Lucy was pregnant, catching Ed totally off-guard. "We've been together all night and you're just telling me now?"

Nate confessed he was so sure he'd screw this kid up before it was ever born he was having trouble telling anyone. Ed insisted Nate would be a great father.

"Unless it's a girl. What the hell do I know about girls? I mean, I figure a guy will handle my crap…but girls, man, they're just so…pink."

Ed told Nate how Libby had adored him from her first moment of consciousness. And now that she was growing up, beginning to sprout little "boob buds" that completely unnerved Ed, she seemed to need him more than ever. She knew he was the parent more likely to allow her the new freedoms she craved so she made him her coconspirator in her ongoing quest to "soften Momma up;" they'd joyfully been plotting together regularly.

"Want the secret?" Ed asked Nate. "Deal with a daughter the way you deal with any woman. Just listen. That's all most of 'em want."

Back at Nate's house, Ed declined an invitation to come in for a nightcap. One encounter with Lucy's disturbing dolls had been enough.

"Listen, I'll make you a deal," Ed said. "I'll cool out and have fun in Washington if you relax about being a dad. You'll be great. I'm really happy for you. It's the one thing in this life that keeps you young while it makes you old, but it's worth every second."

Nate asked Ed to let Lucy be the one to tell Bonnie; Ed tugged a clenched fist across his lips, closing his oral zipper.

Driving home, Ed kept all four windows down and gobbled breath mints. Even though he knew Bonnie would most likely be asleep, he didn't want any chance of her detecting that he'd been smoking. Parking in his driveway, he scooted next door to deposit the rest of the pack in his neighbor's trashcan.

Stocking the pantry for Marsha before they left town, Bonnie was pushing a cart up the cereal aisle at Piggly Wiggly with Ed trailing behind. A man and his ten-year-old son were just ahead arguing over what to buy. The boy was stubbornly clinging to a box of Cocoa Puffs. The aggravated father roughly grabbed his son's arm and twisted it backwards until the kid cried out in pain, dropping the cereal. Ed rushed forward to get in the father's face. "Hey, man, what do you think you're doing?"

Turning to see Ed and the stranger squared off, Bonnie was horrified.

"Mind your own damn business, Mister," the father said.

"I just don't think you need to be hurting your kid like that."

"And, you know what? When I want your opinion, I'll ask for it. Now buzz off!"

"Or what?" Ed asked, puffing his chest out.

The angry man's response was to cock his arm and smash his fist into Ed's cheek directly below his right eye. And then, the father abandoned his shopping cart, grabbed the boy and fled. Bonnie rushed to Ed who was stunned, fighting to regain his bearings.

"Oh my stars, Ed; what in the world were you thinking? Are you okay?" Her voice was high and thin; she was trying to not get hysterical.

"He, he had no right to treat his kid that way."

"And you had no right to butt in. What's the matter with you? This is Texas. You're lucky that fool didn't have a gun."

That evening, Bonnie stood in front of her closet mirror, twirling left, then right in the simple lavender sheath she'd gotten at Dillard's. Nearby, Libby was sprawled on the bed, clutching her *Meet the Beatles* album, mesmerized by the blue-tinted cover photograph. "Is there anybody on Earth cuter than Paul?"

Bonnie unleashed a disgruntled growl. "Why couldn't your dad have saved Eisenhower's life? It would be so much easier to stand next to an old frump like Maime."

Set to depart for Washington in the morning, neither Ed nor Bonnie slept more than a few minutes that night. Ed tossed, endlessly worrying he'd be expected to make some sort of speech. Bonnie had been so preoccupied with her wardrobe, she'd completely forgotten to obsess over the fact that this was going to be her first-ever airplane ride. As she squinted at the glowing bedside clock realizing the sun would soon be up, ten different stressful notions flashed across her interior movie screen. She worried about the plane crashing and Marsha having to raise her children. She wondered what the heck kept a plane up in the air to begin with. She fretted about why her husband had felt the need to get into a brawl with a total stranger.

"Isn't this the most coolest thing ever?" Kenny asked, sitting on his father's lap in the stretch limousine carrying them to the airport.

"Look at these fancy drinking glasses," Libby gushed, holding a cut-crystal tumbler. She lifted the lid of a recessed cooler. "They have Canada Dry! Can we have one? Pretty please?"

"You just finished breakfast," Marsha said.

"I don't guess one little soda pop will hurt," Ed said. "It's a day to celebrate!"

Sitting in the first class cabin of the plane carrying them to DC, Ed and Bonnie felt like they were living someone else's life. A stewardess recognized Ed, remarking on the article about their trip in the *Dallas Morning News*. She and the rest of the crew treated the couple like movie stars. When Bonnie confessed this was her first flight, the stewardess took Bonnie's trembling hand. "Captain Abraham is one of our most experienced pilots; his takeoffs and landings are as smooth as Chinese silk."

Ed, who'd once flown to California to visit relatives and had also gone to Miami for a Beckman Brothers sales convention, was acting like a seasoned veteran. "Have a cocktail, Bon; the rest'll be a piece of cake."

After a romantic night in their luxurious suite at the historic Hay-Adams hotel on Lafayette Square, Ed and Bonnie were nervously getting dressed for the White House. Bonnie fluffed her hair, smoothed her dress. She fiddled with the string of pearls borrowed from Lucy.

"How do I look?"

Plumping the knot of his striped necktie as it rested against his crisp white shirt, Ed gave his wife a smile filled with pride. "Amazing. I'm not lying. Prettier than the day I married ya."

Bonnie gave Ed a kiss. "Okay, sir, let's go meet the president!"

Moving up the walkway toward the portico of the magnificently gleaming building ahead of them, Ed and Bonnie were escorted by a pair of dark-suited officials. Taking Bonnie's hand, Ed tugged her to a momentary halt. "Amazin', right? A hick like me goin' to the White House."

As he pulled his hand free, Bonnie saw Ed's mortified expression. "What's wrong?"

"My palms are all sweaty; they're clammy and disgusting."

Bonnie dug into her pocketbook and gave Ed a linen handkerchief. He wiped his hands once and then again. It was hopeless.

Bonnie looked at him in utter shock. "Did you just pass gas?"

Waving a disgusted hand in front of her face she sent a sly look to their escorts. Oblivious, one of the dark-suited men tugged open the ornate door to usher them inside.

Stepping onto the crimson carpet, Ed turned to Bonnie. "Sorry. My nerves. Jesus, the only thing JFK's gonna remember about today is that his life was saved by a farting Texas moron with sweaty palms and a black eye."

4

THE INTENSE SEPTEMBER SUN hit Rima's cheek like a laser, rousing her from a dream-laden sleep. Turning away from the window and landing on her left side, she let out a moan. Half awake she gripped her right breast. What was making her chest so swollen and sore?

Hearing her husband's rhythmic breathing as he remained asleep beside her, Rima squelched a whimper of panic. She couldn't be pregnant again. The alarm clock went off; Rima slapped it into silence. She sat up and caressed her breasts. She prayed she was overreacting.

Hadi stirred and slowly climbed out of bed, stumbling into the adjoining bathroom. He started the shower; Rima heard the plastic curtain skitter along the metal rod. Down the hall, two-and-a-half -year-old Adiba was yelling to be freed from her crib. The bedroom door opened to reveal a disgruntled Shemma. "Mama, come get Adiba. She's too loud!"

Moving into her girls' room, Rima recalled when Adiba was seven months old and had been wailing incessantly. Rima picked up a potent decongestant from a neighbor who claimed it was an effective sedative and made the impulsive decision to triple the recommended dosage. Addled with guilt, checking on Adiba in the middle of the night, Rima found her struggling to breathe, releasing shallow raspy squeaks.

In a panic, Rima jammed two fingers down Adbiba's throat making her gag. When Rima scooped her up, Adiba spewed out a torrent of violet puke that stained the nursery carpet to this day. After the crisis subsided, Rima cleaned the putrid mess and cradled Adiba until they both fell asleep in the rocking chair inherited from her grandmother. The next morning, Rima told Hadi their daughter was suffering from a twenty-four-hour stomach virus, not daring to confess her sin.

Closing up his tailoring shop, Hadi headed to the home of his sister-in-law Fatima. She'd phoned to report a clogged kitchen sink. Unable to afford a proper plumber, she hoped Hadi might lend a hand. Knowing it was his duty to go, he couldn't stifle his resentment. He longed for his brother's return so he could tell Emad of all he had sacrificed on his behalf.

Knowing it was improper for he and Fatima to be alone together in her home, Hadi made sure her mother would also be present. On his back under his absent brother's sink, he tugged on the crescent wrench gripping the metal collar connecting two sections of the drainage pipes. His nephew, only months older than Shemma, was crouched to watch his uncle work. Fascinated by Hadi's every move, Marwan asked questions nonstop. Seeing the unmistakable resemblance between him and his missing father, Hadi's anger boiled once again. How could Emad abandon his family without even a phone call or letter in two years? How was Fatima to know if her husband was dead or alive?

"Uncle?" The boy's innocent voice brought Hadi back; he was pointing at the metal ring freely turning allowing Hadi to finally get the two pipes apart. The boy asked another spate of questions; Fatima materialized insisting Marwan leave his uncle alone.

"He is fine. A curious mind is the mark of a scholar. If we do not ask, how do we learn?"

Later, as Fatima's mother put the children to bed, Fatima and Hadi heard scurrying sandals slapping the gravel walkway outside. Moving into the front room, they paused in anticipation of the ring of the doorbell or a knock. Nothing came. A fleeting shadow darted past the window getting lost in the darkness. Hadi and Fatima froze.

Terrified, Fatima whispered: "The government spies and soldiers, sometimes they come. They lurk in the shadows or storm inside, convinced Emad has returned."

"It is an outrage," Hadi said trying to summon courage he didn't possess.

"Yet one we cannot resist them without dreadful consequences."

Scanning the room for a weapon Hadi grabbed a copper kettle from a beam between the dining area and kitchen. The front doorknob twisted. Fatima's pulse quickened. The door opened an inch before swinging wider. With a warrior's yell, Hadi made a lunging leap and brought the kettle down into the side of the intruder's head. The large man dropped to the floor. Forcing his eyes to focus, Hadi discovered that the burglar he had bashed was his long-lost brother.

Having just gotten her girls to sleep, Rima was enjoying a moment of peace when Hadi called with stunning news: Emad was back; Hadi would be home late. Rima gave in to the nagging urge to gently massage her left breast, then the right. To her profound dismay, they were as sore as they had been upon waking.

By noon, too preoccupied to eat, Rima had felt nauseous. The feeling subsided only after she ate the flatbread crackers she'd relied on throughout her previous pregnancies. Incapable of denying the truth any longer, Rima now sat in her living room and sobbed.

Emad returned a changed man. The most visible talisman of this mutation was an ugly scar that ran from under his left eye to his upper lip but there were also dark shifts in his moods. He was more cynical, weighted down by secrets. He spoke in the present but his eyes remained miles away. No matter how often Hadi asked, Emad refused to reveal the origin of that scar.

A week after Emad reappeared, he and Hadi sat in their parents' garden with their handicapped father. Preoccupied, trying to reestablish the new normal with his nuclear family while fighting to find a job, Emad had seen his *baba* only one other time since his return. He was having a difficult time reconciling this frail old man in the rusting wheelchair with the family's bellicose lion. Emad had still been in Baghdad when Omar suffered the ravaging stroke that robbed him of his powers of speech and mobility, but during his time away, Emad convinced himself *Baba* must have recovered; he was crushed to discover how wrong he'd been.

Hadi watched with thinly buried jealousy as his older brother kissed the old man's hand and then brought that wrinkled hand to his forehead, repeating the gesture of respect three times; Emad told his father he was glad he had not departed for the next life during his absence. Hadi saw hot tears in the corners of Omar's eyes as he gazed at Emad with undiluted adoration.

Hadi's resentment resurfaced. He didn't understand why he was the one who took care of the entire family and shouldered his father's business after Emad rejected it, yet Omar saved his most naked look of love for Emad.

Returning home that evening, Hadi was seething with anger. Adiba and Shemma were in their room playing with their dolls. Hadi approached Rima who sat in the living room mending his dress shirts. His tone was laced with ire but his voice never rose above a weary monotone.

"It is your fault my father is partial to Emad. Yes, *your* fault, woman." Seeing Rima's confusion, Hadi went on. "You give me doe eyes as if you know not why? Emad blessed my father with an heir. His wife gave him a son. You have created nothing but two worthless girls."

Dropping her sewing into her lap, Rima gaped at her husband. She didn't dare speak; she refused to cry. Hadi's rage was halted by the arrival of his young daughters. Shemma stood paralyzed; Adiba, always the more vocal one, spoke up.

"*Baba*," the three-year-old asked. "Why it is wo'thless to be a girl?"

A month after Emad's return, Fatima spied Rima across the open-air market. Settling up with the meat vendor, she scurried through the clutter of shoppers calling out Rima's name. Perusing stacks of novels and travelogues on a bookseller's table, Rima pivoted to discover Fatima. She grasped the handle of the stroller that held the serenely napping Adiba.

"*Salaam aleikum.*"

"*Wa aleikum assalam.*"

They hugged and traded kisses on both cheeks. Rima self-consciously smoothed the front of her flowing sheath, praying Fatima couldn't tell she was pregnant. She didn't want anyone to know, least of all Hadi. She still hadn't decided if she would bring this child into the world.

Fatima smiled at her sleeping niece. "Look at her, so peaceful."

"A welcome change," Rima said with a hollow laugh.

Fatima expressed surprise at finding Rima browsing through books, wondering when she had time to read. "I have none; yet how I ache to be transported away on a train of words."

Fatima concurred, saying that although it should be the opposite, her life was twice as busy since Emad's return. She had no desire to let Rima know how belligerent and moody he had become; she was constantly on edge. Although she'd prayed for ages for his return, now that he was back, she wished he'd disappear again. Everything she did was wrong. He was critical and cruel to Marwan; he had no patience for their daughter. As Fatima's mind filled with despair, she heard Rima mention a book club.

"We could make a monthly selection and come together to discuss it – you, me, perhaps my mother, a few others – we'd have tea and a light meal. Would it not be bliss, even for a few hours, to speak of something other than our lives as wives and mothers?"

"Emad would permit no such a thing," Fatima said.

Rima deflated before forcing herself to brighten again. "Then we will do it during the day! While our husbands are at work and the children are at school; the men need never know. I have a brain, sister. If I do not begin to use it, it will turn to *gaymer*."

Checking her watch, Fatima panicked. She had to pick up her children and get home to prepare Emad's supper. He'd gotten a job in the outlying oil fields with a new crew. Lacking seniority, all of the dirtiest tasks fell to him and he came home each night exhausted and angry. Fatima said they'd talk of the book club again soon.

Hadi sat at the workbench in his tailoring shop carefully cutting the navy blue fabric for a serge suit. His front door banged open, jangling the overhead bell and Hadi's nerves. He looked up to see Sayed the tobacco vendor.

"Razzaq and the Nasserites attempted a coup to overthrow Arif! It is a mess: gunfights, killing…but, for now, it appears as if Arif and his cronies have won out; they are still in power."

Hadi fought to follow Sayed's rant. The government had been in turmoil for as long as he could remember. Periods of stability were rare. So many competing factions, countless splinter groups, those in support of the United Arab Republic, those who were convinced it would be the death of Iraq…who could keep up? It didn't matter to Hadi who ruled. Whether it's the *Shia, Nasserites, Ba'athists* or *Sunnis*, it was always about enriching those in power.

Sayed declared he tried to keep his nose out of politics yet couldn't help but believe a stronger union with Egypt would be good for all. "The real enemy is Israel. We quarrel, Arab against Arab, while every day the Israeli army grows mightier.

Nasserites are done; count on that. Disloyalty means death. It is why your brother fled. I do not understand why the rest of these upstarts have not learned the obvious lesson."

Sayed departed as suddenly as he'd appeared. Hadi went back to making the blue serge suit for Mister Muntaha.

That night, waking up alone, Hadi touched the still-warm spot abandoned by his wife. Following the stifled sobs, he found her in the living room with her back to him, quietly crying. Even though it was 3:00 a.m., it was still ninety degrees outside. The chugging overhead fan masked Hadi's footfalls. Not wanting to startle Rima, he gently whispered her name. Slowly, she turned with tears filling her despondent eyes. He quietly inquired about the source of her sadness. Rima replied with a slow shake of her head. Sitting down beside her, Hadi watched her shoulders clench with tension. How could she tell him she was carrying a child she already despised? How could she confess she fell asleep each night praying that *Allah* would carry this baby away before it was born?

She'd been with Hadi for six years, yet he remained a stranger. One day he was a loving and kind artist making a delicate purple coat and then he'd turn short-tempered and distant. One night he'd make love like a prince and then the next evening treat her as if she was invisible. She wanted to love and trust him, but she had no idea how to make him let her in.

"It is nothing. Please return to sleep. You have work in the morning. I do not want you exhausted by my frivolous tears."

Rima instinctively folded her linked hands over her belly. She saw Hadi register the gesture, the spark of understanding in his eyes. "You are with child," he whispered. "My love, can you not see this is a blessing?"

Rima looked at him as if his utterance was patently absurd. Hadi put a tender hand on her hands covering her stomach. "This is the son we have prayed for."

Rima winced, wondering what would happen if it wasn't.

As the smoldering September was ending, Fatima stood at her kitchen sink jamming cubes of lamb and cut vegetables onto skewers; she was daydreaming about Heathcliff, the gallant hero of the classic novel she and Rima had chosen to launch their book club. It had not been easy but they'd finally talked Rima's mother Nazik and two additional neighborhood women into joining them. They gave themselves four weeks to finish the tome and then they'd meet to discuss it over afternoon tea. As Fatima imagined herself darting across the moors, being chased by a handsome suitor, she looked up to see a familiar face staring in through the open window.

It was her widowed neighbor Mr. Araf whose wife had succumbed to cancer two years earlier. He had a trio of rambunctious sons he had no idea how to handle. During Emad's absence, Araf would often seek Fatima's advice. He would come to her back window, out of view of the neighbors; she would remain inside and they would talk for hours. Obeying the laws of her culture, Fatima was careful to never invite him into her home.

Araf hoisted his arms to reveal a basket of fresh figs. He and his sons had harvested them from a tree in his front yard and had more than they could eat. Fatima set down a skewer and came outside to accept the gift. They traded pleasantries, chatted about the children. Araf expressed his happiness that Fatima's husband had returned, but his eyes didn't match his words. A moment later, Emad pulled his smoke-belching pickup truck into the driveway. Stained with sweat and grime, he glared through the front windshield flashing a most menacing grimace.

Avoiding eye contact and without another word, Araf swiftly disappeared.

Through dinner with the children, Emad stayed civil but Fatima knew he was seething. Marwan dominated the conversation, chattering about the birdhouse he was building at school. His parents were too distracted to listen. His sister Samira was busy sculpting a mashed potato mountain; undaunted, the boy burbled on.

The moment they were alone, Emad pounced, yelling that ever since he'd come back he'd been struggling to ignore his neighbors' judgmental whispers. "But now you shove your betrayal in my face! He comes to my home bringing you gifts?"

"The figs are for our family. He has more than they can eat; he wanted to share."

"I suspect that is not all he wishes to share. Did you fuck him while I was gone?"

"I will not tolerate such language, Husband. He is a neighbor, nothing more."

Emad ranted, wondering why more than one acquaintance had warned him to be wary of Araf's attentions to his wife. He wanted to know what Fatima did to encourage this affection. Emad again demanded to know if she'd been unfaithful to him. "No, never. Never. How can you even imagine such a thing?"

"If I find you are lying, I will kill him first and then you."

Leaving her gynecologist's office, Rima had confirmation of what she already knew: she was seven weeks pregnant. On the long walk home, she tried to convince herself this pregnancy felt different. She was nauseous day and night, far beyond anything she'd experienced with Shemma or Adiba. She worked to believe that Hadi was right: she was carrying his son. Giving him a male heir would make everything all right.

Rima felt lightheaded from the pounding sun. She'd already consumed the crackers in her purse; she had to get water and needed a piece of fruit. Luckily, she would pass Fatima's house on her way home. Fatima was ironing Emad's underwear when a pale, depleted Rima arrived.

Drinking tea at the dining room table, Rima confessed she was slowly coming to terms with having a third child. In the last month, Adiba had finally started sleeping through the night; she was much less fussy by day. With the entire household more rested, Rima realized there were times when Adiba had become a joy. The toddler was spending two half-days a week with Nazik which was working for everybody. Rima felt she was regaining her sanity and her mother adored having time with her youngest granddaughter. Now that it was a reality, the prospect of another child no longer seemed like a death sentence. Still, Rima spent each of her daily prayer sessions begging *Allah* to send her a son.

Fatima made her own confession: Emad's fury was rising. He had too much time in the oil fields to get lost in his dark suspicions. Every time he saw a coworker glance his way, he was sure they pitied him for having a wife who was a cheating whore.

"What do I do?" Fatima asked. "He speaks constantly of honor killings, about his right as a cuckolded husband to seek justice from our Imam. I have done no wrong yet he demands proof. How does one prove what never happened?"

In the dark café in downtown Baghdad, Hadi and Emad sat at a table with their wheelchair-bound father, each with a tiny cup of Turkish coffee. The brothers had to help Omar get the cup to his lips each time he signaled to them with a grunt. It was rare to get the old man away from home but the brothers felt it was important to provide Omar with outside stimulation; they also knew the benefits of giving their mother a break.

Emad glared at Hadi. "What do you know about my wife and Mr. Araf?"

Hadi's response was truthful and swift: he knew nothing. Emad pressed. Had Fatima said anything to Rima about their neighbor? Had Hadi heard gossip about the two of them?

Emad admitted he'd even interrogated his own children hoping they might spill some deep secret but had gotten nowhere.

"If the court rules it so, it is my right as a husband to have Fatima's life ended for bringing dishonor to my family. The scent of infidelity is as damning as the crime."

"Tell me, brother, you wish to raise motherless children? You were away, she was alone; she spoke with a kind neighbor. I am certain that is all."

"What would you have me do if I learn she opened her legs along with her heart?"

Omar let out a strangled sound that caused his sons to turn. Did he want to comment or merely want more coffee? His eyes flickered, the eyelids fluttered but it was impossible to read his thoughts. Not knowing what else to do, Hadi raised the cup to Omar's lips.

Emad felt a surge of rage. He knew that if he discovered Fatima had lain with another man, he'd swiftly and without regret petition to have her put to death.

5

BRIAN GLANCED UP at the olive-green battalion transport plane ceiling high overhead. Sitting on the metal floor, back pressed against the cold bowed wall, he felt incredibly small and insignificant. Exactly the way his commanding officers wanted him to feel.

It was October 21, 1965 and after so much time it was happening. Following a spring and summer dominated by a torturous air of uncertainty, twenty-year-old Brian Scott and his squad were on their way to Vietnam.

They were all wide-awake but nobody was talking. The only sound was the rumbling howl of the jet engines and the ceaseless monologue inside Brian's head. Instead of the belly-flipping fear he'd felt for weeks before their orders arrived, a new sensation now gripped him: numbness. In his arms, legs, chest, even in his heart, Brian felt inescapably anesthetized.

"I need a job," Nancy announced as she and John grabbed a quick bite to eat at Don N' Bob's before a choral recital at Brighton Junior High; their niece Sandy had a solo in the show. They stood at the counter awaiting their food as acne-dappled teens in paper hats shouted orders to the cooks in grease-splattered aprons at the griddle. "One Texas, that's one. Traveling."

"Two porkers, two ground rounds — hold the pickles — both with fries."

This family-run hangout was famous for its burgers and dogs but it was the addictive chocolate almond fudge custard that kept folks coming back.

John gazed at his wife with a crimped brow. "Why do you need a job?"

"I'm bored. Brian's across the world, Johnny's home about six hours a week, you're always at work. I need to feel more productive."

"Take up tennis. Mike Franklin's wife is a nut for the game."

"Well, I'm glad for her but I want to work."

A kid with butch-waxed bangs frisbeed their food onto their tray. "Two grounds, one with four-alarm sauce, one fries, one rings, a pair of Cokes. Enjoy your meal, folks."

John thanked him and grabbed the tray. Nancy plucked a bouquet of napkins from a dispenser and followed her husband to a booth. "I thought you'd be happy I want to get out and do something useful."

"I just don't get why it's necessary. I make plenty of money, none of the other wives work. Why don't you volunteer at the Red Cross or work with the PTA?"

"John, why are you acting like you're mad at me?"

"I've busted my butt to give you and the boys everything you could possibly need. What will the neighbors think? I can hear them now: 'things must have really gone south at Kodak for the sorry bastard; poor Nancy had to get a job'." Avoiding eye contact, he grabbed his burger and chomped an oversized bite.

"Wait…is this…is all of this about Marsh Ditlow?"

"We're done talking. You don't need to work. Now please eat."

After twenty hours on the plane, with only a brief refueling stop in Japan, Brian and his platoon touched down in Saigon before noon. When the plane's drawbridge door flopped open, they were greeted by a wave of tropical air that encircled Brian like a thermal cocoon. The sweet scents rushing his nostrils were an unexpected gift.

Stepping onto the desolate airfield, Kurt Bitkoff adhered to Brian's side. "It's so fuckin' green," he whispered. "And quiet. Kinda beautiful, get what I'm sayin'?"

"Man, I thought Rochester had humidity, but this shit?"

Around them, most of their fellow soldiers were lighting cigarettes, taking hungry drags. They'd arrived and nobody was shooting at them. Nobody was charging at them with rusty bayonets or screaming in a high-pitched foreign tongue. For once, even their commanding officers weren't barking orders. It was incredibly peaceful – and downright eerie.

Louise Ditlow used to love Friday nights. Now they were nothing but lonely. On the den couch with her two daughters watching *The Addams Family*, she wondered how she'd allowed herself to become caged in this three-bedroom box.

The screaming whir of power tools came from the basement where Marsh was building a coffee table or another pair of bookends nobody needed. The more he used his new hobby to avoid her, the more Louise's home resembled a Ruby-Gordon's showroom.

Hearing the finger-snapping end-credit music, Louise was shaken from her fog; she wrapped an arm around her seven-year-old's shoulder. "Okay, Katie-lady, bedtime."

Ten-year-old Sarah gloated that she got to stay up an extra half-hour to watch *Gomer Pyle*. Snorting over the injustice, Katie grumbled, "What a rook."

After giving her daughter a goodnight kiss, Katie's question stopped Louise cold. "Why do you hate Daddy?"

"I don't hate him."

"Yes you do. I heard you tell Aunt Wendy on the phone. Are you getting a divorce? My friend Jenny B's parents got divorced and she says it's great! She has two neat-o rooms, her father buys her everything and her mom lets her stay up late watching TV in her mom's bed."

"Why were you and Jenny even talking about this?"

"Because you and Daddy never laugh anymore."

In the seven months since confirming her long-simmering

suspicion that Marsh was having an affair, Louise had gone from anger to pain to her current state of resignation. He was who he was, she'd made the choice to marry him and now she had to live with it. She'd spend his money and survive on a rich fantasy life. For most of the past week she'd been lost in daydreams of running away to the Ponderosa where Little Joe and Adam Cartwright would battle for her affections while she secretly longed to be bedded by their stern father Ben.

Down in the basement, Marsh pulled a newly shaped table leg off the lathe and plopped into a chair to sand it. He inhaled the sawdust smell he found oddly comforting.

Louise had no clue Glenda no longer worked for Marsh or that they hadn't seen each other in months. His mistress had discarded him like a piece of junk jewelry the night after she met her current 'real' boyfriend, the man she'd end up marrying. Marsh vowed to never let Louise know how lonely he was. He refused to give her that satisfaction.

After watching ten minutes of the 11:00 p.m. news, Marsh sneaked into his room and was stunned by what awaited him. The dimmed overhead lights cast a golden circle onto the deep green carpet. On the far side of the bed Louise stood wearing a low cut chili-red negligee that pushed her breasts up. Her lipstick was two shades too bright, her eye makeup too dark.

"Hey, you," she said in a Marilyn Monroe whisper. Marsh felt like the floor dropped out from under him like a cheap carnival ride. He staggered to regain his balance. "I don't know what you're trying to pull, Louise…" He might have had the good sense to stop there but he didn't. He went on: "…but you look like a damn clown."

Wet canvas. To Brian, it seemed like the only thing he'd smelled in his entire life. Since they'd set up camp in this desolate outpost it had been raining nonstop. And this was supposed to be Vietnam's dry season. Between their ponchos and tents there was no relief from that singularly distinct odor that now summed up Brian's total in-country experience: wet canvas.

Building their improvised base, it was deeply unsettling to be working alongside local laborers. Vietnamese men and boys, some in their early teens, were helping to construct the open - air mess hall and bamboo latrines. Brian and his buddies had a question none of the officers could answer: when these guys showed up at camp, how were they supposed to distinguish them from the enemy? They didn't wear uniforms, but neither did the snipers in the trees. They all looked the same. Gooks. Commies. Slant Eyes. How were they expected to tell friend from foe?

"Scott, wanna get high?" a guy named Neagle asked Brian the night before.

"On what?"

"Grass. One of our gook buddies got me some kick-ass shit."

Brian had heard a few guys at Fort Dix talking about smoking marijuana but he'd never been near it. The only guy he knew at college who messed with that stuff was a bearded beatnik clarinet player. To Brian, getting high meant pounding back a six-pack of Jenny Cream Ale. "I heard grass gives you brain damage."

"So does a bullet to the head but this is a lot more fun. When me and Bitkoff got stoned last week, he was laughing so hard, he nearly pissed himself."

Brian contemplated. It was raining again. Everything was damp. Depressing. It would be nice to escape the smell of wet canvas. The rest of the guys were asleep. Brian and Neagle slipped into a copse of palm trees providing a canopy of cover. Neagle produced a hand-rolled cigarette and crouched out of the wind to light it. He took a deep inhale and then blew sweet-smelling smoke out his nostrils. A blissful grin overtook his round face. He passed the cigarette to Brian who took a tentative puff but coughed it out. Neagle laughed and snatched the joint back. "Get it deep into your lungs, man. Really inhale, then hold it as long as you can."

Brian tried a few more times without success. Neagle giggled at him with each attempt.

"You getting anything?" The only thing Brian got was a screaming headache.

Now Neagle was in front of him once again. It was late afternoon. The officers were powwowing in the command tent. Brian and his fellow grunts were supposed to be chopping bamboo for a lookout tower. Neagle unfurled his fist to reveal a fresh joint. "Wanna try again?"

"Now, in the middle of the day? What if we get caught?"

"We won't get caught, you pussy."

Minutes later, they were with Bitkoff hidden in the palm trees. Neagle fired up the joint, took a drag and passed it to Bitkoff who knew exactly what to do. He filled his lungs, clenched his lips, let the smoke dance around in his chest. Exhaling, he passed it to Brian. "Do like me. Take a slow steady hit and hold it."

Brian did. On three separate rounds. And then he felt a spiky tingle in his legs that moved up his back to his brain. For a second he thought he saw the palm tree beside him jump to the left. Then he wondered why he'd never noticed Neagle looked exactly like Alfred E. Newman. Alfred. Fred. His brain flashed an image of Fred Flinstone. Brian wondered why Fred never changed his clothes. Wasn't his job at the quarry a union gig? He looked up to find Neagle gawking at him and instantly got paranoid.

"Bri, you in there?" Neagle's face looked like an image through a front door peephole.

Peephole. What a hilarious word. Pee-pole. Suddenly Brian was laughing harder than he had since he was a kid. Kurt and

Neagle dragged him further away from camp, also guffawing hysterically. "Stop!" Brian gasped, "Seriously. You're killin' me; somebody make it stop."

Standing in the Piano City showroom in Penfield, Nancy watched her husband and the salesman negotiate. John argued that if they were going to pay full price for the Baldwin baby grand, the least Smiley Chet could do was waive the delivery fee.

It hadn't been an easy path to get here but now that the negotiation was underway, Nancy was delighted. When they'd left Don N' Bob's the previous Thursday she'd been so angry she was literally seeing flashes of fire before her eyes.

Having made it through her niece's recital without imploding, Nancy wondered if her true calling wasn't to be an actress. She smiled with her sister and praised Sandy with specifics about her performance even though she'd been distracted throughout the show. She teased her brother-in-law about his god-awful tie and even brought John in on the joke despite the fact that what she really wanted to do was cleave his head from his shoulders with a hockey stick. To his credit, John knew how mad she was and raised the issue the instant they were back in the car. "Look, Nance, I don't know what got into me earlier…the whole job thing. It, it really popped my cork. I'm sorry. You were right: all I was thinking about was how that blowhard Marsh would twist this into something to make me feel like shit."

Nancy accepted his apology and he went on, "A while back, weren't you saying you wished you could be a music teacher? Why not give piano lessons out of the house? Put up flyers, tell our friends. You'll set your own hours, still be around for Johnny – I mean, he's not going to college for two more years – assuming he gets in anywhere, but that's a whole other kettle of fish. Anyhow, you'll have your little job and still be home to make dinner. I'll even buy you a new piano."

She leaned over and kissed his cheek. They each got exactly what they wanted. But did he have to refer to it as my "little job?"

The one thing Brian found most unsettling was the buzz of nonstop rumors. North Vietnamese army regulars had hit the nearby Special Forces camp at Plei Me and Brian's unit was being readied to join the aggressive push to drive the enemy out. When they'd be mobilized was still a matter of conjecture but it seemed certain they'd soon be moving into their first full engagement in the foothills of the Chu Pong Mountains. From the moment their sergeant declared it was guaranteed to be a blistering firefight, Brian's mind had not stopped spinning. He wondered how many of them were destined to die.

The paralyzing stomach knot was back. Each night he was dreaming constantly: of explosions mixed with blood-chilling screams, Eric Leyman chasing after his missing leg as Joe Namath hurled it through the air, using the severed limb to score a touchdown.

There was another rumor that nobody was able to confirm or deny: some guys were saying President Kennedy was getting ready to make a major announcement about the US role in Vietnam. Fearing the war was about to escalate, Brian's temples pounded. He hit the latrine six times a day, rarely just to pee. All he knew for sure was he wasn't ready to die.

John was darting through the hall at Eastman Kodak telling his underlings he was heading out early. "The president's talking about the war tonight; my wife and I want to watch together."

"How's your boy doing over there?" a file clerk asked. "Is he sorry he enlisted?"

"No, no, of course not." John's voice dropped. "He didn't really believe there was a war on, but who did? We're just praying he gets home in one piece."

"TV dinners?" Johnny groused. "I'm in training, I need real meat."

"One night won't kill you," Nancy said. "I don't want to be cooking and cleaning up when the president's on. He's talking about the war your brother's fighting in, you know. I'm praying they've come to their senses and are ready to bring our boys home."

"My social studies teacher says Kennedy's probably sending *more* guys over there to stop the commies before they show up here."

Nancy tugged the Swanson dinners from their cartons and popped them into the oven. Moments later, John sailed through the back door. He gave Nancy a quick kiss, greeted Johnny at the table reading *Sports Illustrated*, and moved into the powder room to wash his hands.

As John unfolded the second black tray with the gold floral design and locked its legs into place, the lights overhead flickered…and went out. "Hey!" he cried.

Nancy dashed in. "What happened? Power's out in the kitchen, too."

"Are you running the dishwasher and the dryer again?" When Nancy told him neither one was on, John grumbled, "Something blew a fuse. Where's a flashlight?"

5:16 on a November evening and the house was blanketed in blackness. John followed Nancy into the kitchen as the wall phone rang. Johnny jumped up to answer it.

"Scotts' Morgue; you stab 'em, we slab 'em!"

"Johnny Alexander Scott!" Nancy chided but Johnny continued responding to the person on the line. "Yup. Yup. Us, too. Okay, 'bye." He turned to squint at his parents through the darkness. "That was Mrs. Ditlow. Their power's out, too."

"Great," John groaned, "how're we gonna watch the president?"

Flashlight in hand, Johnny at his side, John went to the edge of their lawn and peered up and down the block. All of the houses were dark; the streetlights were out. It looked like midnight on the moon. When Nancy joined them moments later, John wondered out loud if the entire city had gone dark. They spied Marsh Ditlow hustling toward them, crossing the street with his usual officious stride. "Did you folks hear? Whole northeast is blacked out. Just got off the horn with my sister in Plymouth. New York, New Jersey, all of New England and even parts of Canada – no power anywhere. If you want my humble opinion, it's the Russians."

"Is the President still coming on to talk about the war?" Nancy asked anxiously.

"He's Commander-in-Chief. I'm guessing he'll need to deal with this mess first."

"Maybe Martians are invading," Johnny grinned. "Easier to conquer us if we don't have electricity."

Nancy gasped. "Oh my God, this is so frightening…"

John took her hand and gave it a squeeze. "We'll be fine."

Nancy's voice was thin, tight. "What if we're not? You don't know. Brian's all the way over there in Vietnam, we have no idea what's happening. Think about it, John: what if this is the beginning of the end?"

1974

1

"THE ONLY REASON Kristy Stillman is Alice instead of me is because I have this hideous kinky brown hair and she's blonde!" Ten-year-old Gina Kaufman pouted.

Her mother offered a sympathetic smile. "Honey, the caterpillar is a great part."

"Except he's a boy!" Doing a spot-on impersonation of the droll English tenor in the Disney animated film, Gina rolled out each word to accent her point. "Ah…who…are …hew? Obviously a boy."

"Who cares? The caterpillar gets the laughs. Alice just chases that annoying White Rabbit blathering about being late; she's boring."

Gina frowned. "My costume makes me look like a nerd."

From the kitchen table Debbie chortled. "You are a nerd. Accept it."

Before Gina could erupt, Lisa ordered her to wash her hands for supper. When Gina whirled out of the room like a funnel cloud, Lisa addressed her fifteen-year-old, "Why do you constantly have to antagonize her?"

"Because," Debbie grinned, "it's so easy to make her flip out."

Across town in his USC office, David absently rearranged files on his desk as he waited for the graduate student he hoped to hire as his new teaching assistant. David's original TA had quit due to undisclosed family turmoil. Now he only had a single reader in his class, *The American Experience*, subtitled "Patterns of development from colonial days to the present." With 148 students, he needed another warm body to grade the continual flow of essays and term papers.

Coming through the office door, Greg Milland peeled off his winter parka. "Jeez, isn't this supposed to be sunny Southern California? What's up with the wind? It's frickin' cold!" Raising his gaze to find David staring at him, Greg flushed. "Sorry. What I meant to say was… Good evening, Professor Goldman. I appreciate you meeting with me. How are you doing?

"Fine, thank you. Have a seat."

There was something in Greg's cool, amber eyes peering out from under a mop of dark hair that made David lose focus. It wasn't the first time this happened. Greg was a student in David's graduate level *Era of the First World War* class and habitually sat in the first row. Even while scribbling notes, Greg's piercing eyes stayed locked on David.

"Sir?"

"Sorry. I need an additional TA in my *American Experience* undergrad class. Given the quality of your work and your writing, I'm wondering if you'd be interested."

The instant Greg learned the position paid a $950 tuition stipend he jumped up, shook David's hand and thanked him profusely. Snagging his backpack off the floor minutes later, Greg nodded to David and exited. David brought his hand to his nose and inhaled deeply. Coffee mixed with a trace of "manly-man" cologne: the scent of Greg Milland.

Debbie stormed into her sister's room to find Gina still in bed. "What're you doing, freak? Get up! If you make us late again, I'll pound you."

"Get Mom," Gina groaned. "I can't go today; I have a really

bad headache."

"You're such a faker."

"Go…GET…MOM!"

Rushing upstairs, Lisa marched to Gina's bed. "I don't have time for this today. I have to get you two to school then take Gramma Flo to her heart doctor. She's waited months for this appointment."

"She's Dad's mother; why can't he take her?"

An exasperated Lisa pressed the back of her hand to Gina's forehead. "You're as cool as a cucumber. Is this because you don't want to rehearse after school? Forget that Brody said the caterpillar suit makes you look like a hot dog; just ignore him."

As their brand new Chevy station wagon inched along Ventura Boulevard, a teary-eyed Gina wailed that her headache wasn't subsiding.

"You just took the Tylenol!" Debbie said. "You need'ta give it time to work."

Lisa urged Gina to push through the day. "If you're still in pain after school, we'll go see Dr. Klein."

"I hate Doctor Klein! His nose hair grows into his moustache; it's gross."

"His beard looks like it's made out of pubic hair," Debbie giggled.

"What's pubic hair?"

A week later, Lisa called David at his office.

"How's my Gina-bo-Beena? Any more headaches?" he asked.

"I don't know what's going on. She's fine one minute, in pain the next, she's got a headache, then she doesn't. Mom thinks it might be because her period's coming."

"She's ten!"

"I was only two months older than her when mine started." When David begged her to stop, Lisa chuckled. "Oh, relax.

You men get so touchy about our periods."

"Unless it comes at the end of a sentence, I honestly don't need to hear about it."

Glancing up, David saw his new teaching assistant in the office doorway. "Leese, I've got a student coming in; we'll finish later." Hanging up, David gave a welcoming smile. "Greg …how may I help you?"

David hated the fact that every time he was near this kid, his heart started to race. Greg folded his toned frame into the guest chair.

"FYI, so far so good on the TA thing. Smart kids in that class. Anyway, I'm here cuz I need some advice. I know I want to teach after graduation but I'm not sure if it should be high school or a professor gig."

"Well," David fought to not get lost in Greg's eyes, "great high school teachers can really impact their pupils' lives. But the upside of being a professor is that your students are there because they have a true interest in what you're teaching. High school's all about wrangling."

"That's for sure. Where I grew up, near Dallas, my classes were like a yearlong pep rally. Remember the guy who saved President Kennedy's life, the one that worked at the Book Depository? He lived a few streets over from us; used to see him out mowing his lawn. Anyhow, he spoke at my school one time and said we each have a duty to try to become a hero however we define that."

They debated Greg's future a bit longer until, glancing at his watch, Greg bolted up.

"Whoa, sorry, I gotta go. I'm meeting some buddies for tacos over at Lucy's." Seeing David's blank look, Greg was incredulous. "You don't know Lucy's El Adobe on Melrose? Best Mexican food in LA. Hey, how about I take you there for lunch some Saturday as a thank-you?"

"I'd enjoy that very much."

Weeks later, returning to his tidy house in Silver Lake, David's crimson cheeks reflected his humiliation. In the master bedroom a litter of discarded shirts and slacks only increased his self-loathing. He swept everything onto the floor and flopped onto his bed. A replay of the entire devastating afternoon ran in his head. He'd woken up that morning singing "Something's Coming" from *West Side Story*. This was the day he was meeting Greg at Lucy's. David ate breakfast, showered and splashed on expensive European cologne. For more than an hour, he tried on combinations of clothes at the mirror like a hormonal teenage girl.

Entering the restaurant, he paused in the foyer to let his eyes adjust. Greg was there to greet him. "You found it, Professor. Super."

David's heart catapulted. And then came a voice he instantly recognized but couldn't believe he was hearing. David whirled to discover the still-handsome face of his first real boyfriend, The One Who Got Away. He battled to catch his breath.

"Holy shit, it is you!" Aaron laughed pulling David into a hug.

Aaron grabbed the arm of a man standing beside him and tugged him forward, introducing him as 'my guy.' "David's an old —"

"*Friend?*" David cast a self-conscious glance to Greg. "An old friend. Aaron, you look terrific. Oh, I'm sorry, this is Greg."

A lightning-round of handshakes before Greg excused himself saying he would be right back. The instant he was gone, Aaron grinned at David. "He's cute. Young."

"No, no. It's nothing like that, he's a student."

"I figured. Be careful, David, you don't need that kind of trouble."

"I'm well aware of what I do or don't need, thank you,"

David snapped.

"Anyway…" Aaron vamped, "we need to get going. Great seeing you."

Then, Aaron and his guy were out the door. David felt defensive, angry, judged. Before he could regain his equilibrium, Greg was back. "Our table's this way. I hope you don't mind, my girlfriend's joining us."

Coming home from dinner with friends, Lisa and Martin heard the TV blaring in the den. Making their way there, they found Debbie asleep on the couch. "Honestly, does the TV need to be loud enough to wake the Wellers next door?" Lisa boomed to startle their dozing daughter.

Debbie shot up with a defensive bark. "It's not!" She grabbed the remote, turned down the volume. "Sorry. I got Gina upstairs at nine like you wanted. I think she was on the phone with Uncle David after that."

Fighting a yawn, Martin turned and nearly tripped over Gina who'd silently appeared behind him. "Whoa, where did you come from, babycakes?"

Gina had the telltale squint and flushed cheeks of one who wasn't fully awake. "My head really, really hurts."

"Again?" Martin instantly regretted his irritated tone.

"I can't see right. Everything's, like, two."

Debbie scoffed. "She's faking it!"

"I am not!" Gina moaned. Then, her body went rigid and she dropped to the floor as if she'd been shot. Lisa reacted with a startled scream. Gina began to twitch and writhe on rug.

Martin rushed closer; Debbie jumped up off the couch. Lisa couldn't stifle her hysteria. "What's she doing? What's happening?"

Martin was on his knees beside Gina as she flopped, her eyes rolling back, her jaw locked and clenched. "It's a seizure, some kind of a seizure. Call an ambulance!"

Debbie started to cry. Operating like an automaton, Lisa floated out of the room to the phone. Martin was speaking soothingly, gripping Gina's shoulder as she twitched. "It's okay, baby. You'll be okay. It's gonna be all right."

Two endless minutes later the seizure subsided. Gina's legs quit dancing; her arms ceased twitching. Her unfocused eyes opened. Staring blankly at Martin, Gina asked for her mother. Then her eyes snapped shut and she was still.

David and the Sunday sunrise arrived at Northridge Hospital in tandem. At the reception desk he was told his niece had been admitted to a fourth floor room. David ran down the hall, fighting to keep his emotions contained.

The call from Lisa came just after 4:00 a.m. As soon the first ring jarred him out of a solid sleep, David couldn't help but wonder who was dead. He'd spoken to Gina earlier that evening. She called to complain about her headaches, claiming her parents didn't believe her. David offered sympathy but picked his words carefully; the last thing he wanted to do was get caught in a power struggle between his sister and niece. Now he was tortured with guilt for not having driven right over there to make sure Gina was okay.

Exiting the elevator David saw Debbie in the fourth floor waiting area. She rushed at him bursting into tears; her parents were in with the doctor and Gina was asleep. "Isn't this so scary?"

Lisa and Martin held hands sitting opposite their pediatrician Richard Klein. Nearing twenty-four hours without sleep, Lisa was catatonic. Klein had been having these consultations for decades; they never got easier. How do you tell anxious parents medicine isn't an exact science?

"The difficulty with someone Gina's age is that there's a wide range of things that might be going on. Some children have seizures with no real root cause; it could be related to hormonal changes, a pending growth spurt. More often than not, it's a form of epilepsy; if treated with the proper medications, patients can lead a normal, healthy life."

"Or," Lisa grimly added, "it could be something much more serious."

"At this point," Klein said, "there's nothing to be gained from worst-case scenarios. We'll run an EEG in the morning and go from there."

"Tell me, Dr. Klein, is Gina going to die?"

He hesitated for a beat longer than Lisa could bear. "She'll be fine."

Trying to stay in control, Lisa put in an early Sunday call to her son who was a second semester freshman at Berkeley. Michael had taken to college life without skipping a beat. But now he needed to know what was going on at home. Michael's roommate answered the phone.

"Kirk, I'm sorry to call at such an awful hour, but I need to speak to Michael."

Rolling over in his too-much-beer-last-night haze, Kirk eyed the empty bed across the room. "He's not here. He and Jordan went into the city to see the Dead last night."

Lisa's head was whirling. What city? What "dead"? She couldn't grasp any of it.

Lisa and Martin huddled outside Gina's hospital room with the stoic Dr. Klein. David had taken Debbie home to get some sleep. He promised he'd be back soon to sit with Gina so Martin and Lisa could get a much-needed break. Clutching a clipboard, Klein spoke in a monotone. "We ran the EEG for a full forty minutes and I'm not seeing any type of abnormal activity to indicate epilepsy or Encephalitis…but we still don't know the cause of the seizure or the headaches. I've consulted with a neurologist who feels we should run a spinal tap."

"Isn't that painful? Are you sure it's absolutely necessary?" Lisa gasped.

"There can be a degree of discomfort, but it's an effective tool for ruling out other possible causes for what's happening. If there's bleeding in the brain, the tap will detect it."

"Bleeding? Why would there be bleeding?"

"Any number of factors might cause a rupture. Let's not get ahead of ourselves."

Lisa started to cry again. Martin grasped her hand.

"Dr. Foxboro put in the order for the LP tray; he'll perform the tap first thing tomorrow morning. I believe it's best if Gina spends another night with us so we can keep monitoring her."

When Michael finally stumbled in nursing a monster hangover, Kirk was at his desk. "Shit, man, your mom called early this morning sounding totally freaked out. You need to ring her A-sap."

Michael grabbed the dorm room wall phone and dialed. His dorky sister Debbie answered: "Oh my God, where have you been?"

"What's going on down there? Kirk says Mom was wigged out when she called."

"Gina's in the hospital. She's fully sick. She had a seizure last night. It was awful. She, like, dropped to the rug and started flopping around. You read *The Exorcist*, right? Like that, SO scary! She went to the hospital in an ambulance; today they're running a bunch of frightening tests on her. Mom and Dad are there; I'm home with Uncle David."

"Let me talk to him."

It took David five minutes to calm Michael down. He filled him in on all that he knew and promised to have Martin or Lisa call as soon as they got home.

Sitting at Gina's hospital bedside that afternoon, David was reading to her from *The Day of the Jackal*. His passion for spy novels was something he'd shared with Gina since before she could read. Whenever they had time together, they got busy devouring another tale.

"If the Jackal's trying to kill Charles de Gaulle and we know de Gaulle didn't die, what's the point?" Gina asked.

"The genius is in how the story plays out."

"How about you talk the doctors into letting me go home instead? I'm bored."

"If you're restless, that's good; it means you're feeling better. Now do you want me to keep reading or not?"

Downstairs in the hospital cafeteria, Lisa picked at her chopped salad. "What if something's really wrong, Mart? What if it is a tumor? What if it's cancer? What will we do?"

"Whatever it is, we'll deal with it."

Martin rounded the table, brought Lisa to her feet and pulled her into a tight hug.

"I'm…I'm just saying, Martin, I'm warning you…if Gina dies, so will I."

2

MOVING DOWN A CORRIDOR in the UCLA medical center Neurology Department, Brian felt as if his legs had turned to lead. Everybody had tried to warn him – friends, classmates, even his former pediatrician back home in Rochester – that the one thing he'd remember most about his medical education was that he spent it in a perpetual state of exhaustion. With this being only the first year of his Family Medicine residency, Brian knew he was destined to be a sleepwalker for at least two more years.

His bloodshot blue eyes throbbed; his head felt like it was packed in damp cotton. The good news was his twenty-four-hour on-call shift was finally over. The bad news was his Sunday night stint at Northridge Hospital, where he was moonlighting three times a month to pick up extra cash, was slated to begin that evening. He hadn't slept for more than forty-five consecutive minutes in the last two days.

In the eight months since his residency started, after four years of medical school and a year long internship, Brian had learned more, forgotten more, had higher highs and lower lows than in his previous twenty-eight years combined. His brain was inflated with statistics and probabilities, symptoms and causes, diseases and cures. His girlfriend was little more than a perfumed memory, at least one part of his body was in constant pain – but for some perverse reason he was thriving.

"There's only one explanation," his mother said on the phone earlier that week, "you truly were born to be a doctor."

Driving back to the stale-smelling Westwood apartment he shared with two other medical students, Brian had all the windows of his dented orange Carmen Ghia down. He needed the crisp, predawn March air to keep him awake long enough to get home without killing himself or anyone else. As the

Grateful Dead's "Truckin" poured from the sole-surviving radio speaker, Brian's flickering attention lit on the lyrics, "Lately it occurs to me…what a long strange trip it's been." Brian heartily agreed. Gliding down Wilshire in 6:00 a.m. blackness, he was reflecting on his own long strange trip from the jungles of Vietnam to the halls of UCLA Medical Center.

With a shiver, he recalled being on his belly in the damp leaves of the Chu Pong Mountain foothills beside his buddy Kurt Bitkoff. November '65. Their rifles were aimed, their bodies were rigid; their ears bristled to identify every ambient sound. The enemy was nearby. Rumors of an imminent firefight abounded yet nothing happened. So they waited. And waited. It was torture, lying in silent anticipation of the shit storm that might rain down at any second.

Their pal Neagle materialized out of the darkness. Dropping beside them, he emitted a gleeful hiss: "Did'ja hear? He did it. JFK ended this motherfucking war; he's bringing us home." Brian went into denial, afraid to believe in miracles.

Evidently Neagle was right because by dawn they'd received orders to retreat. All direct engagement had been halted. The final details of a peace accord were still being negotiated but a massive troop withdrawal was set to commence at once. At last, Brian embraced the reality that a foreign stranger wouldn't end up murdering him here. He was reassigned to a provisional security platoon where he spent the next four months helping to ensure the safe evacuation of his fellow soldiers until he finally got the long-awaited word.

On the last Monday in February of '66, Brian was on a chopper to Ton Son Nhut airport.

From there he boarded a plane back to Fort Lewis in Washington State. He could still conjure the thundering roar that filled the plane when the commanding officer announced they'd cleared Vietnamese airspace.

After a month of quarantine and debriefing, Brian got another surprise: although he still had six months left on his enlistment contract, his active-duty combat service had earned him a discharge to the Standby Reserves. For all intents and purposes, he was out.

Taking full advantage of the GI Bill, Brian went to the State University of New York at Stonybrook; the school on Long Island's north shore had a highly regarded premed program. Feeling he'd already wasted too much time, Brian committed to getting his undergraduate degree in three years. Taking packed course loads each semester and additional classes in summer, he exhibited a focused drive his parents admired. "I have no clue what Uncle Sam did to you, son, but I must admit, I like it," John said at the start of Brian's senior year.

"You're working too hard; when do you have time for fun?" Nancy opined.

"Hey, you met his girlfriend," John retorted, "I bet he's having plenty of fun."

After having made it past his nineteenth birthday with his virginity intact, another gift the US Army gave Brian was the confidence to not look back. He surrendered his cherry to a hooker in Saigon and then had a brief intense relationship with a Vietnamese shop girl. Soon after he started at Stonybrook, he fell in love a Jewish fireball from Queens.

Snaking through the empty Sunday morning Westwood streets, Brian was unsure exactly why he'd been so willing to let her go. Maybe he never had a choice. In March of their last year at Stonybrook, he received his acceptance to UCLA medical school, his top pick. Melissa wanted to pursue a Master's in chemical engineering and had several programs to choose from, UCLA among them. Then, on a rainy Saturday before Easter, she wandered out of Brian's bedroom wearing nothing but his Pittsford High baseball jersey. Finding him reading the newspaper in the kitchen, she gave a sweet smile and told him she was headed to Africa.

Moved by an article in *The New Yorker* about the plight of Nigerian refugees, Melissa applied to the Peace Corps on a whim. Once she was accepted, she made up her mind to go. "It's only for two years!" Brian knew in that moment they were done.

When he started medical school, he vowed to remain single. He wanted his full focus to be on his studies. No women, no distractions, just textbooks and test tubes. What he didn't count on was meeting Heather Rusk.

Heather was an insurance executive's daughter from Hartford. She was at UCLA to earn her Master's in Early Childhood Development. She and Brian met in the campus library. Brian later told his roommate Sean he'd fallen in love with Heather the instant he spotted her. They were strangers perusing the clinical psychology shelves when she unleashed a banshee wail of a sneeze. Mortified, Heather whipped toward Brian with an apologetic shrug. "Could that have been any louder? How embarrassing."

"No kidding, it took two years off my life. My heart's still pounding."

He knew it wasn't only because of her sneeze.

A week later they began dating and had been together since. Heather finished her Master's the previous spring and was teaching second grade in Inglewood. Between Brian's residency and his moonlighting gig, they were lucky if they saw each other once a week but they were determined to keep the relationship alive. "Heather just gets me," he told Sean. "We laugh like crazy together. Not to mention she has the greatest pair of legs. Seriously, guy, she's it."

Stumbling into his apartment at sunrise, Brian was greeted by the scratchy yell of static from the living room. He found Sean passed out on the couch while the TV displayed a black and white blizzard. With a sigh, Brian shut it down and staggered to his room.

Peeling off his clothes he snatched a note from his pillow. He knew the precise block printing belonged to his second roommate Ozzie. It was an ongoing joke between apartment mates: how was Oz going to be a doctor with handwriting you could actually read? Scanning the note, Brian groaned. *Johnny called. Give him a holler.*

"It's fucking freezing in here," Johnny wailed at his roommate.

"Well, if we had any fucking scratch, maybe we could afford heat," Jonah said.

Wearing sweatpants and a torn long-sleeve T-shirt, Johnny grabbed his heavy leather jacket from the back of a chair. He zipped it up and turned up the collar. "New York sucks. Being broke sucks. Our shitty band sucks. Our lives suck. I can't even feel my fucking toes."

While rain pelted their brownstone's basement window, Johnny flicked his long dyed-blonde hair out of his eyes and lit a cigarette.

"We haven't had a fucking gig for months," Jonah said.

"Damn you, man; quit bringing me down with your goddamn truth. I'm going back to bed where it's warm."

In the six months since he dropped out of the University of Buffalo at the start of his last year, Johnny lost thirty-five pounds, not because he was on a health kick, he just never had enough money to eat. He'd been an accomplished guitarist since junior high. He was in a couple of high school bands and played with a dedicated Rolling Stones cover group at Buffalo, but it was seeing his first glam-rock concert that changed his life.

Following that show, Johnny spent weeks scouring *The Village Voice* personals until he found a glitter band looking for a bass player. He quit school, dyed his hair platinum blonde, bought a pair of red leather pants and moved to New York City. Two weeks later, his father informed him the parental checkbook was closed. "We love you, we want you to be happy but if you're quitting school a year shy of graduating you're on your own."

Maybe it would have gone better if Johnny hadn't come home wearing blue sequined eyeliner and spandex.

Inhaling a bowl of Spaghetti-Os after a much needed nine-hours of sleep, Brian was on the phone; Johnny asked how Heather was. "If I ever get to see her, I'll let ya know. What's up with you? How's the band?" Silence hung heavy for a long beat. "Okay, Johnny, how much do you need? Residents make squat, ya know, even with my moonlighting gig. I'm…I could maybe send you fifty. A hundred if it's the absolute last time."

"It will be, bro, swear ta'God. Soon as we hit it big, I'll pay back every cent."

The thing Brian liked best about the 7:00 p.m.-to-7:00 a.m. shift at Northridge was that most Sunday nights were fairly quiet. He had patients to look in on, follow-up exams to give but in general it was nowhere near as chaotic as his residency or his recent rotation in a downtown ER. The majority of his Northridge patients were old, many dying and heavily sedated. Since he wasn't their primary physician, he didn't become emotionally attached. He'd offer a few reassuring words, prescribe sleeping meds or, always to his annoyance, have to get up from a blissful nap to hoist an ancient patient off the floor after he'd fallen out of bed.

On this particular night, when he poked his head into room 407 a little after 11:00 p.m., Brian was surprised to find it occupied by a bright-faced ten-year-old.

"Are you really a doctor? You look too young."

"I'm a resident. Dr. Scott. I've got my medical license so I am a real doc, but still in training." Brian moved deeper into the room. "What brings you here?"

"I had a seizure. No one knows why so they're watching me to see if I have more."

Brian asked why she wasn't asleep. "The nurses keep coming in to check the monitors and it wakes me up. My mom says it's because I'm so nosy; I always have to know what's going on."

Glancing at the bedside table, Brian picked up the dog-eared paperback copy of *The Day of the Jackal*. "Wow. This yours?"

"My uncle's reading it to me. Reading spy novels together is our thing. Do you know James Bond? He's my favorite. I'm not allowed to see the movies but the books are marvelous. My uncle buys them the day they come out," Gina said.

"Sounds like a cool uncle."

"He's sensational. Do you have a girlfriend? I'll bet she's pretty."

"She's gorgeous, actually. Wild red hair, freckles, amazing green eyes…"

"Do you two do it?"

"Ya know what, young lady? I think this conversation's over. Seriously."

"I made you blush," Gina taunted. And then, with a startling swiftness, she went rigid. Her eyes rolled up and she started seizing, ferociously flailing and flopping.

Calling up his training, Brian snatched a towel from Gina's tray table and forced it between her clenched teeth to prevent her from biting or swallowing her tongue. He hit the call button to summon the nurse and then pressed down on Gina's left shoulder and right leg to keep her from vibrating off the bed.

The on-call nurse arrived as the seizure was subsiding. A disoriented Gina gazed up at Brian with unfocused eyes. "It happened again?"

Forcing himself to appear in control, Brian nodded. "It's okay. You're gonna be okay."

Then he calmly asked the nurse to phone Gina's doctor.

Waiting for Dr. Klein, Brian sat at the foot of Gina's bed watching her sleep. Her frizzy brown hair ringed her face like a picture frame.

Wearing a rumpled tracksuit and a scowl, Richard Klein tromped into Gina's room at midnight. He demanded to know why he'd been summoned; a confused Brian reminded Klein that Gina had had another seizure. "Has anything changed?" When Brian shook his head, Klein continued. "Then tell me, Doctor, should I wake her up to chat? What should I do that couldn't wait until morning? I'd appreciate it if you could tell me something I don't already know."

Brian wanted to tell him he was an asshole, something he *clearly* didn't know, but he resisted. "The nurse mentioned Dr. Foxboro is doing a spinal tap in the morning. If it's all right, I'd like to stick around to observe."

"6:00 a.m. Sharp. Good-night, Dr. Scott."

Sprawled on the cot in a dark corner of the on-call room, Brian was fretting about Gina's upcoming spinal tap. Worrying about her parents made him think of his own folks.

With the Rochester winter refusing to release its tenacious grip on the pockmarked streets, Brian knew his father would be threatening once again to move. It was an east coast ritual as certain as the swallows returning to Capistrano on the left coast. John would gripe about scraping ice from his windshield well into April. Brian's mother would ask where he'd like to go and John would say he'd never find a new job at his age so what was the point in pretending?

On the other hand, Brian believed Nancy was as happy as she'd ever been. As much as she enjoyed raising her two boys, there were many aspects of the empty nest that definitely agreed with her. Shortly after Brian joined the army, she started giving piano lessons out of their home. These days she had more new student requests than she could accommodate.

Only half awake, Brian felt a hand on his shoulder. Rolling over, he squinted up at a night nurse letting him know Klein and Foxboro were preparing to do Gina's spinal tap.

Still groggy as he approached Gina's room, Brian saw Dr. Klein huddled with a couple he assumed were Gina's parents. The mother's eyes were ringed with dark circles; her unwashed hair was bunched atop her head. The jittery dad looked like he'd consumed too much coffee.

Turning, Klein spied Brian and reacted with the same gruff bark he'd employed the night before. "Young Dr. Scott. Come meet the Kaufmans." Brian knew Klein only added the "young" to keep him in his place. "Dr. Scott is a first year resident picking up extra shifts with us. He requested permission to observe Gina's procedure."

Shaking Martin's hand, Brian used his most comforting tone. "I was with Gina when she had her seizure last night. It passed fairly quickly. How is she this morning?"

"Scared," Lisa said, "like we all are."

Klein grasped her elbow. "We'll get to the bottom of this, I promise."

Lisa didn't look convinced.

After scrubbing up and slipping into a sterilized gown and surgical mask, Brian entered the room where Gina was on her side in bed. He introduced himself to the neurologist Dr. Foxboro. Klein hovered nearby. Gina asked Brian if this was going to hurt. He gave a quick glance to the other doctors. Foxboro nodded to signal he could be honest.

"A little. More discomfort than real pain. But they're going to numb the area before they put the needle in."

"How numb?" Gina asked with terror in her tone.

An all-business nurse readied a syringe with Lidocaine. Foxboro looked to Brian. "Dr. Scott, what are the chief reasons for performing a spinal tap in a case like Gina's?"

Unprepared to be quizzed like an intern, Brian stuttered. "It, they, spinal taps provide a look at the cerebrospinal fluid to check for signs of infection, to see if there's bleeding around the brain and also to look for any other possible causes of unexplained seizures."

"Good." Foxboro shifted to Gina. "All right, sweetie, I'm giving you the numbing shot now. You'll feel a sharp prick, then a brief burning sensation but it shouldn't be too bad."

Gina looked to Brian with pleading eyes. "Hold my hand?"

Smiling under his mask, Brian said he'd be honored. Taking Gina's tiny damp hand, he watched Foxboro expertly pinch the skin in Gina's lower back, insert the needle and depress the plunger. Gina's grip tightened; she closed her eyes. Foxboro withdrew the needle. "There. That wasn't so awful," Brian said.

"Not for you maybe," Gina snapped.

Foxboro picked up a second, more threatening-looking needle. The silent nurse moved into position, poised to hand the doctor a quartet of vials as needed. The doctor told Gina they were about to begin; she requested that Brian hold her hand once again.

Fifteen minutes later the procedure was over. Foxboro had inserted the needle between the fourth and fifth lumbar space of her spinal cord and extracted four vials of fluid, allowing it to drip out at its own pace. While Foxboro worked, Brian kept up a stream of light chatter to distract Gina. He learned she would miss being in her fifth grade production of *Alice in Wonderland* if she didn't get discharged by Friday.

"Well, kiddo, everybody here will do everything they can to get you home as soon as possible. If it works out, I'd love to come see your caterpillar in action."

Preparing the vials of fluid for transfer to the lab, Dr. Foxboro held one up for Brian's perusal and asked what he saw. Brian inched closer, squinting at the clear liquid. "No blood. That's good."

"It's very good," Foxboro agreed. "But it also means we're no closer to knowing what's going on with her."

Gripped by exhaustion, Brian barreled across town to UCLA, worked a full ten-hour shift in neurology and then headed home, once again fighting to stay awake. Rushing into his apartment, he crashed to the floor. Glancing over his shoulder he saw he'd tripped over a discarded pair of motorcycle boots. "God damn it, Oz," Brian bellowed from the carpet. "Seriously?"

Sitting on the couch blithely eating cold pizza and drinking warm beer, Ozzie turned his innocent gaze to his fallen roommate. "What're you doing down there, man?"

"Nice place to leave your boots. And, in case you're wondering, I'm fine."

Getting up, moving the boots to a less hazardous spot, Brian looked from them to Ozzie's motorcycle jacket draped on the back of a recliner. A glint of inspiration filled his eyes. He asked Ozzie if he was on call the next night and whether he was planning on taking his bike. When Oz said he'd ride in with Sean, Brian asked if it was cool to borrow his jacket and boots.

"You thinkin' of gettin' a bike, man?" Ozzie asked with expectant enthusiasm.

"Nope. Just lookin' to add a little kink to date night."

Driving down the southbound 405 after completing another packed day of rounds with cranky patients, Brian was trying to get time with Heather but was now stuck in relentless traffic. Even though they both had to work the next day, they'd learned it was vital to get together whenever they could. They were planning to go out for a cheap dinner near Heather's apartment in Playa del Rey, then back for some "alone time."

When he finally arrived, Brian fought to shake off his irritation. Giving Heather a long kiss, he remembered how much he loved the way she smelled: oranges and cocoa butter. "I'm starving. How about we hit the Shack?"

Draining their second pitcher of beer, which *he* had mostly consumed, Brian gobbled the last bite of his glorious Shackburger (a Louisiana hot sausage atop a cheeseburger with lettuce, tomatoes, onions and pickles). To signal his satisfaction, he rolled out a deep burp. "Life …is good," he said and grinned.

Heather laughed. "I love how little it takes to make you happy."

"Beer, a Shackburger and you? Seriously. How could it get better than that?"

As the sounds of clacking pool balls, and Billy Preston singing about "nothing from nothing," filled the small wood-paneled local hangout, Brian reached across the table to weave his fingers into Heather's wild red hair; he pulled her in for a probing kiss. When they parted, he gave her a lopsided drunken grin. "Feel like playin' tonight, Legs?"

"What d'you have in mind?"

"Thought you might enjoy going home with my friend Jake. He'll be waiting by the car in five minutes."

Coming out to the tiny rear parking lot, Heather took a deep inhale of sea air. With the beach only blocks away, a team of seagulls circled the night sky dive-bombing the dumpster. At the orange Carmen Ghia, Heather found 'Jake.'

Ozzie's Frye boots had replaced Brian's battered tennis shoes; a black bandanna covered his dark hair. He also wore Oz's cracked leather motorcycle jacket. His eyes narrowed, his voice lowered to a deep growl. "Hey, sexy."

"Are you Jake?"

He nodded. "Take me home, school teacher, and I'll deliver a lesson you won't forget."

"You're on, Drunkster. But I'm driving."

With Heather's bedroom swaddled in the flickering bayberry candlelight, Brian began to peel the clothes off her body. Sliding the cardigan from her shoulders, he slowly unbuttoned her blouse. Dropping it to the carpet, he undid the snap of her jeans and carefully lowered the zipper. When she went to ease her jeans down, he halted her with Jake's gravelly tone: "That's my job."

Cupping her taut ass, he used his free hand to slide her pants down her perfect long legs. She stepped out of the rolled jeans and gave him a kiss. Moving his hand off her butt, he tiptoed his fingers up her back and then swiftly undid her bra clasp. Easing it away, he took one round breast in hand and bent to give it a kiss, licking the nipple as he took in a deep inhale of her scent. Still in the motorcycle jacket, T-shirt, bandanna, jeans and boots, he dropped to his knees to pull down her panties. She gasped and grabbed his shoulders as he buried his face in the warm patch of copper fur between her legs. He loved the way she tasted.

"Now let me undress you," she purred.

"We ain't got time for that," he growled. He sprang up swept her into his arms and dropped her onto the bed. Frantically unzipping his jeans, he shoved them down below his ass and made his impatient entrance. Arching her back, gripping his leather-clad shoulders, Heather bucked, as 'Jake' became a human metronome, digging the steel-toed boots deeper into the mattress with each thrust. When they finally exploded within sixty seconds of each other, their exultant cries echoed throughout the apartment. Twenty minutes later, they were at it again.

As Brian drifted off to sleep, Heather pressed her face against his chest.

"Just so you know? Jake can come back and visit me…anytime he wants."

Morning light and harsh reality invaded the bedroom when the alarm woke them at 6:15 a.m. Heather had to be to school at 7:30 and Brian needed to report to UCLA by 8:00.

Attempting to sit up with his jeans and underwear straightjacketed around his knees, Brian felt like hammered shit yet happy and deeply grateful for Heather.

Although her husband thought she was crazy, Nancy Scott could tell when one of her sons was calling. John insisted the ring was always the same but Nancy swore it sounded different to her. And she was positive it was one of her boys on the ringing line now. She snagged the wall phone receiver. "Hello," she sang before reacting to the voice on the other end. "Johnny my rock star! You don't sound good. Are you sick?"

"No. Just broke. The asshole manager at our next gig bailed on us."

"Thank God it's only money; you scared me. Do you suppose maybe it's time to get a real job?"

"Mom, if I'm doing some lame waiter thing, how will I have time to write and rehearse and look for bookings? I can't rely on Jonah; he's a lazy sack of shit."

"Johnny, please! That mouth."

"Is there any way you and Dad could send me, like…a grand? I'll really knuckle down. Write songs, hustle my butt off, find a studio to cut some tracks." Nancy waged an internal debate. Johnny pressed, "You don't have to tell Dad. You've got your own money from your piano lessons, right?"

"I do. And I'll do it, but only this once. You have to promise if nothing happens with the band soon, you'll go back to school and finish your degree. Promise me?" Johnny did but hardly sounded sincere. Nancy persisted. "Mean it, honey. Don't simply tell me what I want to hear."

Sitting in the apartment complex's basement laundry room washing and drying two long overdue loads of clothes, Brian kept thinking about Gina; why would a healthy preadolescent with no prior history be experiencing chronic headaches, blurred vision and seizures? He couldn't help but wonder what her doctors were missing.

Staring at a tumbling dryer, hypnotized by the rhythmic clicking of the metal buttons of his Levis hitting the window with each rotation, Brian had an epiphany. The UCLA neurology department had a new piece of state-of-the-art technology that might help with Gina's diagnosis; the dryer's spinning drum had jogged his memory. Just a few weeks earlier, Brian finished his morning rounds and was darting to the cafeteria when he ran into his mentor.

Dr. Robert Jenkins II was a Scottish neurosurgeon who bonded with Brian as soon as Brian started his neurology rotation at the beginning of term. On this particular morning, Dr. J had news for his protégé: "Did you hear, lad? The EMI scan arrived – it's brilliant. D'ya have time to check it out?"

Brian knew Jenkins had been anxiously awaiting this machine for months. UCLA was fortunate enough to have received one of the first in the United States. The EMI scan was a medical imaging device that created three-dimensional x-rays of a patient's brain. To Brian, the great irony was that EMI's research branch was a division of the company that acquired much of its fortune from being the Beatles' record label. "That noise," as his mother had called the Fab Four's music, played an integral part in facilitating this medical miracle.

Trailing Dr. J into the lab where the scanner was housed, Brian gawked. A large metal barrel protruded from a sleek white cabinet and a raised table waited at the cylinder's mouth, poised to deliver the next patient. "Have you used it yet?"

"Twice. Discovered an undetected malignant brain tumor in a forty six year old high school principal, and bleeding in the cerebral cortex of a female stroke victim. It's pure brilliance, lad. We'll be able to make all manner of discoveries with this baby."

After putting his clean clothes away, Brian grabbed the phone off his much more visible floor and called his mentor's pager. Five minutes later he got a return call.

"Sorry to bug you at home, Dr. J, so I'll cut right to it: do you think an EMI scan might help determine why an otherwise healthy ten year old is having unexplained seizures?"

Hearing the answer he was hoping for, Brian thanked the doctor and hung up. He was devouring a can of chili, watching news of President Robert Kennedy at an economic summit in Paris, when his roommate Sean bounced in seeming overly wired. Spying RFK on the TV, Sean launched off. "I love that guy. Him and his brother? The best. Hey, d'ya ever think what would have happened to your sorry ass if that Dallas dude hadn't stopped JFK's assassination? I mean, where you were in 'Nam? No offense, but if that firefight blew up your baby ass wouldda been smoked for sure, man. Think if that cowboy Johnson was president. No way he wouldda ended the war."

"Appreciate the cheery thoughts, buddy."

"No, I'm just saying – the Viet Cong were such better jungle fighters. You were a pack of kids; you wouldn'ta stood a chance. The timing of the withdrawal? Shit, man. That's what you call *fate*. Somebody up there did *not* want your ass to die. Hey, remember how that same week the whole east coast got blacked out, even up into Canada? Total craziness."

"My brother thought it was the Martians invading."

"Then it turned out to be radicals from, what..Saudi Arabia or some shit? Bringing down the power grid 'cause they hate our Western decadence. Those dudes are all crazy from the heat for sure, man. Happy that shit's calmed down."

"For now anyway," Brian said with a pessimistic growl.

"Well, enjoy your chili; I gotta split for work."

After his ten-hour Thursday shift at UCLA, Brian made a spontaneous visit to Northridge Hospital. He went directly to the fourth floor where he learned Gina had had two more seizures that afternoon. Thanking the night nurse for the update he jogged to room 407. On approach, he heard Gina's anxious parents conferring with the prickly Dr. Klein. Gina's pale face lit up when she saw Brian. "Mind if I join you?" he asked. "Heard it's been a rough day."

Gina's mother battled back tears. "We don't understand why this is happening."

Later, after the Kaufmans left for the night, Brian asked if he could buy Dr. Klein a cup of coffee. Klein said he never had caffeine after three p.m. but grudgingly consented to a cup of herbal tea. Seated in the downstairs cafeteria, Brian began: "Are you familiar with the new EMI scans? Computed tomography. They have a machine at UCLA. Just came in last month."

"Must be wonderful to be so well-funded," Klein said.

"I was thinking it might be a good idea to get Gina over there, do a full brain workup, see what we can find."

"We?" Klein said with deeply arched eyebrows.

"Sorry, sorry. I know this is your case, and Dr. Foxboro's, but Gina's such a great, spunky kid and I just thought—"

"Please don't think, Doctor. Not on my cases." Snatching his tea off the table, Klein rose. "This may come as a shock to you, but I have practiced medicine for over thirty-five years and have somehow managed to treat my patients without expensive, highly unproven machinery. I've put Gina on Dilantin because I'm convinced she's suffering from epilepsy."

Klein marched off without another word. Brian stormed upstairs and found a nurse filling cups with morning meds; he asked when Dr. Foxboro would return.

"Klein's taken the lead on Gina but Foxboro has a spinal cord injury in 411 he checks on first thing in the morning. Usually around 8:15 a.m."

"Please let him know I'll be calling him then."

Well aware that Friday night was always his busiest and most hectic on-call shift at UCLA, Brian struggled to pace himself as he attended to his daytime duties. On this particular Friday, that proved to be impossible. He'd put in a call to Dr. Foxboro as soon as he arrived at the neurology center that morning. The instant he hung up, Ozzie cornered him near the hospital cafeteria. "Do you think Sean has a drug problem? Santoli's been pulling a bunch of shifts with him and she says every time she sees him on the ward he's skulking around the drug closets."

"He has been pretty wired lately," Brian agreed. "Man, the other night he came in and just launched *off.*"

"Still, we can't confront him without evidence. I guess we just have to keep our eyes and ears peeled." Ozzie instantly blanched. "I hate that expression: 'eyes peeled.' Gross. Makes me think of googly bug eyes popping out like grapes."

"Oz, are we done here? I seriously need to start clearing charts."

Brian hadn't gone ten steps when the hallway speaker instructed him to pick up line five.

Putting the phone down minutes later, Brian was shaking from the ass chewing of a lifetime delivered by the excitable Dr. Klein. Brian learned that after he'd spoken to Foxboro, Foxboro called Klein to say Brian presented a cogent case for bringing Gina to UCLA for an EMI scan. Foxboro consulted with Dr. Jenkins and an appointment had been made to transport Gina to Westwood first thing in the morning.

"I don't know who in the holy hell you think you are," Klein roared, "but if you ever go behind my back again, questioning my judgment on a case, I will bring you up on

ethical charges to the AMA. If you have any doubts about my
seriousness, young Dr. Scott, just try me!"

The cacophonous slam of the phone was still ringing in
Brian's ears. Finding his way to the resident's lounge,
exhausted and rattled, Brian was met by a note from Dr.
Jenkins: *Doing the scan on your seizure girl tomorrow, 9:00 a.m. You're
welcome to observe.*

Fearing Klein would also be there, Brian opted to stay away.
Still, he did feel a sense of triumph. Foxboro and Jenkins had
backed his assessment over Klein's.

"Thanks to you," Foxboro told Brian in a Sunday morning
call, "we finally have a diagnosis on Gina. Nothing terribly
positive, I'm afraid. The scan revealed an AVM."

"A cerebral arteriovenous malfunction?" Brian replied with
alarm.

"Chances are it's been there since birth but now it's
enlarged and pressing on her brain tissue causing the seizures.
Dr. Jenkins believes he can remove the cluster, he just doesn't
know if he'll end up killing her in the process. Whatever the
final outcome, Dr. Scott, you made an excellent call – despite
what Klein thinks. Without this scan, it's highly likely the AVM
wouldn't have been detected until it was too late."

Hanging up, Brian pondered the implications of an AVM, a
small grape-like cluster of arteries and veins in the brain that
got knotted together without having the normal capillaries as a
buffer between them. The only way to remove it was through
open brain surgery. Depending on its size and location, there
were countless risks involved in the operation. If left alone, a
whole host of other life-threatening complications might
ensue. Intracranial hemorrhaging could cause an embolism, a
stroke or even sudden death.

The one thing Brian knew for sure with this diagnosis was
that Alice would to be journeying to Wonderland without her
caterpillar.

3

EMAD KASHAT SAT on the front porch of his suburban Baghdad home puffing on a fat cigar. It was a Friday afternoon, normally his day of rest from his brutal hours in the oil fields. However, *this* Friday was anything but relaxing. The power of unharnessed female energy inside his home had driven Emad outside.

In her bedroom, Emad's seventeen-year-old daughter Samira was trembling from head to toe. She tugged one floor-length dress over her head, cast it aside and grabbed another. Behind her, sitting with perfect posture on the bed, Samira's mother could no longer hold her tongue. "What is wrong with that one? You looked lovely," Fatima said. Samira disagreed, claiming the butterscotch gown made her look like a camel.

"But a lovelier camel I have never seen," joked Aunt Rima.

Samira stepped into an orange dress with pale yellow stripes. Fatima sternly reminded her they were running out of time. Smoothing her ebony hair hanging to her perfectly rounded breasts, Samira gazed into the mirror. In tandem, Rima and Fatima pronounced this outfit the winner. Fatima moved to the bureau and extended a yellow *hijab*. Samira balked. "This is truly necessary, *Mama*?"

"Your grandfather says the Azzawis are pious people. They will expect you to cover your head. You only get one chance to make a first impression."

Later in the kitchen, Samira fought to steady her hands as she set her grandmother's porcelain coffee cups onto a silver tray. Fatima stood by arranging a plate of *baklava*. From the main room, they heard the extended family entertaining a quartet of guests. Fatima ordered Samira to quit quaking. "Have you not seen the way the fat auntie glares at me? Clearly I have offended her."

"I have known this woman for ages; she always looks as if she is sucking lemons. Now get out there and serve the coffee so they see you will make a dutiful wife."

Samira took several deep breaths; closing her eyes she asked *Allah* to provide her with the strength to make it through the afternoon. Gliding into the front room, Fatima at her back, Samira used every ounce of concentration to still the trembling tray.

On one side of the room, her father sat beside her grandmother. Rima was on Emad's other side. Seated on the long couch opposite them, a round, stern-faced woman was flanked by her husband, her thirty-year-old nephew and her spindly ancient mother with haunted coal eyes. Clearly, the portly woman in the center was the one in charge. She took the bitter coffee without a smile. "My nephew Waleed is an extremely sought after prospective groom." She jabbed an elbow into her other nephew's ribs. "Show them your brother's photograph."

The young man in the pinstriped suit complied. The aunt snatched the photo and flicked it around for Samira's perusal. Giving the last cup of coffee to the skeletal grandmother, Samira carefully set down the tray. The man staring at her from the glossy photo caused her heart to skip; he was the definition of tall, dark and handsome. Despite being a decade older than Samira, he had a charming, almost reticent smile. Remembering the incessant warnings from her mother and aunt, Samira fought to retain her dignity. She smiled demurely and handed the photo back to the fat auntie.

Coffee in hand, Emad nodded to the two men across from him. "Shall we retire to the porch to smoke, gentlemen, and leave these ladies to their business?" With gratitude, the potential groom's uncle and brother followed Emad outside.

Fat Auntie boasted about Waleed's degree from Baghdad University, his Masters earned in Jordan and his current pursuit of a PhD in economics in London. She also spoke of his strong work ethic and gentle nature despite a fervid determination to succeed. In counterpoint, Fatima spun fanciful tales of Samira's talents in the kitchen. Of course, she failed to mention Samira once nearly set the house on fire boiling the water out of a pot of rice. Fatima told of her daughter's skill with a needle and thread, claiming she inherited her flair from her uncle and grandfather, both renowned tailors. She opted to omit the story of Samira reducing a dress to ribbons in an attempt to alter it.

The back-and-forth continued until, at last, Fatima reminded Samira they had one final bit of business in the kitchen. Samira and Fatima retreated. Rima and Samira's grandmother kept up the polite chitchat with the guests. From the porch, they could hear the men griping about the latest political unrest.

Fatima eyed her daughter. "What we will serve, *habibti*? Bitter coffee or sweet juice?"

Samira was well versed in the significance of each. Dark coffee meant she was rejecting the proposal; to save face, there was no point in the prospective groom's representatives making a formal offer for the couple to meet. Juice indicated the would-be bride was interested in becoming Waleed's wife. The fact that they had yet to meet was of no consequence if the families agreed it was an acceptable match. After only a brief pause, Samira fetched the carafe of peach nectar from her parents' refrigerator.

When Rima returned home that evening, Hadi met her at the door. "There may have been a sighting. Sayed the tobacco vendor was at an outdoor café in Mosul when a pickup truck paused at the curb, its bed packed with old men. Sayed was certain your father was among them. Before he could get closer, the truck sped off."

"There was no follow-up, nothing more?"

Hadi shook his head. Silence filled the room until nine-year-old Mo'ez barreled in with a balsa wood glider. He raced around Rima, zipping his toy plane through the air. "Look what I made, *Mama*! *Baba* helped but I put together the wings and the body – "

"What the airplane body is called?" Hadi prodded.

"Fuse-o-lodge!" the boy bellowed.

Rima felt inexplicably offended by their banter. How could Hadi not be fully focused on the fact that her father might be a prisoner in Mosul? She ordered Mo'ez back to his room and turned to Hadi to ask what they should do about Sayed's report.

"What we can do? It was a phantom sighting, a rumor. Sayed could not say for certain it was your father. We must accept the fact that in all probability Faraj is gone."

Rima was crestfallen. Since her father's disappearance, she had been through more crashing lows and spiking highs than she ever imagined a person could endure. It started on a brutally hot July afternoon. Rima's three children were leaping through a sweeping lawn sprinkler outside. Although Mo'ez was only two years younger than Adiba, his big sisters coddled him like a prized possession. From the day he was born there was tremendous joy and relief that Rima had finally given Hadi a son. As the siblings frolicked, Rima was inside folding laundry. Her mother called in such a state of delirium Rima couldn't make sense of her words. She told *Mama* she would gather the children and be right there.

Arriving at her parents' home, Rima was met by a neighbor who told her he'd been walking in the nearby park where Faraj played chess daily. The man reported that a black car with darkened windows came screeching at them, careened over a high curb and stopped only inches from the table where Faraj and his cronies sat. Young men with military rifles lunged from the car, snatched Faraj and two friends, jammed them into the vehicle and sped away. Despite the fact that there were at least thirty other people in the park, it happened so fast no one had the chance to intervene. The vehicle bore no license plates, no markings. No one knew if the kidnappers were soldiers or militants.

Over the next several days, Rima and Hadi paid constant visits to the local police. The authorities declared that since they had no concrete evidence of a kidnapping, there was nothing to investigate. The Kashats knew exactly what the coded language meant: with the current repressive regime most likely responsible for Faraj's disappearance, the policemen saw no reason to get involved. The Kashats spoke to local politicians but they too were useless. Every avenue Hadi and Rima explored was a dead end. Nazik spent each day at home, glued to the phone, hoping for a ransom call that never came.

The Ba'ath Party was still in control and power had consolidated in the hands of the Tikritis. They were Sunni Arabs from the town of Tikrit, closely aligned with the country's President, Ahmad Hasan al Bakr. Three of the five members of the Ba'ath Revolutionary Command Council (RCC) were Takritis, all related. The most ruthless among them, Saddam Hussein, had started out as the regime's Chief of Security and was now the country's vice-president. Plagued by family tragedies and severe illnesses, Bakr was the nominal leader but had ceded much of his power to Saddam. Known as The Enforcer, Saddam used intimidation, fear and murder to exert control. Anyone perceived to be an enemy could vanish in a millisecond, never to be heard from again.

The thing that bewildered Rima most was that Faraj was not a political activist. During his years as a midlevel banker he focused on making a decent wage and spending time with his family; he could not have cared less about who was in charge. "Leave politics to the politicians" was his oft-repeated mantra.

Rima lay awake many nights wondering if her father was dead or alive. Was he being fed? Was he being tortured? Did anyone bring him his glass of tea before sleep? What about his heart medication? How long would he be able to survive without it?

Sitting alone in her living room well after midnight, Rima wished this latest sighting sparking a flutter of renewed hope had never happened. It only served to revive her torment. She would envision Faraj's corpse, alone and untended, floating down the Tigris, as bloated flesh fell from his bones like an overcooked roast.

Following a night of stressful dreams, Rima was in her kitchen preparing fresh dough for the evening meal's *bistilla*. Turning to grab a rolling pin she collided with Adiba. "Baba says I must stop my schooling next year. I know it is what Shemma did, but for me it is not right! One day I wish to travel, to see the world. *Allah* blessed me with a brain; why I should not use it?"

Rima laughed. "You know, child, I stopped my schooling at twelve, yet I use my brain every day. So does your sister."

Adiba reiterated that she was not trying to be unkind but she wanted to be more than a wife and mother. She wanted to work; she wanted to travel to America. She wanted to be every bit as educated as the boys in her class.

Rima used to joke that the reason Adiba cried for most of her first two years was to make sure the world knew she'd arrived. Staring into the child's fierce eyes, Rima was certain this demand to stay in school wouldn't be dropped anytime soon. She also knew Hadi was the uncontested head of the household. If he decreed Adiba must leave the classroom, there would be nothing anyone could do to change his mind. Frustrated, Adiba retreated to her bedroom.

One of Faraj's chess-playing cronies from the park appeared at Rima's kitchen door. She invited him in and offered a glass of tea he readily accepted. "You are aware your father was a supporter of the Kurdish rebellion? He and his friends would get quite heated discussing this in the park. Some of us tried to warn them: "you never know who is listening; even the benches have ears." Your father was dismissive, claimed he had a right to speak. He thought the RCC had become too oppressive. He had no particular affinity for the Kurds, but felt our country was big enough to accommodate all. "Today the Kurds; who will be next?" he would ask. "We are Shiites, Saddam and Bakr are Sunni; how do we know they will not come for us next?" He railed about this often in the days before…" the man hesitated. "Ayyoob and al-Khodeiri became vocal as well. Now all three are gone."

Rima asked why he was only bringing her this information now.

"I have been afraid. I have a large family, Mrs. Kashat; they depend on me totally. I could not risk speaking out. But now I am hearing Sayed the tobacco merchant believes Faraj to be in Mosul. I know the pain fresh hope must bring; I cannot fathom the torment of uncertainty so I feel compelled to share what little I know. As I believe you heard, Tareq the plumber had been a part of our chess club for years. After your father was taken I learned Tareq's son-in-law is quite high up in the Ba'ath regime, a loyalist. After the kidnapping, Tareq ceased to join us. He claimed an arthritic hip made it hard for him to sit on the wooden benches. But I believe it wasn't his hip that hurt; I suspect a guilty heart."

While Rima grappled with the agony of her father's absence, Fatima's preoccupation fell at the opposite end of the emotional spectrum. Her every waking moment was dedicated to planning her daughter's wedding. In Fatima's world, even the most humble families managed to pull off elaborate nuptial celebrations with enormous guest lists and lavish feasts.

Fatima's daughter Samira was marrying Waleed Azzawi, a handsome, celebrated scholar; anything less than an extravagant affair would be an affront to the Azzawi clan. Fatima's biggest challenge was from the bride herself. Samira craved only a simple wedding.

"Be simple *after* I throw you a celebration that becomes the talk of the city."

When Samira asked why her desires didn't count for anything, Fatima lunged. "Listen to me, Samira. Why it is never my turn? Do I not deserve a chance to make all those who have treated me like dirt envy the beauty and joy surrounding me on your wedding day? You were too young to understand how I suffered. For two long years your father was absent. I was alone with you and Marwan. Your grandparents, your Uncle Hadi…they helped, but in the middle of the night, who was there? Only me, a married woman with an invisible husband. When Mr. Araf befriended me, we became targets of vicious gossip. Your father glided back into our lives threatening to put Araf and me to death over a basket of figs! I endured stares, whispers. I held my head high, took it in stride. Your father never apologized. He was back, and for that alone he expected my eternal gratitude. In all the years since, he has worked and put away money like a miserable Shylock. Did he ever once buy me a fancy coat or a diamond? No. But now that you are getting married, to the much-desired Mr. Azzawi, I will throw you the wedding of the decade and each of our 400 guests will recognize I alone made it happen!"

Adiba stood in her mother's path, defiant arms bent, fists digging into her hips. The eleven-year-old had no intention of backing down. "Have you spoken to him?" Rima hesitated and Adiba pounced. "*Mama*, you promised! You said you would convince *Baba* to let me stay in school."

"I made no such promise. I said I would speak to your father; only a fool would presume she could get that man to change his mind about anything. He is as stubborn as Aesop's mule."

"So will you not even ask?"

Rima reluctantly confessed she couldn't see the point in rocking the domestic boat. She tried to shift focus. "Upper school is more arduous, more competitive than what you experience now, you know. You will have many hours of homework; there will be very little time to play or to visit with your friends. When will you learn to cook and keep house?"

Adiba countered that she didn't care about cooking and housework; she wanted to learn.

"With the endless tension of your grandfather's disappearance, do you truly wish to inflict more stress by raising your father's wrath?"

Giving her mother a steely glare, Adiba's answer was swift and clear. "Yes I do."

On Saturday morning, Adiba was delighted to accompany her father to work. Leaving Shemma and Mo'ez behind, she felt like her father's special apprentice whenever he allowed her to join him at his tailoring shop. Adiba adored its sights and smells: the crumpled yellow tape measure, the bits of soap for marking the fabric, the large bolts of cloth. It was like being in a wizard's lair watching her father turn a few yards of wool into a bright orange dress for her to wear at her cousin's wedding. She loved standing by holding the pincushion shaped like a tomato to hand her *baba* straight pins to mark a hem. As he worked, the tiny circles of sweat dotting his thick black moustache captivated Adiba. When Hadi began to stitch a sleeve, she gently eased her way onto the topic consuming her. "*Baba*, must I really leave school after next year? You know how much I desire to continue."

Hadi paused in his sewing to search his daughter's anxious face. "Already you are such a bright young woman. You truly feel the need to become smarter still? Men do not like overly intelligent women. Protracting your schooling may make it difficult to find a suitable spouse."

"If a man wants a dunce for his wife then he isn't the husband for me."

"Is it propaganda from the west making young women wish to turn into men? This I cannot abide, Adiba. *Allah* purposefully designed a difference between sexes; it is the way it has always been and must continue to be."

"I don't wish to be a man, *Baba*. I want to learn as much as I can so one day when I am a wife and mother, I will give you the smartest, strongest grandson ever."

Rima was applying her nightly cold cream; Hadi appeared beside her. "I have decided it is best to allow Adiba to continue her schooling for as long as she desires."

Rima was speechless. Hadi kissed his wife's cheek. "Our children and the children they create are our legacy. In order to supply them with every tool to build strong families, education must be the cornerstone." To ensure she didn't think he'd gone soft, Hadi growled, "This is my decision. Do not question me, wife. Adiba's education shall continue."

A week before Samira's wedding Rima was having lunch with her increasingly frail mother. It had been fifteen months since Faraj was snatched from a public park by unknown thugs. In the ensuing months, there'd been a rash of unverifiable sightings, a hailstorm of rumors, countless days of lost hope. None of that prepared the family for the new torment that began on this Thursday afternoon. Rima and Nazik were drying the lunch dishes when Hadi appeared at the door. Seeing him pale and shaken, Rima rushed closer with a gasp. "You have news!"

"They have discovered a huge mass grave down south near Al Basrah…"

Rima gaped in anguish. Nazik started to cry. Hadi pressed on. "Bodies piled on top of bodies, most burned beyond recognition – "

"Then we do not know, we cannot possibly know for certain," Rima said.

"We may never know. But some of the bodies, a few among many, were not entirely burned. One still wore a medallion, a trinket, nothing of value or it would have been taken long ago. It was a gift from the man's wife, engraved with their names and wedding date. This medal belonged to Ayyoob."

Nazik let out an inhuman shriek. Ayyoob was one of the men kidnapped with Faraj.

"Ayyoob's son came to me. He met a journalist investigating this mass grave who returned the medallion."

Nazik collapsed into a chair. Rima rushed to envelope her mother in her arms. "We do not know for certain *Baba* was among the corpses. These kidnappers, whoever they are, are animals. We know not what they want so we cannot surmise how they operate. Perhaps *Baba* is being kept alive as a bargaining chip."

"Or," Nazik whispered, "perhaps it is time to embrace reality."

Samira and Waleed, joined an hour before in the *Nikah* ceremony conducted by the *Qadi* from their mosque, sat side-by-side on miniature thrones. Their parents, siblings and immediate families held hands and danced in a circle around them. A ten-piece band played a joyous Arabic tune while the rest of the 400 guests clapped to a rhythmic beat cheering the newlyweds. The hotel ballroom was ringed with buffet tables filled with *bariani, capsi, baklubah,* baked *kube,* and roasted lamb; fresh shrimp cascaded down an elaborate ice sculpture. The party had not started until 10:00 p.m. and was destined to go until dawn. The main meal would not be served for another hour. First they danced. Children were asleep on chairs pushed together around the room, using their parents' discarded coats as blankets and pillows.

Prancing in a spinning circle, holding her mother's hand, Adiba beamed at her cousin with her groom. "Samira and Waleed are like characters from a fairytale!"

Rima replied sharply: "Yet tomorrow they must deal with life's harsh realities." Then she emitted a shallow laugh. "Forgive me, *habibti,* at times the stress of your grandfather's absence overwhelms me — but tonight is about joy and celebration!"

Later, as guests were finally seated to feast, Fatima stood surveying the scene. Everyone she could see was eating, talking and laughing. The women were in their finest gowns, draped in glittering jewels. The men wore crisp suits, many made by Hadi. Fatima was basking in the steady stream of effusive compliments she'd received all evening. Guests repeatedly remarked on what a calm and elegant hostess she was. As Fatima thanked them, her chest inflated with pride. She and Emad would not be able to afford a vacation for decades but she didn't care. She had pulled off the perfect wedding; she was the envy of her community. She eyed Samira and Waleed, pleased that although Samira was a lovely bride, Fatima believed she was even prettier.

Stroking Mo'ez's head as he slept in her lap, Rima watched her extended family dance. Hadi was in a back corner of the ballroom, half-hidden by a curtain of cigar smoke as he chatted with a cluster of friends. Rima's daughters were dancing nearby with a gaggle of cousins.

A distant relative moved toward Rima with urgent steps. It was 2:00 a.m. Rima realized this was the first time she had seen this cousin all night.

"I've only just arrived," he told Rima. "I had business downtown but I have news. My neighbor, he has seen your father. Gaunt and hollow-eyed, in a prison in Tikrit. My friend was there day-before-yesterday. He swears on the *Quran* the man he saw in that cell was Faraj."

4

"TELL YOU ONE THING," Ed said to his pal Nate over the roaring crowd, "walk into any b'ball game in the country and it'll smell exactly like this: sweat, overheated rubber and hot, moist air – the hoops trifecta."

Sitting between his wife and buddy in the packed Irving High bleachers, Ed was trying to get a handle on where the years had gone. It seemed like only weeks ago Kenny was watching his blue and gold Pinewood Derby car race down the wooden track to a second place finish. Now, here he was, playing center for the Tigers, four months shy of graduation.

Nate leaned across Ed to address Bonnie who was gulping down a Tab between handfuls of home-popped popcorn. "What the heck are you feeding the Kenster? I swear, he's three inches taller than he was last week."

Gaining possession of the ball with an elegant steal, Kenny made a furious drive down court heading for the basket. Ed and Bonnie bounded to their feet. With a rival player closing fast, Kenny launched an arcing jump shot that sailed through the hoop with a picture-perfect swish. The home court fans bounced up to scream and stomp. The Ducanville Panthers were sinking fast; Tiger fans were relishing every moment of it.

As his teammate Wayne Fitts nabbed the rebound, Kenny glanced at his folks with a fleeting 'how'd you like that?' grin. Wayne, one of only two African Americans on the team, made a fake-and-go lunge into the clear before passing the ball to their consistent high-scorer. Another two for the Tigers! When the final buzzer sounded it had turned into a rout: Irving 97, Ducanville 78.

Waiting to catch the thirty seconds of high school sports highlights on the local news, Ed heard the phone ring in the kitchen. Checking his watch, he wondered who'd be calling at

10:15 p.m. Seeing Bonnie snatch the wall phone from its cradle, he jumped up to turn down the TV volume so he could eavesdrop.

"Oh hi, honey. What a treat. Is everything okay?"

That was all Ed needed to know Bonnie was talking to Libby, a junior at the University of Texas, Austin. There was a special tone his wife reserved for the kids: sweet, engaged, layered with love. Figuring it couldn't be anything too earth shattering, Ed re-raised the TV volume.

"...after a two-day sojourn to Toronto for meetings with the Canadian Prime Minister, President Kennedy is back in the White House tonight. First Lady Ethel Kennedy continued on to a conference on world hunger in Geneva, Switzerland."

Ed looked up when Bonnie meandered in to join him. "That Libby?"

"She was cute. I'm guessing she had a few beers at the frat party she'd been at. She was missing us and wanted to check in. Sends her love. You coming to bed soon? I'm done-in."

Tossing her turquoise slacks into the hamper, Bonnie was replaying the conversation with Libby, knowing most of it would remain between the two of them. Ed was a wonderful father, more involved than many men she knew, but there were still certain things about his precious girl he didn't need to hear.

For the past eighteen months, Libby had been dating a business major at UT Austin and now they were having sex. Libby started the conversation by announcing she was thinking of getting on the pill. Did Bonnie think it was safe or would a diaphragm be better? Listening to the torrent of questions, it was hard for Bonnie to catch her breath. As close as she was to her own mother, she'd never talked to Marsha about this sort of stuff, not even now that they were both adults living under the same roof. She was flattered Libby felt comfortable enough to broach the topic with her; she just wasn't sure she was ready to hear it.

"Are you thinking of having…you know…" Bonnie stammered. There was a screaming silence. Then, on the other end of the line, Libby burst into tears. "Oh my stars," Bonnie said, "it's already happened. Did you, I mean, did he—"

"Yes! Of course. We're not idiots."

Bonnie allowed herself to start breathing again. "Good, that's good. If you're truly at this point, Lib, just be smart and safe." She lowered her voice. "I'm ready for lots of things but being a granny isn't one of them. And, of course, your daddy doesn't need to know any of this."

They agreed Libby would visit the campus clinic to obtain birth control pills and then together they'd see Bonnie's gynecologist when Libby was home on spring break. "Thanks for being cool, Mom."

"It's all an act, believe me."

Arriving at school the following Friday wearing the white shirt, blue tie and letterman's sweater that was the team's required game-day uniform, Kenny was shocked to find Wayne in a nylon windbreaker. "What're you doing, man?" Kenny asked. "Where's your sweater?"

"On my closet floor. Got a two-game suspension. It's bullshit."

Wayne had to get to class but promised Kenny they'd discuss it further at lunch.

Pushing the lump of mystery meat around his plate, wondering why he hadn't ordered the Friday fish fry, Kenny listened as Wayne spewed. "You know I don't like to play victim, but if I was a white boy, none of this would be happening." Wayne paused to exhale. "I been goin' out with Helen Furgeson, right? We ain't hid it from nobody – except her parents cuz that's how she wanted it. Well, they know now and they're raining all kinds of shit down on me. Her father's some Mr. School Board. Seems like everybody be afraid of that

cat and he's playin' it to the hilt. Last week, night before
Ducanville, Helen told her folks she was studying at a friend's
house only her and me went to grab dinner. Then – this is
where I'm such a dumb-ass – I brought her home and we were
out front in my Buick having us a little goodnight kiss and
whatnot—"

"How much whatnot?"

"No, man, it was innocent, just making out is all, I swear.
Comin' home from her bridge game, her old lady caught us
and, Jee-zus, the way that woman carried on, you'd a thought
we were buck-naked doing the nasty. She dragged Helen's dad
outside – you seen that guy? Abe Lincoln without the damn
stovepipe. Swear if he'da had a rope, he'd a'lynched me right
there."

"I'm still not getting what this has to do with you playing
ball."

"He told Helen she weren't allowed to see me no more, she
said she couldn't make no promises and then he came after me;
I start throwing out every 'yes, sir, no, sir," hopin' to get clear.
Next day, he goes to Coach Pete and tells him I was out past
curfew and need to be punished. First Coach said nobody
obeys curfew so he didn't think it was fair to single me out;
then ole' School Board must'a laid down the hammer 'cause
Coach called me in, saying he didn't agree with none of it, but
had no choice 'cept to put me out for two games or all hell
would break loose. Now Helen isn't speaking to her parents,
her mother's on pills for her nerves and my black ass is gonna
be sittin' on the bench when I should be helping y'all win
division."

Later, the instant the final bell rang, Kenny bolted out of
school and caught a bus to nearby Plano. A half hour later, he
was in the washer-dryer section of Beckman Brothers talking
with his dad while Ed kept an eye out for customers.

"How often have I been out after 11:00 the night before a game? Nobody checks; nobody cares. It's bogus. We both know this is only happening 'cause Wayne's black."

"What's he thinking dating Helen? Her father's practically a grand wizard of the KKK."

"But she's not like that. She's dating Wayne 'cause she really likes him. C'mon, Dad, you think this is bogus, right?"

"Sure," Ed said. "But I don't know what you expect me to do about it.

That night over dinner at Denny's before Kenny's team took on the Cedar Hills Longhorns, Ed, Bonnie and Marsha were assessing the team's chances without Wayne Fitts.

"So how is it Helen lied to her parents but Wayne's the only one suffering any consequences?" Bonnie asked.

"Wayne and the whole team," Marsha added. "They've worked so hard this year …now it all might be for naught if Wayne's out again next week against Grand Prairie."

"Clayton Furgeson is and always has been a bully," said Ed. "Sure he's on the school board, acting like he's God's gift, but y'all know it's always his way or the highway. Maybe I need to talk to Coach Pete."

"Ed, stay out of this. Please. Despite what you've apparently come to believe, you do not need to be a hero every day."

"Where's this coming from all of a sudden?"

"Oh," Bonnie shot back, "do you not recall getting a black eye from that guy in Piggly Wiggly when you tried to tell him how to parent? Or how about when you gave your suit jacket to the homeless man and then found out you'd left our car payment in the pocket!"

"He needed it more than we did, Bon."

"Really? Is that why we ate nothing but Kraft dinners for a week tryin' to make up the loss? Sometimes, Ed, I just don't understand what's gotten into you."

Pulling into his driveway a few minutes before midnight the Tuesday after the Longhorns left the Irving Tigers in the dust, Ed realized he hadn't been so exhausted in years.

The parents' meeting he'd set in motion was slated to last forty-five minutes but had gone on for nearly four hours. The principal promised to announce her decision by noon the next day as to whether or not Wayne would be permitted to play in the final game. The thing that shocked Ed most was how quickly passions had ignited. It was a verbal brawl from beginning to end. Ed asked why, if no one had been previously penalized for curfew violations, did it make sense to start with Wayne? Furgeson wondered how one wrong justified another. He asked if it was the desire of the parents and faculty to turn out a generation of lawless savages. As he spit out that last loaded word, he glared at Wayne. Only Ed voiced objection to Furgeson's thinly veiled attempt to ignite a race riot.

Through it all, Wayne sat erect in his pressed white shirt and dark tie, his sport coat fresh from the cleaner's. Flanking him were his sister and single mother silently eying the charges and countercharges getting swatted back and forth.

Stiffly climbing out of his car due to a sharp ache in his bum knee, Ed fought and lost his fight to refrain from having a cigarette. These days, he was down to a pack a week but, no matter how hard he tried, he couldn't quit entirely. He kept a carton of unfiltered Camels in the trunk under the mat that covered his spare tire. In part it was to hide it from Bonnie but also to make it more difficult for him to get to them.

Slipping into the bedroom, Ed saw Bonnie open a sleepy eye; she asked how it had gone.

"The Alamo meets Hiroshima. Not a man left standing. The principal's making her call tomorrow but let's just say Clayton Furgeson and I won't be dancing a tango anytime soon."

Ed was showing off the in-door ice feature on the newest Whirlpool side-by-side to a pair of newlyweds from Arlington when a fellow salesman approached. "Pardon me, folks. I hate to interrupt, Ed, but Bonnie's on line two sounding pretty upset."

Ed asked his coworker to take over with the couple and bolted for the wall phone in the customer service area. Grabbing the receiver, he punched the flashing line. "Hon, what's up?"

Bonnie fought to control her hiccupping sobs. "Mom and I…we came home from the grocery and… and…"

Ed was going out of his mind. "Is it one of the kids?"

"No, no. It's the garage door. Somebody spray-painted it, Ed."

Standing in his driveway, Ed was trying to take in what he was seeing; it wasn't some hasty scrawl, it was bold and incongruously neat. It covered the entire garage door.

NIGGER

LOVER

Marsha, who was beside Bonnie and Ed, asked if they'd called the police. "You have to; it's a crime, pure and simple."

"I know that, Mother…but all I want is to have it gone."

"It will be," Ed promised, "as soon as it's on record with the cops."

Ed went down to Sears with a paint chip from the garage door while Bonnie waited for the local sheriffs. It would take at least three or four coats to cover those thick black letters and Ed intended to get a jump on it the instant the policemen were gone.

Later, after the first two coats had been applied and they were breaking for dinner, Kenny informed his family that Principal Lafferty had made her ruling. She felt bound to stand by Coach Pete's original decision: Wayne would miss the final game.

"So me and a couple of the guys are boycotting Friday night. We're not gonna play in solidarity with Wayne. We've violated curfew more than he has; what's fair is fair."

"But you have a championship on the line," Marsha reminded.

"Granny, aren't principles more important than trophies?" Kenny snapped.

"Don't be fresh," Bonnie scolded.

"Sorry. But it's a load of bullshit and I wanna do something about it."

"Now you're cussing at my dinner table?" Bonnie whirled to face Ed. "I hope you're proud of yourself, Mister. This is all your doing."

"Me? I haven't said a word."

"Aren't you the one who called that parents' meeting getting everybody riled up? I swear, Ed, I do not understand this Hero Complex! Who ever told you it's your job to save the world?"

Bursting into tears, Bonnie swatted her napkin onto the table and bolted out of the room. Stunned, Ed looked from Kenny to Marsha. "Did I miss something?"

"It's been a terrible day, Oak. She's just upset and taking it out on you."

"Should I go talk to her?"

"Eat your lamb chop, darlin'. You should know by now, when she gets like this, best to steer clear. It's the only way I survived her teenage years."

"It's bleeding through again," Kenny moaned as he and Ed applied a fourth coat of paint to the garage door. With the late February moon rising above them, they worked under the inelegant glare of a floodlight Ed clamped to the edge of the gutter.

"Then we'll have to wait 'til tomorrow and go at it again."

Hearing the sound of a coasting motor behind them, Ed turned to see a Channel 8 news van gliding to the curb. Its huge antenna was reaching for the inky sky; its side door slid open. Ed had an urge to bolt but stayed put. A field reporter Ed recognized from TV was coming at him. A second man shouldering a large black camera trailed. "Excuse me, Mr. Callahan?"

Ed nodded. Kenny stood frozen, paint roller in hand.

"John Rottman, Channel Eight news. May I speak with you a moment? I've been informed your home was vandalized this afternoon. Apparently in retaliation for a recent stand you took on certain racial tensions at Irving High?"

"Look, I'd rather not get into it."

Kenny erupted. "What? Why not, Pops? People in this town need to know what kind of bigots they're living with."

Rottman pivoted. "Are you Kenny Callahan?"

"Yup. You can interview me if you want."

"Great." The reporter turned back to Ed, "but since you're already a bit of a local legend, sir, I know our viewers would like to hear from you."

Heading to the kitchen for a glass of water, the bright light outside caught Bonnie's attention. Working to stay hidden, she pulled back the dining room curtain. In the driveway, she spied Ed and Kenny talking to a television reporter with a camera aimed at their faces. Seeing the Channel 8 van at the curb, Bonnie's anger flared anew. *What, they won't be happy until they've blasted our private pain out to the entire city?*

After 10:00 that night, Ed trudged toward his bedroom to make peace. Taking Marsha's advice, he hadn't seen Bonnie since she fled the dinner table. Now he hoped she'd had sufficient time to cool off and realize that, from the start, he was only trying to do what he thought was right. Entering their bedroom, Ed found Bonnie packing a suitcase. "What're you doing?"

"I need to go, I need to get away from you. Talking to a reporter, going on television? Is it, what, you won't be happy until somebody *firebombs* us?"

Ed rushed closer to take her into his arms but Bonnie dodged him. "Don't touch me."

"Where will you go? It's not like you can run home to mother – she lives here!"

"You think this is funny? It's all some big joke to you?"

"No! Look, I – that TV guy ambushed me. I think you're overreacting."

"No, Ed, I'm not. I'm sick of this; sick to death of you never caring about what I want."

"Honey, that's not true!"

"Oh really? I happen to think you'd rather be a hero than a husband and I'm sick of it. I'm going to Libby's. Work will survive without me, and so will you."

Ed made one last feeble attempt to stop her but Bonnie wouldn't be deterred. The next thing he heard was the squeal of rubber as she jetted out of the driveway in her Volkswagen bug.

Knocking on the door of the apartment Libby was renting with her best friend, Bonnie realized she should have called ahead. When Libby opened the door, Bonnie had never seen her look so shocked. "Mom! Oh no, what's wrong?"

"Why didn't you ask who it was before you opened the door? I could've been a serial killer."

"We have a peephole," Libby pointed to it. "But why are you here? Is everything okay? Oh Lord, is it Granny?"

"Everyone's fine. I just, I'm really angry with your father right now and I had to get away. I didn't know where else to go. I'm sorry."

"No, no, it's cool. I'm glad you're here. I want to hear everything but, um…oh gawd, this is so humiliating. I'm actually having a really horrible day myself."

On the sagging plaid couch that was once the centerpiece of Ed and Bonnie's living room, Bonnie and Libby sat sipping mugs of steaming tea. Bonnie filled Libby in on all that had happened in Irving – Wayne's suspension, the parents' meeting and the ugly garage graffiti – now it was time for Libby's tale of woe.

"Okay…this is way more than you ever wanted to hear about your precious girl but you're here and I'm freaking out." Libby's voice cracked. "This is what you get for showing up unannounced."

Bonnie wondered why she suddenly had an elephant sitting on her chest.

"I'll just say it but you can't freak out. Nick and I were having s-e-x this afternoon; he was wearing a condom like always 'cause my stupid pills still haven't come and when we were done, he pulled out but the…it…the condom didn't."

Returning from the nearest Skillern's where she used her employee discount to purchase three boxes of Summer's Eve, an exhausted Bonnie sat on the bed while Libby was in the adjoining bathroom. Bonnie couldn't fathom how her life had come to this.

And then, Libby's ebullient "Bingo!" rang out from behind the bathroom door.

Downing a soup tureen of Wheaties before school the next day, Kenny asked Ed when he thought Bonnie might return.

"When she's good and ready. I'm suspectin' it'll be a day or two. Libby can handle it. Listen, I was thinkin', if you feel boycotting the game is the right thing to do, I'm with ya, Ken. Integrity's important. A man can be a lot of things, but what you don't wanna be is full of shit."

Walking from Chemistry to English, Kenny was deep into it with the three teammates who were also considering sitting out the final game against Grand Prairie. After much debate, only their small forward Chihuahua was prepared to stand with Kenny. At five foot nine, he was the shortest but fastest guy on the team. "Okay," Kenny said, "looks like it's me and Chee."

Kenny and Chihuahua stood uncomfortably in front of Coach Pete.

"We know you only did what'cha had to do; it's the same with us. We're not trying to screw over the team but bottom line? We're sitting tomorrow night out."

"Well, Kenny, that's about the biggest bunch of bullshit I ever heard," Coach Pete said.

Chihuahua cleared his throat. "Can I ask one thing, Coach? How come you ended up suspending Wayne in the first place?"

"Off the record? Furgeson said if I didn't, he'd slash next year's budget to shreds. And know what, boys? He's the kind'a prick that makes good on his threats."

Returning from work, Ed was relieved to see Bonnie's VW in the driveway. He found her in the kitchen, shakin' and bakin' chicken. "Hi." She gave an icy hello. He tried again. "You okay?"

"Been better."

Ed kissed her cheek. "Look, Bon, I don't wanna live in a Cold War. I'm sorry, okay? I swear to you, I was only trying to do what I thought was right."

"I know. So let's just agree to drop the whole thing. No more meetings, no more interviews; we'll put it to rest and move on. Can you do that?"

Ed said he could and then added, "I don't think Kenny's playin' tomorrow night."

"That's his prerogative."

"You still seem mad."

"I'm tired, Ed. I'm just really, really tired."

To no one's surprise with Kenny, Wayne and Chihuahua on the bench, the Tigers lost to the Gophers, 110-82. Opting out of the game, Bonnie made Ed take her to a Barbra Streisand movie. Man, he thought, when my wife wants to punish me, she really knows how to drag me to hell.

Returning from the movie, Ed and Bonnie found Marsha poised like a panther ready to pounce. "We need to get to Parkland. Kenny got into a brawl after the game; he's there getting stitched up. He's the one who called so it can't be too bad. Just sounded like some nasty scrapes and bruises."

Seeing the angry glare Bonnie was shooting at him, Ed made a preemptive strike: "I know, go ahead and say it: this is all my fault."

"It was stupid," Kenny spit as his anxious parents hovered. "A guy went after Chihuahua saying we flushed the season, then Wayne went to defend Chee and it erupted. Kids I've never even seen before were kicking and punching like lunatics."

The emergency room doctor was finishing a neat row of stitches to close the deep gash over Kenny's right eye. Kenny stated, not for the first time, that it was no big deal.

"Is that why we're in the emergency room at midnight? Cuz it's no big deal?"

Ed took a step closer. "Bon, calm down."

"No! I will not calm down. This is a nightmare. It's a nightmare, plain and simple."

"It's over, Mom. It's done."

With her chest heaving and her temples pounding, Bonnie looked to Ed. "And don't think I don't know you're still smoking! You can sneak all you want, Mister, but that doesn't keep your entire closet from stinking like a barroom ashtray!"

In all the years they'd been together, Ed had never known Bonnie to drink alone. But that was where he found her at 2:00

a.m: in the dark kitchen drinking white wine, crying quietly. He sat down across from her. "Ya know why I first fell in love with you?" she finally asked. "Because we both wanted the same things: kids, a house, a simple, solid life. I didn't need to be on Broadway, I didn't care if you ever played in the Super Bowl or took me to Paris. All I wanted was security and love."

"But we have that, that's exactly what we have!"

"Is it? I'm not so sure anymore. Ever since Oswald, you've changed, Ed. You have this restlessness, this…it's like me and the kids are no longer enough for you. I see you, ya know, upstairs some nights. Taking out your Presidential Medal, staring at it like it's a long lost lover, like you're aching for something I can't give you. And I have to tell ya, it breaks my heart." She took a long pause before continuing, "Honestly, the way it's going, the way it's been lately… I'm not sure I can do this anymore."

5

ENTERING THE UCLA Medical Center's basement cafeteria searching for his sister, David was consumed by a single thought: why must hospital lighting make everyone look like an extra from *The Legend of Hell House*?

Seated in a back corner, Lisa was the personification of David's thesis: bloodshot eyes, limp hair and colorless cheeks. Adding insult to injury, she was bathed in harsh white light. Reaching her, David insisted on getting her something to eat, despite Lisa's claim that she wasn't hungry. He asked how Gina was.

"She has a brain tumor, David; how would you expect her to be?"

"It's not a tumor, it's an AVM."

"Call it what you will, it's all horrible."

Delivering a bowl of matzo ball soup for Lisa and turkey-on-rye for himself, David pulled a rolled sheath of papers from his sport coat pocket. He'd spent the morning in the USC library doing research on Gina's condition, compiling questions for Lisa and Martin to ask the surgeon. Biting into his sandwich, David shuffled the pages as Lisa eyed her soup like it was alien technology. He prodded her to eat while it was hot. Lisa half-heartedly lifted her spoon.

"Everyone says that with cases like Gina's, you have to be your own best advocate. Doctors only tell you so much because they're terrified of malpractice suits. Take this sheet into your meeting with Dr. Jenkins; if you're not up to it, have Martin ask the questions. It's things like 'how many times have you performed this procedure, what's your success rate' – it's imperative to determine if he's the best man for the job."

"Okay, David, you need to stop. I know you mean well, but I can't breathe right now."

Lisa dropped her soupspoon as if both she and her hand had lost the will to hang on.

"Leese, I agree this is awful but going in blind won't help."

"I know," she barked. "But it's, you're…it's too much. It's *too much*."

Martin and Lisa sat in Dr. Jenkins' office waiting from him to arrive. Having raced there from work, Martin was in the crisp navy blazer and red tie he wore to sell Chevys. Engulfed in anxiety, the Kaufmans' eyes stayed fixed on the neutral space ahead. They knew the intimacy of facing one another might push them over the emotional cliff.

"Michael asked if he should come home but I didn't know what to tell him. I'd rather he stays up at school but he's worried, he wants to be with us. It's very dear," Lisa said.

"We'd have to buy a plane ticket, somebody would need to pick him up at LAX… Besides, he should be attending classes. I'll give him a call when we finish here."

Walking in, Robert Jenkins jammed the tails of his white shirt into his slacks as his loosened tie hung around his neck. "Sorry for the delay, folks. I just got out of surgery."

He launched into details of the operation but Lisa didn't hear a word. She was riveted on a splash of crimson on his forearm below his rolled right sleeve; it was clearly blood.

"I'd like to do the procedure day after tomorrow, first thing." And then for emphasis he added, "Thursday, 6:00 a.m."

Lisa blinked away the blood drop and forced herself to concentrate. Recalling David's prompts she asked, "How long do you expect the surgery to last, Dr. Jenkins?"

"With an AVM approximately 3.5 centimeters in the frontal lobe…I'd venture to say we're looking at about seven or eight hours."

"For the operation? My god, isn't that an awfully long time?"

"This is the brain we're dealing with, folks. It's vital that we move as deliberately as possible. We have a strong indication of the AVM's size and location from the EMI scan, but there are always variables that can only be confirmed once we open her up."

Lisa's head swam. *Why is he talking about my precious daughter like she's a can of tuna.?*

"With this surgery, there's an inherent risk of swelling on the brain, hemorrhaging, additional seizures, a stroke—"

"A stroke. In a child?" Martin asked.

"Rarely. But it does occur. Since we're dealing with the frontal lobe, there's also a chance Gina's speech or memory might be impaired but I assure you we'll do everything in our power to see that none of those things happen. Any questions?"

"Yes," Lisa exhaled, "why is this happening to us?"

Brian splayed his cards onto the tray table bridging the bed between him and Gina. "Gin."

"Again?" Gina growled. "You cheat."

"Nope. I'm just better than you. Deal with it."

Brian collected and shuffled the cards. Gina blurted, "Will my operation hurt?"

"Not before and definitely not during. You'll be totally conked out. But your head will be pretty sore afterward. Probably itchy, too – especially around the incision."

"That's disgusting. Will I have a big ugly Frankenstein scar?"

"Naw. Once your hair grows back, it'll totally cover it. Most of it anyway."

"Grows back?"

Brian couldn't believe no one had talked to Gina about his. "They, they have to shave your head to do the surgery. It'll be okay. You'll get hats. Great hats. Ya know, all kinds of cool things to wear 'til your hair grows in. With your face, those eyes, you'll be beautiful. Seriously."

"Or maybe I'll just get really lucky and die."

"I can't believe Dad got Mom to leave the hospital long enough to have dinner with us. She hasn't done that since they moved Gina to UCLA," Debbie told David.

"Your mother needs a break. She looks awful to me, just awful."

Debbie's eyes glistened. David touched her elbow in sympathy. "It's been tough, huh? You're the one getting left by the wayside. At least Michael's a bit removed up in Berkeley. You do know I'm here for you, right? Whatever you need."

"I'll get the olives for the salad."

"Something smells good," Martin said, when he and Lisa returned.

Debbie set the salad bowl in the center of the table. David filled her tumbler with milk as Martin grabbed a beer from the refrigerator. Snatching a pair of quilted potholders from the counter, David moved to the oven. Standing at the table, Martin used silver tongs to hurriedly shovel a mound of salad onto his plate.

"Where's the fire?" Lisa asked.

"Lakers are on. I'm gonna take this into the den and watch the game."

"No you're not," Lisa said. "David and Debbie prepared this beautiful meal and we're going to sit down and enjoy it together."

Wishing he were invisible, David put a trivet onto the table and set the steaming casserole on top of it. Debbie was in her chair; the adults remained standing.

"Babe," Martin persisted, "It's game three of the western conference semifinals against the Bucks. I've been waiting all day to watch it."

"And you may. As soon as we finish dinner and you help me clean up."

"Look, I'm not one of the kids; I don't need you telling me what to do." As tension blanketed the room, he snatched up his plate and spooned out a hefty helping of the casserole.

"We haven't had one civilized meal in weeks," Lisa hissed.

"And that's my fault?"

"It's not anyone's fault, Martin, it's simply a fact. Now please do me a favor and sit down with your family."

"Why are you pushing this? All I want to do is watch the game."

"Sit…down!" Lisa screamed.

Even though he knew Lisa was talking to Martin, David dutifully dropped into his seat. Martin, on the other hand retorted, "Screw you!"

Clutching his plate, he left the room. Lisa sped after him. David and Debbie remained frozen. The next thing they heard was the reverberating slam of a door.

In the den, neither Martin nor Lisa had the control to extinguish the sizzling fuse of the bomb that had become their life. "Have you gone completely insane?" she asked.

"Have you?" He stomped to the television and flicked it on, furiously slapping the channel buttons until he found the basketball game. Lisa moved to turn it off but he jumped in front of her. "Don't…you…dare."

Blocking her access to the TV, Martin started to shovel tuna casserole and salad into his gaping mouth positioned at the edge of his plate.

"You're an animal," Lisa hissed.

"At least I'm not a goddamn control freak."

"All I'm trying to do is hold this family together!"

"Well, if you ask me, you're doing a piss poor job of it."

In a violent rage, Lisa slapped Martin's dinner from his hands. As food flew in all directions, the plate of their Noritake wedding china hit the edge of the coffee table shattering into ceramic hail.

Martin cranked up the volume on the TV. Chick Hearn rattled off the play-by-play. Lisa lunged, snatched the remote control off the shelf and turned the set off. Martin dove at her but she dodged him. "Give me that! You really have gone crazy, Lisa. Give me the fucking remote."

Rearing back, Lisa fired it as his head. Martin ducked; the remote exploded a crystal vase on the shelf behind him. Losing all control, Martin vaulted over the coffee table and was inches from grabbing his wife by the hair when the door flew open to reveal David and Debbie gawking in horror. Lisa and Martin froze.

Tuna, noodles and salad littered the rug garnished with broken bits of china. Shards of shattered crystal glinted on the bookshelf. Debbie saw her parents looking wild-eyed, electrified. Streaking across the room, Martin broke the titanic silence. "I'm going out to watch the game."

Unable to bear the stunned faces of David and Debbie, Lisa excused herself. David was turning to comfort his niece when the phone rang. She bolted out to answer it. David dropped to his knees, grabbed a wicker wastebasket from the corner and began to collect the bits of broken plate and wasted dinner.

With her hands trembling as she held the phone, Debbie listened to Michael calling from his dorm room in Berkeley, demanding to talk to their mom or dad. Debbie said they couldn't come to the phone. He asked when they were operating on Gina; Debbie told him it was set for very early Thursday morning.

"Debbie, what's up? You sound weird. I mean, even-for-you weird."

"They've gone crazy, Michael. It's horrible. Mom and Dad are fighting and screaming; they're completely flipping out."

"I need to come home. I'm sure I can find a ride down."

"Wait, don't. The last thing we need is for them to be even more stressed out. I'll make sure Mom calls you later, I promise."

Slowly moving up the stairs, David paused outside Martin and Lisa's closed bedroom door. "Leese?" Creeping into the room, he found her in a straight-back chair, catatonic. He sat on the bed in the humid silence.

"I'm so scared, David. What are we going to do? How will we survive this?" The doorbell rang twice in rapid succession. Lisa jumped up. "Maybe Martin's come to his senses."

Downstairs, Debbie unlocked the front door. The pair of intertwined voices they heard made Lisa's heart seize.

"Oh God," David said in disbelief. "That cannot be Mom and Dad."

Peggy and Len Goldman hated to travel. They hated airplanes, the smell of taxis, and sleeping in other people's beds. Locked in an ongoing nightmare, Lisa perched on the edge of the living room sofa gaping at her parents on the loveseat.

"We couldn't take it another minute," Peggy said, "sitting in Murray Hill on *schpilkes*, not knowing what's going on, not being able to help…"

"How could you not let us know you were coming?" David asked.

"We knew you'd try to talk us out of it," Len said; even when he wasn't angry he sounded pissed off.

Peggy was gaping at Lisa. "You look terrible."

"Thank you, Mother. That's very helpful."

"May I go upstairs?" Debbie asked. "I need to do homework."

"Of course," Lisa said. "Come give me a kiss." Debbie complied, making the rounds.

"You've put on weight," Len said as Debbie leaned down to kiss his leathery cheek. "Your arms look fat."

"Leonard!" Peggy admonished. "How many times have I told you? You don't make comments about a woman's weight."

"I'm just saying she looks big to me." Len shrugged.

Sprinting for the stairs, Debbie turned back to her mother. "Excuse me while I go kill myself – and don't forget you need to call Michael."

Hoping to dispel the high-voltage tension, David chirped, "All righty. How about I take Mom and Dad to my place?" Peggy insisted they'd stay with Lisa but David wouldn't relent. "Mother, she and Martin have enough to deal with. It's best for everyone if you come with me."

"With those tiny guest beds even the seven dwarves couldn't fit into?"

"You'll survive, Dad. Let's go."

As David marshaled their parents toward the front door, Lisa caught his eye and mouthed two simple words: "Bless you."

The minute they came into David's immaculate home in Silver Lake, his mother asked why he still wasn't married. David insisted he was happy with his life as it was.

"And if you wanna stay happy, you'll *remain* single. Christ, this suitcase weighs a ton. Your mother packed every pair of shoes she owns."

David directed his parents to the guest bedroom.

"There they are, the famous dwarf beds! Good thing we got home before Dopey!"

Lisa was alone in the middle of her queen-size mattress, staring at the shadow-streaked ceiling when Martin returned after midnight. Slipping into the bedroom, he spied Lisa's open eyes. They stared at each other for a long beat but neither spoke. Finally, Martin shook his head and went into the adjoining bathroom. Frozen in bed, Lisa listened to him wash his face and brush his teeth. Then he was flossing. Lisa was certain she could hear each excruciating second tick by despite the fact that the bedside clock was digital. Now Martin was at the toilet, peeing for an eternity. Great, he probably had a million beers, and then drove home like an idiot.

The toilet flushed and started to run. Martin jiggled the handle. Repeatedly. The metallic clanging was piercing Lisa's brain. He came back into the bedroom.

Martin undid his belt, pulled it through the loops in one tug, fuming, wondering why he always had to be the one to make the first move. Tonight he wasn't in the mood. He ducked into the closet and undressed. Lisa was rigid in bed, fighting an urge to scream. Martin slid under the covers, turning his back to her. Intense heat radiated from their bodies. Lisa wondered how silence could be so loud. "Martin...what are we doing?"

"I have no clue." He rolled onto his back; they were two planks laid side by side.

Very slowly Lisa moved against him and took his hand. He gently entwined his fingers in hers. Even though she was mute, Martin knew she was crying. After one more soundless gap, he inched closer to nestle his head against her shoulder. Lisa let out a muted sigh.

Exhausted and famished, Brian had finished his ten-hour shift in the UCLA neurology center but needed to make one more stop before going home. Retrieving a shopping bag from his locker, he went upstairs. He found Gina propped up drinking cranberry juice. The wild brown hair that usually surrounded her face was gone; it took Brian a startled moment to realize it was tucked up under a weathered Dodgers cap.

Her parents were seated in side-by-side chairs on the far side of the bed while an inane family drama played on the mounted TV. Seeing the handsome resident striding toward her, Gina lit up. "Yay! Dr. Scott."

"Hey, beautiful. Nice hat. And just so you know, I come bearing gifts!"

Gina clapped. Lisa turned off the TV. "Brian, you didn't need to – "

"Well, actually, my girlfriend did the shopping, but it was my idea."

"What'd you get? Let me see." Gina was jumping out of her skin.

Brian set the shopping bag on the bed, milking the presentation like he was P.T. Barnum.

"First off, I know you're planning on becoming a spy when you grow up..."

"Definitely. CIA or FBI."

"So you need to look the part. And every woman of mystery needs..." Brian reached into the bag letting the suspense build. He banged on his thigh creating a drum roll. A moment later, he whipped out...

"A black beret! Marvelous!" Gina squealed. She snatched the hat from Brian, removed her Dodgers cap and plopped the beret in its place. "How do I look?"

"Like a movie star," Martin said.

"Here," Brian stepped closer and tugged the hat down a bit so it was cocked over one eye. "Now you're Bond. Jane Bond."

Returning to the bag, Brian dug in once more. "This is for your international stakeouts, when you need to hide your eyes but still see." He yanked out a brown '40s-style felt hat with a floppy brim. "Heather, my girlfriend, said it's a Trilbie."

"Like Rosalind Russell used to wear," Lisa added.

"Whoever that is," Gina snorted. She took the hat from Brian, replaced the beret and tugged the Trilbie low. With a saucy tilt of her head, she faced her parents.

"Wow," Martin exclaimed. "Move over Mata Hari."

Brian said, "Last one: for when you need to infiltrate a band of dirty hippies at a sit-in." With the flair of a magician, he produced a tie-dyed bandanna.

"You are going to be the most stylish fifth grader in the Valley," Lisa declared. "Thank you, Brian. How incredibly thoughtful and sweet."

"Will you be there tomorrow when they operate?" Gina asked.

"I won't be participating but I'll be observing. Somebody's gotta keep Dr. Jenkins on track. You'll do great. We'll have you back in school in no time."

Seated at his Berkeley dorm room desk, Michael was staring at his Hendrix at the Fillmore East poster. "He had no clue he was gonna die so young. My poor sister. I mean, fuck, man — brain surgery? That's serious shit."

Reading on his bed, Kirk turned to him. "They must be pretty sure they can save her or they wouldn't be doing it."

"They've got no choice. If they leave it alone and it bursts she's a goner for sure."

Michael let out a slow, ragged breath. "Fuck, man. I should be there."

Except for a silent Korean couple in a corner, the extended Kaufman-Goldman clan took up the rest of the surgical waiting room. Martin and Lisa had stayed with Gina until the last possible second while Debbie, David, Len and Peggy insisted on collecting in the cafeteria at 6:00 a.m.

Lisa held Gina's hand as the nurse clipped away the girl's kinky brown locks depositing them into a plastic barrel. It was only when she took the electric clippers to Gina's exposed scalp that tears came; Lisa and Gina sniffled in two-part harmony.

Now, staring at the faded waiting room carpet, Lisa was trying to remember the last thing she'd said to Gina before they wheeled her away down that long cold hall to the operating room. Lisa's mind was blank. She couldn't hold a thought. Fleeting images flipped through her head like a TV with someone sitting on the remote.

"Who wants coffee?" Martin asked. No one responded. He moved to the pot on a hot plate against the wall. Refilling his Styrofoam cup, he hoped no one noticed his shaking hands. Len stood up; Peggy asked where he was going.

"Out for a cigar."

"The sun's not even up."

"What does that have to do with the price of tea in China?"

Martin sat beside Lisa trying to imagine how they were going to survive the day. Dr. Jenkins expected the surgery to last at least seven hours. With any complications it would go longer. Jenkins promised to send a nurse out with periodic updates.

The elderly woman at the desk looked unnervingly like Alfred Hitchcock in a burgundy wig; she had a loud, too-cheery voice that grated on Martin's nerves every time she answered the phone. "Surgical waiting room," she sang with the lilt of an opera diva.

Hovering at the back of the bustling operating room, Brian was fighting to stay awake. He'd finished his morning rounds and then slipped in, hoping to watch Jenkins pull off a miracle.

After his year as an intern and seven months as a resident, Brian was relatively used to losing patients. Especially during his internship, he'd been present for a death or two a week but most of them were old, terminal cases from the minute he met them. What Brian couldn't face was losing someone who hadn't even confronted puberty.

Compelled to get a better look at what was happening, he inched closer being as unobtrusive as possible. Dr. Jenkins was aided by a team of nurses, the anesthesiologist, the technicians, and other surgeons moving around the operating table with the precision of a well-drilled platoon. A portion of Gina's skull had been opened. Jenkins was in the slow, precise process of clipping the arterial vessels bringing blood to the AVM. So far, all of the data Brian could see on the monitors looked very encouraging.

"I'm not taking no for an answer. What, better we should sit here and go crazy?" Len was on his feet in front of his family in the waiting room. "We're playing charades, guys versus gals. I'll start." He put a curled fist to his eye; with his other hand he made a cranking motion.

"It's a movie," Debbie said.

Len held up two fingers to indicate the number of words in the title. He exuberantly waved an open hand from side to side.

"Hello," Peggy called out.

Len shook his head. Lisa guessed 'howdy' and Martin tried 'greetings' but Len wagged his head and waved even more frantically until Peggy finally said, "Goodbye!"

Len nodded; Peggy called out "Goodbye, Mister Chips!"

"That's three words, Nana. Papa said it's only two."

"Folks," the Hitchcock doppelganger chimed, "please keep your voices down."

"Fine," Len barked, not lowering his voice one bit. He held up two fingers; he was going for the second word. Len stood erect, gazed forward and put a flat hand to his forehead like an Indian scout. He swiveled his neck as if scanning a distant horizon. No one responded. Stomping to recapture their attention, he stood stiff, bringing two curled hands up to his

left eye as if using a telescope. A couple of silly solutions were
shouted out, raising Len's frustration.

"For Christ's shake, it's *Goodbye Columbus*!' I was
Christopher Columbus discovering America!"

Lisa grabbed a donut she didn't want to eat. "Why haven't
we heard from the nurses?"

Apparently her simple query was all it took. A surgical nurse
materialized. "Dr. Jenkins asked me to let you know things are
going very well. He clipped the arterial vessels feeding the
AVM and is now removing the veins draining the cluster. It's
slow going but Gina's a trouper, her vitals are strong – she's
doing great. There's still much left to do but we're on
schedule."

Lisa rushed to Martin and threw herself into his arms. "So
far so good."

The surgical nurse reappeared just before noon to say
they'd removed the AVM's nidus, the abnormal connection of
the clustered arteries and veins. They were hoping to have
surgery wrapped up within the next ninety minutes.

At 2:17 p.m., seeing Dr. Jenkins striding toward her with a
wide smile, Lisa's legs started to quiver so violently she was
afraid to stand.

"We did it. It was challenging and took a bit longer than we
anticipated, but she's in recovery, the AVM is gone; there
doesn't appear to be any collateral damage. She's still pretty out
of it so we can't be one hundred percent certain her speech or
her memory weren't affected but the preliminary signs look
good."

Len shook the doctor's hand and ducked out for a cigar.
Debbie ate another donut.

As the sun sank, Gina was moved to the ICU. When it
became clear only her parents would be permitted to see her,
David left with Len, Peggy and Debbie. They were worn out,

each craving a hot shower. "Who wants to stop for Chinese?" David asked.

Len and Peggy were on board but Debbie begged off. "I've got a ton of homework; I need you to take me home."

An hour later, Debbie opened the back door to tug her ruddy-faced classmate Norm Fitzpatrick into the kitchen. Year round, no matter the temperature, Norm's rose-colored cheeks made him look like he'd just come in from the snow. Producing a brown paper bag from under his nylon windbreaker, he proudly held his prize aloft. "Wodka!" he declared, with a put-on Russian accent. "Are you sure your parents won't be home?"

"My mom's spending the night at the hospital and Dad'll stay 'til at least eleven."

Later, sitting on the living room couch trying to get her head to stop spinning, Debbie heard Norm ask, "Can I touch your boob?"

"I don't know," she said with a giggle, "can you?"

Over-enunciating to make his words conform to his thoughts, Norm replied. "I mean, may I touch your boob, Mrs. Blazey?" he asked, using the name of their militant English teacher.

Debbie gave him permission to go for it. Norm quickly grabbed her right breast.

"Ow! Gentle, okay? Don't be an ape." Norm awkwardly gave her breast a squeeze. "Oh my God, you're terrible at this." Debbie placed her hand on top of his and moved it in a gentle massaging circle. She emitted an unanticipated moan.

"Touch my pecker."

Keeping her eyes closed, Debbie eased her hand down to the crotch of Norm's corduroys. Feeling his pulsating penis she recoiled, but then splayed her fingers across his straining zipper.

"Can I touch you...down there?"

"No! You already got boob; I'm not a slut. It's our first date."

At 10:30, Debbie shoved Norm out the door making him take the vodka bottle so her father wouldn't find it in the trash.

"I'm glad your sister's gonna be okay."

Without responding, Debbie swiftly closed the door. Feeling the unholy trinity of corn puffs, liquor and orange juice cartwheeling in her belly, she sprinted for the bathroom. Grasping the pink toilet bowl, she vomited with such fury she was afraid she might dredge up a kidney. When the puking finally subsided, she took two aspirin, brushed her teeth and passed out.

Checking on Debbie when he got home just before midnight, Martin was surprised to find her in bed on top of her covers, wearing her flannel nightgown – and red Keds.

I guess it's been a long, hard day for all of us.

Although she wasn't allowed to sleep in the intensive care unit, the hospital staff set Lisa up on a cot in an adjacent on-call room. Working to block the ceaseless hospital noise, she'd done her best to grab some fitful sleep. Opening her eyes just after 7:00 a.m., she spied Dr. Jenkins in the hallway. Instantly, Lisa was on her feet, raking her fingers through her hair, trying to shake out her wrinkled clothes.

"How's our girl this morning?" she asked the doctor as she caught up to him.

"I'm on my way to check on her now."

David finished teaching his morning *Era of the First World War* class and got to the hospital as quickly as possible. After the weeks of tension, with the interminable surgery behind them, he'd had his first decent night's sleep in ages. Even his mother's incessant chatter through breakfast didn't quash his buoyant mood. That was why he was finding it impossible to comprehend what Lisa was saying to him. "What do you mean she had a stroke? How? When?"

"Sometime in the night. They warned us it was one of the potential complications but I didn't let myself think about it. She's, it's…her face and speech seem fine, thank God. I mean, some words are slurred and you can see her straining for certain thoughts but it's mostly her left arm and leg…" Lisa stopped. David expected her to dissolve into tears but Lisa confessed she was all cried out. "They're saying it might only be temporary, she might get at least ninety percent of her motor skills back with lots of physical therapy but they don't know, they don't know anything. Martin's with her now; he's being so great. Listen, David, you have to keep Mom and Dad away today. I can't handle them, with their questions, their confusion…I can't—"

David promised to take care of it, right after he got to see his Gina-bo-beena.

Leaving math class, Debbie was intercepted by her best friend. "You let Norm Fitzpatrick feel you up?"

"Oh my God…how do you know that? I am going to rip his dick off and club him to death with it."

Coming up behind him on the way into their sixth period English class, Debbie socked Norm in the kidneys with enough force to drop him to his knees. "What the f – " He sprang back up, whirled and froze when he saw Debbie.

"You're the most disgusting yuck-face ever! I'm going to tell everybody in this school your penis is the size of a Munchkin's pinkie toe."

Brian was glad he'd stopped at Jenkins' office to get updated on Gina's condition before going to the ICU. It would be easier to act optimistic armed with facts. When he arrived in her sterile alcove, Gina's mother had stepped out to use the phone; her father was down in the cafeteria. Gina was pale and groggy. Still, she managed a meager smile for her favorite doctor. "You heard I stroked out, right? Isn't it sucky? What am I, some old granny?"

All of the beautiful light and energy had disappeared from Gina's face. She was paper white, vulnerable. "No FBI for me now, ya know. No way they'll want a useless gimpy spy."

1984

— 1 —

"LUCY, CALM DOWN; breathe. I can't understand a word you're saying." In a back corner of the busy showroom of the Beckman Brothers in Plano, Ed was battling to make sense of the garbled words filtering through the phone. Seconds later, two words registered with a clarity that knocked the wind from his chest. "Nate's dead."

"He can't be. We have Astros tickets."

"But he is!" Lucy wailed. "They called from the diner. He was doing inventory in back and—" She was bawling so hard Ed had to pull the phone away from his ear.

He knew she had to be wrong. Nate wouldn't do that; he wouldn't just up and die.

Pulling into the driveway of Nate and Lucy's faded yellow ranch house, Ed had no idea how he'd gotten there. He didn't remember leaving the Beckman Brothers' parking lot. This isn't real. Those fucking morons at the diner must be pulling an idiotic prank.

Before Ed raised a fist to knock, Lucy yanked open the screen door and flung herself into his arms. Her normally perfect blonde hair had been caught in an emotional monsoon; her face was streaked with black lines of mascara under vampire eyes.

"We have to get to Parkland. That's where they took the

body."

"Where's Kendra?" Ed asked, thinking about Nate and Lucy's pain-in-the-ass daughter.

"No idea," Lucy sobbed. "As usual. She's not here and we need to go."

Ed took in the fact that the always-impeccable Lucy was in a frayed housecoat and slippers at 2:00 on a Friday afternoon. "Don't you want to get dressed?"

"What's the point? It won't make Nate any less dead."

Driving to the hospital, Ed's mind soared back to time a decade earlier when Ed and Bonnie found themselves in the throes of serious marital discord. Bonnie accused Ed of having developed a Hero Complex after he'd achieved notoriety saving JFK's life. By the mid-'70s, she thought Ed had gotten so consumed with his desire to save the world he'd forgotten how to take care of his own family. She blindsided him with a threat to end their marriage. With no clue how to respond he went to Nate.

"Take Bonzo away for a long weekend; make it all about her. Wine and dine her, do spa shit, buy her jewelry, the whole shebang. Convince her you've seen the error of your ways and know you can't possibly ever thank her enough for loving your worthless ass all these years."

And that's exactly what Ed did. He and Bonnie spent three days at a secluded spa in Taos. They got massages, ate grilled fish, and drank expensive wine; they had sex several times a day at odd hours in new positions. They also spent lots of time talking. About their lives, the kids, their unrealized dreams. The other important thing they did was laugh. A lot. They reconnected. They fell back in love. And their whole path to healing had been suggested by Nate.

Identifying the body was one of the most painful experiences of Ed's life. Before they went into the curtained basement morgue, Lucy worried that she might pass out and crash to the concrete floor, orphaning Kendra. "Although it would serve her right given how she treats us." With sudden force, Lucy grabbed Ed's hand. "C'mon, let's get this over with."

At the Callahan house that evening, Bonnie and Marsha couldn't sit still. They zipped around serving, cleaning, and answering the constantly ringing phone. Maybe if they didn't stop moving, they wouldn't have to face the awful truth that Nate was gone. The minute Ed called to relay the unfathomable news, Bonnie launched into Earth Mother mode. She sent Marsha to Piggly Wiggly to stock up on groceries for a communal dinner. She went to Nate and Lucy's to intercept nineteen-year-old Kendra so she didn't have to learn about her father's death from a random neighbor.

Waiting for Kendra, Bonnie called Kenny. He'd graduated from Oklahoma University in '79 and for the past two years had been employed in the Applications department at Electronic Data Systems fifteen minutes from where Ed worked. No matter how many times Kenny explained what he did for a living, his parents still didn't get it. "All I know," Bonnie would say, "is that it's something to do with computers and clients and storing information. I find it as confusing as all get-out but he seems to adore it."

Hating to be dumping this awful news on her son at work, Bonnie heard a car door slam in the Stokesberrys' driveway. "Honey, I gotta run; Kendra's here. Do me a favor? Call your sister. She doesn't know yet." Glancing at her watch, Bonnie tried to conjure Libby's schedule. "The restaurant opens in an hour; she's probably there doing prep. This'll be horrible for her, like it is for all of us. If she can get someone to cover, tell her to come to the house. You, too. We'll eat together, be together. I love you. Gotta run."

The front door pushed open as Bonnie came into the foyer. The sight in front of her stunned her. Kendra's formerly chestnut hair was black, very black, cropped short, like a punk rock Peter Pan. And she was incredibly thin and frail. "Aunt Bonnie. What are you doing here?" It was evident the girl already knew something was horribly wrong. "Where's my mother?"

"Sweetheart, I have news. Bad news. Your father…he passed away." Kendra's eyes lost focus. "Your mother and Ed are at the hospital trying to find out what happened."

"But he's dead? He's definitely dead?"

Bonnie nodded. Remaining rigid, Kendra couldn't manage to cry.

Marsha whisked away plates of half-eaten Bundt cake as Bonnie refilled glasses of iced tea. Kendra and Lucy flanked Ed on the couch, having taken great pains to ensure he sat between them. Libby was in a chair across the room. Kenny was on the phone letting his roommate know he'd be staying overnight with his parents.

Determined to keep her emotions buried, Kendra was flipping through a yearbook from Ed and Nate's high school senior year. "How have I never seen this? Dad was quite the stud. Football hero, prom king…he's practically on every page."

"Can I please get you a piece of cake, sweetheart?" Bonnie asked, hovering.

"I don't do cake."

"Since when?" asked the heavily sedated Lucy.

"Ages, *Lucy*. You'd know that if you paid attention."

Wide awake, watching the digital numbers change to 3:00 a.m., Ed was thinking about all the great times he and Nate shared over the years. Having an aching need to conjure images of his friend alive, Ed kept hearing Nate's deep, unguarded laugh: on camping trips, playing shortstop for their softball team, knocking back beers at the Double Wide as he relayed his favorite dumb blonde jokes.

Ed knew people often talked about a hole in their heart after a loved one passed but he'd never quite gotten it until now. His parents were gone, and he definitely missed them, but they'd each lived a nice long time and passed away before falling apart. It was the natural order, to be expected. But this…Nate was only fifty-four. Grabbing onto a specific memory Ed chuckled, quickly swallowing his laughter so he wouldn't wake Bonnie.

He, Bonnie and Nate were out to dinner at a gourmet pizza parlor downtown. There was a thirty-minute wait but since they could order beers, the guys didn't mind. Trouble was Bonnie had eaten an early lunch, wasn't drinking to save calories, and was beginning to feel light-headed. When the hostess went off to seat another party, Nate stepped up to the podium. As soon as the hostess returned, she called their name and took them to a comfortable booth in the back. "I don't get it," Bonnie said. "I thought there were still two or three parties ahead of us."

Responding with a Dennis the Menace grin Nate replied, "There were. But you needed to eat, darlin', so I went up and crossed their names off the list."

That was Nate: the gallant friend, the impish mischief-maker, and audacious provocateur. No matter what else you might think of him, he was always entertaining.

Suddenly, Ed felt an urgent need to have a cigarette. Since he'd gone back to being a fulltime smoker a few years ago, despite endless attempts to quit, Bonnie had forbidden him from smoking in the house. He squinted at the clock again: 3:17 a.m.

Standing in his backyard in his boxer shorts and wife-beater, Ed took a ravenous inhale of his Camel drawing the smoke deep into his lungs. He exhaled luxuriously; his nerves began to calm. Taking another greedy drag, he was rocked by an inescapable truth: despite the nicotine's momentary relief, Nate was still dead.

Ed and Bonnie planned all aspects of the viewing, funeral and burial. Unable to handle it, Lucy gave them her blessing. She spent the week secluded in her bedroom, crying and drinking wine. Kendra was off with unknown friends, impossible to reach, physically and emotionally.

"I do believe that girl's on drugs," Bonnie said.

"D'ya think Aunt Lucy's gonna be okay?" Kenny asked.

"If you want my opinion," Marsha said, "that gal hasn't been okay in years."

"I wish it was her instead of him that died." Sitting on the floor of a friend's dirty apartment, Kendra took one more drag from her French cigarette and exhaled a perfect smoke ring. "You know she'll totally work the widow thing. That bitch'll buy every black dress in Nordstrom's. At least my dad left a shit-ton of life insurance. Plus we can make a killing selling his stupid diner."

"Um, this might be creepy to ask but did you see the dead body? Was it scary?"

Kendra shrugged. "Not really. It wasn't him. Just like…more like seeing the empty box he came in. I did kiss his cheek though." Absently licking her lips as they curled in disgust at the memory, she went on: "It was like kissing the wax fruit my grandma kept on her dining room table. Not that I kissed that shit, but you get what I mean." Stubbing out her cigarette, Kendra jumped up. "I'm bored. Let's go to Twyla's and steal her mom's diet pills."

Slowly, steadily, life began to inch onward. Several times a day Ed would think of something he couldn't wait to tell Nate and then feel a pain grab his heart as it registered that this wasn't an option. He took to calling Bonnie regularly from Beckman Brothers to be reassured by the sound of her voice. One Thursday afternoon during a smoke break, Ed called Kenny at work to invite him to dinner. Ken asked what the occasion was.

"I need a reason to see my son? I thought it might be nice, just the two of us."

"Ribs at the Smoke House? I was gonna see Molly but I'll do it tomorrow night."

When Ed asked if it was getting serious between them Kenny deflected, saying he was in no rush to define the relationship. Ed reminded him he was married with two kids at Kenny's age. Kenny's response was swift and unambiguous: "Sucker!"

Wiping grease and sauce from his face with a massacred napkin, eying Kenny across the table, Ed felt warm contentment in his sated gut. He was proud that Kenny was working and living on his own. Even through the teenage years, he'd rarely caused them much grief. Ed knew much of this was due to Bonnie's parenting skills; his biggest contribution had been keeping out of her way.

Ed smiled. "Hey, what's up with Chris these days? I saw him at the funeral but we didn't really get to talk."

Chris Ebersol was Kenny's roommate in the two-bedroom apartment they shared in Addison near Kenny's job. Chris, a friend from high school, was an aspiring screenwriter who worked with Libby at the Italian restaurant she managed. "He's still tryin' to be the Next Big Thing. He's up at 7:00, writes for hours, works out, has lunch, then comes back and writes 'til he has to go to work."

"Your sister says he's one of her best waiters."

"Not surprised. No matter what he's doing, that boy's a working machine."

Ed downed the rest of his beer. It grew quiet. The

surrounding tables had emptied; their waiter wasn't hovering. The silence lingered. Kenny stared at his dad. "How're you doing…you know, with the whole Uncle Nate thing?"

"I never guessed it would be this hard."

Angelo's Restaurant in Highland Park had been a neighborhood fixture for years. After graduating from UT Austin with a degree in hotel and restaurant management, Libby took a summer job there and stayed on. She was the current night manager, working 4:00 p.m. to midnight, Tuesday through Sunday.

A year earlier, she'd broken up with a guy she'd been seeing for nearly three years after he gave her an ugly pink sweater from K-Mart for her twenty-ninth birthday in lieu of the expected marriage proposal. These days she used every spare moment at Angelo's to jot down ideas and recipes for her own restaurant. It was going to be elegant, intimate, a place for couples in love to celebrate special occasions. She even had the name: *Eros.* She spent her days off sampling menus all over the greater Dallas-Fort Worth area. She was hoping to find the perfect chef – and then lure him away with her passion and spirit of collaboration. She joined the Chamber of Commerce and befriended investment bankers to help recruit the needed backers. Libby was determined to bring her dream to life.

"So what d'you do for fun?" Kenny's roommate, Chris, the writer/waiter asked as they cleared the last tables after closing.

"For me working *is* fun."

"That's a little sad."

"Why, because I don't care about hanging around bars getting my heart-broken?

"John Steinbeck or Mark Twain?"

"What?"

"Don't think, just answer: who do you like better, Steinbeck or Twain?"

"Steinbeck's *Grapes of Wrath*, right?" Off Chris's nod, Libby replied, "Then him. I always thought Twain was a little racist. All that N-word Jim stuff."

"Hey, he was a product of his times – and a total genius."

"You asked my opinion and I gave it. Now keep moving and let's get those dishes into the back." Chris picked up one gray tub of dirty plates and silverware; Libby grabbed the other, following him into the restaurant kitchen.

"If you could trade bodies with anybody on the planet, who would it be?"

"What are you implying? I like my body."

"Great. But answer the question."

"No. Women need to learn to accept themselves, flaws and all, so it's a stupid question and I'm not answering it. Whose hair would you like to have?"

Skimming a hand over the receding bristle atop his head, Chris chuckled. "Wow, man, low blow!" He self-consciously scratched the stubble that perpetually shaded his cheeks and chin. "Oilers or cowboys?"

"Neither."

"Come out and have a drink with me."

"What?"

"You need to learn to relax. Come out and have one drink with me."

"Chris, you're my brother's roommate, I've known you since you were ten, we work together. Not gonna happen."

Rolling over, colliding with unexpected naked flesh, Libby catapulted out of the bed to grab a nightgown from her closet. Slowly turning back she hoped she'd hallucinated. She hadn't. Naked and drooling, Chris was in her bed.

"Shit. Shit, shit, shit."

Walking past her mother's bedroom on a late-August Friday morning, Bonnie spied Marsha folding a pair of green velour pants into the suitcase on her ottoman. "Heading off with Mr. Miles?"

"He has to be in New Orleans for a few days and asked me to join him."

"I'll never understand why you refuse to marry that dear man."

"I do believe, Counselor, that question has been asked and answered ad nauseam."

As impossible as it was for Marsha to comprehend, she'd been in a relationship with Miles Ludwig, the ladies' handbag salesman from Oklahoma City, for twenty-one years. When their whole affair – for that's what it was, no matter how hard Marsha tried to deny it – started, he was a married man. He told her on their second date he had no intention of leaving his wife and Marsha was fine with that. She loved his company but also coveted her freedom. Seeing him seven or eight times a year, usually for a few days at a time, worked for them. The only thing Marsha feared was her daughter's judgment. With deft evasion and a slight twisting of the truth, she managed to keep Miles's marital status a secret for a full decade. Bonnie may have had her suspicions but it was a topic mother and daughter studiously avoided.

In the fall of '75 Marsha's card-tower of white lies tumbled down. Miles was supposed to come to town to host a birthday party for Marsha at her favorite steakhouse. Kenny was coming home from his sophomore year at OU for the weekend. Libby had graduated the previous spring and was working locally. At the last minute, Miles canceled. When Bonnie pressed her mother to find out why, Marsha dissolved.

"He's married, isn't he? Has been from start." With her head hung lower than Eeyore's on his worst day, Marsha nodded. "Well, Mother," Bonnie scolded, "what are you thinking?"

"I'm thinking that as long as it works for us I don't give a *hoot* what anybody else thinks. He's been honest with me from the get-go, he treats me like a queen and it beats the tar out of being alone."

The thing Bonnie now found perplexing was that seven years ago, Miles's wife passed away. Six months later, he flew to Dallas, took Marsha out to an expensive brunch and asked her to marry him. She firmly declined. Later when Marsha relayed the conversation, Bonnie asked, "But what about a bit of security, more constant companionship…"

"What about having to cook his meals and iron his shirts? Not to mention wiping his rear when he's old and feeble. In case you've forgotten, my dear, I already buried one husband, may your father rest in peace. I don't care to do it again."

"Can I say one thing?" Chris asked Libby a week before her parents threw Kenny a surprise birthday party at Double Wide Bar & Grille. "Mightn't you be overthinking this?" Libby shook her head. "So you're breaking up with me?"

"Let's not get all dramatic, Chris. We went out a few times; we were never officially 'together,' so we can't be breaking up."

"But you have fun with me, right? And the sex…" he grinned. "You're not gonna tell me that's not great." Libby blushed. "So what the hell's the problem?"

Libby took a breath. "We'll go to my brother's birthday party and either we have to agree to ignore each other all night or we'll make some awkward announcement, then Kenny'll freak out that we're dating and my mom'll ask a million questions and everybody will get all invested in us as a couple. Then eventually it'll go bad, we'll split up and I won't be able to go to my own brother's apartment because you live there, and you'll be out of a job because I'll fire you for breaking my heart. Or we can totally avoid it all by making the rational choice to end it now."

Jammed into the back room of the Double Wide six nights later, Bonnie and Ed were taking inventory to make sure all of Kenny's best buddies were there. Libby and Chris, unable to make the break from each other, huddled in a corner reviewing their battle plan. They'd decided that somewhere in the course of the party they'd make an off-hand comment about the fact that they'd been seeing each other and see what happened.

Capturing the revelers' attention Bonnie announced that Kenny and Molly would be arriving momentarily. Molly told Kenny they were going to dinner at his favorite seafood grille but his dad had asked them to stop by the Double Wide for a birthday beer first. Since it had been Ed's eternal hangout, everyone agreed this was the ploy least likely to arouse suspicion.

Positioned on a barstool providing a sightline to the front door, Ed turned to the gang in the room behind him, "Quiet now. Here they come." He glided to the entrance with a kiss for Molly and a hug for his son. "C'mon, kids; Mom and I grabbed a table in back."

Kenny was confused. "How come the lights are off?"

On cue, the lights flashed on. "Surprise!"

Kenny gasped and laughed and looked genuinely blown away.

Molly beamed. "Oh my God, we did it! We pulled it off. I don't think he had any idea!"

From the crowd another voice was heard. It was an old buddy who'd been pounding back shots of Yukon Jack. "Wanna even bigger surprise? Your sister and your best bud are boning!"

Hearing a clatter down the hall, Lucy rolled over in bed and groaned. The thick mauve curtains blocked out all light but she knew it wasn't early in the day. She opened one crusty eye to peek at the digital clock: 12:29 p.m.

Kendra bounced in. "Why are you still in bed?"

Brutally hung over, Lucy pushed herself up on the stack of decorator pillows.

"You look like shit," Kendra snapped.

"Good morning to you, too, dear heart."

"Where's my Burberry suitcase? I'm taking the money Daddy left me and going to Europe tomorrow. It's all booked. I'm going alone and I'll be there 'til the money runs out."

"You didn't think this was something you needed to discuss with me?"

"Please don't start acting like you care all of a sudden. For once in our lives, let's be honest: I hate you, you hate me; I'm moving to Europe and we'll both be happier."

Lucy shoved herself upward yanking away a lock of matted hair stuck to her caked-on lip-gloss. "Why do you work so hard to break my heart?"

There was something in her mother's plaintive tone that knocked Kendra off-balance. For a fleeting second, she felt a tug of sympathy for this veritable stranger who'd birthed her. "Karma's a bitch. Shitty mom begets a little shit for a daughter; oh my god, what a shock!"

"Are you on drugs?"

"Yes! Anything I can get my hands on. Know why? Because I learned it from you: when in pain, self-medicate."

Lucy shot up, fueled by her indignation. "I have never taken drugs in my life!"

"Oh, that's right, you're just an alcoholic."

Opening her kitchen door, Bonnie was taken aback to find Lucy there with a plaid kerchief over her platinum hair; her eyes looked like they'd suffered tandem bee stings. The instant Bonnie invited Lucy in, a wail rose up from her gut.

An hour later, both women were spent. Lucy told Bonnie about Kendra's tirade and her furious departure; she had no idea when or if she'd ever hear from her only child again. Lucy was alone and what she wanted more than anything was a tall glass of Chardonnay. "Bonnie, do you think I'm a drunk?"

Bonnie picked her words carefully. "Well…I mean, especially since Nate passed…it does seem to have gotten a bit out of control, your drinking."

"What will I do? I'm so ashamed, I'm like to die."

Bonnie hopped up and forced a smile. "No more talk like that, all right? There's plenty of help out there and we're going to find it for you together."

"Terrific" Lucy scoffed. "Then I can be *sober* and alone. Whoop-dee-do."

"I'm seventy-four years old, Miles. Why would I want to get married again? I've told you, my dear, I see no reason to mess with success."

Strolling along the Miami Beach shoreline, Miles persisted. "Will you at least consider my proposal? Truth is, it would make me extremely proud to tell the world the beautiful gal on my arm is my wife."

Marsha felt herself blush. That was the danger of dating a man like Miles: he always knew exactly what to say to weaken a gal's resolve.

For the past six years, Labor Day weekend meant only one thing to Bonnie: time to dust off her lesson plans and prepare for a new school year. After working at Skillern's Drugs for most of her adult life, the day they packed Kenny off to college in the fall of '75, Bonnie knew she needed a new challenge. "Idle hands," she said to Ed. "After all these years of being a mom and checkout gal, it's time to start using my mind again."

When Bonnie decided to go back to school to get her teaching degree, Ed couldn't have been more supportive. After a five-year program at Texas Wesleyan University, wading through classes with students half her age, Bonnie graduated with a teaching credential and an eagerness to get to work. She was starting her fourth year as a seventh and eighth grade science teacher. Unlike almost everyone else she knew, Bonnie adored being with the angst-ridden, acne-riddled teens. She found them to be as interesting as they were hormonal. Ed teased her that, fighting to keep her students engaged, she spent half her salary on materials for which she was never reimbursed. "Still beats the tar out of ringing up Juicy Fruit and tampons at Skillern's."

Driving to his sister's apartment after work, Kenny couldn't help but wonder what he was walking into. When Libby invited him, saying she had a new Veal Piccata recipe she was dying to try out, Kenny asked if she wanted him to invite Molly along but Libby said she preferred it be just the two of them. Since they were always with Bonnie and Ed or Molly and Chris, Libby thought it might be nice to have some sibling time.

"Why do I feel like Wile E. Coyote heading into one of Road Runner's traps?"

"Years of conditioning, thank you very much. But this time it's only dinner."

As Kenny praised the veal, Libby urged him to take seconds. "I know it was weird for you when Chris and I started dating; believe me, no one's more shocked than I am to hear these words coming out of my mouth but I really like him. I mean, to me he was always your goofy friend with the taped-together glasses talking into his shoe doing Maxwell Smart impressions. But since he's grown up and been writing…he's…I'm kinda—"

"Jesus, are you falling in love with him?"

"Maybe. Look, I don't know where it's going, I have no idea what'll happen but…I… we…wherever it might be headed, I wanna make sure you're okay with it."

Kenny chuckled. "Okay, first off – *shocked* you care, but listen, would I live with Chris if I thought he was a dick? You could definitely do worse – and so could he."

"Thanks." A lump caught in Libby's throat. "So how's it going with Molly?"

Kenny said that things were terrific and, for the first time, he was feeling as if he was with the woman that would probably become his wife. Libby lifted her wine glass. "Wow, look at us! Turning into grownups."

A few days before Halloween, Marsha was in Denver with Miles. Ed was at the kitchen table paying bills while Bonnie emptied the dishwasher. They were debating how many bags of candy to buy for the upcoming onslaught of trick-or-treaters when the phone rang. Bonnie dashed to answer it. Ed paused in his check writing to eavesdrop.

A moment later, Bonnie was squealing. "Oh my stars, what wonderful news! Yes, yes. Congrats! I'm thrilled. Do you know when?" Bonnie listened to the response. "Sure; he's right here. He'll be as tickled as me."

Hanging up the phone, Bonnie rushed toward Ed, grinning from ear to ear. "Well, my dear, cancel any plans you have for next Valentine's Day. We have a wedding to attend!"

2

DIGGING THROUGH A BIN of bootleg VHS tapes at an open-air market on the far side of Baghdad, Adiba Kashat Ahmed glanced over her shoulder to confirm no one she knew was in sight. The thick gold hoops in her ears accented her dark feathered hair, cut to bounce above her shoulders. At five foot eight, she was taller than most of the women in her family adding to the air of authority and confidence that accompanied her gliding gait. She resented feeling like a common criminal; why should she feel it necessary to travel thirty miles to pursue a harmless hobby?

Gazing at the cover of the videocassette in hand, a picture of an outstretched alien arm with an extended finger connecting to the finger of a young boy in front of a glowing moon, Adiba grinned. She'd read about this one in her American magazines. Even though she found the alien frightening, the director was one of her favorites. She didn't care if her husband Hazem thought movie viewing was blasphemous; she couldn't wait to share this one with her film club.

At home that evening, with the videocassette buried in a bureau drawer, Adiba finished making the *tahini* to go with the *falafel* and fresh baked pita prepared earlier. Because Hazem was an orthopedic surgeon at a military hospital in central Baghdad, Adiba never knew when he'd get home. Although she preferred to wait so they could dine together, on many nights she had to eat a small snack to sustain herself. Dismayed by how little he saw her consume, Hazem feared she'd developed an eating disorder. In her deep, smoky voice, Adiba would assure him she had a small but healthy appetite; she couldn't admit she'd already eaten, lest he think she was a disloyal wife.

A dozen years older than Adiba, Hazem was two inches

shorter and except for patches of ebony fringe over his ears, had been bald since the age of twenty-five. Being an acclaimed surgeon, he provided his wife with a large home in a desirable neighborhood. Adiba's extended family envied her upscale life. The only cloud over this bright domestic picture was the fact that they'd been married for two years and Adiba had yet to give her husband a child.

With great ceremony, Nazik lit a candle under the portrait of her husband. Its black wooden frame hung on the living room wall. It was more than a decade since Faraj was kidnapped from a public park but his fate remained unknown. There had been countless rumored sightings over the years; none led to a definitive conclusion.

For Nazik it was an ongoing nightmare. As long as there was no corpse to bury, she refused to surrender hope; she was a married woman living in tortured limbo. For Adiba, Faraj's disappearance only increased her determination to escape to America one day. She longed to be in a place where unknown cowards in dark cloths didn't leap out of cars to snatch innocent civilians off the streets. She ached to be in a country that allowed both men and women to pursue their most audacious dreams. Flipping through the western fashion magazines she purchased at a sequestered booth in a hidden alley at the outdoor market, Adiba marveled at the models' power and poise. She ached to be with them in a white wicker chaise at the edge of a glistening beach sipping a frothy cocktail.

Bringing her grandmother two jars of homemade blackberry jam, Adiba was struck anew by how ancient Nazik looked. She was only months past her 60th birthday but her virgin-white hair and inflated dark sacks under her eyes gave her the appearance of a ninety-year-old crone.

Almost by rote, Nazik asked if Adiba was pregnant yet.

"Why must everyone assume that the instant an Arab woman has a ring on her finger the only thing she is good for is to become a baby oven? I am but twenty-one years old. I desire time to get to know my adult self. I want the opportunity to get acquainted with the stranger I married. Even Saddam urges women to attend university, believing we have much to offer our country."

"What he believes in is the opportunity to indoctrinate another mass segment of the population. His schools are an avenue into your mind. Young women there learn only what he wishes them to learn. You must quit being so naïve."

"That still does not mean I am ready to be with child."

When Nazik asked if she was refusing to be intimate with Hazem, Adiba blushed. She'd always been close to her *BB* but they rarely discussed such personal topics. Adiba confessed that she obliged her husband whenever he demanded it.

"This is good. It is a woman's duty. The sooner you accept this, the sooner you will lead a righteous life."

Hazem's jiggling leg was shaking the table. Oblivious, he used a wooden pointer to explain an upcoming surgery to a severely wounded soldier's family. He pointed to jagged blotches on the x-ray above the base of the young man's spine. "Shrapnel that lodged in the spinal cord has shattered two discs causing his pain and difficulty walking. He is lucky he is not paralyzed. The surgery will replace these discs with synthetic ones. It is a risky procedure, but if all goes as planned he will be back on his feet in two months."

Hazem wished he felt half as confident as he sounded. His knee continued to bounce; his mind whirled. He'd been an orthopedic surgeon for six years and everyone told him he was a skilled and gifted doctor; the problem was he never truly believed it. He worried constantly about the inevitable day when he'd turn a formerly robust twenty-something into a cripple for life.

Hazem bolted up begging the indulgence of the patient's parents. Sprinting into the men's room, he darted into a stall and threw up.

With his country engaged in war with neighboring Iran since September of 1980, Hazem knew it was only his capricious decision to pursue orthopedics that kept him out of active military duty. He was certain if he'd stuck to his original plan to become a general practitioner, he'd currently be on the front lines. The war started when Iraq launched land and air attacks into Iranian territory. Saddam claimed the invasion was in retaliation for an assassination attempt on his foreign minister yet most felt the true reason for the aggression was to gain control over the Shatt-al-Arab waterway. Saddam declared the river must have its Iraqi-Arab identity restored as it was throughout history. Subtext? Time to expand his sphere of influence over the entire Middle East.

Regaining composure, Hazem returned to the soldier's unsettled parents and apologized for his absence. He'd perform the surgery at sunrise.

Setting the dinner plate in front of a weary Hazem, Adiba announced that her father had offered her a job in his tailoring shop; she wished to take it. Adiba explained that Hadi was having a difficult time finding a suitable apprentice. Her nineteen-year-old brother Mo'ez, who'd been in line for the position, was in the Air Force training to become a pilot. Most of the community's other young men were now also in the military. Adiba said that with so many men off fighting, women were needed to keep the nation functioning. She would still be at home each evening to prepare Hazem's supper; nothing about his routine would change.

"I will take this request under advisement and shall render my verdict in a day or two. If I permit you to work, you will be forbidden from measuring the male customers. My wife shall not be running her hands along the inseams of strange men."

It was more than a week, pushing Adiba's patience to the limit, before Hazem granted her permission to go to work. Making love that night he was unusually aggressive, pinning Adiba's wrists to the sheets as he slammed into her. She felt he was reasserting his dominance but Hazem had another agenda: I will get her pregnant this very night, then she will have to be home raising my son, instead of working like a common laborer's wife. When he finally came, his orgasm was so powerful he convinced himself he could feel his sperm invading Adiba's unsuspecting eggs.

Seated on a stool in her *baba's* tailoring shop, Adiba felt ten years old again. The sight of the two ancient Singer sewing machines, the crumpled yellow tape measure, the chunks of soap to mark the fabrics…these were all pieces of deeply engrained memories from her childhood. Some of Adiba's happiest Saturdays were when she alone got to come into work with Hadi while her brother and sister were off elsewhere.

On slower days Hadi would make a new dress for one of her dolls or a flowing scarf for her teddy bear. Adiba could inhale even now and conjure the odor of his ever-present cigar. A mild heart attack two years earlier had forced Hadi to quit smoking but Adiba swore that pungent aroma remained embedded in the shop's every pore.

The clearing of Hadi's throat returned Adiba to the present; he was pointing to the shelves where fabric bolts sat in jumbled disarray and asked her to convert that chaos to order. He would begin work on a dark brown suit for Noor the fish peddler.

Adiba's first week was enjoyable and uneventful. In her second week, things took a dark turn. After watching her father create a beautiful calf-length wool coat for the dentist's wife, Adiba came to work that Wednesday with two American fashion magazines. *Vogue* was all about the latest trends in women's wear; *Gentlemen's Quarterly* focused on styles for men. Adiba showed both to Hadi. "*Baba*, you do such exquisite work but your patterns…they are from the days when *Jadda* Omar, rest his soul, ran this shop. Nothing has changed in ages." Turning the pages of the *GQ*, she landed on a department store advertisement. "Look. Double-breasted they call it. Is it not marvelous?"

"That man looks like a cheap gangster."

Adiba asked Hadi when he'd turned into such a stodgy old man. Expanding his product line would expand his customer base. New styles meant younger clients. Local women would clamor to have access to chic designs from the US and Europe. She could use these magazine ads to create colorful sketches to frame on the shop walls as inspiration for the clientele.

"If you are so anxious to become an American, why not pack a bag and go? Otherwise, do not ever again tell me how to run my business."

Returning from the park across the street where she'd eaten lunch, Adiba saw the *Vogue* and *GQ* ripped to shreds, stuffed into a trashcan near the door. The rest of the week was a tense waltz of deference. Hadi remained distant; Adiba couldn't get him to make eye contact.

Friday afternoon, while Hazem was playing tennis with a fellow doctor and Adiba was at home doing laundry, Rima appeared at Adiba's door. "Whatever you have said to your father, you must apologize."

Adiba felt a tightening in her chest and thumping blood in her temples. "All I did was offer innocent suggestions on how he might increase his business. I was not impertinent, I showed no disrespect – he acts like a crazy man; I refuse to apologize for his bad behavior!"

The women became a pair of dogs chasing their tails. The more Rima talked of a child's duty to honor her parents, the more Adiba's ire escalated. "If anyone needs to apologize it is *Baba* yet no one ever challenges him. We cower, we quiver…you wait on him hand and foot; even his customers bow to his will. Why should he bend? You know I revere you, *Mama*, but I am not like you. I will not submit to rudeness from my father or my husband. I demand to be treated with the same kindness and credibility we give our men."

"Then you, my *habibti*, are destined for a life of turmoil."

At Hadi's insistence, Adiba's workweek was cut from five days to three. Their frosty standoff continued. Hadi treated her more like an employee than a daughter. Most working hours were spent in silence. Adiba was saddened by the estrangement but wouldn't capitulate. Hadi had ignited this feud; it was up to him to make things right.

The first Monday she was free, Adiba called a meeting of her Women's Secret Film Society. It had been a month since their last gathering. The group consisted of Adiba and four longtime friends. Each was married, three of them had children in elementary school; the fourth was six months pregnant. Adiba alone remained childless.

They met in the late morning, always at Adiba's house since she was the only one with a VCR. They would watch a film, have lunch and catch up on the latest gossip. It was a rare and welcome escape from the regimentation of their daily lives.

The movie Adiba selected starred a young American actor who undeniably excited her. Gazing at magazine photos of him caused prickly beads of sweat to dot her hairline. Sometimes when she and Hazem made love, she'd imagine him to be the movie star, begging him to say her name so she could pretend her idol was passionately crying out for her. It was always a rude disappointment to open her eyes and find her short, bald husband on top of her.

With lunch leftovers littering the coffee table, the five women were absorbed in the film's climax. A polite tapping on her front window pulled Adiba from her cinematic bliss. She spied Shemma peering in. Despite the vociferous protests of her riveted guests, Adiba paused the tape and opened her front door. Shemma had been married for six years and had two young children sixteen months apart. Her husband was a contractor in Saddam's army. Adiba's sister was a traditionalist, a devout Muslim content with the role their culture had ascribed to her. She dropped out of school at fourteen, married at seventeenth and never experienced a day of regret.

While the sisters had an inherent affection for one another, they were not close. Adiba didn't invite Shemma to join the film society, knowing Shemma believed Western cinema to be a celebration of shameless women flaunting their bodies. Shemma begged the guests' forgiveness for her intrusion. She eyed the frozen screen where a beautiful American actor was clad in a white military uniform. Shemma's gaze shifted back to Adiba; she explained that her husband was taking her out for their anniversary and she was hoping to borrow something elegant from her affluent sister. Adiba escorted Shemma to the bedroom and told her to help herself. With her guests on a tight timetable, she needed to get back to finish the film.

Ten minutes later, as the movie star swept his leading lady into his arms to the swelling soundtrack, Shemma emerged from the bedroom, aghast. She demanded to speak to Adiba in private. The movie watchers offered to pause the tape again but Adiba insisted they go ahead.

Sequestered in the bedroom, Shemma accusingly thrust a packet of small white pills at her sister. "These are what I am suspecting them to be?"

Adiba nodded and confessed that a friend living in London had sent her the pills. "She said just because I am a married woman, I should not have to be pregnant until I am ready."

"Your husband has no idea of this deceit?"

"It is my body, not his."

"If you do not give him a child, he will have your marriage annulled. Are you out of your head? You must flush these down the toilet at once and stop this foolishness."

Adiba snatched the packet from her sister. "I will not do that."

"You must. You must tell Hazem and beg his forgiveness. You are committing a mortal sin. Do not misunderstand my seriousness, sister; if you will not tell your husband, I shall."

3

ENTERING THE ORNATE red and gold bar in the Sir Francis Drake Hotel in downtown San Francisco, Dr. Brian Scott paused to assess the night's prospects.

Two attractive women in tailored business suits were locked in an intense conversation oblivious to everyone around them. A blonde seated at the bar was sipping a martini, reading *The Wall Street Journal*. Brian thought she'd be much more attractive if both the drink and the paper didn't look quite so much like props. Another woman caught his eye. She was under a sconce at a table against the red velvet wall. Her wild strawberry hair was wrangled into a bun. She wore black-rimmed reading glasses and had smoke colored stockings disappearing under her tight black skirt. She was lost in *The World According to Garp* and appeared to be alone.

Brian inhaled to fortify himself. This was why, when out of town on business, he never stayed near the hosting venue. He preferred anonymity, the ability to prowl. And he certainly didn't want to have to worry about sparking gossip. He loped toward the woman under the light. Absorbed in the novel, she sipped a clear fizzy drink Brian couldn't identify. "Great book. Don't you love Roberta Muldoon?"

The redhead laughed. "She's a trip."

"Look," Brian said, "I don't want to be obnoxious but may I buy you a drink?"

She raised her glass. "Gin and Sprite with a lime twist."

Returning, Brian delivered her drink; he had a tumbler of scotch for himself. "Hope you don't mind me saying this but you have a stunning pair of legs."

"I'm married," she said. "And judging by your bedside manner, I'm going to guess you're in town for the medical convention."

"You got it. And for the record? I'm very married, too."

"Okay then. Since I've seen how you are *beside* the bed, I'm curious to know how you are in it." She raised her drink. "Bottoms up, Doctor. I'm not a woman who believes in procrastinating."

The instant the door closed behind them, it became a flipbook of flying clothes and primal groans. They touched and rubbed and stroked. Compliments layered their laughter; shared sweat seeped toward the squeaking springs. The headboard banged against the wall like some romance novel cliché. Noisy joy accompanied their volcanic release. When all was silent they lay entwined in the twisted bed sheets. Eden evaporated with the ring of the bedside phone. "You need to answer that," she said. "It's after midnight. Might be an emergency."

"Shit." Brian grabbed the receiver. "Hello?" A beat. "Mom. What's up?"

The redhead was up on her elbows, "Is it the kids?"

Brian signaled her to hold on.

"When was the last time he pooped? Are you sure? Okay. In the cabinet beside the tub in our bathroom there's a jar of suppositories. He does this fairly frequently; all anxiety goes to his bowels." He listened to his mother's query before replying: "You just kinda have to insert it with your fingers and push it up, like jamming a bullet into a peashooter."

When he finally hung up, Heather was at the mini-bar pouring a Diet Coke over ice asking if Brian's mother would be able to handle the task.

"Are you kidding? Johnny was a chronic puker. A little suppository? Cake!"

"At least she was kind enough to call after we finished."

"Are we finished?" Brian asked wiggling his eyebrows.

"You burned me down, Dr. Scott. This lonely slut needs her sleep." She slid back into bed. Brian pulled her close; she rested her head on his chest. "Was Russell in terrible pain?"

"Who wouldn't be? He hasn't taken a shit since Friday. He'll be okay." He quoted his mother who said their other son Joey was with Poppa John: "Even when Russell was howling like a wolf, they never stirred; a pair of peas slumbering in their proverbial pod."

Heather turned to kiss Brian's shoulder. "Thanks for the sexual healing, Doctor."

"Thank you for being my horny businesswoman."

In the seven years since they'd gotten married, this was only the second time Brian and Heather had managed to pull off a week away together. Brian finished his residency weeks before their summer of '77 wedding and joined a general practice in Santa Monica after they returned from their Hawaiian honeymoon. That fall they bought their first house, a two bedroom relic from the '50s on Meier Street in Mar Vista. By Christmas, Heather was pregnant.

Russell was born in September of '78, arriving via emergency C-section. The delivery had been going smoothly until the baby rolled over onto his umbilical cord, cutting off his oxygen supply. Before they grasped what was happening, Heather was rushed into the operating room to be, as she later described it, "gutted like a trout." Russell was lifted out, Brian cut the cord and Russell's siren cries began.

Three years later, they had Joey, the dream baby. He was easy to feed and a rabid sleeper with beautiful blonde ringlets surrounding crystal blue eyes. As soon as he could sit up, he had the ability to amuse himself, perfectly content to push a toy car across the rug for hours.

Heather resigned from her teaching position in Inglewood to be home with the boys but by the start of the current school year she was onto her next career. Through each pregnancy she'd become more aware of the importance of prenatal care. From her five years of teaching in a low-income area, she knew many of her students' mothers couldn't afford proper healthcare and often didn't see a doctor until their babies were full-term. It seemed immoral to Heather that the richest country in the world had such an inequitable system. She decided to do her own small part to change that.

One of the things Brian loved most about his wife was that once she got an idea into her head, it would take an act of God to deter her. Doing copious research to uncover available government funds, grant money and private donations, Heather and a friend opened the Inglewood Family Health Clinic just after Labor Day. The clinic's mission statement announced a goal to "offer education, health and human services to low income families to enhance their ability to become robust and productive members of the community." Brian recruited several doctor pals to donate six hours a week; along with them, Heather, her partner and their staff provided much needed care and counseling to those who'd previously gone without. Heather felt a deep sense of pride and accomplishment now that the clinic was thriving. They'd moved to their current four-bedroom Spanish-style hacienda on 17th Street in Santa Monica in early July.

Waking up to a spectacular, clear October Bay Area morning, Brian decided to blow off the day's flu vaccine workshop to spend the time in the city with Heather. While he showered, she checked in at home. Nancy happily reported that Russell had unloaded "an enormous BM" two hours after she gave him the suppository and immediately went back to sleep. He'd gone off to kindergarten that morning with a big smile. Joey and Poppa John were outside looking for four-leaf clovers while Nancy was having her coffee watching the *Today* show.

Delighted and relieved, Heather was perusing the San Francisco guidebook when the phone rang again. It was her brother-in-law Johnny. "I feel like a dickwad bothering you guys on your getaway but Mom told me where you were and I…I'm going crazy; I didn't know who else to call."

Brian emerged from the bathroom naked, drying his hair with a towel. He heard Heather say, 'Hold on. Your brother's right here.'

After the call, Brian turned to Heather with a heavy sigh.

"Did Olivia leave him?"

"Worse. He came home early from driving his cab last night 'cuz of a big thunderstorm and caught her in bed with the sculptor from upstairs. Get this: the guy's a nose artist! He makes masks with weird noses and calls it art."

Sitting at his rain-streaked front window, Johnny finally spied what he'd been waiting for: his wife and her greasy-haired lover the nose artist exited the building and hopped into a waiting cab. Johnny went to the building super with a bogus story about needing to borrow a plunger. When the guy went to fetch it, Johnny swiped the ring of master keys beside the front door.

Now, he was unlocking the nose artist's apartment grasping his prized Mickey Mantle bat. He ducked inside turning the lock behind him. Gazing around, he found it impossible believe the guy actually sold this shit.

WHAM! The bat came down on a pale plaster mask with a Danny Thomas proboscis. It shattered into a disassembled mosaic. WHAM! He destroyed a glazed purple mask with the aquiline nose of an English aristocrat. Shards skittered across the floor. Johnny felt high on the power of wanton destruction. When he was finished, a year's worth of inventory was dust. He returned the plunger to the manager and covertly put the purloined keys back on their hook.

Getting ready for work, Johnny heard a devastated male scream from above along with Olivia's high-pitched sobs. Moments later, a furious pounding pelted Johnny's door.

"What the fuck did you do, man? What the fuck? You ruined everything!"

Johnny had never in is life felt calmer. "Prove it."

While Johnny was hip-deep in misery, Brian and Heather reveled in the San Francisco sun. After crab legs at Fisherman's Wharf they sat on a Golden Gate Park bench watching a flock of Cal students playing Frisbee. A boy with hair to his shoulders made a diving catch. "We'll blink and that'll be Russell, ya know." Brian gave a melancholy sigh. "I can't believe he's in kindergarten already." A wistful beat. "So where to next, Legs?"

Heather laughed, "You haven't called me that in years."

Returning to LAX the next day, Brian was hailing a cab when someone called out, "Is that the famous Dr. Scott?" Spinning toward the voice as Heather came up behind him, Brian knew he knew the face but it took him a moment to place it. "Sean?"

The guy coming at him in the American Airlines skycap uniform was extending a hand for Brian to shake. Wow, Brian thought, I know we haven't seen each other in a decade but what the hell happened? Didn't we used to be the same age? "Honey, you remember my old med school roommate Sean Pembroke."

Heather and Sean shook hands. Brian knew from his wife's tight tone she was as shocked as he was. Sean heard they'd gotten married and asked how it was going. They told him about their young sons. Brian asked Sean how he was doing. "I'm a forty-year-old med school dropout working as a goddamn sky-cap. Living the American fucking Dream."

It was during the first year of their residency when Brian was living with Sean and their classmate Ozzie that Sean had gotten hooked on prescription drugs. It started with stealing speed to cope with the long hours and intense pressure. Being wired on uppers meant he soon needed downers to sleep. The insidious cycle spiraled into a meltdown. When he got busted,

Sean was ordered into rehab and given a second chance. Unfortunately, his addictions escalated. By year's end he was thrown out of UCLA. He stayed in touch with Brian for a bit before falling away.

Not knowing what to say next, Brian fumbled. "So, are you, ah…"

"Still a drug addict? Depends on the hour. But at least I'm holding down a job. You take care, Bri, all right? Good to see ya, Heather. I've got…"

He gestured to a couple at the curb anxious to check in. Brian urged his old pal to be good. Sean's matter-of-fact retort broke Brian's heart: "I try, man. Every single day."

As they rode toward their comfortable Santa Monica home, nestled together in the back of the musty-smelling cab, Brian couldn't shake his unsettled feelings. "Could that have been more awkward? He looks like he's aged a hundred years."

Heather reached over and intertwined her fingers in his. "We're so lucky…"

"Seriously."

Later, as Joey played with his new Ghirardelli Chocolate delivery truck and Russell worked with Poppa John on the Golden Gate Bridge jigsaw puzzle, Heather, Brian and Nancy got down to the subject weighing on them all.

"Johnny's devastated," Nancy said. "Olivia's already gone, you know; moved in with that awful artist. What sort of fellow takes up with his neighbor's wife?"

"Enough folks that they had to make a Commandment about it." John chimed in. "Hey, he's better off cutting his losses now instead of ending up like Marsh and Louise."

"Oh my God," Brian laughed, "they're still married?"

In bed that night, Brian filled Heather in on the sordid history of the family that continued to live across the street from his childhood home. He told her about Marsh's many extramarital affairs and how, one way or another, Louise found out about all of them. Their oldest daughter Sarah was pregnant at seventeen, living in her parents' basement raising the baby alone. Their other daughter Katie went to college in Hawaii and never came back. Her annual Christmas cards arrived without a return address.

Seated at his office desk for the first time in a week, Brian was overwhelmed by the huge stack of mail in front of him. He'd come in an hour before his first appointment in anticipation of this paperwork avalanche but now had no idea where to begin.

Spying one envelope addressed in a neat cursive slant, the Washington DC return address captured Brian's attention. It was from Gina Kaufman, the girl whose AVM he'd helped diagnose a decade earlier. Awash in curiosity, Brian ripped the letter open and pulled out the lavender stationary covered by a torrent of words.

Gina was writing to let Brian know that in three months she'd graduate from Georgetown University, earning a BS in history with a focus on the politics of the Middle East. She'd done hours of research on how and when to apply for the CIA or the FBI, the culmination of her childhood dream. Both agencies required candidates to first acquire a few years of practical experience in the civilian work force. As a result, Gina was chasing a position at a DC think-tank in need of translators. Having minored in Middle Eastern languages, she was hoping she was a natural fit. She wrote that as she was writing the personal statement for her application, she formulated a thought that hadn't crystallized until that moment:

You, Dr. Scott, are the reason I'm still alive. I figure it's finally time to say thank you.

4

"Mom, stop. I can make my own bed. Please. You've been amazing, but now you're stressing me out."

Lisa finished stuffing the pillow into its butter-yellow case and tossed it onto the half-made bed. "I'm done."

Gina gave her mother an appreciative kiss. "I'll finish putting everything together later but now I'd much prefer you buy me dinner before I drive you to the airport."

Looking around the next-to-new one-bedroom apartment off Dupont Circle in the nation's capital, Lisa was struggling to digest the fact that her baby was a twenty-one year old college graduate starting her career. It was three weeks before Christmas and Gina had finished at Georgetown at the end of fall semester earlier that week. On the coming Monday, she'd start work at the Brookings Institution, 3,000 miles from her family. Even though Lisa knew Gina was fully recovered from all the after-effects of the stroke she'd suffered as a child, that didn't stop Lisa from worrying. She hated that Gina wanted to work and live across the country but also knew it was the price she and Martin paid for raising such a strong, confident young woman.

When Gina first fell ill, Lisa didn't know if she'd ever be able to live on her own. It was only through eighteen long months of arduous speech, occupational and physical therapy that Gina managed to regain control of her body. Watching her daughter now it was hard for Lisa to remember how fragile Gina had been. For months after the catastrophe she spent most days in a wheelchair. She had home tutors to accommodate her rigorous physical therapy schedule. She missed the last three months of fifth grade and the first half of the following school year. Of course Gina had her dark days but her Uncle David had an almost magical ability to shake her out of those periodic depressions. The two of them had been a team from Day One. It was David's love of spy novels that first sparked Gina's interest in becoming a government agent. Gina's dogged pursuit of that dream spurred her to heal.

Sharing a large bowl of peel-and-eat shrimp, Lisa and Gina talked nonstop. Their last hour together was precious even though they'd be reunited in a few weeks when Gina came home for the holidays.

"Let's pray your sister's finally found a major she'll stick with. As is she's got another year-and-a-half to go. She'll be graduating with so much debt…"

"You and Daddy *had to* cut her off. Nine years to attain a B.A? Please."

"I just wish she'd lose some weight."

In San Diego, Debbie sat naked in an unfamiliar bed. Her mouth felt like it was filled with dirt, her clothes were littered across the floor. From an adjacent room, she heard raucous laughter and hard-edged rock and roll. She had no idea where she was. She spied a shriveled condom stuck to the sheet between her legs: Oh, that's pretty. Oh well, at least I won't turn up pregnant.

Rolling over to snatch her underwear off the floor, Debbie felt her stomach rolls flap against the stale-smelling sheets. She grabbed her dress and tugged it over her head. Creeping toward the door, the voices she heard were all male: drunk talk, guys giving each other ceaseless shit. There was no way she was going out there.

Squeezing her considerable bulk through the bedroom window, Debbie dropped to the grass darting through sweeping sprinklers. Reaching a familiar street, soaked from head to toe, she headed for her apartment. Streams of strolling students were staring at her, fighting to suppress erupting giggles. A few rudely laughed out loud. Debbie knew she was wet, drunk and fat but was it really necessary for these kids to laugh in her face?

Rushing into her apartment, she dashed into the bathroom. Seeing words scribbled across her forehead in black marker, appearing backward in the mirror, it took her a second to decode them: **TWO TONS O' FUN.**

Up in Los Angeles, David questioned the man snuggled against him on the living room couch: "If we're buying a place together, where would *you* want to be? You must admit there's more to do around here than in Baldwin Hills."

"Why, because my neighborhood's filled with *schvartzas*?" his partner asked.

"I just think if we're starting fresh, it should be on neutral turf."

Even though they'd met four years earlier at a Centennial celebration at USC, David had only been seriously involved with Cyrus Ralston for eight months. Cyrus, class of '59, was a tall black man originally from Atlanta who'd caught David's eye immediately. They talked, toasted to one hundred years of Trojan power, flirted and then went their separate ways. Six months later, David got a call in his History Department office. When Cyrus offered his name, an embarrassed David couldn't place him. "Trojan champagne on the lawn last summer…"

"Of course. Cyrus! How may I help you?"

"I was wondering if you'd be interested in having dinner with me."

Reflecting on it, David didn't know why it had taken them so long to become a duo. It was probably about timing and David's unabashed commitment phobia. The thing that scared him most about buying a house with Cy was that he'd finally have to come out to Lisa and Gina.

Marshaling his courage, David called his "Geena-bo-beena" in DC.

"Uncle David! How are you?"

"I'm…ah – I'm gay."

"You do know this isn't exactly breaking news, right?"

The conversation lasted an hour and when it was over, David felt as weightless as a space walker. Not only was Gina nonjudgmental, she was truly elated. She was glad they could finally be completely honest with each other. She needed David to know he was and forever would be one of the most important people in her life. "I can't wait to meet Cyrus. I love that he's black. How scandalous! Have you told Mom yet?"

"No. You were my test case. And you passed with flying colors. I love you."

"I love you, too – even if you are a big old queen. Oh no, wait, was that insensitive?"

"Honey, you can call me a queen any day; what hurt was that you called me old."

Monday morning, dressing for her debut at the Brookings Institution, a prominent left-leaning think tank in downtown DC, Gina stared out at the falling snow. She slipped into her navy topcoat, tugged on the stylish wool beret she'd gotten from Brian Scott a decade ago, and sailed to the Metro stop. Catching her reflection in a coffee shop window, Gina was startled to see a twin to Mary Tyler Moore's career girl alter ego gazing back. She thought about changing but then decided the advantage of working with a pack of Ivy League eggheads was that most them probably didn't even own a TV.

"Well, if it isn't Mary Richards," quipped Gina's boss Geraldine Krassner the instant Gina rushed through the office door. "Welcome. You look adorable, all pink-cheeked eagerness and wide-eyed innocence. Don't worry; I'll beat some healthy cynicism into you soon enough. Take off your coat and let's get started."

When Gina interviewed for the job three months earlier, she thought it was a sign that she and her prospective boss shared the same initials. She decided against bringing it up for fear of sounding like a nitwit, but then Geraldine addressed it almost immediately. She declared them to be kindred spirits: two liberal Jewish gals with twin initials and hair that looked like corkscrew pasta. Geraldine's take-no-prisoners manner enthralled Gina.

"The Middle East is a hot-bed of dysfunction, has been for centuries and always will be. Our job is to help the Powers That Be create policy to make a volatile region a touch more stable but anyone who thinks there'll ever be a true lasting peace is blind or an imbecile – or both."

As one of Geraldine's three fulltime assistants, Gina was hired to do translations and research as directed while also providing administrative support. It was a two-year appointment and at the end of the term Gina would either be promoted or let go. With one eye still firmly focused on the FBI, Gina figured this was the perfect way to gain the experience she needed by eavesdropping on some of the most brilliant progressive minds in the capital. Now all she had to do was learn how to mix a perfect martini. "I expect a drink on my desk every day at 5:00 p.m.," Gerry commanded.

"Shaken not stirred?" Gina said and laughed. Seeing Gerry's befuddled reaction, Gina blushed. "James Bond."

"Forgive me if I don't follow the exploits of chauvinistic fantasy that's an affront to women everywhere. Pussy Galore? Honestly! Now go see Virginia on desk two; she'll set you up to review today's position papers on Egyptian trade policy."

Buoyed by his success in opening up to Gina, David booked a Saturday lunch at the Bullock's Wilshire tearoom with Lisa. The waiter arrived, they ordered two Waldorf salads, and then David reached across the table to take Lisa's hand. "Leese, may I talk to you about something?"

"Oh God, you're not sick, are you? I couldn't take it."

"No! Well, according to the Christian right I am. I'm gay."

Lisa's expression went from concern to confusion. "How long have you known?"

"Since Mother took us to see *Gone With the Wind* when I was nine. Blame it all on Rhett Butler."

With her mouth hanging open like a seal awaiting a tossed fish, Lisa's eyes filled with tears. "David, I'm really, really angry at you."

"What? Why? I can't help any of this, it's just who I am."

"I know that. I'm not some ignorant hillbilly. I'm mad that you felt the need to lie to me. For ages. Does this mean Martin was right way back when? Aaron was your boyfriend?"

Nodding, David kept his gaze riveted to the pink tablecloth.

"And Cyrus, too?"

"That's why I'm coming clean. Cy and I are looking to buy a house."

Lisa's tone retained its chill. "Mazel tov."

Sitting at his desk at the nonprofit Camp Mariposa Foundation, Martin was scrutinizing the coming year's operating budget. This whole enterprise began with a one-line announcement from Lisa the year Gina started high school. "Our kids are grown; it's time to give back."

After exploring various options and a few wild pipe dreams, Lisa hit upon the idea that stuck. "When Gina was going through rehab, we went from one facility to the next, met hundreds of doctors and therapists and assistants — but never had a place that felt comfortable and safe. None of it was ever fun."

Out of that declaration Camp Mariposa was born. Now in its seventh year, funded solely by private donations, the two-

month summer program provided a joy-filled environment in
which kids from five to eighteen could convalesce from serious
illnesses. Camp Mariposa's Olympic swimming pool, running
track and stocked athletic fields were there to help them heal.
Lisa got the ball rolling, Martin helped when he could, and all
three of their kids had worked there over various summers.
Once Martin retired, he became the foundation's Chief
Financial Officer and, each summer, its head track coach.

Lisa and Martin pulled into their driveway simultaneously.
After thirty years of marriage, the instant he saw her face he
knew the right question to ask: "What's wrong?"

"My brother's gay."

Martin worked to stifle a triumphant laugh. "He finally
admitted it?" Lisa nodded, upset. "C'mon, honey, you can't be
shocked."

"I'm not. I'm just hurt he told Gina before he told me."

On the last day of work before Brookings shut down for a
two-week holiday, Gina was lunching in the company cafeteria,
reading *The Wall Street Journal*. Sensing someone hovering, she
glanced up. "Hi," the tall, skinny kid beamed. "I'm Gordon
Teisch. Gordy. I work on Latin America. You cover the
Middle-East, is that correct?"

Gina nodded. For a moment, they both froze. Gina
managed an uneasy giggle. "Would you mind sitting down?
I'm breaking my neck looking up at you."

Gordy sat, complimenting Gina on her ability to work for
Geraldine Krassner; he found her "scary as hell." Gina told
him the trick was to not take things personally. "I take
everything personally. Wanna maybe grab dinner or a movie
sometime?" Gina said she was heading home to LA the next
day. "A west coast girl, wow. So can we maybe get dinner after
you're back?"

Gina gave a noncommittal reply; with an embarrassed nod, Gordy rose and shuffled off. Gina started mentally pummeling herself. Why am I always so quick to chase guys away?

In her cubicle buried in policy papers, she couldn't focus. After her clumsy encounter with Gordy she was obsessively reviewing her entire romantic history. Always a serious student, she hadn't yet had a real boyfriend. In high school she was extremely shy. Her parents suspected her medical issues and long recovery left her feeling too vulnerable to open herself up. She went to her junior *and* senior proms but there was never that one guy she really connected with. Georgetown wasn't much better. Those guys were either egomaniacs or beer-guzzling goons.

She spent her junior year fall semester in Amman in an intense Language and Culture program at the University of Jordan. Having several other Americans in the program inspired Gina to make a calculated decision: wanting to get it over with, she just picked a boy to have sex with, a Jewish kid from Brown. She couldn't remember if his name was Mark or Mitchell.

Returning from lunch, fumbling to get his office door unlocked, David was surprised to see Cyrus coming down the hall visibly upset. "I…I ran into Cameron today. He's HIV positive. He and William are absolute wrecks. We all know it's a death sentence."

"Not necessarily. "

"Quit your denial, David. As long as it's 'gay cancer' do you honestly believe the medical establishment will squander their genius keeping a bunch of queers alive?"

This new epidemic had only been on the international radar for eight months. Already David and Cyrus knew a dozen men with the disease; two had recently passed away. There were myriad rumors about how it was transmitted, how it spread, but everyone agreed it was an awful way to die. Cyrus insisted he and David get tested.

"Thank you, but I'll pass. For the first time ever, I'm truly happy. I love you, I'm out to my family…well, most of my family, but my point is I'm free and would sincerely like to hang onto my ignorant bliss as long as possible."

Readying to leave her downtown office, Gina wished Gerry a happy holiday. Scooting around a corner, she collided with a man who stopped her heart. Glancing up as he grabbed both of her elbows to keep her from crashing to the carpet, Gina experienced an electric connection unlike anything she'd ever felt before.

"Sorry," she said, locking her knees to prevent them from buckling.

"My fault. That's what I get for thinking I can read and walk at the same time."

He smiled. Gina felt a hot current flood her body. She tried to decide how old he was: Forty, at least; with Warren Beatty hair.

"How rude of me," he stuck out a hand, "Tucker Edwards."

She shook his hand, feeling as tiny as a toddler. "Gina Kaufman." He asked if she worked for Gerry; Gina nodded, unable to banish her dopey grin. "Do you, ah, work here, too?"

"No, no; just doing a bit of consulting work. I'm actually an agent at the FBI."

5

TUGGING DOWN THE BLACK skirt of her waitress uniform, Adiba moved to the lone customer at a window table in her station. Being an avowed anglophile, she was delighted to discover he was an American. She didn't need to hear him speak; merely taking in his clothes, his haircut and his expensive Nike athletic shoes told her he was from the United States. The instant he replied to her formal greeting with a chipper 'What's happening?' any lingering doubt vanished.

In the six weeks she'd been working at Rick's Café in downtown Baghdad, Adiba quickly came to know that Americans were the most generous tippers. The small diner with décor from the '40s was based on the place Humphrey Bogart's character owned in *Casablanca*. As soon as she learned it would be opening, Adiba became determined to get a job there. The new establishment featured framed black-and-white stills from the movie with an upright piano in back; during the lunch hour, an elderly African man played a parade of tunes, beginning and ending each shift with "As Time Goes By."

When Adiba initially saw the café was hiring a wait staff, she was working three days a week at her father's tailoring shop. Although the pair had been close when Adiba was young, their relationship had grown strained. Hadi expected the women in his life to be obedient and deferential. Unfortunately, that had never been Adiba's way. As an infant, her endless wailing affirmed her need to be heard; growing up she inevitably spoke her mind. Working with her *baba* she found it impossible to hold her tongue when she believed he was being unfair. The tension between them escalated until Adiba found it untenable. Although Hadi didn't want her to quit, he refused to beg her to stay.

It had not been easy for Adiba to convince Hazem to allow her to work at Rick's. He was a successful surgeon at al-Karkh Hospital. It was bad enough his wife took a menial job in her father's shop but at least there she was working for family. How would it look to have a doctor's wife waiting tables? Adiba didn't care. She was severely under-stimulated and hated being trapped at home. All her husband desired was for her to hurry up and give him a son.

After Shemma discovered Adiba was taking birth control pills imported from London, she threatened to tell Hazem if Adiba didn't confess her sin. Not trusting her sister to follow through, Shemma insisted on witnessing Adiba flushing every last pill down the toilet. Now Adiba spent the last days of each monthly cycle praying her womb remained empty.

Taking her customer's order, she learned he was Tommy McBride from Cleveland, an AP reporter covering the Iran-Iraq war. He looked to be in his early thirties with an athlete's toned arms and broad shoulders. When he asked Adiba how she'd been impacted by the now four-year-old war, she told him her brother Mo'ez was stationed near the Iraq-Iran border. The last time Mo'ez wrote home he talked about the recent death of one of his closest platoon mates. The two were yards apart when a rain of enemy bullets invaded their trench. Mo'ez whirled around to find his friend lacking a head. Mo'ez ended his letter saying the one thing he knew for sure was that it was absolutely insane to have a war where Muslims were killing Muslims.

Checking the x-rays of a soldier with a shattered wrist bone, Hazem fought to mask the wince provoked by a pain piercing his belly. He could see on the patient's face that his grimace had not gone unnoticed. Afraid his insides were about to explode like a detonated firecracker, Hazem jumped up, mumbled an apology and bolted out. Desperately clenching his butt cheeks to ward off an embarrassing accident, he lunged into the nearest water closet. Charging into the stall, he locked the door while his trembling hands fumbled to unhook his uncooperative belt buckle. Frenzied, he yanked down his zipper, unbuttoned his pants and collapsed onto the toilet seat a millisecond before he unloaded a witch's brew of gas, blood and diarrhea. His eyes stung; his temples throbbed. Everything bloating his tender stomach and fiery colon had been evacuated in a muzzle flash. The unyielding cramps felt like a gnarly claw scraping his stomach from inside.

Exiting the bathroom, Hazem was shocked by the ghost staring at him from the mirror.

Dabbing his forehead with a monogrammed handkerchief, he returned to his patient. The soldier asked if he was all right; Hazem replied with an unconvincing nod.

Driving home, Hazem's cramps had eased but he was suffering from an unquenchable thirst. His growling belly felt hollow but the thought of eating made him nauseous. He was subconsciously clenching his ass to ward off a new explosion. He'd become a human volcano in efficacious denial that something was very wrong. His wife claimed doctors made the worst patients; Hazem was living proof.

Adiba and Hazem sat at the table wrapped in an oppressive silence. She watched him move the rice and marinated lamb in circles without bringing the fork to his mouth. "The meal is no good? I did not cook the lamb sufficiently?"

Hazem kept his eyes on the lace tablecloth. "It is fine. I have no appetite."

"Hazem—" He angrily cut her off. Adiba would not be deterred. "You hardly eat anymore. Your mother thinks I am starving you. You look like a walking bag of bones and she blames me."

He locked his dark eyes on her. "I have enough stress at work. I do not need stress in my home. I am fine, I have told you! I do not wish to speak of this again."

Adiba was half asleep when Hazem slipped into bed. She reached out to touch the hairy back turned to her. As her fingers connected, his shoulder blade tensed.

"I only question you out of concern, Hazem. "

His words were marinated in condescension, "In case you have forgotten, woman, I am a doctor. If something was wrong I would know."

"Knowing it and doing something about it are two entirely different things."

Paying his check, Tommy McBride stood with Adiba at the pass while she waited for her next order; he asked her why she looked so exhausted. She sighed. "It is my husband. "

"Wait, you're married? I thought you were, like, sixteen."

"I have recently turned twenty-two. Women in my country marry early. My sister was a bride at seventeen."

"So no college for you? Just dad's pad to hubby's house?" Adiba nodded and he went on, "Would it be possible for us to meet away from here sometime?"

Adiba felt her face flush. She told him that would not be appropriate; in fact, it could be dangerous – for them both. Absorbing her discomfort, Tommy laughed. "Whoa, relax. I only want to interview you for that piece I'm doing about the war's impact on civilians. I talked to this one cat at a government ministry. An Iranian rocket ripped right through his office wall. Missed him by a few yards but the impact blew him out of his chair and slammed his ass, I mean, his – him – ya know, it knocked him into a wall. Messed him up pretty good, mentally and physically. It's Looney Tunes, right?"

Adiba grabbed the plate of fish and chips from the window and nodded. Tommy asked again if they might get together, assuring her it would be strictly professional. Adiba told him she was off on Thursdays; they could meet at the very public cafe across the street: 10:00 a.m. the day after tomorrow. "It's a date," Tommy said with a wink.

"No," Adiba corrected, "it is a formal interview. Nothing more."

Changing out of her sweat-stained waitress uniform, slipping into a lightweight cotton sheath, Adiba darted to the ringing phone in her kitchen. Her mother Rima was choking out words between sobs. "Mo'ez was wounded. I have no details. He's being airlifted to al-Karkh."

Struggling to remain composed Adiba made plans to meet her parents at the hospital. She called Hazem to give him the scraps of information she knew and asked him to find anyone at the hospital that might be able to uncover an update. She'd pick up Shemma and be there soon.

Confusion and chaos dominated the night. Adiba, Shemma and their parents huddled in the hospital waiting room. Around midnight someone reported that the military transport bearing Mo'ez had landed at Baghdad airport. The wounded were being transferred to ambulances. Through all the long hours, no one had been able to give them a clue about Mo'ez's condition.

The hospital air conditioning system overloaded and shut down. Even at 1:00 a.m., the temperature outside was 102 degrees; the air draped them like a velvet curtain. Adiba was exhausted, frustrated, aching to dissolve into tears. Her father wouldn't look at her, her husband resembled a cadaver in black Oxfords, and her only brother might be dead or dying.

Hadi cried out, "Here he comes!"

The family charged toward military drivers wheeling the gurney carrying Mo'ez. Adiba reached him first. He was pale and glazed but alive. Spying his sister, he grabbed her hand; the escorting soldier told him they needed to keep moving. Adiba eyed an expanding crimson blot on the sheet covering Mo'ez's leg.

"It is my upper thigh," he muttered as the rest of his family arrived. Their anxious scrum was making it difficult for the emergency room personnel to do their jobs.

At 3:00 a.m. Hazem emerged with an update. The bullet had demolished Mo'ez's femur from hip to knee. It was repairable but would require at least two, possibly up to four, surgeries to put it right. None of the damage was life threatening but his recovery would be grueling. Mo'ez had been sedated and moved to the surgical ward. Hazem was slated to do the first surgery in morning. His supervisor needed assurance that, being the patient's brother-in-law, he'd be able to maintain the necessary objectivity. Hazem argued that his emotional investment was the strongest reason to believe Mo'ez would be in the best possible hands.

Standing at Mo'ez's hospital bedside, Adiba was shocked by his dark humor. "I hope Father and Mother are not disappointed I failed to earn them a new Toyota Corona."

The car Mo'ez was referring to was an absurd "reward" Saddam was giving to all families who lost a father, son or husband in the war.

Before dawn the next day, Hazem was in his sterile scrubs; a surgical cap covered his dark hair. A male nurse told Hazem that Mo'ez wished to speak to him before they administered the pre-anesthesia shot to begin putting him under. When Hazem entered the austere preparation room, Mo'ez asked the nurse and the young anesthesiologist to give them a moment alone.

"I need you to make a mess of this operation," Mo'ez pleaded. "Do whatever you can to ensure I will never recover full use of my leg." Hazem could only stare in utter shock. "If I recover, they will immediately send me back to the front. I cannot do that. The things I have experienced, the terror I have felt...I have murdered total strangers, Hazem. Before their bodies hit the ground I see the widows and fatherless children...inconsolable parents, ruined lives, unending grief…for what, borders and inflated egos? What does any of that mean to me? I cannot return to the madness. Rig it so the bone does not repair properly; let me be forced to walk with a cane or a limp. Can you understand? I need you to make a crucial error."

The surgery took nearly four hours. Hazem repaired the bit of broken bone closest to the hip joint. The single bullet had shattered or nicked several portions of the femur and Hazem needed one area to heal before he could judge what the next damaged piece of the bone required.

Despite a few shaky moments when nerves started to get the better of him, and one emergency interruption to relieve his bloated bowels, Hazem was pleased with the outcome. He was able to knit the upper portion of the bone back together aligning the pieces perfectly. He knew that the only one who would not be pleased was Mo'ez.

Adiba looked forward to her appointment with Tommy as a welcome break from the previous days' stress. Mo'ez's second surgery would come at the end of the month. For now he appeared to be relatively comfortable.

In the open-front coffeehouse where Tommy and Adiba met, most of the patrons were old men sharing ornate hookahs stuffed with pungent tobacco. Clouds of blue smoke hovered near the inlaid brass ceiling. The sweet smelling smog irritated Tommy's allergies but Adiba found it comforting; it reminded her of her missing grandfather. When Tommy asked if Saddam's repressive regime had a tangible impact on her life, Adiba told him about Faraj's abduction. "My grandmother lives without a moment of relief. For me, his absence is daily a hole in my heart. I pine for the man who gave my sister and me sweets when we were children. I can conjure the feel of his scratchy beard against my cheek when he would hug me and tell me I was the sunshine in his soul." She went on to relay a tale she'd heard from her husband. "Two of Hazem's colleagues, esteemed physicians with years of lauded service to our town were together at a recent party. They assumed they were among colleagues and friends. Relaxed, enjoying themselves, the doctors began to mock Saddam's dyed hair and too-black moustache; they joked about his sexuality doing crude impersonations of the tyrant. The next thing anyone knew, they were arrested, imprisoned and executed for treason. No trial, no jury of their peers. It was revealed that a member of the Republican Guard also attended the party and covertly taped the incident. He scored personal points by showing the tape to Saddam. As a result two valued doctors are dead. So, yes, the regime's policies affect us all every day."

Processing what he'd just heard, Tommy's green-and-gold eyes studied Adiba. Turning from his gaze, she quietly said, "Tell me, Mr. McBride, is America truly a place where women are the equals of men?"

Tommy laughed. "I'm guessing that would depend on who you ask. Ya see, more and more women are making strides in the workplace, in politics, at colleges across the country…but they still don't earn the same as men and some guys are pretty threatened by ladies trying to get their fair share—"

"And yet, women there have far more freedom than in my country."

"Certainly looks that way to me."

The wistful look in Adiba's eyes told Tommy she was already mentally packing her bags.

At Al-Karkh Hospital, Mo'ez was two days away from the second surgery to repair the femur destroyed by an Iranian soldier's bullet. Despite his pleas to Hazem to botch the initial surgery, Hazem did a perfect job. When Mo'ez's commander paid a visit, he quipped that they'd have Mo'ez back in fighting form in no time. The young soldier didn't see this as good news.

In the hall outside his sterile room it was uncommonly quiet. Mo'ez's roommate, a soldier with a badly mangled spine, was asleep. Mo'ez's leg was in a hip-to-toe cast but he was able to get around on crutches. He wasn't supposed to even go to the commode without a nurse or an immediate family member at his side but, in this moment, Mo'ez didn't care. He had a pressing solo mission to execute.

At the top of a walled-in hospital stairwell, he attempted to steady himself on his wobbling crutches. It had required an enormous amount of exertion to get out of bed, into the corridor and to the elevator at the end of the hall. With so much time spent flat on his back, his upper body strength was severely compromised. Now, peering down the steep concrete stairs, he was fighting to fortify his trembling arms and rattled nerves. He would do anything to keep from being returned to combat.

Serving Tommy a late breakfast of scrambled eggs and hash browns, Adiba remarked that he seemed unusually subdued. She asked if everything was all right.

"John Kennedy died today. Only sixty-seven years old. Turns out he's had Addison's disease since the '40s but they kept it quiet. Ya know, he was the first president I actually cared about."

"You respected this man?"

"How could you not? He was a great looking athlete, had a beautiful wife, fought for civil rights -- and he ended a war that was destined to cause nothing but heartbreak. A real leader. Sure he was a Boston Brahman, but he empathized with the Average Joe."

"This for me is not possible to imagine," Adiba said. "Living in a place where powerful men care about more than simply enriching themselves."

Poised at the top of the steep hospital staircase, resolved to fling himself down the entire flight, Mo'ez was startled by a door opening behind him. He whipped around to find a young orderly greeting him with a broad smile. "This looks like a really bad idea. Are you trying to kill yourself? Wherever you thought you were headed, friend, why not forget it and let me help you back to bed."

Standing at her bedroom mirror brushing her feathers of dark hair, Adiba was immersed in a daydream. What if she told Hazem she was going to visit cousins in Kuwait and once there, applied for a visa to the United States? She could start a new life, attend a university and perhaps pursue a career as a writer or a film critic. She might even change her name to Marilyn.

Then she felt it: a strange yet somehow recognizable flutter in her belly. How can I be pregnant? Hazem and I have hardly been together. Except for the night last month when he was desperate to convince me he is not ill.

Adiba raced to a cabinet under the bathroom sink where she stored her beauty products. At the very back she found what she was looking for.

Clutching the plastic stick, she couldn't stop staring at its bright blue tip.

Surrounded by her elated family, Adiba felt a wave of calm wash over her. Confronting the reality of her pregnancy had created a change of heart she never could've imagined. She tenderly rubbed her belly as the party at her parents' house percolated around her.

"At last you have come to your senses," Shemma whispered.

"You flushed my pills and nature did the rest."

Shemma's four-year-old charged at Adiba to grab her dress with chocolate-stained hands.

"*Baba* says my new cousin is inside your belly." The little girl attempted to dive under the hem of Adiba's floor-length garment. "May I see her?"

Laughing, Adiba tugged her dress down and moved the child aside. "I am afraid you will have to wait. We need to let the baby grow."

Rima gathered the partiers into the backyard. A bountiful spread of food covered the long table set up under a canopy at the rear of the house. Looking from Adiba to Mo'ez, Rima wiped away a tear. Mo'ez, still fragile and pale with a cast from his hip to his knee, sat in the shade of a huge palm tree. Even at twenty, he was still Rima's baby.

Seated amid the gallery of relatives, Adiba gazed at Hazem across from her. He looked awful. If he is so thrilled he is finally going to become a father, why does he still refuse to deal with what is ailing him? Seeing Adiba eying him with such tender sadness, Hazem forced himself to eat several unwanted bites of food. Adiba noted his listless nibbling. She recalled the dream she'd had the previous night. She was holding a beautiful baby boy with fat rosy cheeks as she stood at the edge of Hazem's open grave.

Despite the resistance she knew would meet her, it was time to summon her courage and confront the husband she wished to save. After the party, alone at home with Hazem, Adiba commanded him to sit. "This cannot go on one minute longer. We must talk."

With uncharacteristic surrender, Hazem dropped into his favorite chair. Adiba pulled a footstool in front of him and took his hands into hers. "Do you love me? You are happy we are having a child?"

"Yes, yes. Have I not told you repeatedly? I could not be more thrilled."

"Then for my sake and the sake of our baby you must find the proper doctor to determine what is wrong with you. We need to get you well."

Hazem did something Adiba had never seen him do before: he erupted in heaving sobs.

First thing the next day he made an appointment with a gastroenterologist. It took weeks of tests and one humiliating sigmoidoscopy to reach a diagnosis: Hazem had ulcerative colitis, an acute inflammation of the large intestine. It was chronic but treatable with dietary changes and medication; he'd never be fully rid of it but if he adhered to his doctor's recommendations and learned to manage stress, this probably wouldn't kill him.

Proud of herself for confronting Hazem, Adiba was hugely relieved. She felt a profound new affection for her husband. His vulnerability in dealing with his illness made him more appealing. She quit her job at Rick's Café to focus on having a peaceful, robust pregnancy. She knew from the start her notions of escaping to America were nothing but idle fantasy. She'd never leave her parents. She couldn't abandon her tormented grandmother. Instead she'd become a caring, devoted mother as all the previous generations had done before her.

And then, nearing the end of her first trimester, Adiba suffered a jolting miscarriage.

Visiting the hospital that night, Shemma stood at Adiba's bedside. Hazem had gone for a cup of coffee. "You know why this has happened, sister: because you took those horrible pills. *Allah* is punishing you for thwarting his will. You have desecrated your womb. You will never carry a baby to term. You have brought upon yourself a lifelong curse."

2001

— 1 —

TRAPPED IN THE UNMOVING TRAFFIC on Lincoln Boulevard, Brian was anxiously drumming the heels of his hands on the steering wheel of his year-old BMW 320i. "I thought if we were out by 6:30 we'd be fine; what the hell's going on today?"

In the passenger seat, Heather twisted her red hair, now flecked with gray, into a knot, securing it atop her head with a tortoise shell clip. "Put on 'traffic on the ones.' There must've been a wreck."

Sixty seconds later they had their answer: a three-car crash on the westbound Santa Monica freeway sent cars scurrying for the surface streets; Brian and Heather were victims of the fallout. Heather asked if he was going to miss his plane.

"I guess that depends on how fucked we are, doesn't it?"

"Hey, I didn't cause this mess so please don't take it out on me."

Brian apologized for being a snapping turtle all morning; everything about the trip he was embarking on was stressing him out.

"I couldn't say this to anyone but you," Heather admitted; "but as tragic as the situation is, it's also perversely hilarious to me. Am I a terrible person?"

"I get it. I mean, Jesus, she stabbed him through the heart with a samurai sword."

A combination of luck and good karma allowed Brian to catch his flight to Chicago with seconds to spare. The early

April weather cooperated, they landed on time and he easily made his connection to Rochester where once again the gods smiled; a predicted late-season snowstorm didn't materialize. He arrived at this parents' Woodside Lane home by 9:00 p.m.

It had only been four months since Brian had seen his mom and dad but as soon as they opened their door, he realized they looked noticeably older. John's eyes were ringed by a bandit's mask of fatigue; Nancy appeared thin and frail. When Brian asked about their health, his mother waved a dismissive hand. "Listen, Doctor, your father's eighty-one, I'll be seventy-nine in July. What can I tell you? We're old. At least we didn't end up like Marsh."

"That sorry son-of-a-pup got exactly what he deserved," John said.

When his mother called Brian about the unfolding neighborhood drama three months earlier, Nancy was having a hard time controlling her gasping breath. "There are police cars and paramedics – it looks like a scene out of one of our programs. Something awful happened, mark my words. Sarah arrived an hour ago; she's as big as a house! I want to see if I can help, but I'm afraid of what I'll be walking into. Goodness me, now a coroner's wagon just pulled up."

"I'll bet Louise finally killed the old prick."

"Brian! You know I don't like that language. Please."

"Sorry. Look, Mom, I've gotta get back to my patients. Call me later."

Heather told Brian the whole twisted tale that evening. Not wanting to disturb her son at work again, Nancy phoned her daughter-in-law to fill in the blanks. For the past two years, their across-the-street neighbor Marsh had been collecting antique Samurai swords. He'd retired from a long career at Xerox a decade ago and spent the intervening years jumping from one hobby to the next to avoid spending time with his wife. Everyone knew they'd been estranged for eons but neither

Marsh nor Louise ever mustered the energy to move on.

"I will never understand why they didn't simply get a divorce before it had to come to this," Nancy huffed at Heather. "Can you imagine?" Nancy relayed the full account she'd gotten from the Ditlows' daughter Sarah: as Louise started the dishwasher that morning, it made a loud grinding noise, groaned, and then emitted one puff of smoke before it died. Finding Marsh in the den watching the *Today* show, Louise reported this latest domestic setback, insisting the washer was too old to repair; they needed a new one. Without taking his angry eyes off the TV, Marsh informed his wife that unless she had two broken arms he wasn't aware of she was perfectly capable of washing dishes by hand.

A livid Louise glanced to the wall where Marsh had a half-dozen antique swords mounted in polished chrome brackets. She argued that if he could find money for four thousand dollar swords, he could damn well buy her a new dishwasher. Marsh glared at his wife and asked what would happen if he refused.

Sarah told Nancy that her mother claimed that, in that moment, everything around her went dark. Louise remembered sailing across the room to grab a curved carbon steel sword from its mounting, she recalled screaming creative cuss words and then…all she could see was blood.

The first policeman on the scene told Louise she'd made the 9-1-1 call herself but Louise had no memory of it. She was sitting in the kitchen sipping coffee when the officers arrived. Together they found the sixteenth century Hiromitsu sword piercing her dead husband's heart as he sat impaled into the back of his Barcalounger. When asked why she committed such a violent crime, an emotionless Louise simply replied, "He refused to buy me a new Kenmore."

Hunched at her desk paying bills in the office that was once her younger son's bedroom, Heather was surprised to hear a car door slam in the driveway. She glanced at the digital clock: 9:15 p.m.

Coming downstairs, she was delighted to find twenty-three year old Russell stepping inside.

Instantly, her joy was supplanted by apprehension. "Honey, is everything okay?"

"Everything's great. I was just at an awesome screening on the Promenade. Jack had to get back to school but I'm starving. Dad's at Gramma and Poppa's, right?"

"Yup. He got in on time, everybody's good; G & P are set to testify tomorrow or the day after. I have leftover steak and a baked potato I can nuke; how's that sound?"

Scraping the last bits from his plate with the gusto of a refugee, Russell said, "This screening – I mean, you would've hated it; the movie's dark and weird but SO cool. The lead's this new kid, Jake Gyllenhaal. He was there. Cool, right? It's exactly the kind of a movie I wanna make, Mom, not the formula crap the studios are doing. Hey, any ice cream?"

Scooping chocolate Haagen Dazs into a little silver bowl, Heather couldn't help but smile at seeing her son so revved up. After getting his undergraduate degree from the Tisch School of the Arts at NYU a year earlier, Russell was in his first year of the MFA Producing Program at USC. Although she and Brian had no idea if their boy would ever make a living as a filmmaker, they'd long ago decided to support his dream. He was focused, hard-working and had been a natural storyteller since elementary school. Seeing how undirected many of their friends' kids were, Heather and Brian were grateful their first-born had a passion.

Their second son Joey was a junior at UC Santa Barbara. He'd started college thinking he'd follow his dad into medicine but lately he'd been considering becoming a pharmacologist.

"So he can become a legit drug dealer," Russell quipped to his folks a week earlier.

Seeing his mother's horrified face, he added. "Mom, it's a joke."

Heather wished she could be sure. Joey had always been the more "adventurous" of the boys; he was a good kid yet had a way of perpetually pushing boundaries. His incredible charm saved his hide at every turn. He wasn't just good-looking with golden ringlets and his father's blue eyes; he also had an irresistible twinkling grin. And he milked those assets mercilessly.

In the Monroe County Criminal Courthouse in downtown Rochester, Nancy caught her first glimpse of the defendant and whispered: "Goodness me, I can't believe how ancient Louise looks."

From the bench, the judge doled out instructions to the jury. John was instantly asleep. Brian nudged his mom who reacted with a resigned chuckle. "What took him so long?"

Calling Heather to deliver the day's report after pork chops with his parents, Brian was surprised by how wiped out he felt. He knew a lot of it was due to the fact that he'd been forced to sit still during the endless hours of courtroom testimony. It was probably the longest he'd been immobile since he started med school in the early '70s. Brian was a mover, a doer. As a doctor, a dad, a bed partner, he was a man in motion. Heather swore he was never even at rest when he slept. They had to ship their newlywed waterbed off to Johnny after four short months because it was impossible for Heather to sleep without Dramamine.

For Brian, the time in court was torture. The same questions were asked twelve different ways as lawyers jockeyed to score legal points like it was one big game. Lost in the theatrics was the fact that a seventy-three year old woman's fate was at stake. When John took the stand, he won the jury over after his first few answers. His matter-of-fact replies were disarming.

"Did I know the Ditlows had marital troubles? Lady, everybody in Pittsford knew. Louise confided in my wife all the time. Marsh cheated on her, treated her like she was a moron – which couldn't be further from the truth, by the by. Marsh Ditlow simply needed to convince himself he was the smartest guy in any room."

Half of the folks in the jury box stifled the urge to laugh.

"You should've seen him, Heather. He worked the crowd like a pro. They called Mom to the stand at the end of the day. She was only warming up but she'll be back up there in the morning. She's already convinced everything she said was wrong. She told them Louise used to come over for a glass of wine some afternoons and now she's sure the jury will think Louise is an alcoholic. You know my mom, if there's a way she can beat herself up she definitely will."

After Heather and Brian told each other they loved and missed one another and hung up Brian slipped into his parents' garage and pulled out his old ten-speed bicycle.

Whipping through his former neighborhood, seeing most of it looking exactly as it had when he was a kid, Brian was overcome with nostalgia. It seemed like only weeks ago he was lying on his bed inhaling the scent of Karen Peterman's panties and now he was the father of two boys who were suddenly grown men. What the hell?

Coasting back onto his parents' street Brian looked to the Ditlows' house where Sarah was living with her fifteen-year-old son while her mother sat in jail and her father lay buried in Saint Mary's Cemetery. Katie, the one who went to college in Hawaii and never returned, was on Kauai, married to the manager of a Poipu restaurant. Their eighteen-year-old son was a pro surfer. They had a quiet, peaceful life far from the insanity of Katie's childhood.

Sarah told Nancy that after the murder, she tracked her

long-estranged sister down to give her the grim details of their
mother's crime and urged her to come home for the trial; Katie
refused. Calling Louise in jail to offer support, she explained,
"You people are too toxic for me. I'm doing what I need to do
to survive."

Thinking about all of it, Brian felt incredible gratitude for
his life.

As Nancy's testimony resumed the following morning,
Brian's mind drifted to another trial, the one some folks called
The Trial of the Century. When football star O.J. Simpson was
arrested for killing his wife Nicole at Christmastime of '94,
Brian wasn't paying much attention to the media circus
surrounding the case. Even though the Rockingham estate
where the murder took place was only a few miles away,
Brian's growing medical practice and busy family life left him
little time to get consumed by the pop-culture feeding frenzy.
But he did remember one night earlier that year when he and
Heather were out to dinner and spied the Simpsons at a nearby
table.

"What's up with that?" Brian asked, "I thought they were
divorced."

"*People* magazine says they're back together."

And then Brian forgot about the whole thing, leaving
Heather to follow the murder and its aftermath. That abruptly
changed the morning she appeared brandishing the front page
of *The Los Angeles Times* as Brian was shaving. "Look who's a
media star."

The second he saw the picture of his burned out med
school roommate Sean, there was only one question for Brian
to ask: "What'd he do?"

"Apparently he's the guy who found O.J.'s murder weapon
at LAX. They're calling him the prosecution's star witness."

On the day Sean was brought to the stand, Brian hustled

home to watch a tape of Sean's testimony. Heather and sixteen year old Russell crowded onto the couch with Brian; Joey was across the street playing video games. Brian filled Russell in on his history with Sean, explaining they lived together for two years before his buddy got into trouble with prescription drugs. Brian relayed how he and Heather had last seen Sean a decade earlier when they ran into him at LAX where Sean was a skycap.

"That sucks. Going from almost being a doc to hauling people's luggage? Grim."

"That's why drugs are so dangerous," Heather scolded.

"Got it, Mom. Hold on while I run upstairs to flush my heroin."

Watching the testimony, the Scotts saw the seasoned prosecutor lead Sean through his description of a limousine pulling up to the curb in front of his American Airlines podium days before Christmas of 1994. Being a rampant football fan, Sean was thrilled to recognize the man scrambling out of the car. He recounted tagging two bags and a set of golf clubs while a distracted 'Juice' covertly stuffed something into a nearby trashcan. "What happened once Mr. Simpson went into the terminal?"

"Well…I'm a nosy guy. Couldn't help but wonder what he tossed away. Thought it might be something I could sell to a sports memorabilia dealer or something. So I waited 'til there was a lull, then went to that trashcan and pulled the bag out."

"And you opened that bag?" the attorney asked.

"Wouldn't you?" Sean shot back to the amusement of the jury.

"Mr. Pembroke, please tell this court what you found."

Sean sat up straighter. "There was white towel with something reddish-brown and sticky all over it. I unfolded it…and this…knife fell out. I gotta tell ya, I had no idea what had gone down, but seeing that thing hit the sidewalk, I damn near had a heart attack."

And then it was the defense's turn.

"Mr. Pembroke, were you a one-time student at the UCLA medical school?" When Sean admitted he was, the masterful attorney took a dramatic pause to smile slyly at the jury. "Are you currently practicing medicine, Mr. Pembroke?"

"No, sir, I'm not."

"May you please tell this court why not?"

"In my first year of residency, I became addicted to prescription meds."

For the next two hours, the slick lawyer did everything in his considerable verbal power to annihilate Sean. He called him an unreliable liar, a thief and a criminal desperate for personal rehabilitation. To Brian's delight, Sean stayed strong and credible. When the attorney finished his most vicious attack, Sean's response was clear and simple. "Everything you said about me, sir, is true. But it doesn't change the fact that O.J. Simpson stuffed that bag in the trash and I pulled it out and found a bloody knife."

"Wow," Russell said, "it's so cool you know that guy, Dad. He's awesome!"

"Ironic, huh? If O.J. gets convicted, Sean'll wind up being a bigger hero by *not* being a doctor than he probably ever wouldda been if he hadn't blown it."

In the end, Orenthal James Simpson was found guilty of premeditated first-degree murder and sentenced to life in prison without the possibility of parole. At the chaotic press conference following the verdicts, the prosecutor delivered a long list of thank-yous and concluded with a final mention: "As compelling as the evidence was, we believe we might not have reached this fair and just outcome without the curiosity of football fan Sean Pembroke. He gave us the murder weapon and helped the DA's office achieve the justice Nicole Brown

Simpson deserves."

The banging of Judge Vener's gavel brought Brian back to the present in the Rochester courtroom as his mother was dismissed from the witness stand.

"She did great, huh?" John said a bit too loudly as Nancy moved toward them.

Too embarrassed to admit he'd mentally been 3,000 miles and seven years away during most of his mom's cross-examination, Brian nodded and smiled. Slipping into the gallery bench beside them Nancy was near tears. "Louise is going to hate me. Everything I said was wrong."

The next morning, Brian asked his mother if they really wanted to put themselves through another long day in court. Nancy was whipping up her famous scrambled eggs-with-cheese. A pair of crisp English Muffins jumped up in the toaster.

"The judge said it's likely the last day. They're bringing Louise to the stand. We need to be there for support."

Watching Louise testify, Brian was amazed by her serenity. She never choked up; she delivered her answers with crisp clarity. Whether it was her own lawyer or a member of the prosecution confronting of her, Louise maintained direct eye contact and occasionally glanced at the jury. She was aware of what she'd done and felt no need to deny it. "Mrs. Ditlow, did you love your husband?" the defense attorney asked.

"Once, a long time ago. Before he became a cold, cruel man who treated me like the maid. Actually, that's not true. Most days, he was nicer to our housekeeper than he was to me."

"Why didn't you divorce him?"

"I had no skills, two young daughters, no self-confidence. How would I support myself? Please understand, I'm not liberated like you, ma'am. I had no place to go. Do I have remorse for killing him? I'm sorry I took a human life; that's against everything I stand for. But he drove me to it, belittling me until I snapped. I'm sorry I committed a terrible crime but I'm not the least bit sorry I never have to see his miserable face again."

Caught up in the moment, Nancy and John exploded in applause. Judge Vener hammered his gavel demanding order. After impassioned closing arguments, the case went to the jury.

As much as she loved her work at her Inglewood Family Health Clinic, on this particular night Heather returned from her nonprofit job depleted. It didn't help that Brian had been gone for four days leaving her lonely. After a long soak in peach-scented bath beads, sipping a glass of her favorite Merlot, she slipped on only a pair of sexy black panties and her most cherished spiked heels and went down to make dinner. With her hair clipped atop her head and Carly Simon pouring from the stereo, Heather glided about the room like a pornographic Ginger Rogers, creating a masterful Lobster Fra Diablo-for-one. Refilling her wine glass, she glanced down at her bouncing bare breasts, cursing time and gravity.

As her voice blended with Carly's, Heather stirred lobster bits into the spicy red sauce and reveled in the joy of feeling sexy and free; she harmonized with her heroine declaring she didn't have time for the pain. And then she froze, thinking she heard something. As the song ended, she heard it again: "Mom?"

Heather's heart slammed against her breastbone. She glanced down at her naked torso, her sheer panties and her black stilettos. Knowing that both the coat closet and the staircase to the second floor were between the kitchen and the front door, she was trapped. Seconds later, Joey crept into the kitchen. "Um…Mom…why are you wearing the tablecloth?"

"Sweetie…" she gasped, "why aren't you up at school?"

"Me and the guys came down to see Punk Skunks at the Roxy. I told 'em it'd be cool to crash here tonight. It's just Justin, Kurt and Willie."

"Oh, is that all?" Her tone was laced with flat-lined horror.

After asking Joe to take his friends outside long enough for her to make her way upstairs to get dressed, Heather grabbed her Italian heels from the Tupperware drawer, drained the pasta and dashed to her bedroom.

Nancy made Brian promise he'd call as soon as he was on the ground in LA. He declined her offer of her scrambled-eggs-with-cheese; all he wanted was a bowl of Wheaties. He'd grab coffee at the airport. "If Sarah calls with the verdict, leave a message on my cell, okay?"

"You really think they'll decide that quickly?" John asked.

"How hard can it be? She admitted she did it; the only thing left is to decide whether it's murder or manslaughter."

Pouring milk onto his breakfast of champions, Brian's attention was drawn to the television. At the *Today* show news desk, the anchorwoman lowered her voice to deliver the next item with somber reverence.

"Last night in Irving, Texas, the man credited with saving the life of President John Fitzgerald Kennedy in November of 1963 passed away after a lengthy battle with lung cancer. Edward Kenneth Callahan heroically prevented would-be assassin Lee Harvey Oswald from pulling the trigger on President Kennedy as his motorcade passed the Texas School Book Depository in Dallas where both Callahan and Oswald had been employed. Mister Callahan was seventy-one years old."

2

"MY FATHER WAS MANY THINGS: a hard-working, truly decent man, a modest hero who saved a president's life, a good son, a loyal friend and a lifelong Cowboys' fan — but what he was above all else was a great husband and an awesome dad."

Gripping the cedar lectern at the front of the packed church on an unseasonably warm April morning in Dallas, forty six year old Kenny Callahan paused to will back tears. He looked to his mother and sister in the front pew clad in their black dresses holding hands. Their eyes were fixed on him as they smiled despite both having tears gliding down their cheeks. Clearing his throat, Kenny continued. "I always knew I was lucky because, unlike so many of my friends, Dad was around for my sister and me. Working on my Pinewood Derby car when I was a Cub Scout, attending Libby's tap dance recitals, he took a genuine interest in what we were up to. He knew our friends, encouraged us, and supported everything we dove into. He was also there when we screwed up. He knew we weren't perfect, never expected us to be. There were times when we pushed him to the limit and he let us have it, but guess what? It was always because we deserved it. The way my sister and I fought sometimes…okay, let's not go there today."

Several mourners chuckled.

"My father was cool, in every sense of the word. He was a guy who didn't discuss his emotions much, didn't tell you every little thing he was feeling; naw, that's more Libby's style," Kenny paused to chortle. "But again I digress. Point is, Dad was a guy who showed you how he felt through his actions. He never left in the morning without giving my mom a kiss. After my games, Little League, high school b'ball, whatever, he'd give me a clap on the back or a pat on the shoulder. Sometimes he'd go all out with a, 'Good game, son' when he was really proud, but no matter how he expressed it, we always knew he cared. We knew he loved us. When Libby got married, he really wanted to do a great job with his toast, worked on it for weeks; wrote it, rewrote it, practiced in front of my mom, in front of the mirror, but then when he got up to deliver it, he looked at Libby, looked at Chris, raised his glass and said, 'Be nice to each other and you'll do okay.' That was it. But you know what? We got it. He didn't need to say more; all you had to do was check out the love in his eyes." Kenny exhaled. "It'll be tough without you, Dad. But we'll be all right because you'll be in our hearts every day. Be at peace – and, for your sake, I hope you've found the smoking section in heaven."

Back at the house on Jimmydee Drive, the living room, dining room and den were packed with folks comforting one another as they celebrated Ed's life. His work buddies were in the backyard around an iced tub of Lone Star. His four grandchildren were in the guest bedroom looking at family photo albums, drinking Coca Cola as they devoured a purloined plate of their granny's chocolate éclairs.

Glancing to the front door, Bonnie saw someone entering she hadn't seen at the church. She needed a moment to recognize the face. Appearing at her mother's side, Libby whispered: "Oh my God, is that Aunt Lucy? What's she done to herself? She's pulled so tight she looks like a conga drum with eyes."

As Bonnie fought to repress a startled laugh Lucy was on them. Her voice was too loud, her tone too theatrical; she lunged at Bonnie and yanked her into a too-tight hug, offering her "sincerest" condolences. Releasing her stranglehold, she placed her altered face directly in front of Bonnie's. "Sugar, I do hope you'll forgive me for missing the service but I had a doctor's appointment I couldn't skip; woulda had to wait a year to reschedule. But enough about me, how the Sam Hill are y'all holding up?"

"We're okay, thank you. For better or worse, we've known this was coming so we've had plenty of time to make our peace."

"Unlike when I lost Nate. Alive and kickin' in the morning, dead as a doornail by noon. Shocking, it was just shocking; no two ways around it."

"I'm sorry Lionel's not with you," Bonnie said.

"He's working. As usual. Asked me to send his regrets and deepest condolences. He adored Ed. Who didn't?" Taking a quick look to her left, Lucy reacted. "Oh good gracious, Libby! I didn't even see you there. Come give your auntie a hug."

Another lunge, another peck. Libby forced a smile. "How have you been, Aunt Lucy?"

"Bored and ignored. Serves me right for marrying a mogul." Gazing past them to the makeshift bar on the kitchen table, Lucy brightened. "Now if you ladies will excuse me, I need a glass of wine."

Libby leaned into her mother. "One more lift and she'll be Asian." For the first time since Ed passed away Bonnie laughed.

When Lucy married Nate, Bonnie made a silent vow to find a way to get along with her even if they had nothing in common. She'd do it for her husband's sake, and for Nate whom she loved like a brother. Lucy was a true Southern Belle with a sugary drawl and batting eyelashes. She outwardly deferred to the men in her life and then did exactly as she pleased behind their backs. She gave birth to a daughter purely out of obligation despite not having a maternal bone in her body; she once admitted she carried a grudge against Kendra for ruining her figure.

Kendra was nineteen when her father died and shortly after that awful day, she packed a bag for Europe and never returned. The last time Bonnie asked about her a decade earlier, Lucy's reply was stunning. She assumed Kendra had probably gotten into some awful trouble and was most likely dead but Lucy couldn't muster the energy to care. "Why would

I? The only thing I ever got from that girl was pain; started in childbirth and never quit."

Two years after Nate died, Lucy married a Dallas real estate tycoon everybody knew and nobody liked. Ed once remarked, "I guarantee you the iceberg that sank the Titanic gave off more warmth than Lionel Coot."

Despite it not being a storybook romance it seemed as if they'd both gotten what they needed: Lionel acquired a stylish bit of arm candy and Lucy got a deep pocketed financier for her obsessions: pinot noir and cosmetic surgery. Without Lionel paying enough attention to put the brakes on, Lucy Stokesberry Coot looked like a gargoyle embalmed in Paul Masson.

In the bedroom where Ed and Bonnie's grandkids were examining an ancient photo album's yellowed pages, thirteen-year-old Sierra was mesmerized by an official-looking 8x10. Flanked by her identical twin brothers Eddie and Patrick, Sierra took in every detail of the glossy, faded print. "Turn the page already!" ten-year-old Patrick snapped. "Who wants to look at Poppy shaking hands with some guy who's all hair and teeth?"

"It's President John F. Kennedy," Sierra replied. "Wasn't he so handsome?"

From the corner of the room where he was playing Pipe Mania on his Game Boy, the kids' cousin Jimmy chimed in. "Poppy got to meet him because he saved the president's life."

"Poppy wasn't a Secret Service man," Eddie scoffed. "He sold washing machines and refrigerators."

"But one day, a very long time ago," Sierra said as if reciting a fairytale, "Poppy stopped a very bad man from shooting President Kennedy's head off."

Blonde and bubbly Sierra looked so much like Libby at this age it took Bonnie's breath away. She and her eldest grandchild were never happier than when they were working side-by-side on some hands-on lesson plan Bonnie was creating for her junior high science students. Now that she was approaching seventy, Bonnie knew she should think about retirement but couldn't bring herself to file the paperwork. She still loved being in her classroom, loved the kids and knew she had plenty more to give. Especially with Ed now gone, the last thing she needed was too much time on her hands.

The post-funeral reception was winding down. Libby, her sister-in-law Molly and a few neighbor ladies were cleaning up. The men were out back pledging to polish off the remaining beer in Ed's honor. Bonnie retreated to her bedroom, took off her black beaded jacket and sat in the straight-back chair beside an open window. She thought about a day seventeen years earlier when a phone call interrupted the conversation she and Ed were having about Halloween candy. It was Libby calling to announce she and Chris were engaged. They were married on Valentine's Day '85 in a twilight ceremony in Bonnie and Ed's backyard. The celebration brawl happened that Saturday night when they took over the Italian restaurant where Libby and Chris worked; the party lasted until dawn.

Six months later, the newlyweds moved to Los Angeles. Although it was hard for Bonnie and Ed to see them go, they knew Chris needed to pursue his dream of becoming a screenwriter. Libby became a sous chef at a gourmet restaurant on Melrose. Chris waited tables by night and wrote for hours every day. He sent out scripts, met with agents, and had a few promising nibbles before getting buried under a mound of rejection slips. A year later they were back in Dallas.

"Hey," Chris said, genuinely devoid of regret, "At least I gave it a shot."

Libby revisited her plan to open her own restaurant. After months of intense work and an orchestrated seduction of investors, *Eros* became a reality. She and Chris were partners in the venture and together they turned it into a popular, elegant eatery. When Sierra was born, Chris became the fulltime manager so Libby could be at home with the baby. Once the twins arrived three years later, Libby's involvement was basically reduced to working with the chef to plan each new menu. Still, Chris always made time to write and was currently working on an historical novel. Reflecting on all of this, Bonnie looked up to find Sierra in the doorway.

"The boys and I were looking at your scrapbooks. Tell me about when you met Jackie Kennedy; was she amazing?"

Yanking up the memory, Bonnie chuckled. "I know I was a wreck the entire month before we went. Oh my stars, I cried like a crazy woman. I felt so dowdy standing next to her. It was terrifying. But you know what surprised me most? Y'all have to remember this was before every little news clip showed up on the on-line like it does now – "

"Grammy," Sierra laughed, "you don't say 'on the on-line,' it's just 'on-line'."

"In any case, the big shock was what a whispery voice Mrs. Kennedy had. I realized I'd never heard it before. When she said hello, she sounded like a little girl. Mostly we talked about your mom and Uncle Kenny since we each had a girl and boy. For all her power and beauty, it seemed she cared most about being a good mother. I found it so sweet."

"Did you get to talk to the president, too?"

"A smidge. There in the East Room with those gorgeous crystal chandeliers and the portraits of George and Martha Washington. It was simply astonishing being inside the White House, thinking about all the history that had happened in those very rooms. The whole meeting, the medal ceremony…it was over and done in a blink. Then Poppy and I were back to being pumpkins. You know, like Cinderella? One minute you're dancing with the prince then, poof, your coach is just an old gourd."

Joining Bonnie and Sierra, Kenny asked his mom how she was holding up; Bonnie admitted it had been a long day. "Well, everything's cleaned up and put away. We stacked the rental chairs, dishes are done, leftovers are in the 'fridge. Need anything else before we go?"

The trio returned to the living room. Libby, Molly and Chris were watching the evening news. The three boys were out front playing Frisbee. "Actually," Chris laughed, "Pat and Eddie are throwing the Frisbee; I'm sure Jimmy's busy trying to deconstruct the aerodynamic principles allowing it to fly."

The adults shared a knowing laugh. From the moment he could walk, Jimmy had been what his father lovingly called "a science nerd," something neither he nor Molly could relate to. Still, they stocked their cellar with chemistry sets and engineering books, making it Jimmy's private paradise.

Although she knew it would be difficult, Bonnie insisted on facing the task alone. Sorting through Ed's clothes, deciding what to keep, what to pass on and what to donate to charity was something she needed to do at her own pace, devoid of unsolicited advice. Many of the work shirts, slacks and ties were from Sear's or Dillard's, holding no sentimental value at all. They were the first to go. But there were a number of things Bonnie couldn't bear to part with. She stood in their shared closet absently rubbing her thumb along the brim of the sweat-stained Dallas Cowboys cap Ed owned for all of their forty-nine year marriage. It quickly got tossed atop the "keep" pile. In an old pair of khakis she found the engraved lighter that had been a long-ago birthday gift from this parents.

Going through Ed's wallet Bonnie found credit cards to cut up, a laminated 1998 Cowboys' schedule and a discount coupon from an extinct pancake house. Behind his soon-to-expire driver's license, she found a photograph that broke her heart.

The color was bleached to faded pink and yellow; the beaming boy and girl were young and bright-eyed. He stood with his shoulders broadened to superhero proportions by the pads he wore under his high school football jersey. She had a pert ponytail held by a Scotty dog clip above her luminescent smile. They'd been dating for just a few weeks when Bonnie's father shot this photo with his Brownie Bulls-Eye after a game against Cedar Hill Ed's senior year. She couldn't believe he'd carried it in his wallet all these years.

Thinking about Marsha's passing just two years earlier, Bonnie knew how lucky she was to have had her mother in her life for as long as she did. Her dad died when she was a newlywed, but when Marsha suffered a fatal heart attack at eighty-nine as the two of them trimmed green beans in the kitchen, it was devastating.

Bonnie's recollections were cut short by the ringing telephone; plucking up the receiver, she was happy to hear Libby on the line. With the all-consuming chaos of Ed's final illness and death beginning to ebb, Libby, Kenny and their spouses were considering a three-day trip to New Orleans for Jazz Fest; Libby was inviting Bonnie to join them. Declining, Bonnie offered to look after the grandkids while the couples were away. Libby hesitated. "At least Sierra's old enough to help…but those boys with their energy… are you sure you're up to it?"

"I handled you and your brother; I can do three days of Jimmy and the twins."

"Behave!" Molly called from the back seat of her brother-in-law's SUV. "Listen to Grammy and don't give her any lip! We want a good report on all y'all."

As Kenny backed down the driveway, the quartet inside gave one last set of vigorous waves to the quintet on Bonnie's front lawn.

"Oh God," Libby groaned. "What have we done to poor Mom?"

"The only thing my dad cares about is being shit-faced all

weekend."

"Patrick Lloyd Ebersol! Don't let me hear that kind of language from you again. I won't tolerate it."

"Sorry, Gram. My bad."

Tucking the twins into bed in Kenny's old room that night, Bonnie recalled the days when this add-on was built. Until Libby hit puberty, she, Kenny and Marsha shared a single room across the hall from Bonnie and Ed. Once Libby started to develop breasts and a rabid crush on Ricky Nelson, her parents decided it was no longer appropriate for her to be sleeping in such close quarters with her brother. With money as tight as their square footage, Ed proposed that he and Nate build the needed new bedroom themselves. They bought several *How-To* books, drew up detailed plans and set to work.

One week later, they hired a general contractor to finish the job. Ed said he and Nate could have gotten it done but there wasn't a snowball's chance in hell they'd still be friends when it was over. So, they called in the pros. Kenny got his own room and Libby and Marsha continued bunking together until Libby went to college.

With her third beer of the morning in hand and her hairdo a fallen soufflé courtesy of the New Orleans humidity, Molly was downright giddy. "I can't believe we've never been here before. It's like Disneyland for grown-ups! Who should we hear next?"

"Let's check out the Gospel Tent," Libby said. Off they went.

Even though folks had spread blankets or carried in folding chairs, Libby didn't get how anyone could sit still while the rollicking gospel choir filled the stage. The singers' voices soared, their arms waved, their sweat-saturated robes swayed on their joy-filled bodies. The infectious ebullience permeated every inch of the large white tent. Despite the heat and the slosh of beer in her belly, Libby was gyrating like a cheerleader surrounded by 200 kindred spirits.

"How can this not be heaven on Earth if even my brother's dancing?"

As the sun sank that evening, with a slur in her words Molly asked Libby if she'd seen Kenny lately. "I thought he was with Chris but Chris's there and I'm not seeing your hubby."

Joining them, Chris confessed he hadn't seen Kenny in over an hour. "But he's a big boy. Don't worry, Bo Beep; leave him alone and he'll come home – "

Libby finished, "Wagging his drunk-ass tail behind him.

Planted onstage at the historic Saenger Theatre, staring out at the glow-stick waving crowd, Kenny shook his head and rubbed his eyes. He couldn't quite get why the musicians and the entire audience were acting like it was perfectly normal for him to be a part of this big time rock band. The guitarist nodded his approval as Kenny banged a rattling tambourine against his throbbing thigh. He remembered being in line to pee with the guy who was now playing organ, sharing vocals with the mandolin player. He said he was in a band called String Cheese Incident and invited Kenny to their gig. They ended up doing Jello shots near the pavilion honoring Louie Armstrong's 100th birthday…and now Kennny was on stage playing tambourine. How pissed is Molly gonna be when I finally find her again?

The song ended and the crowd erupted. Kenny felt the adulation wash over him. He twirled to slap a high-five with the guitarist. "Keep it going, bro. You're killing it."

Feeling an unwanted wave rise in his stomach, Kenny bolted. Dropping the tambourine with a jingling clatter, he raced to a corner backstage and threw up in an unsuspecting band member's guitar case.

"At what point do we call the police?" Molly asked a little before midnight.

"Let's go back to the hotel. Maybe he got partied out and crashed," Chris offered.

Two hours earlier, Molly had called her husband's cell phone, jarred to hear it ringing in her purse. Digging it out, she also found Kenny's wallet. "Great: he's in a sea of a half-million people with no phone, no money, and no ID."

Molly wanted to return to the hotel then but Chris assured her Kenny was fine. "Besides, Buckwheat's about to play. Maybe we'll find our boy there."

They didn't. But, caught up in Buckwheat Zydeco's Cajun rhythms, Molly danced like a maniac. Now that Buckwheat was gone and Kenny was still missing, it was time to pack it in.

Anxiously hustling down the third floor hotel corridor with Libby and Chris trailing, Molly made a beeline for her room. In the hallway outside their door she saw a crumpled lump on the carpet. Passed out, barefoot and with his face painted in bright-colored Zulu warrior squiggles, Kenny was snoring like a St. Bernard.

Up with the birds, Eddie and Patrick found their grammy on the porch with her newspaper and coffee. They eagerly asked if they could build something in Poppy's workshop. Bonnie said perhaps they could all get her garden ready for spring planting but the twins dismissed that notion as "girl stuff." They wanted to build.

"I'll work in your garden with you, Gram," said a sleepy-eyed Sierra emerging into the sunlight. "Sounds fun."

Before setting the boys free Bonnie told them to only use wood scraps in the box under the workbench, no power tools, no cutting with anything but a hand saw. "Can we take apart that baby tricycle?" Jimmy asked. "We'll use the wheels and pedals to make a go-cart!"

"Fine. But you may not dismantle anything else without my permission."

Under their cousin Jimmy's exacting supervision, Eddie and

Patrick were converting an old shower rod into the front axle of their cobbled-together racecar. "If we're usin' this for front wheels, what about the back ones?" Eddie asked.

"Poppy won't need his lawnmower no more. Let's take those wheels!"

When Patrick asked where the pedals would go, Jimmy eyed a striped beach umbrella. "We don't need pedals. I'm rigging this puppy so it can fly!"

Stomping the pitchfork into the dirt to unhinge a cluster of leafy weeds, Bonnie looked to Sierra on her hands and knees using a trowel to dig out the roots of last year's tomato plants.

"Those boys have been awfully quiet. Why don't you go check on them while I make some fresh lemonade."

Coming around to the front of the house, Sierra couldn't grasp what she was seeing. A tall ladder in the center of the driveway was angled up to the sloping garage roof. Backing up to get a clearer view, she spied the twins, with Patrick in front and Eddie directly behind him like a two-man bobsled team, sitting in their homemade craft at the roof's crown. There was an open beach umbrella affixed to the back of the cart like an inflated antenna; Jimmy was crouching behind them on the rear slope of the roof, poised to give the vehicle a launching push. Sierra heard him ask his grinning cousins if they were ready.

"NOOOOOOO!" she screamed with equal parts terror and disbelief.

It was too late. Patrick clutched the cart's wooden frame; Eddie held onto Patrick. Jimmy gave a vigorous shove. The rickety little vehicle went clattering down the red-shingled roof heading for its edge. Patrick cried with a true believer's glee. "Fly, you sucker! FLY!"

3

ALTHOUGH SHE HATED to admit it, Gina still smiled in quiet pride each day when she arrived at work. Even after thirteen years, walking under the silver words WILLIAM MARK FELT FBI BUILDING adhered to the chrome facade over the front doors, she was endlessly awed by the privilege of living her dream.

"Good morning, Ms. Kaufman."

Gina smiled at the coworker whose name she couldn't conjure and ducked into the elevator filling with colleagues. There was reserved chitchat about the early summer humidity and the palpable influx of tourists around town. "Apparently President Conrad's ad campaign is working. 'DC means Destination Central.' I hear those commercials in my sleep."

The elevator stopped on the seventh floor. Gina hustled out, straightening her navy pencil skirt, tugging down her matching blazer. She pulled a briefing book from her shoulder bag and pretended to read it as she hurried through the maze of hallways, sweeping the corkscrew curls from her forehead.

Swiping her security badge, she swiftly tapped her entry code on the keypad beside her office door. When the lock clicked, she entered to find her clerical assistant at her desk. Gina complimented Margaret's new blouse and asked if there were any bureaucratic fires to put out. Margaret reported all was quiet.

"That won't last," Gina affirmed as she grabbed her mail. She slid into her adjoining office, closed the door, and offered a silent prayer of thanks to Margaret for having her back. A tall black coffee waited on the desk in an insulated aluminum cup. Removing the cap, blowing on the steamy elixir her body craved, Gina recalled that it was Tucker Edwards who'd first gotten her hooked on black coffee. She wondered what had become of him in the years since they'd lost touch. She knew she was destined to become involved with that man the instant he reached out to steady her after they collided in the corridor of the Brookings Institution just before Christmas of '84.

Tucker was forty-two when he met Gina who was half his age. Divorced with a ten-year-old son, he was an FBI Special Agent in Charge sporting a steely self-confidence bordering on arrogance. Even having grown up in Los Angeles where it was common to spot movie stars lunching at Nate N' Al's, Gina thought Tucker was the most handsome man she'd ever seen. Sleek black hair, dark eyes and custom-made suits…he took her breath away. He wasn't married, they were together for three years, but whenever Gina thought about him she considered him her "wild affair." Maybe it was because he taught her how to dine in elegant restaurants, how to dress, and how to have mind-blowing orgasms. Thank you, Tucker Edwards.

He also instructed Gina on how to use her time at Brookings to ensure it would be a *fate accompli* when she was ready to apply to the FBI. Four months before she submitted her agent trainee application, Gina broke up with Tucker. To her surprise, he was devastated.

"We both know I have to do this, Tuck. I can't go there believing I was only accepted as a favor to you. It's imperative that I succeed or fail on my own."

With a deep sigh, Gina refocused on the stack of morning briefing papers waiting in her in-box. Given her background in Middle East issues and her proclivity for Arabic languages, she was a member of an anti-terrorism task force charged with reviewing all manner of intercepted intelligence communiqués.

Her job had recently taken on a new level of urgency following the bombing of the USS Cole in port in Yemen the previous October. A small explosive-laden boat with two suicide bombers on board rammed the Cole portside while it was refueling in Aden harbor. The blast ripped a huge hole in the ship's hull. The impact struck the galley where the crew was lining up for lunch. Seventeen sailors were killed; thirty-nine others were injured. Osama bin Laden's al-Qaeda terrorist organization instantly claimed credit.

At a briefing a few weeks after the blast, Gina was informed that FBI agents sent to Yemen to investigate the bombings entered a decidedly hostile environment. Yemen Special Forces soldiers met them at the airport with assault rifles. The agents felt constantly threatened. There was no cooperation regarding the sharing of collected evidence. While the on-site investigation progressed, Gina remained at her DC desk collecting and analyzing reams of data.

Now there was a spike in terrorist chatter once more. The consensus on Gina's team was that bin Laden and his band of thugs were getting ready to strike again. The challenge was to try to figure out the where and when before it was too late. She was reading over a new report on the analysis of the method of attack in the Cole incident when Margaret buzzed to say Gina's husband was on the line. Smiling, Gina punched the flashing light and picked up. "Good morning. I was surprised you were up and out so early; what's up?"

"The Carlton case is driving me batty. I couldn't sleep so I figured I'd go in while it was still quiet enough to hear myself think. Anyway, we'll work it out. I'm really only calling to say good morning."

In the two years since she'd gotten married, Gina was constantly amazed she'd found the last true gentleman in Washington. Noah Zager was an environmental lawyer from Boston. He'd earned his undergraduate degree at Brown, went to law school at UVA and moved to DC after being recruited by one of the country's top environmental firms. He was eighteen months older than Gina and, to her mother's delight, Jewish. Aside from the boy she'd surrendered her virginity to in Jordan, he was the only Jew she'd ever dated. "Didn't I always tell you?" Lisa said. "Jewish men make the best husbands. They know how to earn money, they don't run around – and if they do, the wife comes first!"

Ending her conversation with Noah, Gina couldn't regain her focus. Surrendering, she called David in LA. "I just had the most marvelous idea! Why don't you and Cyrus come spend the Fourth of July with Noah and me next month? You won't believe who else is going to be here: Brian Scott and his wife." When David drew a blank, Gina went on: "Dr. Scott, the resident who helped diagnose my AVM? I think that was the first time I suspected you were gay because you kept talking about how cute he was."

"Wait, that kid from UCLA? He *was* cute. But, honey, that was thirty years ago. How are you still in touch with him?"

"I tracked him down in the '80s to finally say thanks and we've exchanged holiday cards ever since. Anyway, he and Heather are coming to town for a conference in Bethesda, so I invited them to spend the Fourth with us. It'll be fun. You know Noah and I are a pair of poker players: never happier than when we have a full house!"

David asked when they were going to start filling those empty bedrooms with babies. "Those eggs won't stay fresh forever, dolly. Especially not when the incubator's pushing forty!"

Gina reminded him she was only thirty-seven, then jumped back to pressing her case for a July visit. David said he'd check with Cyrus and let her know.

Snatching a feather duster from a cabinet drawer, David darted to his bookshelf to attack the layer of dust that had captivated his attention while he was on the phone. Taking in every corner of the room, he sighed. At seventy-one, David was the oldest member of the USC History Department by a decade. He knew it was time to contemplate retirement but decided he'd only do it if Cyrus promised he wouldn't force David to take up golf.

Putting away the duster he chuckled at a framed photograph that sat among many atop the cabinet. It was of his middle-aged nephew Michael astride a majestic black mare in the Rocky Mountains. Michael was wearing a denim jacket, a battered black Stetson and a steely scowl. David laughed to himself: Seinfeld meets the Marlboro Man.

The thing Michael loved most about his current life, after more than a dozen years in corporate banking, was that he could wake up every morning, put on jeans and commute less than a hundred paces to the barn down a dirt trail. His business partner was his wife; his employees were trusted friends. The air was clean and crisp. His biggest stress came from whiney tourists or an occasional sick horse but after nine years at it, Michael had learned to handle both with equanimity. His wife Bootsy, given name Ruth Ann Evans, grew up on this dude ranch in Loveland, Colorado that she and Michael now owned.

In the late summer of 1991, Michael convinced two pals to accompany him on a weeklong stay at the Rocky Echo Ranch. They had cookouts and camp-outs, took daily rides into the foothills and spent evenings drinking, singing and telling stories around a crackling campfire. Michael fell in love with the mountains, he fell in love with the wide-open spaces, and he fell in love with the rancher's daughter. Ten months later, he and Bootsy were married behind the barn amid a sea of wildflowers waving their approval.

While her brother dealt with horses and hay, Gina was 2,000 miles away, awash in a jigsaw puzzle of intercepted intelligence. If you managed to link the pieces properly you'd be left with a clear picture for everyone to admire; but if things weren't lined up, if a few pieces were missing or you worked too hard to cram them in where they didn't belong, all you got was an unreadable mess. She knew there was something crucial she wasn't seeing. What were the missing links?

She closed her eyes, willing herself to envision what she'd overlooked. Her eyes sprang back open. It was the names! Many were similar but a few kept popping up over and over, in unrelated cables and disconnected places. She knew she had to follow the names. With a renewed sense of mission, Gina signed in to her most secure portal where she stored top-secret files for her eyes-only. She opened several windows showcasing multiple reports filled with data she was using to compile an ever-evolving assessment of the on-going Cole investigation. Scanning them, she had no idea what she was looking for but had a fervent feeling she'd know it when she saw it.

Khalid Almihdhar.

She went to the first file and did a search highlighting that name each time it appeared. She repeated the process through all the open windows, finding the same appellation seven or eight times which led to a new epiphany. She buzzed her assistant who dashed in a moment later.

"Margaret, we received a report a while ago on an intercept from the phone line of that safe house in Yemen…from late '99 or early 2000. About an al-Qaeda meeting in Malaysia, very high-level. Can you locate that file, please?"

Margaret vanished. Gina felt her heart racing; her breath shortened. She scanned a few more recent reports, found Almihdhar's name in a half-dozen other places. Who was he? What was he plotting? Margaret was back with a briefing folder. "Here it is. December '99." Gina snatched the file and started reading; Margaret knew it was her cue to disappear.

'Khalid Almihdhar and an associate known as Nawaf'… Gina had no idea if that was a first name or last… 'planning to attend an important al-Qaeda meeting in Malaysia in January of 2000.'

Gina wondered if this was when they began plotting the Cole attack. The timing made sense. But then she recalled something she'd seen in the last few days. Sorting through the files on her desktop she opened an updated report on Khalid Almihdhar stating he'd been in the US but left for a brief trip to Germany in June of 2000. If or when he returned wasn't immediately clear. She wondered where he was now.

Gina navigated to a site that allowed her to access the current terrorist watch list. She entered Almihdhar's name but he wasn't tagged. Neither was anyone named Nawaf. Digging deeper into the file on the Malaysia meeting, Gina found a full report compiled by the CIA. It stated that the gathering took place from January 5-8, 2000. It was described as "a top-level al-Qaeda summit." The report concluded that the meeting's primary goal was to plan an undefined attack somewhere in Southeast Asia. Was that all that happened there? She didn't understand why every person who was known to have attended that meeting was not now on a watch list. What more did they have to do? Almihdhar, Nawaf... if they were at a top-level al-Qaeda summit, why would they not be considered known enemies of the United States?

That thought triggered another flash of recollection. Gina grabbed her keyboard, typed in the name of a well-connected Muslim transplant working with the FBI in San Diego: Abdussattar Shaikh. A briefing paper popped up. As she scanned it, Gina was shaken by a chilling tingle. She read that in September of 2000, Shaikh invited two young Arab immigrants to share a room in his home: Khalid Almihdhar and Nawaf Alhazmi.

At dinner that night, Gina was too distracted to focus on her husband's report on his day.

"I know something's brewing, Noah. Obviously I can't say more – "

"Well, you could but then you'd have to kill me," he said with a chuckle.

"I don't understand why I'm the only one seeing it."

"Listen, before you work yourself into an anxiety pretzel, let's finish eating and take a walk. I'll clean up when we get back."

Strolling hand-in-hand, Gina and Noah loved that they lived in one of the most vibrant cities in the world. As they walked up Connecticut Avenue, the evening was alive with tangled traffic moving to the soundtrack of urban life. It was a beautiful June night; the warm air was devoid of the ballast of humidity that tended to weigh the town down.

Though neither of them stated it, Gina knew they'd walk the mile to the White House. They loved seeing the presidential residence awash in golden floodlights. They were always amused by the combination of tourists and protestors adhered to the sidewalk against the black wrought iron fence bordering the executive mansion.

Noah said it was the perfect way to take the nation's political temperature: listen to the out-of-towners, scan the placards and you instantly knew what the pollsters worked tirelessly to discern. If signs of support outnumbered the messages of dissent, the current occupant was having a good week. If middle fingers flew while cameras flashed, the president might need to recalibrate his current course.

"Wouldn't it be wonderful to have David and Cyrus and the Scotts here for the Fourth? Since it's on Wednesday, I've already put in to take Thursday and Friday off."

"Good. You could use a break. By the way, have you talked to Debbie lately?"

"I left a message. I'm sure that awful woman she works for keeps her hopping."

In her current life as a grossly overweight, forty two year old 'executive assistant' to a Hollywood producer with a serious chemical imbalance, Debbie was constantly reminded of an old joke: 'What do I do for a living? I work at the circus, trailing around behind the elephants cleaning up their shit.'

'That sounds disgusting. Why don't you quit?'

'What, and give up show business?'

Absorbed in typing notes from the day's meeting with the pair of writers penning what everyone hoped would be the company's next comedy blockbuster, Debbie knew her boss was hovering before she actually saw her.

"Is it...too much to expect...that I might have my meeting notes printed out and waiting on my desk by the time I'm ready to leave at 7:00 p.m.?" Lydia asked with a sneer. "Just because *you* have no life doesn't mean I don't have plans; I have a dinner to get to."

"I know. I made the reservation. Seven thirty at the Palm with Xavier Riley."

"Which means I should have been...out the door...five minutes ago."

"Go. I'll finish the notes and email them; they'll be waiting when you get home."

"But then *I'd* have to print them out. You know I don't read things on the computer. Finish the notes here, print a copy and drop it at my house on your way home." And with that, Lydia was gone. Debbie admitted to herself that it would be easier to be offended if Lydia wasn't right: she didn't have a life. Her biggest thrill in months had been delivering a script to a movie star's mansion in Beverly Hills.

Later, locking the office door from inside, Debbie returned to her computer to call up her favorite "romantic entanglements" chat room. She trolled through the lines of insipid romantic banter from participants with screen names

like HOTJOHNNY and MESOHORNY27. At last, she found
a posting that appealed to her. LUKE69: No frills, no bullshit.
Who's down 2 meet?

After a brief back-and-forth in a private chat window,
DARINGDEB and LUKE69 agreed to meet: midnight,
behind the tennis courts at Balboa Park in Encino.

"Has anybody ever told you you're fat?"

"Why no, Mr. Sensitive, you're the first."

"I'm not complaining. More cushion for the pushin'. I dig
it. How about I bend you over this picnic table and come in
from behind?"

"Only after I see you put on a condom."

"No glove, no love. I ain't stupid."

"We could debate that, but why waste the time?"

Less than fifteen minutes after they'd met, Debbie watched
Luke69 disappear into the moonless darkness; she pulled a
clump of tissues from her dress pocket and wiped herself. She
always made a point of locking her purse in the trunk before
these anonymous encounters. She didn't particularly care if she
got murdered, she just didn't want to get robbed.

The minute she arrived at her office the next morning, Gina
was back on her computer working to find more information
on Abdussattar Shaikh, the FBI "undercover asset" who'd
offered housing to Alhazmi and Almihdhar in September of
2000.

When Margaret charged in to put the sweating aluminum
cup of black coffee on Gina's desk, she was startled to find
Gina already at work, lamenting that this case was driving her
insane. Margaret reminded Gina that her gut was her most
valuable asset; she needed to listen to it. Preoccupied by the
files filling her screen, Gina nodded. Margaret ducked out.
Scanning one open document on Shaikh, Gina found what she

was looking for: the name of his main bureau contact in San Diego.

"Agent Fuentes? This is Special Agent Gina Kaufman calling from FBI HQ in DC. Do you have a minute?"

After going through their respective security checks, verifying they were on a secure line, Gina got down to business. She asked if Fuentes was the point person on Abdussattar Shaikh.

"Yes, ma'am. He's proven to be an invaluable resource. Extremely tied to the local Muslim community in Southern California," Fuentes said.

"Are you the one he initially told about his association with Almihdhar and Alhazmi?"

After Fuentes confirmed all of Gina's initial suppositions, she asked him for a favor he knew was more like a subtle command. "If you could please go through your notes and files on all encounters with Shaikh over the last twelve months, I need you to send a memo – strictly between the two of us at this point – detailing every mention Shaikh has made regarding his dealings with those two."

Reviewing the ten-page dossier that arrived by courier late the following afternoon, Gina instantly fixed on two paragraphs on the fifth page that made her eyes bulge. She reread the section three times to be sure she was getting it right. Agent Fuentes recounted a conversation with Abdussattar Shaikh the previous summer. During that encounter, the contact reported that his friends Almihdhar and Alhazmi had visited a small flying school twenty miles south of San Diego in May of 2000. They said they went there "hoping to learn how to fly Boeing airliners." Fuentes reported the name of the place: Kelso's Flying Club.

As an adrenaline surge made her temples bulge, Gina grabbed the phone and connected with a 4-1-1 operator. Minutes later she was on the line with an instructor at Kelso's who had a very distinct memory of the two Muslim men Gina was inquiring about.

"Actually, there were three of them who came, all of 'em, you know, Arabs or Persians or whatever they call themselves these days. I think the third guy's name was Hami or Hani, something like that. He never went up in the plane, just the other two. They claimed they wanted to be commercial pilots, fly the big jets, but of course, that's pretty much what everybody says. The thing with those two, they were so clueless about the most basic aspects of how an airplane works it was almost comical. At one point, I asked the one guy – Almihdhar, I'm pretty sure – he was the one who didn't know much English. No matter what I asked, I got the same blank look and then, 'Very good. Very nice.' That's what he said to everything, 'Very good. Very nice.' Anyhow, I asked him to draw me a picture of the kind of plane he wanted to fly and the guy draws one with the wings on backwards! I'm telling you, it was strange."

"But you actually did go up with them?" Gina asked.

"Two of the three, like I said. Hami/Hani stayed on the ground. And the two I did take up didn't do the piloting, I did. We went up, I showed them, you know… the basic operations, how the instruments work, what did what…"

"Did they seem to comprehend it?"

"Hard to say. I mean, if you want my honest opinion, and it wasn't only the language barrier; there was something about the pair that made me call 'em the Two Stooges. As soon as they left, I go to my boss, 'there's no way those clowns are ever gonna make it as commercial pilots.' That was how I felt. No chance. They were the Two Stooges."

Gina finished the call and immediately jumped back on the line with her assistant. "Hold my calls, Margaret. I'll be down with Dan."

Gina's immediate supervisor, FBI Assistant Special Agent in Charge Dan Mottola, was a sixty-two year old career agent marking his days until retirement. After being pulled from the field at the mandatory age of fifty-five, he'd been reassigned to a desk job that he found to be confining and humiliating. He was eligible to cash out, but if he hung on until age sixty-five, he'd escape with a full pension and benefits that would leave him sitting pretty. Despite his burnout, Dan firmly believed the extra perks were worth the additional years.

With his military crew cut and cold green eyes, he was the poster boy image of a classic G-man. One time years ago Gina had made the mistake of calling him a walking cliché and Dan snapped: "All stereotypes start somewhere, lady. And if you and your women's-lib gals want to lump me in with macho cops from Elliot Ness to Dirty Harry, go ahead – make my day."

At home that night, Gina was still incredulous. "He actually said that, Noah. With a straight face: Go ahead, make my day!"

Seated opposite Dan in his office filled with plaques of praise and framed letters of commendation, Gina knew she probably wouldn't get the support she wanted. "Look, I agree, these guys sound like creeps. But everything you have is circumstantial. INS says their papers are in order, we've got no violations of any kind, no criminal complaints – they've never even gotten a parking ticket. I don't understand what you'd have me do."

"Every fiber in my body tells me these men need to be under twenty-four-hour surveillance, Dan."

"Do you have money for an operation like that, Agent Kaufman? I don't. Maybe your rich lawyer husband wants to kick in. I mean, everybody wants us to keep an eye on the bad guys but nobody wants to fund it; right now our operating budget is stretched thinner than nylons on a fat lady's thigh. I'm sorry but facts are facts."

"You're making a huge mistake."

"Then I guess it's a damn good thing I never claimed to be perfect."

"I have a question: do you feel it's been harder to be black or gay?"

From the couch where he sat watching TV, Cyrus squinted at David. "How can I answer that? I've always been black and I've always been gay; both have their challenges but how can I separate one from the other?"

"All right, which have you been called more, the n-word or 'fag'?"

Cyrus grabbed the remote and muted the TV. "Are you trying to be offensive?"

"No. I'm preparing tomorrow's lecture for my *History of the Turbulent '60s* class and it made me realize you've had a deep personal stake in two of the era's most protracted struggles."

"After seventeen years together, you're only realizing this now? The sad reality is I've been called both of those despicable names more times than I care to count; but if you're asking me to be purely objective, I'd say it's harder to be black. You can hide your sexuality but your skin color's always out there for all to see."

David stared at his partner feeling a deep surge of love and empathy. "Look," Cyrus said, "life is hard for all of us. Believe me, I'm well aware I've had it easier than most. I grew up in suburbia, went to college when it was still a novelty for black men to be there, and worked in a business where my sexuality wasn't an issue. The struggles I faced were an inevitable part of life – but I'm also wise enough to know that, in the big picture, I have nothing to complain about."

David rolled out a long, growling fart, provoking Cyrus to tack on an addendum: "Except for your excessive gas."

All her life, Gina Kaufman had been a rule follower. She never talked out of turn in school or disobeyed her parents' curfew; she seldom drove above the speed limit even now. At various times over the years, her siblings had tried to get her to smoke pot but as long as the drug was illegal, Gina would not partake. But this decision was different. It might violate protocol to go over a superior's head but if Dan was refusing to hear anything she was saying, Gina felt he was leaving her no choice.

It was Monday July 2; David and Cyrus were scheduled to arrive late the next evening. Brian and Heather would show up around noon on Wednesday. Gina was looking forward to her first consecutive vacation days in more than a year but before the respite could begin, she needed to survive two more days at the office. She told Margaret, "If I ignore all my training and instincts and several, maybe even hundreds of people wind up dead that will be on me alone."

Picking up her phone, Gina had Margaret connect her with Agent Fuentes in San Diego. As soon as he was on the line, Gina asked if he had an update on the current whereabouts of Khalid Almihdhar or Nawaf Alhazmi.

"My latest information concerns Almihdhar's June 10 departure for Frankfurt, Germany. My sources cannot confirm if he's back in this country and no one seems to have a fix on Alhazmi's current location. The last time we know for sure they were together was when they visited Kelso's Flying Club last May."

"It may well be in the report you sent previously, Agent Fuentes, but off the top of your head, do you know when the two of them first arrived in the US?"

"The first concrete acknowledgement of their presence in our area was in November of '99. They flew into Los Angeles and were met by a man named Omar Albayoumi; he drove them south to San Diego and brought them to the Parkwood

Apartments, even paid their first two months' rent. What Albayoumi's connection is to the two men has never been determined."

Fuentes tipped Gina off to a section in his initial report that gave further details on Almihdhar and Alhazmi's time at the Parkwood apartment. As soon as she was off the phone, Gina dug out the report and reread the portion they discussed. She discovered detailed information on the two from a tenant at Parkwood.

"My name is Special Agent Gina Kaufman and I'm calling from FBI headquarters in Washington. Do you have a few minutes? I'm doing a very preliminary investigation of two gentlemen whom I believe were or are your neighbors – "

"Are we talking about those Arab fellows?" the renter asked.

"Khalid Almihdhar and Nawaf Alhazmi," Gina confirmed.

"Odd dudes. Come and go at all hours, seems like they travel a great deal; been here for more than a year-and-a-half but still don't have any furniture beyond a TV and two plastic lawn chairs. Always on their cell phones, leave their door open most of the time. I go out, you know, ten, eleven at night to walk the dog and they're either on their phones talking Arabic or playing crazy flight simulator games. You know, those video games where you act like you're the pilot? Calling the shots, bringing the plane in for a landing under all kinds of stressful conditions. Seem real serious about it, too. Transfixed. Like kids high on dope."

"Do you know where Alhazmi and Almihdhar are now?"

"The chattier one, Alhazmi, I think…he's been around lately but I haven't seen the other guy in a while. Tough to know where he might be. Except for dealing with folks that sometimes show up late at night in limos, those two stick to themselves."

"Have you ever caught a glimpse of the people inside the limousines?"

"Not really. The cars pull up, the guys come out, get into the limo and it leaves and then comes back thirty, forty minutes later. I know all this 'cause it's a pretty modest neighborhood, Agent Kaufman. Limos with blacked out windows get people's attention."

Standing in Dan Mottola's office, Gina declined his offer to take a seat. "I'm here strictly as a professional courtesy. If you still feel you can't help on this matter, I believe it's only fair to let you know I'll be going over your head to Warren Cuppinger."

"Why the hell would you want to piss me off? You know how bat-shit crazy Cuppinger gets when we violate chain of command. You've got an issue with me, work it out, Agent Kaufman. That's how it's done."

"But you're *not* working with me, you're totally shut down to this, Dan. Every single thing about the way these guys are living, the way they're traveling, their peculiar contacts...they are sending up every flare we've been trained to look for. And yet they're disappearing for weeks and sometimes months with no one tracking them. It's ludicrous. Absolutely outrageous."

"Yet they still haven't done one thing you can pinpoint that's outside the boundaries of the law, am I right? So it sounds to me like we're back to square one: you're petitioning to place Almihdhar and Alhazmi under twenty-four hour surveillance and, as previously stated, I am denying your request."

"And I'm walking out of here to go directly to Cuppinger."

"You do that, lady. But let me warn you: you go over my head and I can pretty much guarantee it will be the beginning of the end of your career."

4

THE THREE SPELLBOUND GIRLS sitting cross-legged on the woven rug gazed at Adiba as she read from a beautifully illustrated picture book in her lap. It was a tale of two adventurous storks basking on the banks of the Tigris River in Baghdad, capital of all Islam, City of Peace.

"We live in Baghdad!" one of the eight-year-olds exclaimed.

With a nod, Adiba showed her young charges the illustration. When she finished the story, one girl declared that no matter how much fun it might be to fly, she'd never want to be turned into a bird because they had to eat worms and snails.

When the pupils' mothers, all friends and neighbors of Adiba, arrived a short time later, Adiba gave each child a hunk of the date-and-nut bread she'd baked that morning; she urged the departing girls to read every evening with their parents.

Adiba's short-lived solitude ended as her own two children charged through the front door tangled in a boisterous debate over whether or not girls were inherently smarter than boys. Adiba's daughter Qamar, a self-possessed fifteen-year-old, enjoyed steamrolling her brother at every turn. Dark-eyed and passionate twelve-year-old Zayd was badly in need of a growth spurt, sick of being called Runt by his peers. Often when Zayd and Qamar were locked in one of their frequent verbal battles, he'd bounce and hop at her side in an attempt to obtain direct eye contact.

"He's so irritating," Qamar would cry. "It is like conversing with a kangaroo."

Despite the mean-spirited prediction Shemma made at Adiba's bedside following her devastating miscarriage years earlier, declaring that Adiba's secret use of The Pill would keep her from ever bearing a child, Adiba was pregnant again that winter. Hazem was reluctant to share the news with anyone.

Even when Adiba looked like she'd ingested a basketball, people would ask when their baby was due and Hazem would coyly reply, "What baby?"

Qamar was born in August 1985. In the months preceding her arrival, Adiba and Hazem had grown unexpectedly close. Escorting his wife through her minefield pregnancy, Hazem accessed a buried vein of tenderness; for the first time since they met days before their arranged marriage, Adiba fell in love with the man who'd shared her bed for the previous four years.

Qamar had just celebrated her second birthday when Adiba learned she was expecting again. Hazem spoke often to her swelling belly, talking to the son he was certain was growing under his mother's soft brown skin. Adiba asked what would happen if it turned out she was carrying another girl but Hazem avowed that this baby was a boy. He was right.

From Zayd's initial moments on Earth he had a determination in his eyes and a way of shaking his clenched fists that made his maternal grandmother Rima guffaw. "Never have I seen a child who looks and acts so akin to his *Mama*. He is you to a tee, Adiba; I am sure he will be just as smart and twice as stubborn!"

Almost instantly, Rima and Zayd developed an unbreakable bond. Rima had five other grandchildren but Zayd was the undeclared favorite. When he started school, he began each day by phoning Rima, always signing off with, "My love for you, *BB*, is bigger than the stars, sun and moon combined."

Each year as Zayd matured, Adiba kept expecting the ritual calls to end but he never wavered. Even now as his voice was cracking and spiky stubble dotted his chin, Zayd launched every weekday with a call to *BB*.

Rima was widowed in the winter of '99. Hadi suffered a fatal heart attack at the sewing machine in his tailoring shop. After the ritual year of mourning, Adiba began to notice subtle changes in her mother's behavior. Rima became extremely forgetful; some days she was unusually combative. Occasionally, she would lapse into deeply unsettling baby talk. "No need to worry," Rima told Adiba one afternoon, "I will not be late to Friday lunch because…" Her voice jumped a gleeful octave: "I am a good girl!" Those last four words held the lilting cadence of a five-year-old.

When Adiba tried to make Shemma acknowledge that something was happening to their mother's brain, Shemma opted for fervent denial.

"It is more than the natural aging, sister. Last night she told me she was dining with Bashir and Aziza. Bashir has been dead for a decade!"

Two weeks later, Adiba received a panicked phone call from her mother claiming her automobile had been stolen. Rima explained she returned from the market, put away her groceries and went to retrieve her purse but the car wasn't in the driveway.

"Mother, are you sure you did not drive to the market and leave the car there?"

It turned out that was exactly what had happened. The following day Adiba and Shemma sat at the kitchen table with their spouses.

"Hazem, you are a doctor. Please tell my sister our mother's lapses are not typical for someone her age."

Hazem conceded that despite being an orthopedic surgeon and no expert on dementia, he did feel Rima was experiencing something beyond normal age-appropriate absentmindedness. When Shemma deftly switched the subject to her daughter's upcoming school play, Adiba knew she'd be facing the challenges of her mother's declining health without her siblings' help.

Their brother Mo'ez was living in India. After surviving six years in the military during the protracted Iran-Iraq war, Mo'ez returned home with scars more emotional than physical.

Disillusioned by his government's penchant for violence, no longer finding solace in the religion he was raised in, Mo'ez converted to Buddhism. This led to tempestuous encounters with the disapproving Hadi who cut off his only son. Despondent, Mo'ez fled to Mumbai to begin a new life as a spiritual healer.

When Hadi dropped dead, Adiba and Shemma begged Mo'ez to return for the funeral. He sternly declared that the father he loved died the day he rejected his only son so Mo'ez saw no reason to honor him now.

Sitting in his grandmother's backyard having honey cake and tea, Zayd asked Rima if he'd ever get the chance to know the uncle he regularly corresponded with but had never met. Rima remarked that she had no idea what the universe had in store. Zayd wondered if it was hard for her to never see her son. In an increasingly rare moment of lucidity, Rima said she'd long ago accepted that Mo'ez needed to forge his own path. She didn't want to be a parent who crippled her children with unfair expectations or guilt. "He was deeply disturbed by what he witnessed in that awful war. His conscience is tormented by things he was commanded to do. Now, my love, he is off on a spiritual quest to find inner-peace and so it must be."

"But I very much hope to meet him one day," Zayd sighed.

Rima looked up at her grandson with far-off, clouded eyes: "Meet who?"

"Why I have two siblings but feel I am an only child? I write my brother to inform him *Mama* is drifting further away with each passing day and in return I get a Buddhist axiom? 'Life is the joyful participation in the suffering of mankind.' This should comfort me? And Shemma the ostrich sticks her head in a dune rather than see that our mother asks the same questions twenty times in one hour. Today when I visited, *Mama*'s refrigerator was stocked with twelve bottles of salad dressing but no lettuce. Her silverware was in plastic bags and the bulbs had been removed from her lamps but she had no idea why. She never eats and her face fills with panic when I ask basic questions. I am sorry, Hazem; I no longer feel it is safe for her to live alone."

Hazem's simple answer caught Adiba completely off guard: "I agree."

It was no easy task convincing Rima to give up her home to move in with her daughter. It was even more difficult for Rima to accept that she could no longer drive. More than once Adiba caught her mother scouring the house for her car keys despite the fact that her Kia had been sold months earlier. The situation was difficult but manageable – until Rima took a hard fall landing on her tailbone. The doctors said it was only a severe bruise; Rima sharply disagreed. "Those doctors are idiots. My back is broken. It is unwise for me to move."

One evening Adiba was washing dinner dishes, Hazem had returned to the hospital to check on his post-op patients and Zayd was sitting with *BB* watching a pirated American film he picked up at the open-air market.

"I must use the commode," Rima barked, sprawled on her back on the couch.

When Zayd offered to help her up, she called him a fool and told him she was incapable of moving. He asked how she planned to relieve herself; Rima ordered him to stop being stupid and fetch a bedpan. Unaccustomed to hearing his beloved *BB* speak to him so harshly, Zayd reminded himself she wasn't in her right mind; that didn't keep him from feeling hurt.

"I am sorry, *BB*. We have no bedpan here."

Rima impudently responded by flooding her dressing gown and the couch cushions in a torrent of urine. Springing up in shock, Zayd raced to the kitchen to summon his mother.

Later, after she had scrubbed the couch cushions until her forearms ached and gotten her mother into bed, Adiba sat staring at Rima with equal parts pity and love. Rima lapsed into the baby talk that made Adiba's jaw clench. "Do not fret, Missus. From now on, I will be a good girl and use the potty."

Four months later, Rima looked like the Holocaust survivors in Zayd's history books. She had quit eating completely. Three times her doctors had inserted a feeding tube into her stomach but Rima would get agitated or confused and rip it out. Standing over her emaciated mother's hospital bed installed in the living room, an exhausted Adiba's head was pounding. Her neck was locked with tension; a churning anxiety filled her belly. Unwittingly, she erupted in noxious rage. "You simply need to die now, old woman! Before you kill us all, please, do everybody a favor and *die*."

Adiba immediately tried to reel the words back with a sucking gasp. Rima did not seem to register the verbal assault but Adiba was consumed with burning guilt.

Watching his beloved grandmother waste away, Zayd was beside himself.

"She is done," Adiba said one afternoon. "She wishes to join your grandfather in the next life. Perhaps it is time we accept that."

"No!" Zayd roared. "If we give up so will she."

"I believe, *habiti*, she already has."

When Shemma visited that afternoon, spouting myriad excuses as to why she'd been so invisible, her majestic denial was firmly in tact. She declared that her mother would pull out of this and soon be home baking honey cake.

Four hours later, while Shemma shopped for expensive spiked heels she could ill afford, Zayd sat at Rima's bedside holding her hand. Hearing a whirling rush of air leave his *BB*, he was relieved she was at last sleeping peacefully – until he noticed her chest had stopped rising and falling. Coming completely unglued, Zayd began to wail. Adiba rushed in; Zayd retreated to his room and collapsed into a fetal ball.

For the first several days of mourning, nothing but water passed his lips. He didn't talk, he didn't sleep, he only cried. Adiba was too enveloped in her own grief to pay Zayd much mind but Hazem was deeply concerned. Coming into his son's room he paused. Zayd's eyes were clamped shut but Hazem could tell he wasn't asleep. "Zayd, darling, please let me fetch you something to eat. It is time to rise up and honor BB's wonderful life."

"That is crap. She was taken too soon. And now she will never get to visit me in America where I shall one day live."

Shemma and Adiba ritualistically cleansed Rima's body in a scented bath one last time before carefully wrapping her in the *kafan*, clean white muslin sheets. When Rima's corpse was taken to the town square for *Salat Al Janazah*, the mourning prayers attended by the entire community, Zayd donned his late grandfather's finest suit and wore dark sunglasses to hide his swollen eyes.

Following another prayer session at the local mosque, the body was taken to the cemetery for burial. Only the men were permitted to participate in this ritual but Zayd declined to join his father, uncle and cousins. He knew he would not be able to handle seeing his coffin-less grandmother, wrapped in her *kafan*, lowered into the cold ground. She would be set on her right side facing Mecca as the men shoveled dirt on top of her. The mere thought of it sent Zayd's heart racing; how could he possibly witness it?

"His grief is too excessive for a young man," Hazem told Adiba a few days later.

"His grief is his grief; we must honor it."

"I am worried he is making himself sick."

Adiba put a gentle hand on her husband's cheek. "When you were so very ill with colitis, did your doctor not tell you the damage you were inflicting upon your body was due to stress and stifled emotions? Zayd is expressing his pain, feeling his despair—"

"It is not manly. It demonstrates weakness."

"No!" Adiba snapped, startling herself with her intensity. "It is the opposite: it shows the power of his love and connection to my dear mother. It is most beautiful; we must embrace it."

Hazem did not agree but was wise enough to let it drop.

Tracking Mo'ez down to inform him of their mother's death, Adiba was stunned by his current address. For years, Mo'ez had been in India pursuing his path as a spiritual leader in his adopted Buddhist faith. He communicated with his family rarely so it had been difficult to find him after Adiba's initial letter came back unopened. Only through dogged perseverance did she learn Mo'ez was now a resident of New York City. In America. Where Adiba had longed to go since she was a child.

Despite the fact that it would be a prohibitively expensive call to make, Adiba needed to hear her brother's voice. When they finally connected, they chatted for an hour. In Mumbai six months earlier, Mo'ez had met and married a woman on holiday from the United States; together they returned to her small apartment in Brooklyn. He apologized for not keeping his sisters in the loop but claimed he'd been too consumed by the romance, the move and a job hunt to find time to sit down and write.

When Adiba told him of Zayd's deep grief and the difficult time he was having recovering from Rima's death, Mo'ez made a generous proposal: "Why not let him visit me in New York? You have both always told me of his love for all things

American; perhaps this will be the cure he needs. It is a city of such vibrancy, how could he not be reawakened? What do you say, sister? The plane ticket will be my gift. I would deeply cherish time with this nephew I have not yet had the opportunity to get to know. I could take him to my favorite spot at the top of the World Trade Center. It is called Windows on the World; it is truly astonishing what one can see from up there. He should come for my birthday in September."

5

AFTER THE UNCOMFORTABLE STANDOFF with Dan Mottola, Gina spent a sleepless night and a conflicted Tuesday struggling to determine her next move.

"Maybe it's good you've got a five-day break ahead," Margaret offered. "Don't think about any of it for a bit – "

"Oh sure, that'll happen," Gina responded with a sarcastic chortle. "You know me, the queen of letting go. No matter what, I've lost all credibility with Dan. I didn't storm off to Cuppinger, I certainly can't let this drop, so instead I'll come off like a spineless wimp."

"Hardly. You're conscientious, trying to come to a measured, well-informed conclusion – instead of exploding in a rage like the men around here."

Reaching the baggage claim area after the flight from LA, David rushed to Gina and Noah with Cyrus trailing. Gina threw her arms wide to pull David into her hungry embrace; reveling in their overdue reunion they fired endearments at each other. Noah clapped Cy's arm. "You look great, my friend. How the hell are you?"

"Fat, happy and very glad to be here. If I'd known retirement would be this good, I would've skipped the whole working part in the first place."

Back at the Kaufman-Zager townhouse, David and Cyrus quickly unpacked before the quartet reconvened for a midnight snack. As soon as Gina took her first sip of Sharaz, David groaned in realization that she wasn't pregnant. Cyrus swatted his arm, chiding David for being so rude. They spent the better part of an hour catching up before everyone faded. As they wound down, Gina spilled the next day's agenda.

"The Scotts arrive around noon, we'll barbeque, then head over to the Capitol. It's a real scene but everybody should experience it once. The National Symphony Orchestra plays, pop stars perform and then the grand finale: fireworks over the Capitol dome. How could it get any more Yankee-Doodle-Dandy than that?"

"Oh, you just wait," Cyrus chuckled.

"My God," Gina squealed at David, "you do not still have the flag shirt?"

"You bet your bippy he does," Cyrus said. "In all its Old Glory! Pun intended."

On the west coast, the Fourth of July delivered a glorious day to the San Fernando Valley. Lisa and Martin rose early to make breakfast for their three visiting grandchildren, letting Michael and Bootsy sleep in. When Martin asked who wanted whipped cream atop the strawberry pancakes Lisa delivered, eight-year-old Calvin and three-year old Scout responded at once. Mimi, the cautious middle child, asked what it tasted like. At a loss for words, Martin turned to Lisa. "How would you describe whipped cream?"

"Yummy, yummy, yummy!" said Calvin.

Requesting a sample, Mimi swiped it onto the tip of her finger and raised it to her extended tongue. Seeing her hesitation, Calvin jumped to his feet. "Jesus-fucking-Christ, just taste it already!"

"Your mother and I about died," Martin told Michael and Bootsy later. "It was hard not to bust up laughing. He sounded so much like you, buddy, it was scary."

Across town, Debbie gave an indelicate poke to the bearded stranger under her sheets, telling him he needed to go. He flopped onto his back. "We could fuck again."

"Thanks anyway, Romeo."

"Ya know, you're a bitch in the morning. Can I call you again sometime?"

"Please don't."

In the walled-in patio of Gina and Noah's townhouse, Brian Scott proposed a toast: "To old friends, new friends and to the long and winding road of life!"

"To the eternal flag shirt!" Cyrus laughed. "Long may it wave."

On cue, David pulled the ripcord under the hem of his sateen flag-patterned shirt; its fifty white stars, made from tiny twinkle-lights sewn into the layers of fabric, lit up.

At the grill, Noah asked Brian if he made a habit of staying to touch with all his patients the way he had with Gina; Brian admitted his bond with Gina was unique.

"Personally, I think he gets off on bragging to our friends that he knows a real live FBI agent," Heather said with a laugh.

"Seriously, guys, that's a huge part of the draw," Brian admitted. "I tell everybody she was this little kid reading *The Day of the Jackal* and now she's kicking ass hunting terrorists."

By the time they got to the west lawn of the Capitol, the area was a rolling sea of humanity. Gina and company miraculously found a spot in the shadow of the Capitol dome.

A little before nine, with the sun melting into the horizon, it was time for the main event. Gleeful children darted around brandishing sparklers. Marijuana smoke danced in the balmy air. When the first silver shower burst into the starless sky, the crowd let out a thundering roar. Staring up, watching starry pops with sizzling white tails chasing overlapping explosions of percolating color, Gina's eyes filled with tears. What a glorious night! She was with beloved family and friends; everything was perfect. Until some maniac detonates a dirty bomb and kills us all.

With more than two hours until sundown, the party in Martin and Lisa's west coast backyard rolled on. Lisa and Bootsy sat in the patio swing, cocktails in hand, keeping watchful eyes on the kids in the pool. With inflated water wings hugging her upper arms, Scout sat on a step in the shallow end with a bucket, happily scooping water into it with its matching shovel.

At the deep end Debbie was throwing a beach ball for Calvin to catch each time he took a running leap into the water. Michael was crashed out in a lounge chair; his father tended to the hot dogs and burgers on the Weber under a palm tree. A John Philip Sousa CD boomed out of the portable stereo.

After several loops marching the family German shepherd around the pool waving one of Lisa's ubiquitous mini American flags, Mimi pooped out. She hooked the leash around a grill leg and threw a chew toy into the water intending to dive in after it. Unfortunately, the dog assumed it was his invitation to play. He bolted for the pool dragging the grill behind.

Toppling into the pristine water, the grill sent up a huge splash; hot dogs, burgers and spicy sausages, accompanied by an army of sizzling coals, bobbed or sank below the surface as the Sousa tune reached its cymbal-crashing crescendo. Debbie broke the stunned silence with the only question that seemed relevant: "So Ma, does Guiseppe's deliver on holidays?"

The next day, despite having no set agenda, Gina was up making coffee at 6:25 a.m. The rest of the townhouse remained dark and silent. Noah and the Zagers' guests were still asleep. After taking a full half-hour to read the morning's *Washington Post*, savoring her self-allotted two cups of black coffee, Gina slipped into her master bathroom to snag her workout clothes and swiftly dressed. Noah's droning snores never skipped a beat. Trotting back into the kitchen, Gina was surprised to find Brian at the table with the *Sports* section. He invited himself on Gina's jog.

Running side-by-side on the shaded trails of Rock Creek Park, Gina and Brian chatted nonstop. A complimentary match in physical prowess and mental acumen, neither had the slightest idea they'd been gone for over an hour. They were deeply engrossed in discussing the realization that they'd both been on a singularly directed career path since they were kids.

"Funny we each got our initial spark from an uncle," Brian panted as they ran, "You had David and his spy stories and for me it was my doctor uncle Nelson. I was seven, maybe eight when I first saw his vintage '52 Cadillac Coupe…cherry red, white vinyl convertible top…God, that thing was a beaut. When I put it together that being a doctor allowed him to afford a ride like that, I was sold." Laughing, Brian went on. "Seriously. My draw to medicine had nothing to do with wanting to heal people, I just wanted a big house and a hot car. Of course, the irony is that big bucks in medicine are long gone, but luckily I love what I do so it's all good."

Once the Scotts departed before dinner, Gina and Noah used the rest of the long weekend to run David and Cyrus from a free concert at the Kennedy Center to a full day at the National Portrait Gallery before an elegant dinner at the Occidental Grill. Sunday afternoon, Noah and Cyrus were watching the Orioles-Phillies game. Gina and David took a neighborhood stroll.

"It's been so wonderful having you and Cyrus here. It's never enough time. I'm thrilled to see you two so content. Cy's a doll." A long beat passed. "How can I ever thank you, David, for everything you've given me over the years? For always being so present and supportive. You're a constant inspiration whether you know it or not."

David took her hands into his. "Well, dolly, it's high-time you knew I literally owe my life to you. It's true. There was a night, years ago, I was so conflicted about my sexuality, in constant fear of being outed, ashamed of everything I did and felt. I left dinner at your parents' – you were just a baby, an infant – I was hating myself, filled with self-loathing…"

As he choked back his emotion, Gina studied her uncle's quivering face. "Oh my God, you were contemplating suicide?"

"The only reason I didn't go through with it was because I got this…this flash of your gorgeous little face and your precious giggle and I…" His voice dropped. "I had to stick around to see you grow up."

Gina's colleague FBI Special Agent Priscilla Ogilvey was the only female agent on their floor with more years of service than Gina. As soon as she arrived at work on the Monday after the holiday, Gina ducked into Priscilla's office to seek counsel.

Gina launched into a recitation of her recent collection of troubling intelligence on Khalid Almihdhar and Nawaf Alhazmi. She revealed what she knew about their strange travels, their midnight visits from unseen men in blacked-out limousines, their oddly unfurnished apartment. She told Priscilla of her unshakable instinct that these two men needed to have twenty-four-hour surveillance but had hit a brick wall with their boss.

"Dan's a jackass. But if you're convinced it's unwise to make an end-run around him, don't. You have an independent operating budget. True you lack the authority to initiate a surveillance operation so invent a way it isn't surveillance. Make it a 'fact finding mission' or 'field research' – call it whatever you can to make it fit under a billing area no one will have reason to question. Don't you know this by now? You can get everything you want around here if you learn a few simple tricks of creative bookkeeping."

By the meeting's end, Agent Fuentes had the authorization needed to put the Parkwood apartment of Alhazmi and Almihdhar under the watchful eyes of two of his top men.

"And the beauty is," Priscilla told Gina, "Dan never needs to know."

The next day, Gina was reading through her morning briefing papers when a new memo caused her heart to seize. It was from an agent in Phoenix and was titled "Zakaria Mustapha Soubra: IT – OTHER (Islamic Army of the Caucasus)." It carried a subtitle of 'Osama bin Laden and Al-Muhjiroun supporters attending civil aviation universities and colleges in Arizona.'

In the body of the report the agent detailed recent interviews with and observations of several students from Pakistan, Algeria, Saudi Arabia and other Middle East hotspots. He had heard numerous hostile comments about the United States and was alarmed by the fact that many of these men were suspiciously well informed about security measures at US airports. At least ten of the men had direct ties to Al-Qaeda.

Although she didn't immediately recognize any of the names in the report, what Gina did see was the beginning of an emerging pattern. Why were so many Arab immigrants turning up at American flight schools? Putting what she'd learned about Alhazmi and Almihdhar at Kelso's Flying Club together with this latest information had to set off alarm bells for even the most jaded observer. Some nefarious plot was definitely hatching. At the end of the communiqué, the agent recommended the FBI ask the State Department to supply visa data on flight school students from Middle Eastern countries that could facilitate the FBI tracking efforts. Gina didn't believe even Dan Mottola would be able to ignore this new incriminating data.

"Did you read this memo?"

"I did," Dan growled. "And did you notice it was marked 'routine,' not 'urgent'? Once again Agent Kaufman, you are treating conjecture as fact."

Gina threw up her hands in exasperation. "I give up."

"About damn time."

Later, after another lengthy internal debate, Gina decided she wouldn't approach Dan again until she'd put together a report so packed with connected dots it would be impossible for him to remain blind. Contacting an old Georgetown classmate who was a high-ranking official at State, she gathered the flight school student visa information she was seeking. Checking in with Agent Fuentes in San Diego, she learned that Almihdhar had returned to the US on July 4 and was back at the Parkwood Apartment he shared with Alhazmi. What Fuentes didn't know was where Almihdhar had been or with whom he'd been meeting.

Searching through a classified file on recent communiqués from the FAA, Gina made one more startling discovery. One of the men mentioned in the July 10 memo, Hani Hanjour, was also the subject of an alert to the FAA from an Arizona flight school called JetTech. They expressed concern that Hanjour lacked both the English and the flying skills necessary to have obtained the commercial pilot's license he already possessed. The JetTech manager relayed that he could not believe Hanjour acquired this license legally given his limited abilities. It was the manager's assessment that the matter warranted further investigation. Reading through the rest of the dossier, Gina couldn't find an iota of evidence that any follow-up had been done.

Intensifying her investigation of Hanjour, she learned he'd never been reexamined; in February he began advanced simulator training, an even more intricate task than he'd had to deal with in getting his commercial license. In all, Gina flagged five separate flight school alerts ignored by the FAA. She was incredibly frustrated that all these agencies were gathering all this data – but there was absolutely *no* integration of information between them. It got collected and then instantly disappeared into a black hole.

"Am I ever going to see you again?" Noah asked when he reached Gina at her office after 10:00 p.m. that Thursday. "Have you had dinner yet?"

Glancing at the half-eaten BLT on her desk, Gina groaned. "I never even finished lunch. Something is about to happen, Noah. Something terrible." When he told her it was time to bring a few more colleagues into the loop Gina responded furiously. "Not yet!" Noah was so silent on the other end of the line Gina asked if he was still there.

"Yeah. I'm just afraid that no matter what I say you'll bite my head off. Look, I know you're tired and I know you're trying to do the right thing, but that doesn't mean you should kill yourself. Come home, get some sleep."

"I will. I promise. Soon."

Gina finally made it to their townhouse after Noah was dead to the world. Lacking the energy to brush her teeth, she undressed, clicked off the muted TV and climbed into bed beside her husband. She was back at the office by 7:00 a.m.

In midafternoon, Margaret popped in to tell Gina she had a visitor.

The man explained he was a CIA officer assigned to the FBI. He was having lunch with Priscilla Ogilvey on an unrelated matter when she mentioned Gina's ongoing investigation of the Middle Eastern students attending US flight schools. "Am I correct in assuming you're familiar with the January 2000 Al Qaeda summit in Malaysia?" he asked.

"Intimately. I've been on the Cole investigation since its inception."

"Then you'll certainly want to hear what I found out this morning. I was finally able to confirm that Khallid bin Atash was at that meeting in Malaysia. And given that we know bin Atash is a major league killer, I believe it would serve you to go back and review every CIA cable we have regarding that summit."

"I'll need your authorization to gain access."

"Done." As quickly as he'd shown up, the agent was gone.

Combing through classified files that afternoon, Gina received one more mind-bending jolt. In the packet of materials on Khallid bin Atash, whom the FBI considered to be a principal planner of the Cole bombing, she found pictures of him with a top bin Laden operative, Fahad al Quso – posing beside two other men Gina instantly recognized as Alhazmi and Almihdhar.

Galloping into Priscilla Ogilvey's office, Gina fought to catch her breath. "We have photographs – not hearsay accounts, not speculation, not unattributed chatter – black-and-white photos of these men with the top operatives of the world's most lethal terrorist organization – " Gina could no longer mask her outrage. " – yet they have never even ended up on a No-Fly list! They get visa extensions, come and go as they please…is this insane?"

"No, honey," Priscilla replied, "it's our government bureaucracy at work."

For the next five weeks, Gina was forced to play a tension-laced waiting game. She was too wired to sleep, too distracted to eat; Noah grew more concerned daily. "Please, can't you just take a break? You're a mess. Yesterday you drove off with your purse on the roof of the car."

"I got it back," Gina said defensively. "Noah, I know this is hard, I know I've been a preoccupied bitch but I'm close, I'm getting so close I'm just—"

"Unable to tell me more or you'd have to kill me," he retorted without humor.

On August 21, a report from Agent Fuentes in San Diego caused every hair on Gina's arm to stand up. Fuentes called to alert her to the transcript of a wiretap he'd just sent. In the recorded call, Nawaf Alhazmi told an unidentified cohort that he and Almihdhar had been in Los Angeles in January of 2000. Gina instantly grasped the significance of this. During that period, a man was arrested entering the U.S. from Canada with a trunk-load of explosives. He was charged with plotting to blow up the Los Angeles International Airport on 1/1/01 and was now serving a twenty-two year sentence in federal prison.

Two days later, Gina headed into a top-level meeting of the FBI's Senior Anti-Terrorism Task Force, an assembly she set in motion. Unwilling to risk additional rejection from Dan, fully prepared to weather his wrath, she'd worked up a detailed report on her recent findings and sent it to the FBI Assistant Director in charge of the task force who immediately acknowledged its urgency. After handing out bound copies of Gina's exhaustive findings, along with a succinct document summarizing the report's most provocative bullet points, the director announced he had his own breaking news. "Prompted by the exceptional and exhaustive legwork of Agent Kaufman, I've been in close touch with my CIA counterpart. One hour ago, I was cc'ed on a warning received by the CIA this morning from Israel's Mossad. In it is a list of nineteen names of known terrorists currently residing in the U.S. whom Mossad believes are in the final planning stages of a lethal attack on an unspecified domestic target. At least four of these names, Nawaf Alhazmi, Khalid Almihdhar, Hani Hanjour and Mohamed Atta, appear in Agent Kaufman's report. All of them, as well as several others on the list, attended US flight schools within the last eighteen months."

As a chill shot up Gina's spine, the room was abuzz; everyone had a theory to espouse. The director had to shout above the din to restore order. "As of this afternoon, all nineteen of these men have been added to the Terrorist Watch List."

"Have we also added them to the No-Fly roster?" someone asked.

The director's cheeks reddened; he'd have to get back to them on that.

"Shouldn't they also be tracked down ASAP and put under 24-hour surveillance?" Dan asked with a smugness that made Gina want to slug him.

"Absolutely," the director agreed. "And thanks to Agent Kaufman's fancy footwork, two of these men are already being tracked."

From that moment on, after weeks of Gina plodding through her paces with methodical precision, everything moved as if they'd made the jump to hyperspace.

Agent Fuentes deciphered enough chatter to know a high-level meeting was planned for the Parkwood Apartments on August 27. Almihdhar and Alhazmi were coming and going several times a day. An unknown visitor arrived late on the 24th but hadn't been seen since; he was presumed to be holing up inside the apartment.

Several members of the FBI HQ Anti-Terrorism unit were sent to San Diego to assist Agent Fuentes. Gina was ordered to remain in DC to monitor communications from the CIA, the FAA and the State Department as well as any relevant documents being generated internally. She lovingly told Noah she might not see him for days.

Arriving in San Diego on the morning of August 26, FBI Assistant Special Agent in Charge Dan Mottola made it clear he was the uncontested leader of this covert operation. The goal was to take down Almihdhar and Alhazmi along with any other co-conspirators that were present. The mission quickly mushroomed into a joint effort between the FBI and local law enforcement with the National Guard on standby should additional assistance become necessary.

Dan was in his glory barking orders, reviewing wiretapped communications coming from the Parkwood apartment, making snap decisions without affording room for debate. It was his operation and no one should dare to challenge his authority.

On August 27th, shortly before midnight on the east coast, Gina got the call she'd been awaiting. Knowing the planned raid was imminent, she was in her office when the bell of her telephone rattled her raw nerves; she yanked up the receiver.

"It's going down," Agent Fuentes said. "At least six or seven guys from the Mossad list are present. Started filing in about an hour ago." The sounds of sirens and whirring helicopter blades drowned Fuentes out. His strained bark snapped in Gina's ear: "I'll call you back."

Asleep at her desk, Gina was roused at 4:00 a.m. by the phone ringing anew. "We got 'em. And when you hear what they were plotting, Agent Kaufman, pardon my French but you are gonna shit."

Battling to stay awake at 5:00 that afternoon, Gina was in her bathrobe, leaning against Noah on the den couch. Staring blankly at the TV, they were awaiting the start of a press conference in San Diego where the local police chief and the FBI's Dan Mottola would be making a major announcement.

"I cannot believe they didn't fly you out there for this," Noah groused.

"Look at me. Do I look like I'm in any shape to be winging across the country?"

"That's beside the point. They at least should've had the decency ask. The fact that they didn't makes my blood boil."

She patted his leg in an unspoken thank-you for the support.

When the press conference started, the police chief congratulated his department for pulling off a smooth and safe operation. He acknowledged the supreme coordination between his men and the federal authorities before casually mentioning that, thanks to their amazing efforts, countless lives had been spared. He turned the mic over to Dan.

"Jesus," Noah growled. "Look at him, with his $200 haircut and designer suit. He's eating this shit up."

"I hate to admit it but he looks good," Gina said.

On the TV, Dan adjusted the mic and cleared his throat. "Ladies and gentlemen, members of the media, citizens of this great nation…it's my privilege to tell you that due to the remarkable work of law enforcement personnel at every level across this country, all Americans can sleep more securely tonight."

Dan went on to disclose that after a preliminary review of the seized computers, physical evidence, and intelligence gathered during the raid on the Parkwood Apartment of Nawaf Alhazmi and Khalid Almihdhar, a major international terrorist plot with ties to Osama bin Laden's Al-Qaeda network had been foiled. He said these men were planning to simultaneously crash multiple commercial airliners into targets in New York City and Washington, DC. Eight men were in custody with twelve others being sought. All were expected to be in law enforcement hands by day's end. An unconfirmed report that one of the suspects had committed suicide in Florida was currently under investigation.

Dan declined to take questions; further information would be released as the investigation progressed.

"Isn't he going to thank you?" Noah shouted, jumping to his feet. "This whole thing never would have been prevented if it wasn't for you! Are they kidding me?"

Gina shrugged. "It would be a whole different ballgame if I was a man."

2009

— 1 —

SITTING AT HIS PARENTS' kitchen table, Zayd Ahmed knew he had important forms to complete but couldn't focus. Blank only minutes before, the paper in front of him was now populated by cartoon monkeys clutching banana-blasting bazookas. The doodles were rich in amusing detail but Zayd was keenly aware they weren't helping him to finish his pressing task.

Wiping her hands on a dishtowel as she peered over her son's shoulder, Adiba clucked her tongue. "Silly me, why I was not aware a visa application required cartoons?"

Zayd groaned. Adiba pulled out the chair opposite him and sat, keeping her tone judgment-free. "How long have both you and I dreamed of spending time in America? Now that such an opportunity is looming for you, is this procrastination perhaps a bout of cold feet?"

"Not for a moment," Zayd declared. "Do you not recall how much I loved every second of my trip to New York with Uncle Mo'ez? That was when I knew I must return to attend university in the US."

He met up with the newly married Mo'ez in September of 2001; together they took in all the incredible attractions of the bustling city. The highlight of the trip was an elegant breakfast at the Windows on the World restaurant on the 106th floor of the World Trade Center; Zayd recalled it was the 11th of the month, his uncle's birthday. The breathtaking views of the city, the harbor and area beyond provided a stunning perspective. In Baghdad, the tallest building Zayd ever visited was the eight-story hospital where his father worked.

He applied to four American universities and was ultimately rejected by NYU, waitlisted at Brown and accepted by UCLA and the University of Pennsylvania. Two months prior to this July afternoon, Zayd sent a letter of acceptance to Penn.

"I need not remind you that none of it will matter," Adiba chided, "if you do not apply for and receive a never-guaranteed visa to leave Iraq."

Zayd's sister Qamar, his senior by five years, was a public librarian in the heart of Baghdad. Being an insatiable reader, the best part of her job at the information desk was that every minute she wasn't needed to answer patrons' questions she was free to burrow into a nest of words. No matter how much activity swirled around her, when her eyes fixed on a printed page, Qamar was always more present in that world than in the corporeal one.

Unlike most of her family and friends, Qamar managed to marry for love. Her parents, grandparents and aunts all entered marriages arranged by their elders, meeting their spouses weeks, sometimes days, before they were wed. Qamar met her husband of three years on her first day as a student at the University of Baghdad. He was a fourth year engineering major; she intended to focus on literature. Unable to find an assigned classroom, she asked him for directions and sparks ignited.

Ghazi Rahim had a receding hairline and an elongated face with close-set eyes but also possessed a deep bass voice and an energetic charisma that was tough to ignore. When Adiba first met him, after months of hearing how sexy Ghazi was, she fought to hide her shock. Expecting a movie star, instead she

got a popcorn vendor but after their first encounter Adiba
came to understand why Qamar was so smitten. Ghazi's inner
confidence and innate intelligence erased any physical deficits.
Both Adiba and Hazem were forced to acknowledge their
daughter had defied tradition and found a suitable match.
Ghazi graduated near the top of his class with an engineering
degree but the country's economic downturn thwarted his
career plans. Unable to find work befitting his education and
intelligence, he took a menial job on a construction crew
swiftly working his way up to project foreman.

Although Qamar and Ghazi had separate and mutual
friends from their university days, they found it difficult to
meet couples to socialize with. Most of their friends were in
traditional marriages so the men were considerably older than
their wives. Many of Ghazi's pals were still single while
Qamar's friends had husbands twice their age. It was lucky the
young couple was so compatible; the majority of their time
away from work was spent together or with family.

Ghazi's construction crew finished six-months on a
condominium project and was awaiting their next assignment.
The boss came on site wearing an expression as dark as his
sunglasses. Real estate development had plummeted. The firm
put in bids on several projects but didn't win any of them. The
one job they did secure required only a skeletal crew. Everyone
else was being let go. Ghazi was devastated to find his name at
the top of the list. If the situation improved, the boss would
hire back as many people as possible but couldn't make any
promises.

Attempting to share the news with Qamar over dinner,
Ghazi fought to get the words out.

He seemed so tortured Qamar feared he'd fallen in love
with someone else. Finally unable to bear it, she wailed,
"Please, Ghazi, tell me what is troubling you before I lose my
mind!"

When he finished his anguished confession Qamar felt nothing but relief. She assured him he would get another job soon, hopefully as an engineer. It was his destiny.

Ten days after Zayd mailed in his application, he received an order to report to the visa bureau for an interview. Adiba offered to accompany him but Zayd demurred.

"One piece of maternal advice: do not be a wise guy there. Our government agents are not known for their sense of humor."

Ushered into the visa administrator's office, Zayd was completely intimidated. The room's gray interior and the official's matching expression nearly convinced him he was guilty of some terrible crime he didn't remember committing. In the silent room the agent studied the papers before him. It was a full three minutes until he uttered his first words: "What you will study at the University of Pennsylvania that you cannot undertake in Baghdad?"

Zayd reviewed each word in his head before he let it dance across his lips. "I have a keen interest in the history of cinema."

"Are you aware that American films spew blasphemy and decadence?"

Zayd wanted to cry out that this was *why* he couldn't wait to see as many of them as possible but remembering his mother's words, he resisted. "I believe that only by studying foreign cultures are we able to gain an understanding of them."

"What you plan to do with a degree in cinematic history?"

"I do not yet know," Zayd honestly replied.

The official asked Zayd if he would be willing to sign a loyalty pledge promising to return to serve Saddam's government once his education was complete.

"Of course. Without question."

The clerk went back to perusing the documents on his desk.

After several long moments, he swallowed his sole word with a sneer: "Film." The minister made notes, asked Zayd a few more perfunctory questions and scrawled one last concealed memo.

"Thank you, Mr. Ahmed. Expect to hear from my office in three to six weeks."

Although there was no practical reason why he couldn't sleep in, Ghazi rose with Qamar each morning to make her breakfast while she got ready for work. He would walk her to the bus stop, then head to a corner café to meet with a coterie of unemployed friends. They'd scour the papers and trade tips on possible leads. They'd smoke too much and drink coffee until they were as jittery as a pack of pugs. Their gallant attempts to bolster each other up often devolved into a full-blown pity party.

By noon, he'd tire of the men at the café and wander home. Inside his cool dark house he was too distracted to read, too agitated to watch the state-run television so he'd sleep for several hours every afternoon. He repeatedly offered to make dinner but Qamar insisted it was her job to cook the evening meal; moving around the kitchen helped her to unwind after a long workday.

On a late September afternoon, Zayd came to his sister's door looking for Ghazi. The insistent knocking roused the unemployed engineer from a deep sleep. "I was in back," he stammered, "working on…there is much to maintain as a homeowner."

Lost in his own drama, Zayd didn't realize he'd woken Ghazi up. "They turned me down. My visa application was denied."

Ghazi called a friend who had a friend who worked in the visa administrator's office. The man promised to look into Zayd's case and report back.

The next night, Qamar and Ghazi joined Zayd and his parents for dinner. Adiba prepared a sumptuous lamb roast with rosemary potatoes. As the women cleaned up and Hazem stepped out to smoke, Ghazi filled Zayd in on what he'd learned. "You must file an appeal. Tell them you have decided studying film would be a waste of time; declare that you have realized it will be more productive to major in chemical engineering or nuclear physics—"

"But I do not wish to study those subjects."

"It is not about what you want. It is about how to best serve our government. It is about acquiring the skills they wish you to possess so you can help Saddam build weapons."

"This is crazy. Why I would want to contribute to that?"

"Quit playing the innocent," Ghazi snapped. "The privilege to leave comes at a price." When Zayd said this wasn't fair, Ghazi went on: "Years of a crippled economy is also unfair, as is the ruination of our infrastructure or my inability to find employment. Life is filled with inequities. You are a spoiled young man who needs to wake up."

Coming in to collect the last few dishes Qamar saw Zayd looking stung. Responding to her questioning gaze, Ghazi replied, "Your little brother has received a slap of truth and it hurts."

Over the next week, Zayd knew he had a crucial decision to make. If he wanted to get to America he'd have to tell the visa officers what they wanted to hear. Would it be worth it? Could he tolerate studying physics and chemistry? Upon return, would he be bound to a job in a corrupt government developing lethal weapons? Unlike Ghazi, at least he'd have a job.

Tormented, Zayd confided in his mother. He loved and respected Hazem but his father was a pragmatic doctor who worked at a government hospital. He'd long ago accepted the regime's extensive reach; he'd tell Zayd to switch his major without hesitation. Adiba was more likely to see both sides Zayd's dilemma.

Walking with his mother to the open-air market Zayd laid out the entire scenario. Adiba was pleased Ghazi had been able to provide Zayd with this crucial inside information. Zayd told her his reservations about returning home to be a government scientist. Pausing at a fruit stall, Adiba examined a mound of dates, telling the vendor they looked dry.

"Here, here," the eager merchant responded; he used metal tongs to pluck up one of the fattest samples. "They are fine. Taste for yourself."

Adiba snatched the date from the pincher nodding toward Zayd. "He does not deserve a taste as well?"

The vendor groused but plucked up another plump date for Zayd. Devouring the offering, Adiba grinned. "You were right, I was wrong; we'll take a kilogram." As the merchant weighed and bagged the fruit, Adiba whispered to Zayd: "I knew they would be delicious. I also knew one good insult would earn us each a free treat!"

Moving on, Adiba refocused: "Your decision is not easy, *habiti*. None of us can see the future. Four years is a long time. Will Saddam still be in power when you return? Will his spies monitor your every move in the US? Would you be able to fulfill the government demands and still pursue your goals? Who can say? But remember Uncle Mo'ez's mantra when you met in New York City? He implored you to live life free of regret, and I agree." She lowered her voice to a confidential whisper. "Through you, I will at last vicariously get to live my dream."

Despite being exhausted from her day at the library, Qamar knew she and Ghazi needed to talk. She found him slumped on the living room couch staring at the television he wasn't watching. She moved behind him to rest her hands on his shoulders, beckoning him to bed. He remained silent. Qamar glided around in front of him wearing the plum-colored silk robe he'd given her for her birthday. She smiled coyly. "If you are not yet sleepy, I was hoping you would let me to make you tired."

His sigh sounded more like a groan. "Not tonight."

"That is what you tell me every night for weeks."

Ghazi's temper flared like a match hitting flint. "I have too much on my mind!"

Qamar lowered herself to the couch resting a hand on his knee. "I know you are worried. I know this job hunt consumes you…but I love you, I miss you. Please, my sweet, come to bed."

Ghazi was on his back. Qamar unbuttoned his shirt and eased it off. She stripped him of his trousers and boxer shorts. His cock was hiding like a soldier in a wiry foxhole. Qamar rested her head on his thigh and slowly began to stroke the recalcitrant penis. She used the palm of her other hand to cup his testicles and wiggled her fingers to initiate a gentle massage. Slowly, the cock unfurled, stretching like a waking child as she continued to play with it. When it was fully upright, Qamar brought it into her mouth and slid her hugging lips up and down.

After a jaw-cramping period of devotion, Qamar felt rippling tremors traveling from Ghazi's toes to his pelvis to his shoulders. As the quaking escalated, his vibrating moans grew louder: agony entwined with the pure pleasure. His orgasm erupted with convulsive force; he lunged into a half-sit-up as he released a primal wail. He crashed back to the mattress but kept on twitching. Finally finished, Ghazi cried and laughed in tandem. Five minutes later he was asleep.

Qamar nestled herself against him and rolled onto her side. She stuck the middle two fingers of her left hand into her mouth, hungrily licking them to make them moist. A moment later she delicately worked them into the folds of her neglected clitoris.

"Comb your hair. Look presentable. You need to appear to be a serious young man, even if I know better," Adiba teased.

Moving to the open front door, Zayd saw Ghazi waiting for him outside. He greeted him, kissed his mother's cheek and departed.

Adiba remained staring after her son. Did they not used to call him Runt? When did he grow so tall and sturdy? With those black caterpillars he calls eyebrows and that ivory smile that dazzles each room enters. How will I be able to let him go?

She knew if they granted this appeal Zayd would be gone for at least four years. Now that their shared fantasy was closer to fruition, reality was setting in. He'd be living in a land where everyone owned a gun. Young girls wore skirts no bigger than a dishtowel, often with bare arms covered in hideous tattoos. But it was also a place of ideas and energy and the freedom Adiba coveted. This is a mother's curse: wanting the best while imagining the worst.

The official Zayd met with wasn't the one he'd spoken to originally. This man didn't fire questions at Zayd as if using him for target practice. "Why for you have requested this second application review?"

"I have given careful consideration to the course of study I shall pursue at the University of Pennsylvania. I have realized film is a frivolous area of focus affording me no practical path to employment upon my return."

When asked what he now intended to major in, Zayd took in a breath, hoping to convince himself so he could convince the official. "I wish to study nuclear physics."

"A wise choice." The official gave Zayd a wink. "America is a challenging place. I know; I completed my studies at Princeton. I sincerely hope this works out for you, Mr. Ahmed. I believe you have the potential to be an asset to our great nation." Once again, there was a wink.

"Fate is a funny thing," Ghazi said when he and Zayd reunited. "While you were inside, I happened to speak to a random fellow who knows someone that might be able to get me a job. His friend runs an engineering firm; two of their most promising employees recently fled to Saudi Arabia. The firm is interviewing replacement candidates next week. How did it go for you, our budding scientist?"

"Who could imagine a devil's bargain would be sealed with a wink?"

The letter arrived four days later. Not only was Zayd granted a student visa, a second letter promised full government funding for his four-year education. In exchange for Zayd's commitment to study nuclear physics, Saddam's regime would pay his tuition, room and board along with a modest monthly stipend. He simply had to sign a loyalty oath pledging to work for the state-run Scientific Development Center when he came home.

Hazem was thrilled. Zayd would get to follow his heart and set himself up for gainful employment. It would have been disingenuous for Hazem to deny he was also happy to learn this $200,000 investment would not have to come from his own pocket. Adiba was more ambivalent. She needed reassurance that Zayd wasn't boxing himself into a lifetime of misery.

"*Mama*, you are the one who told me the future is unknowable. I am certain that if I make it to America, the proper path will reveal itself."

The night before Zayd's December departure, Adiba and Hazem threw a party for their extended family. All of the aunts, uncles and cousins came to wish Zayd well. Ghazi, who'd recently started work as an apprentice engineer at the firm he'd learned about during Zayd's visa appeal, collected everyone for a toast. He credited Zayd's desire to study aboard with facilitating his own recent good fortune. He saluted the Ahmeds as the epitome of a loving, supportive family. He wished Zayd the adventure of a lifetime.

Sipping a glass of mint tea, Zayd gazed around at the faces he'd known since the day he was born. What would happen if he fell madly in love with the United States and decided to never come home?

2

"Wait, the Biltmore for New Year's Eve? Jeez, that must be costing you guys a damn fortune. Don't ya know you're squandering my inheritance?"

"That's why we're doing it, pal," Brian told Russell. "Just to piss you off."

"Actually," Heather chimed, "how much is this little getaway costing? Mary said the Biltmore's gotten ridiculous."

"It has, so what? What's the point of working so hard if I can't spoil the woman I love?"

"Just make sure you bring Mom along, too," Russell quipped.

"Funny guy, huh?" Brian eyed Heather. "Aren't you glad we raised a comedian?"

Spooning her frittata into a serving bowl, Heather gazed at Russell. "You know, babe, you're thirty one now; you might have better luck finding a wife if you cut the comedy."

"Might also be easier if women weren't so fucked."

Later, packing for their overnight escape up the coast to Santa Barbara, Heather asked if it was time to worry about their first-born's hostility toward women.

"It's only been two months since the Julia debacle," Brian reminded. "Of all the guys, why did it have to be Perk?"

Matthew Perkins was Russell's best friend since their days at Franklin Elementary. Even after graduating from Santa Monica High with Russell going off to NYU while Perk headed to UC Davis, they remained close. After they finished graduate school and Perk moved back to LA, they ended up sharing a two-bedroom apartment in Ocean Park. Russell started pursuing his filmmaking career while Perk got a job in hotel management. Working as an Assistant Director on a low-budget horror film, Russell met and fell in love with the lead actress. Six months later, Russell helped Perk find a new roommate so he and Julia could move into a tiny one-bedroom flat on the Venice boardwalk. To Brian and Heather, they seemed like a great match: two passionate artists talking film into the early hours of the morning.

And then, two months ago, Russell came home from a truncated production meeting surprised to find Julia and Perk sharing a bowl of Thai noodles. He was even more surprised to notice that it was his USC shorts and *Conrad for President* T-shirt Perk was wearing; Perk's own white shirt and navy business suit were in a rumpled heap at the foot of Russell's bed.

"I talked to him about therapy," Brian said. "But he's so consumed with trying to pull his movie together he barely has time to eat. He's flying to DC this afternoon; Joey's driving him to the airport. Any idea what Joe's doing later?"

"He's clearly excited about his plans but being very mysterious."

"In that case," Brian laughed, "we should probably have bail money on hand."

Caught in a tangle of traffic on the 10 Freeway, Joey looked to his brother in the passenger seat. With his cellphone smashed to his ear, Russell was shouting at his caller about flakey financiers and immovable deadlines. "If we can't start by Valentine's Day we lose Jennifer and if we lose her, we lose Josh and then we're cooked. It's over. All the shit we've put up with for the last year-and-a-half will have been for no fucking reason. I don't care if it's New Year's-fucking-Eve; they have to make a fucking decision!"

Seconds later, Russell punched his iPhone to end the call. Gazing out the window he gave a frustrated sigh. When Joey sarcastically commented that his brother's business sure sounded like fun, Russell's retort was vehement. "The only reason I do it is because I don't know how to do anything else."

Riding on in silence Joey could hear the acid churning in his brother's stomach. Russell asked Joey where he was headed later.

"Party in Malibu. Some friend of Kyle's. Guess who I'm going with?"

"Rita Hayworth."

"She wishes! No, dude, Sadie Sweet. She finally said yes. Sexy Sadie. Hot damn, right?"

"I guess. As long as you know she'll eventually rip your heart out and stomp it like a bunch of fucking grapes."

Driving up the Pacific Coast Highway, Brian glanced at the crystal-capped waves in the bordering ocean. The sky was clear and cloudless. The temperature was in the upper 60s.

"December 31st. Ya see, Legs, this is why we live in Southern California."

Agreeing, Heather flicked on the BMW's CD player. Brian unconsciously grinned as she sang along to "Lady Madonna." And then, in the next second, they nearly died.

It was Heather's terrified scream that got Brian's attention. Glancing to the right he saw the enormous boulder that had come loose from the cliff side and was bouncing toward them like an earthly asteroid. Acting before thinking, he swerved into the opposite lane and stomped the accelerator. By some miracle, the southbound corridor was clear. The huge rock skipped across the road inches behind Brian's rear bumper. Behind them, the Scotts heard squealing brakes but no metal crunching sounds of a collision. Propelled by its own momentum, the rock tumbled out of sight down the ocean-side embankment. When Brian checked his rearview mirror, it appeared as if everyone on that busy stretch of highway had avoided the potentially fatal catastrophe.

"Let's get to the hotel, lady. I need a drink."

Working on his Macbook as the half-empty plane winged its way to Washington, Russell was growing evermore exasperated. No matter how he tried to juggle the numbers he'd been given by his line producer, he couldn't figure out how they'd accrue the needed one-and-a-half-million dollar budget. He'd already rewritten the script four times, called in every favor, made endless compromises and all but sold his soul to enlist Jennifer Durazo as his leading lady. Having her onboard pulled Josh Alexander in but that meant their million-dollar movie instantly inflated to 1.5. It was that extra $500,000 they still lacked.

The project was designed as Russell's directorial debut. The script, which he'd originally written with a USC classmate seven years earlier, was a romantic comedy set in the nation's capital. At its inception, the climax took place during the annual Cherry Blossom Festival but after having gotten caught up in the excitement surrounding the campaign and election of Barack Obama, Russell relocated the movie's finale to the incoming president's inauguration.

Knowing there was no way he could bring his stars and an entire crew into the middle of such a frenzied event, Russell decided to simply show up at the swearing-in with a single digital camera and an endless supply of *chutzpah*. He'd shoot background footage there and then later insert his actors into a more controlled recreation of the event on a soundstage. The trouble was, even to pull off this modest plan he needed a hefty chunk of his budget in the bank.

It was no accident Russell had booked himself on a plane scheduled to land at Dulles at 11:40 p.m. With no cause to celebrate, he was hoping to be with a gang of strangers in baggage claim when the crystal ball dropped in Times Square.

In their cottage-like room at the Four Seasons Biltmore in the moneyed Santa Barbara enclave of Montecito, Heather was meticulously hanging up her party dress. Brian was in the bathroom unpacking his toiletry kit. As he often did at the end of the year, he got lost in reflecting on all that had happened in the past twelve months.

"You okay in there?" Heather called.

Brian reappeared. "What d'ya say we go downstairs and grab a cocktail?"

One drink turned to three and suddenly the Scotts' plans were out the window. Finishing a second bowl of complimentary Oriental party mix as she sipped her third mojito, Heather smiled at Brian snuggled against her in the bar's leather booth. "I sure don't need a five-course dinner after this."

"We could grab take-out and have a picnic on the beach. You've got your big wool coat, we'll take the extra blanket from the room…get a bottle of wine, sushi – maybe those chocolate cupcakes with the little white squiggles. It's New-Year's-goddamn-Eve, Legs. Let's go nuts."

"Dude, wait: you're cooking? Isn't that dangerous?" Joey's roommate asked.

Standing at the counter in their narrow apartment kitchen, using a rubber mallet to pound the daylights out of a pair of defenseless chicken breasts, Joey grinned. "No, man, it's genius. Every restaurant in town, like, triples their prices tonight so why buy into that shit? See, me doing the cooking is like, 'look, Sexy Sadie, I'm a sensitive male who can whip up a killer chicken parm; how can you not ball my brains out'?"

After prepping the meal, Joey showered and gelled his hair into a perfect messy-casual hipster sweep. He put on skinny jeans with a denim button-down. Sadie Sweet rang the buzzer downstairs as Joey zipped up his battered brown boots. She was wearing a tight black mini-dress and a frayed jean jacket. Joey told her she looked hot and kissed her cheek. With electronic jazz pouring from his iPod he handed her a glass of red wine. She raved about how wonderful the dinner smelled as Joey slid garlic bread into the broiler.

Splayed on the bed in his room at the Red Roof Inn on H Street, Russell was staring at, but not really watching, the flat screen where some teen queen was prancing across a stage in Times Square. A blast of the Beatles' "I'm a Loser" ringtone trumpeted from his iPhone. He squinted at the caller ID: Lazlo.

Russell turned to the bedside clock. It was 12:41 a.m., 9:41 p.m. in Los Angeles. Russell braced himself. Lazlo Polchek was the line producer on their upcoming film. If he was calling at this hour on a holiday evening, the news he was delivering was either very good or very bad. Russell knew from experience it wouldn't be anything in between.

"I am interrupting?" Lazlo asked in his thick Eastern European accent.

"Lazlo, I'm alone in my hotel room watching TV. What's going on?"

"Distributor: out. They call this afternoon. I didn't vant to tell you before you took off; vas afraid you'd jump from plane. I know this mean ve don't have distributor but ve will. Zoon. Have faith. It is already New Year where you are, yes? So – new year, new start. No'ting to vorry about. Get sleep. I call you Monday."

On a blanket abutting a sandbank ten yards from the inky ocean, Russell's parents watched the neon waves reflect the moonlight. Taking a long pull of Merlot from the bottle, Heather touched her head to Brian's. Although a few folks were strolling the narrow path bordering the road far behind them, there were no other people in view on the beach. Heather was wrapped in her calf-length wool coat; Brian flicked up the collar on his leather duster but it was the four cocktails each and the shared three-quarters of the bottle of wine that was really keeping the chill at bay.

"Wanna do it?" Brian asked with a puckish grin.

"Out here? No. God no. I might be drunk but I'm not insane."

Brian asked where her sense of adventure had gone. Heather quipped she'd left it back in the mid-'70s. Brian continued to beg and cajole; Heather reminded him they were old enough to be grandparents.

"I ate cupcakes with the shelf-life of enriched uranium tonight; why not double down and go for broke?"

Readjusting the blanket in the nest he'd sculpted in the sand below the protective screen of waving reeds, Brian yanked off his coat and beamed at his wife kneeling nearby. He sounded as excited as a virgin frat boy. "This is so fun!"

Taking off his shirt, he rose onto his knees, waddled to Heather and pulled her close. They hugged, kissed. He unbuckled his belt, flopped onto his butt and tossed his pants aside. Dropping onto his back Brian pulled Heather on top of him. As their frenzied kissing resumed, she deposited her heavy coat onto the blanket. Brian hiked up her dress and gingerly worked her cotton panties down to her thighs. A moment later, with Heather on top, they became linked.

"What in the name of Jesus H. Christ do ya think you're doing?"

Snapped from her bucking reverie, Heather let out a startled scream. Brian froze like a victim of Midas's touch.

"You're on a public beach, for the love of Mike."

Heather molded herself into Brian and closed her eyes, refusing to look up. Brian let his lids slowly rise to take in the looming police officer. "Now I've seen everything. Fornicating senior citizens. A living Viagra ad minus the bathtubs."

Brian quietly retorted, "Actually, I'm pretty sure the bathtub thing is Cialis."

Standing in a stranger's Malibu kitchen mixing a pair of potent rum-and-Cokes, Joey felt his phone vibrate in his pocket. Pulling it out, he was startled to see his father's face on the incoming call screen. 2:32 a.m. Even through the fog of rum he realized this couldn't be good. "Dad, what's going on? You sound freaked."

"Mom and I are in jail. Up in Santa Barbara. You need to come bail us out."

Feeling a warm, curvy body pressing into his back, Joey turned to find a drunken Sadie Sweet nuzzling his neck. Joey held up a finger in a plea for her indulgence. "What the hell did you do?"

"We, ah…see – we were making love on the beach. That alone wouldn't have been so bad; it's, your mother has this thing with authority figures. Anyway, the cop busted us for public lewdness or some crap and was gonna let us off with a warning but then he made a stupid crack about us being old enough to know better and added that nobody needed to see your mother's 'saggy old white ass bouncing in the moonlight.' As you can guess, she wasn't pleased…so she slapped him. Then he went for her, I jumped between 'em…who knows what went on; it got totally out of hand and here we are, which is why we need you to come get us."

"I can't drive, Dad. I'm trashed. And…I'm…I'm with a date."

"Joey, you really want us sitting in a cell in the Santa Barbara sheriff's station all night? It's humiliating. Oh, by the way, Dylan Klosterman says hi."

"What the fuck?"

"He's on the cot above me in the drunk tank. I think a couple more of your old frat brothers are here, too."

"Whatever you do, don't tell them what you're in for or this whole thing'll be on Facebook by morning." Brian urged Joey to focus. "Don't know what more I can tell ya, Pops. I'm in no shape to drive so you're just gonna have to chill. I'll be there by noon – at the absolute latest. Happy New Year!"

Being led back to his holding cell, Brian looked through the bars to a disheveled Heather in the adjoining tank. "He's not coming 'til tomorrow. Too drunk to drive."

"Wonderful," Heather replied in a crepe-flat tone. "Nice to know one of us is exercising good judgment tonight."

"Hey, you're the one who lost her temper."

"That pig had no right to talk to me that way. I'm at the gym six days a week. My ass might be white, but it sure as hell isn't saggy!"

The drunks in both the men's and the women's cells, most of them closer in age to the Scotts' sons, broke into raucous applause. Down but not out, Heather stood up and took a bow.

Pulling up his parka hood to cover his stinging ears, Russell couldn't fathom why anybody lived in this climate by choice. Making his way down the Capitol steps heading for Independence Avenue, the temperature on the first day of the New Year was in the mid-20s. The icy wind chapped Russell's lips and bit at the corners of his eyes. His digital camera was buried deep in his coat pocket to keep the lens from cracking. The next distracted step he took wound up dumping him onto his butt on the frigid sidewalk.

A hung-over yet high-stepping Joey arrived at the Santa Barbara Sheriff's station shortly after 11:30 a.m. armed with the emergency Mastercard his parents kept hidden in their pantry. Taking one look at him, the desk sergeant gave a lopsided grin. "Come to retrieve Dr. Scott and his bride? Ya got the same dimple as your old man. Lucky for all of yiz, Officer Friedel woke up in a generous mood and dropped the most serious charges. Trust me, it's easier to move on from a few misdemeanor counts of public lewdness than to try to get beyond an assault on a police officer."

After a mound of paperwork and a pair of four hundred dollars fines, the Scotts were free.

With Joey at the wheel, they drove to the Biltmore to retrieve their belongings. Entering the room, Brian exhaled. "You know what really burns my ass? Paying 600 bucks for a room we didn't even sleep in."

"Hey, Russell tried to warn you not to squander our inheritance."

"Why are you so darn perky today?" Heather asked Joey.

"You mean aside from the fact that I can hold this bail run over your heads for years? I am the man who welcomed 2009 with – in the Biblical sense, wink-wink – the luscious Sadie Sweet. My number one Fox hunt for years; now the minx is mine."

Before Russell went to D.C., Brian urged him to look up his old friend Gina. He told Russell about her life at the FBI, reminding him of her integral part in heading off the planned terror attacks of 2001. He pitched her as a vital resource during Russell's location scout and mentioned that she and her lawyer husband knew all the city's power players. In his current people-hating state, Russell wasn't sure he could get it up to make contact.

He paused on the bottom step of the Lincoln Memorial to take an incoming call. Lazlo informed him that, even though it was a holiday, he had just gotten off the phone with a friend who had a solid 'in' with the president of production at Guy at Work Films. "I give him whole spiel, told him vhy dis is perfect GAW movie. Heading to him now vit complete package: script, board, budget. He vill read tonight; if he like, he give strong recommend. Boom, bang, bam."

Russell praised his producer for his dedication and urged Lazlo to take the rest of the day off to be with his family. Lazlo promised he would – right after he made calls to the principle actors to wish them a Happy New Year from Russell and himself.

By the afternoon of January second, while Russell sat on the toilet in his room at the Red Roof Inn, the Guy at Work president of production was reading his script. An answer was due by the end of the day. A 'yes' meant they'd stay on track and have the necessary funds to do their guerilla-style shoot at the Inauguration. A 'no' would cause the pieces of their package to tumble away like discarded debris from the space station.

At 7:15 that evening, Russell's phone finally rang. Lazlo was calling.

3

GINA HAD NO IDEA how she could have given birth to the planet's most willful child. "Ryan, I put your hat on for a reason. Either put it back on or we're not going anywhere. Do you want your ears to snap off and get lost in the snow?"

"Ears can't do that," Ryan scoffed.

Zipping the puffy black parka Gina had gotten him for Hanukah, Noah chimed in: "Please listen to your mother and put your hat on. Or we're going to cancel your party, take back your presents and you can spend your birthday sitting in your room wondering why you're such a defiant little—"

"—boy," Gina finished in a preemptive strike.

"Can we please go? I'm burning up!" begged six and a half year old Danielle.

Pivoting, Gina and Noah burst out laughing. With a knit cap pulled below her eyebrows, her knee length coat zipped to her chin and her neck swaddled in a red scarf, their daughter looked like the Michelin Man with flushed-pink cheeks.

Tugging Ryan's hat onto his head Gina barked: "Everybody out. Let's go."

Scrambling out of the Metro at Union Station on the first day of 2009, corralling her children with Noah beside her, Gina was feeling truly blessed. In the seven-plus years since she'd been intimately involved in heading off the most potentially lethal domestic terror attack in US history, Gina's life had changed radically. Examining the bone-chilling details of the upended attack gave her a new understanding of life's fragility. She and Noah agreed right then that they were ready to try to become parents.

Less than ten weeks after the press conference in San Diego that exposed the diabolical plot, Gina and Noah learned their first child was on the way. Danielle debuted on an unusually chilly June day in 2002. With forty firmly in her sightline, Gina was pregnant again nine months later. Ryan came into the world, willful from the start, on January 2, 2004.

For Gina, who'd been on a single-minded career path since she was ten, the adjustment to motherhood was difficult. Luckily, Noah was a natural, calm and confident from the start. There were times when his competence secretly irked Gina. She didn't understand why her spouse was a better 'mother' than she was.

Ultimately, it was sheer exhaustion that taught Gina how to embrace her new role. After six months of constant self-doubt, she began to unwittingly fall asleep, day or night, every time Dani breastfed. Gina would snap back awake to find her plump, serene offspring clamped to her breast, deep asleep, warm and safe.

Gina reduced her hours at the FBI and stepped away from a few of her more high-pressure assignments. She started putting in only forty weekly hours instead of sixty. Noah, too, reduced his caseload. The Zagers had many more evenings and weekends together, allowing them to discover something amazing about their life: they really liked it.

Standing at the base of the Capitol steps, Gina and Noah looked at the half-constructed inaugural platform taking shape. Dani and Ryan scurried around trying to make snowballs from the feathery powder that had fallen earlier.

"Honestly," Gina asked Noah, "did you ever imagine a day when this country would elect a black president?"

"I'm still afraid we'll wake up to find T-bag Tanner being sworn in again."

"Bite your tongue. Lucky for us the only thing scarier than a skinny black freshman senator with a Muslim name was the prospect of a Norman Tanner second term."

On the other side of the country where it was a balmy sixty-five degrees, David sat on his Palm Springs patio, holding his throbbing head. Eying him with a palpable lack of sympathy, Cyrus groused, "I'll never understand why every idiot who barely takes a drink all year feels compelled to act like a teenager on New Year's Eve."

David tried to blame it on their friend Mitchy but Cyrus wasn't having it. He told David he was old enough to just say no.

"I'm also old enough to be dead, so be glad I'm still here and get off my back."

Eying the afternoon light dancing across the San Bernardino Mountains, David asked if Mitchy was coming to dinner, admitting he'd been too loaded the previous night to remember her reply to his invitation.

Five years earlier, six months after he retired as the senior-most member of the USC history department, David longed to be living someplace that didn't require him to jump in the car just to buy a newspaper; he was ready for a smaller, simpler life. Since it was his nature to reject any idea that wasn't his own, when Cyrus first suggested Palm Springs, David balked.

"The summer's there are a literal living hell."

Cyrus quietly insisted that just this once, it might be nice for him to get his way. On Christmas Day '03, they were in Cy's ten-year-old Volvo following the moving truck down the 10 Freeway to their new home on Tamarisk Road.

While Cyrus prepared chicken curry for New Year's Day dinner with David and their pal Michelle "Mitchy" Pelico, David was on the phone with Gina, trying to convince her he wasn't as hung over as he sounded. Refusing to believe him, she expressed concern for her mother. "You know she and Dad were supposed to come for Ryan's birthday but cancelled. Debbie says Mom doesn't look well and she *never* says stuff like that."

"Well, dolly, your mother's no spring chicken. And this getting old business? It ain't for sissies, trust me." Before they hung up, Gina made David promise he'd try to convince Lisa to see her doctor. "She's so great at taking care of the world but she never takes care of herself."

Shoveling in a forkful of chicken curry, Mitchy Pelico looked across the table to David and Cyrus. Clearing her throat she affected her best stand-up comedienne tones. "Did you hear about the Little Dutch Boy who stuck his fingers in the dike? He promptly got the shit beat out of him by her girlfriend."

David laughed. Cyrus grimaced. "It's a bit crude."

"I'm doing comedy for a bunch of drunk gays at 11:30 on a Saturday night. If I'm not crude, they'll have my ass."

The banter-filled camaraderie binding David and Cyrus to Mitch had its origins in their first day in Palm Springs. When Cyrus and David arrived in the desert, Mitchy was a sixty-year-old fireplug working in a local hardware store plumbing department. Despite the fact that it'd been fifteen years and forty pounds since she retired from the US Marines, she never lost her military bearing or clipped cadence.

David and Cyrus were in search of a flapper for their guest toilet when Mitch approached. Not yet acclimated to their new environment, David wore a shirt and tie; Cyrus was in pressed Dockers with a tucked in Polo shirt. Mitchy told them they looked like black Gilligan and the Professor and implored them to loosen up; in that instant, a fast and furious friendship was born.

On Ryan's birthday evening, Gina and Noah took the kids to T.G.I. Friday's. The wait staff harmonized through "Happy Birthday," Ryan had a blue balloon tied to his chair and, after the meal, got a free thick slab of Chocolate Peanut Butter Pie with a blazing sparkler on top. What more could a newly minted five-year-old want?

Standing in her front hallway a little before 10:00 the next morning, with Ryan bundled up at her side, Gina eyed Noah and Dani at the den coffee table blanketed with art supplies. "We're off to pick up the pizzas and birthday cake."

Noah stayed focused on drawing a perfect nose-less Mickey Mouse on a sheet of poster board. Dani announced: "Me and Daddy are making Pin-the-nose-on-Mickey, then we'll blow up the balloons!"

Forty minutes later, searching through CDs in anticipation of the afternoon's game of Musical Chairs, Noah was jarred by a shriek so startling he was certain rouge coyotes were shredding his son. Bolting into the foyer, he found Gina bearing a stack of pizzas and a guilty expression. Ryan's tear-stained mug was contorted in agony. "My Goofy cake. It's all ruined!" He launched himself to the floor, kicking and wailing. Gina stepped over him to set the pizzas down. Noah followed.

"I'm an idiot," Gina said. "I don't know what I was thinking. The cake was in the back with the rest of the groceries, I had to make a sharp turn on Canal because some moron in an Escalade — have I told you how much I hate those things — was on her phone; she would've hit us if I didn't swerve. The fruit punch flew out of the bag and landed in the middle of the cake like an A-bomb!"

"But everything's okay? You didn't have a wreck? Nobody got hurt?"

"The only casualty is the cake. But according to your son, he'd be happier if I'd gotten killed. Noah, *I mutilated his cake*! I've ruined his birthday party. He hates me."

Coming into her parents' condominium in Encino, Debbie stopped when she spied her mother sitting in her bathrobe at the kitchen table. "Mom, you're yellow." Lisa tried to deflect her; Debbie persisted. "Don't blow me off, you're yellow!

Where's Dad? Does he think you look jaundiced?"

"I could light myself on fire and do a naked can-can and he wouldn't notice. Now c'mon, sweetheart, let me make you something to eat."

Returning from the market with a multitude of cake decorating tools, Noah rolled up his sleeves, summoned his inner forensic surgeon and set to work. Armed with Krazy glue to mend the broken plastic clubhouse, plus multiple tubes of gel and icing, he worked on the mangled Goofy cake until moments before the guests arrived.

Covering Ryan's still-swollen eyes, Noah steered his son to the edge of the table and whipped his hands away like a magician flourishing his cape. As Gina and Dani beamed, Ryan gawked in disbelief. "Wow, Daddy. It's perfect!"

When Martin got back from his country club lunch, Debbie followed him into the den; Lisa was upstairs napping. "Something's wrong, Dad. Can you honestly tell me you don't think Mom looks like a banana?"

Martin froze looking so vulnerable it broke Debbie's heart. His tears crested like the afternoon tide. "Oh no, you see it, too? What in God's name are we going to do?"

Wrangling fourteen five-year-olds high on a sugar rush from the resurrected Goofy cake, trying to calm them down long enough to explain the rules of Musical Chairs, Gina was sure she was trapped in The Never Ending Birthday Party.

"After this we have Pin-the-Nose-on-Mickey, then he can open presents," Noah said, "and then if it's still not five, I say we pop in a DVD and start drinking."

At her desk in the FBI building before 8:00 on Monday morning, Gina was relishing the quiet. She scanned the morning briefing papers, read the latest threats against the incoming president and digested the updated security plans for the inauguration. Margaret came in with Gina's daily tall black coffee. They talked about their respective holidays, caught up on office scuttlebutt and reviewed the day's agenda.

As they were finishing, Gina's colleague Priscilla Ogilvey appeared, looking tanned and relaxed from ten days in Aruba. She told Gina a friend on the transition team had gotten her two tickets to the inauguration, but Priscilla just learned she was being dispatched to Kabul; she wondered if Gina and Noah would want to attend the swearing-in in her place. Gina was thrilled.

Studying a report on a possible terrorist plot to set off a bomb at the foot of the Capitol steps during the inauguration, (an action that could, if successful, take out most of the federal government,) Gina was jarred by the buzz of her phone. Margaret said David was on the line. His stiff tone alarmed Gina immediately. "Your mother saw Doctor Bonham this morning – it's not good."

That evening, after spending a distracted afternoon trying to absorb the shock of David's news, Gina was in her bedroom with Noah. "No one escapes pancreatic cancer. You die, usually very quickly. I have to get out there. I need to be with her. But I also need to cover the kids, I need – I didn't get to tell you: Priscilla gave us tickets to the inauguration but now…who knows if I'll even be in town? But I can't be gone indefinitely. What about you, the kids, my job? Maybe I should wait."

"Until what? She'll only get sicker. Honey, it's all out of our control. She might go down hill then rally…who knows about any of it? The most important thing is to do what's best for you so you don't have any regrets. Please, just this once, let yourself be the priority."

4

FINDING HER PARENTS on the den couch on a chilly January afternoon, Sierra waited to capture their attention. Her mother was flipping through a magazine while her father was fixed on the TV. The Ravens were battling the Dolphins in an AFC playoff game; Chris was riveted. Even though Libby's eyes were on the passing magazine pages, Sierra knew her mom's mind was elsewhere.

"Hello? Anybody alive in here?" Libby and Chris returned to Earth. Sierra took a tentative step closer. "Have you guys thought any more about what we discussed at breakfast?"

Chris scooted next to his wife and patted the couch on the opposite side. "Ravens are winning; wanna watch with us?"

"No. I want to know if you're gonna let me go to Washington."

Releasing a pent-up sigh, Libby closed the magazine to meet Sierra's unrelenting gaze. "You'd be missing the first few days of classes, you said."

"So?"

Chris chimed in, "It's the first week of your last semester; why should you be in DC when you belong in Austin?"

"To witness history, Dad. It'll be amazing and totally educational. Missing this once-in-a-lifetime opportunity? No bueno."

"It'll be a circus; it probably won't even be safe. What if there's a terrorist attack?"

"What if?" Sierra scoffed. "It could happen anywhere. Any time. Should we all just crawl in a hole and hide? Ya know, if you don't let me go, the terrorists win."

With his focus back on their fifty-two inch plasma flat screen, Chris growled, "Can we do this later, please? Not that anyone cares, but I'm trying to watch the game."

Throwing up a hand up in exasperation, Sierra stormed out.

Libby sighed. "Maybe we should let her go, Chris. Meeting the Kennedys was a highlight of my parents' lives."

"She knows we have no money to contribute to this excursion, right? I still can't figure out how we'll cover her tuition this semester."

"She says she saved every penny she made at the restaurant over break, plus they'll stay with Gilly's family friends. I mean, she is twenty-one. And it's Sierra we're talking about. I'd be much more terrified if it was the twins."

"Amen. Get those two on a bus to DC and the whole country would have to worry. Christ, remember when they nearly sailed off your mother's roof in that homemade go-cart?"

"I still have nightmares. I just thank the good Lord my father's spirit saved them."

"Lib, it was the string of Christmas lights wrapped around the axle that kept them from flying off the roof."

"I know: Christmas lights that were still up at the end of *April* because my father never got around to taking them down before he passed. We're talking about a man who every other year had those lights put away on New Year's Day."

Across town, Kenny was peeling shrimp for the gumbo he was making while Bonnie sat nearby doing the Sunday crossword puzzle. Kenny's wife Molly was at the mall with Jimmy, buying him a wool topcoat before he returned to Case Western Reserve. Having spent his first eighteen years in the mild winters of central Texas, Jimmy had not been prepared for the intensity of the frigid Cleveland temperatures he'd endured as a freshman. Now, older and wiser, he announced he wasn't going back without all the cold weather gear he could convince his parents to buy him.

Looking up from her puzzle, grappling to find a ten-letter word for cutlery, Bonnie stared at the back of Kenny's head. "I'm worried about your sister. She seems stressed to me. I don't know if it's the boys or something with Chris—"

"It's the restaurant."

"Why, what has she said? You two have talked about this?"

"Mom, things are tough. Everywhere. When the economy's in the crapper the first thing people do is stop going out to eat. That's why they started closing on Sundays and Mondays, to save on staff. She hasn't said anything because she doesn't want to worry you. I'm sure they'll work it out."

"My stars," Bonnie said, "they've poured their heart and soul into that place. Maybe I should start working there."

"Oh yeah, that's what you need – to be a seventy seven year old waitress!"

"I could hostess. Work three, four nights a week. They wouldn't need to pay me; it's the least I can do. You'll see with Jimmy; you never stop worrying about your kids."

On cue, Jimmy burst in from the garage laden down with shopping bag. Molly was close behind. Eying his father, Jimmy laughed. "Good thing you got a bonus this year!"

In his decrepit downtown Dallas apartment, Jimmy's cousin Patrick was guzzling a Lone Star and rolling a joint as he waited for his twin brother to arrive.

With his head shorn to brown stubble, three small silver hoops in each ear and a tattoo of black ivy crawling up the side of his neck, Patrick cut an intimidating figure. He kept a set of weights at the foot of his futon bed and pumped for an hour three times a week. His arms were huge, his stomach was flat; he and his twin were six feet tall. Eddie's hair was more grown out, his biceps less developed and the only tattoo he sported was a cigar-smoking raven on his right bicep. Everyone called Patrick "The Bad Twin," a nickname he despised.

When Eddie arrived a little after six, Patrick's face lit like a Chinese lantern. "Dude, I'm pretty sure I met the world's most gullible chick and I came up with the all-time greatest plan but I need your help. Gimme your coat and put this on."

Patrick snagged a black zip-up hoodie from the floor; he tossed it to Eddie who brought the jacket to his nose and took a deep whiff. "It smells like shit."

"You smell like shit. Just put it on and shut the fuck up."

As Eddie reluctantly obeyed, Patrick removed his earrings and crammed them into a pocket. Snatching a wool cap from the couch, he yanked it down to cover his bristly hair and pierced lobes before slipping on his twin's motocross jacket. With a sweep of his hand, Patrick ushered Eddie out the door.

In a back booth of the Denny's downtown, Eddie sat with the hood up on his brother's sweatshirt, eyes downcast as he picked at a lukewarm chicken potpie and eavesdropped on the conversation in the abutting booth.

Lola, the girl sitting with her back to Eddie, arrived to rendezvous with Patrick. In Pat's own delicate phrasing they'd "met at a lame ass party last night and fucked like rabbits."

"So…'member you said you'd give anything to get rid of that hideous dragon tattoo your loser ex-boyfriend talked you into?" Eddie heard his brother ask. Patrick slapped a label-less jar onto the table. "Got your miracle right here. A hundred bucks for the whole jar and that tattoo'll be history, no expensive lasers; no painful burn-off. Slather this gunk on, wait five minutes, adios dragon."

"That can't be true!" Lola exclaimed with a protesting giggle.

At the next table, Eddie fought to keep from losing it. Patrick worked a little longer to sell his story and then, acting as if he'd just gotten a brilliant idea, he told the naïf he'd be willing to demonstrate the product's potency before she handed over a nickel. He said his black ivy tattoo had started to seem tired and he'd happily remove it to illustrate the cream's effectiveness.

"I'll go do it in the bathroom, 'kay? Ya know, so the smell doesn't bother anybody and whatevs. You got the hundred bucks if you decide you want the jar?" Lola told him she could go to the ATM down the street. "Sweet. Back in five."

Patrick disappeared into the bathroom. Perfectly content, Lola ate her cherry pie. Totally off the oblivious girl's radar, Eddie slid out of his booth. Reunited in the men's room, the twins stripped to their underwear and exchanged clothes. Eddie tugged on Patrick's wool cap to hide his longer hair and took the white jar from his brother. A moment later he dropped into Patrick's seat and offered Lola a radiant grin. Gazing at her, he pivoted to show off his unadorned neck.

"Check it out. No mas tattoo."

Lola's eyes were cylinders of disbelief. "Wow, like total magic, right? And you'll really sell it to me for only a hundred bucks? That's so generous!"

Eddie lowered his voice. "It's bootleg from Mexico. If I wanted to be a dick, I could probably sell it on e-Bay for a grand."

Within the hour, Patrick and Eddie were back in Patrick's apartment getting annihilated on the premium tequila they'd purchased with a chunk of the evening's spoils.

Eying her laptop screen, Sierra gaped at her friend Gilly. "It's a bus, not a rocket ship! How can a round trip ticket cost so much? Are they joking? It is so not fair!"

"My 'rentals would kick in the extra bucks if I begged; how 'bout yours?"

"I don't dare ask. The restaurant's struggling, they're way stressed; all they talk about is how broke they are."

"What if we blew off the bus and hitchhiked?"

"So we can get raped and killed and chopped into fish chum? Pasadena."

"Then how about we post an ad online? Tons of kids must be going to the inauguration; some have to be driving. This is the Obama Age, right? All the freaks will be too busy making big-eared voodoo dolls to go to Washington. I know the perfect ad: two hot chicks, with belts both black and chastity, seek a ride from Dallas to DC to celebrate Hope and Change."

Returning from driving Bonnie home, Kenny entered his darkened kitchen and stopped short. Jimmy was sitting on the floor across the room, back against the refrigerator, legs outstretched. He was methodically tearing matches from their paper pack; he lit one after another, flinging them into the cat's metal water dish at his feet. As each match met its mark, the tiny flame died with a rhythmic sizzle. Aware of Kenny gawking at him, Jimmy continued his ritual without pause.

"What the heck are you doing?"

"I like the sound they make when they hit the water."

Eying the two dozen matches floating in the dish, Kenny said, "Looks like you been at it a while."

One match missed the dish, landed on the linoleum and went out.

"Let's not burn the house down, okay?" Kenny cautioned. "Is Mom upstairs?"

"I guess." Jimmy lit one more match and hurled it forward. The sizzling whisper of fire meeting water followed. "I don't think I'm going back to school. I hate that weather. Plus, I could teach most of my classes better than the professors."

"If you quit, your scholarship goes away, ya know. For good. It's not like you can take a semester off, decide you made a mistake and get it back. They were very clear about that, Jim. The money's on the table only as long as you're a fulltime student."

Another errant match hit the floor but didn't immediately flicker out. Before Kenny could lunge to stomp it into submission it died of natural causes. "Could you quit doing that, please?"

"It relaxes me."

"Yeah, but I'm the guy who pays the fire insurance around here so knock it off."

Jimmy petulantly slapped the matchbook down. Kenny moved to the refrigerator Jimmy was blocking. "Want a beer? I'm thinking we need to talk."

Jimmy scooted to one side to clear the refrigerator door. "I'm good."

"If you drop out you'll have to get a job, ya know. You're not coming home to lie around waiting to 'find yourself.' We'll expect you to get to work."

"In this economy? Yeah, right. Who knows if I could even get a job?"

"All I'm saying is the free ride ends if you're not in school."

Kenny grabbed a beer and pried the cap off. He took a long slug. "What happened, Jim? You're such a crackerjack student. I thought you were lovin' Case."

"Honestly? I'm fried. I just don't think I can get it up to sit there and read and take notes and listen to all the blah, blah, blah."

"This won't make your mother happy. Are you sure you're not just having a bad day?"

Kenny felt painfully aware that, as a father who should know best, he was coming up short. He drained his beer. "What do you say we continue this tomorrow?"

Leaving the room, Kenny heard the snap of another igniting match.

Sierra and Gilly sat in Starbucks as Sierra's fingers tickled her laptop keys; she logged onto their account to check the latest responses to their "need-a-ride" posting. An earlier batch of replies personified the girls' worst fears: "How about staying right here in Dallas to ride my lap?" asked one. "Wanna take a trip on my personal pogo stick?" asked another. "Manage-a-trois a plus!"

Logging onto their page, Sierra told Gilly this was going to be their day. She could feel it. Finding two new messages, she excitedly wagged her crossed fingers. The first reply was from three long-distance runners from Texas Tech; they included their non-threatening photo in team shirts and shorts. They were so lean and gangly Gilly guessed they probably didn't weigh three hundred pounds combined. "They're kinda cute — in a take-'em-home-to-granny sort'a way."

"Pasty runners?" Sierra replied. "No bueno. What if they're cross-country vampires?"

The other message was from a pair of married graduate students at Texas Christian University in nearby Fort Worth. Their email was packed with so much detail that by the time Sierra finished reading the dense paragraphs out loud, she and Gilly felt like Dennis and Rachel were their new best friends.

"Wow," Sierra said, "if they give up this many deets in an email, imagine what we'll know by the time we get to DC! I never knew you could *write* perky. Jesus freaks for sure."

"Texas Christian U. What was your first clue? But the good news is they're married so we won't have to worry about getting hit on."

"Unless they're jaunty Mormons shopping for sister-wives."

Jimmy's decision to quit school created a ridge of high-pressure that hung over the Callahan house all week. While Kenny kept hoping his son would snap out it, Molly was focused on their boy's mental health. "Remember Geoffrey Friedlander? He was a high-achiever like Jimmy. I'm not saying Jimmy's suicidal but you never know. I mean, is he talking to you? Because he's sure not talking to me. I'm lucky if I get a good morning and a goodnight."

"I don't understand why he couldn'ta decided this before we spent 500 bucks on a new winter wardrobe," Kenny grumbled.

"Truth be told, I think it was the clothes that pushed him over the edge. Facing the reality of fighting his way across campus in a blizzard again. I asked if he'd see a shrink; he said he didn't get how hearing his parents think he's crazy is supposed help his depression."

Reacting to the irate pounding on his apartment door, Patrick hissed, "Dude, don't answer it."

Eying Patrick cowering on his belly on the floor like a Mafia capo taken to the mattresses Eddie asked, "Who's out there, the Big Bad Wolf?"

"It's that crazy chick Lola. Tattoo-removal girl. She's pisseder-than-pissed and wants her hundred bucks back but fuck that. Losers-weepers."

"I can hear you in there! Open up or I'm calling the police!"

Sitting upright, Patrick tugged on one of the silver hoops in his ear. "Dude, can she do that? Can she get my ass arrested for fraud or some shit?"

Later, lowering the volume on the Ravens-Titans division championship game, Eddie whispered, "It's been quiet for a while. D'ya think she died?"

"If I'm lucky. What if it's a trap? She could be laying low like some Incredible Bitch Hulk!"

"Incredible Bitch Hulk? Dude, that's brilliant! You have'ta write the comic book. I'm fully serious. Make a zillion bucks, return her money: a win-win for everybody."

Patrick stiffly pushed to his feet, crept to the door and put an eye to the peephole. No one was there. With the care of a

Swiss watchmaker, he disengaged the lock. As he gingerly opened the door, he heard a lunging thump followed by a hissing spray. Reeling, blinded by a cascade of burning tears, Patrick felt Lola's wild energy gallop past him as she screamed, "Fuck you, you fucking fucker! Die blind!"

Patrick slammed the door and crashed into Eddie who'd come to his aid. "What'd she do? What happened?"

"Pepper spray or some shit. Help me, man, I'm dying."

For the next forty minutes, Patrick stood at the kitchen sink splashing a stream of cold water into his blazing eyes.

"I hope the damn tequila was worth it," Eddie said from the couch as he played a noisy video game. "Guess this gives a whole new meaning to blind rage."

"Mother," Sierra said as she and Gilly stood in the Dallas Greyhound parking lot wearing long down coats and stuffed backpacks, "we'll be careful, we'll be fine. It'll be amazing."

"Just promise you'll keep your cell phones on. And call as soon as you get there. You both have scarves and gloves? The weatherman says it's going to be brutal."

Sierra laughed in disbelief, "Mom…are you crying?"

Libby sniffed back her tears and gave a quiet chuckle. "It's just…you getting to do this… thinking about my parents meeting JFK…"

"Well, I doubt if we'll exactly be sitting down to tea with Barry and Michelle but it's still super cool. Thanks for letting us go."

"That's all we do from the day you're born," Chris said. "We let you go."

"Stop or you'll make me cry! You two need to leave now, okay? I love you."

"We'll wait 'til you're on the bus," Libby said.

A jolt of panic hit Sierra's heart. "No. Please. We're gonna use the restroom, maybe grab a snack. We really appreciate the ride but now it would be great if you'd go and let us do our thing. Please," Sierra said sweetly but firmly.

Surrendering, Libby grabbed her daughter and hung on. When her parents were finally out of hearing-range, Sierra turned to Gilly. "Geez-Louise, I didn't think they'd ever leave."

"I was *freaking out*. What if they were still here when the Jesus freaks pulled up? The jig totally wouldda been up! Wait, is that them?" Gilly pointed across the lot to a newly washed-and-waxed red Buick LaSabre.

Sierra pulled out the printed email bearing a photo of Dennis and Rachel's car. "Time to say 'hola' to our new best buds!"

The minute they were on the interstate, Mr. Prepared announced the game plan and trip rules. It was clear he was the commander; the three women were his lieutenants.

"It's 12:57 p.m. We have twenty-four hours of drive time ahead, factoring in gas stops and meal breaks. Everyone will empty their bladder at each scheduled stop to avoid undue delays. Rachel and I will be the primary drivers, with no shift lasting more than three hours to avoid unsafe fatigue. If need arises, we will call upon one of you to fill in. The goal is to arrive in the greater metropolitan DC area tomorrow evening allowing ample recuperation time before the Big Day Tuesday. We will meet at a designated location at six a.m. Wednesday to begin our return journey. If all goes as planned, Rachel and I will drop you ladies in Ft. Worth to catch your bus to UT early Thursday. Comments or questions?"

Gilly stayed silent. Sierra saluted.

By the time they had dinner in Memphis, Gilly and Sierra hadn't spoken more than ten sentences each but, if quizzed, could divulge every tiny detail of Rachel and Dennis's lives.

"We originally thought we'd wait until after graduate school to get married but we were so in love," Rachel sighed, "and we made a promise to God that we wouldn't succumb to temptation until we were husband and wife…"

"But we sure did succumb on our wedding night!" Dennis chortled.

"You hush up now," Rachel blushed.

The sun was peeking over the horizon, Gilly and Sierra were deep asleep in the back seat and Rachel was at the wheel. In the copilot chair, Dennis's head rested against the frost-coated side window. He was deep in a dream about an elderly female Republican Senator dancing in a cone-shaped bra when an urgent voice pierced his revelry. "Papa! Wake up!"

Cracking one eye, Dennis saw the windshield before him shrouded in smoke.

Rachel managed to guide the belching vehicle off the northbound I-81 onto a side street. Returning to consciousness as she felt the car jerk to a halt, Sierra eyed her cell phone: 5:42 a.m. Poking Gilly who reluctantly woke up, Sierra pointed to the front of the car where a geyser of hissing steam spewed from under the hood. Banks of plowed snow lined the roadside.

Rachel was trying not to cry. "I didn't do anything, Papa! I promise!"

"Looks to me like we overheated. Might'a blown a hose."

Gilly had an urge to make a crude joke but refrained. She pressed a hand to her window; it was freezing outside. "Where are we?"

Being told they were in Virginia, Sierra asked, "You guys have Auto Club, right?"

"Of course." Dennis pulled out his wallet, rooting through the slots for his card. Rachel waited for him to realize what she already knew. As his fingers gripped the AAA plastic, the dime dropped. "This is one of the bills we didn't pay, isn't it? Our card's expired." Rachel nodded. Dennis closed his eyes and counted to ten. "Let us bow our heads and pray."

Myrt's Family Restaurant in Lynchburg became the scene of an unanticipated, not-so-civil war between the college coeds and their new/now former best friends. Although no actual blood was shed, for a time it appeared as if it could go either way.

Dennis hired a tow truck to haul them into town to get the LaSabre assessed. After checking under the hood, the driver saw that the radiator had sprung a major leak and would need to be patched or replaced. He estimated they were looking at a three to five hundred dollar repair bill. Because the mechanics didn't report to work until 8:00 a.m. and it wasn't even 7:00, the quartet retreated to Myrt's to escape the bitter cold.

After they ordered hot breakfasts to help dispel the embedded chill, Dennis offered Sierra and Gilly his most Christian smile. "I hope y'all aren't going to mind splitting the cost of the repairs." Sierra asked why they would be expected to do that. "That was our deal. We agreed to bring you to Washington in exchange for sharing expenses."

"Yeah," Gilly snapped. "GAS money. We never signed on for more than that."

Rachel argued that the radiator wouldn't have blown if they hadn't been driving for twenty-four hours straight. Sierra wasn't buying the logic. And things didn't improve from there. Halfway through her corncakes, Rachel discarded every pretense of Christian charity. She ranted about debt and death and disloyalty. Tightly gripping his wife's hand, Dennis glared at the girls across the table. "If you're not willing to split the repair bill, we feel you two should leave."

"And go where?" Sierra asked. "We're in Lynchburg-fucking-Virginia!"

"Do not cuss at us. Honor our deal or you can find your own way to DC."

"You," Sierra barked, jumping out of the booth, "can kiss my all-American ass!"

With that, she yanked down her pants and wagged her naked behind in Dennis's stunned face. Rachel slapped a hand over her husband's eyes. A redneck at the counter dropped his coffee cup.

Ten minutes later, encircled by freezing 8:00 a.m. air, Sierra and Gilly were on an on-ramp to US-29 clutching a hastily assembled red-white-and-blue sign.

WASHINGTON OR BUST.

5

"I WOULD HAPPILY OFFER a cogent explanation if I could but I cannot," Zayd told his Penn roommate, "I know only that I feel an inexplicable pull to be present. My Uncle Mo'ez reminds often that one should live a life devoid of regret – so I am off."

Nestled into his Greyhound bus seat, heading from Philadelphia to DC, Zayd was writing in the journal he was determined to maintain during his time in the States.

Perhaps I am romanticizing it, but having been raised amid ceaseless oppression, to be in this country at this moment, after the people have freely elected a young black man as president with a woman vice-president…this day in America feels to me like a miracle. It is why I must be in DC. My sole fear? How I am to survive when the bus station clock declared it to be 19 degrees Fahrenheit? Never previously had I known such frigid air actually exists.

With a weighty exhale Zayd closed his notebook and then closed his eyes.

Roused by the bus's hissing brakes, stiff from the three-and-a-half hour ride, he checked his watch. It was 1:20 a.m. as they pulled into the Massachusetts Avenue station. Beside Zayd, the previously silent woman who smelled like maple syrup gave a serene smile. "Coming to town for the inauguration, I imagine?"

"Yes, ma'am. How best I am to find the United States Capitol? I am a student at the University of Pennsylvania and have only been in your country for three weeks."

"You're not a terrorist, are ya?" the woman asked warily. Zayd promised he wasn't so she went on: "Capitol's about a fifteen, twenty minute walk. Get out to 1st Street and follow the signs. 'Course nothing's happening for hours and it's freezing out there; I'd bring ya to my son's place but, to be frank, he's not keen on you Arabs. Says it's the price you're charging for your oil that's driving our country to the poorhouse."

Not knowing how to respond, Zayd went mute. The woman glided off to find her son.

Stepping onto her front stoop to collect the morning paper, Gina wondered if she'd made a critical mistake. Even with the sky still dark, a rumble of distant voices rolled off the horizon; more cars than usual filled the neighborhood streets.

Back inside, Gina found her houseguest Russell Scott at the kitchen table. Clad in a thick robe and Ugg slippers, he sported a three-day beard and a nest of bed-hair.

"I hope we haven't miscalculated," she whispered as her husband and children slept upstairs. "Seems the whole city's already on the move. With the crowds and security and all the craziness they're anticipating, I wonder if we'll still be able to make it to our designated spot?"

"Swearing in's not 'til noon; we'll be fine." Russell poured himself more coffee.

The path from Los Angeles to Gina's Georgetown kitchen had been a twisted route for Russell. There were many recent days when he was fairly positive he wouldn't be returning to Washington at all. Lazlo Polchek, the line producer on what was hoped to be Russell's feature film directorial debut, had reached Russell at the DC Red Roof on January 2nd to report that he'd secured replacement funding for the budget they'd lost the previous week, but that had hardly been the end of the challenges.

One top-billed supporting player got busted for his second DUI and was ordered into a forty-five day rehab, forcing him out of the movie. His departure sparked a bout of cold feet from leading lady Jennifer Durazo. Immediately after Lazlo got her placated, the first assistant director got into a fender bender on Fairfax. His air bag deployed, breaking his arm in two places. The required surgery and recovery would keep him, too, off the production.

In the meantime, Russell had contacted Gina. He was returning to Washington where his film was set to shoot footage of the inauguration. In an effort to cut expenses, he hoped Gina might offer him a place to crash. Once they connected she did all that and more.

At her husband's urging, Gina promised Russell a coveted ticket to the VIP area at the foot of the Capitol steps, the closest civilian vantage point to the ceremony. An FBI colleague of Gina's had given the Zagers her tickets after learning she'd be overseas on Inauguration Day. Hearing Russell was arriving camera in hand, Noah insisted Gina take the young auteur in his stead. Noah promised he'd be quite content, and a whole lot warmer, watching the pomp and circumstance on TV. Russell was ecstatic.

Given the way her year had started, Gina was grateful for the distraction the inauguration and Russell's visit were providing. At the beginning of the month, she'd learned her mother had terminal cancer that started in her pancreas and spread to the liver. Gina had flown to LA to spend a week with her mom; as she was leaving, she promised to return in early February. Of course no one knew how much time Lisa had left but even in the week Gina was with her, her rapid decline was heartbreaking.

Sitting at her mother's bedside, watching her sleep through most of a Wednesday, Gina had a difficult time reconciling this nearly translucent figure with the formidable woman who had raised her. She recalled when, as a ten-year-old, she'd suffered multiple seizures induced by a potentially lethal knot of blood vessels on her brain. Lisa fought like Godzilla to ensure Gina received the best possible care. During the arduous months of recovery and rehabilitation that followed, Lisa never wavered in her determination to fully restore her daughter's health.

Now, despite wishing there was some miraculous way to return the favor, Gina was forcing herself to accept that Lisa was slipping away. Decades at the FBI taught her how to skillfully mask her emotions but on that cloudy afternoon in LA, Gina took her sleeping mother's hand and allowed herself a long cry.

Russell's announcement that he was heading up to shower brought Gina back to the present. She advised him to dress in every bit of flannel and thermal he had. "All I keep hearing is how unbearably freezing it'll be out there all day long."

Walking up 23rd Street as the sun began its post-dawn climb, Sierra smiled at the shivering Gilly. From every direction, steady masses of wrapped patriots were floating along multi-pronged paths toward the Capitol. "It's looks like *Night of the Living Dead* out here." Sierra said with a laugh.

The people around, ahead of and behind them were swaddled in scarves, knit caps, hoods or festive 'church hats' and huge coats; fleece-lined boots encased their feet. Many clutched miniature American flags. Several were festooned with Obama campaign buttons, hoisting signs declaring the dawn of a new era.

A man with a card table at the edge of the sidewalk hawked boxes bearing the incoming president's beaming face. "Ten bucks! Don't miss out," he barked as he uncorked a glass bottle and waved it in the air. "Obama Cologne! Smell the hope!"

Pulling her plaid scarf across the lower half of her face so only her eyes were exposed, Sierra was relieved to have made it to Washington in tact. Standing on a freeway ramp in Lynchburg in the early-morning frost, she wasn't sure how things would turn out. After fleeing from the crazy Christian couple demanding payment for auto troubles Sierra and Gilly had no hand in causing, the girls spent three arctic hours waving their "Washington or bust" sign before a car stopped. It was a late-model Lexus driven by a traveling salesman who looked better suited to be riding Seabiscuit. Later when they talked about it, Sierra chuckled to Gilly in disbelief. "Wasn't he the teeniest man ever? Not like a midget or a dwarf – perfectly proportioned! I wanted to stick a lantern in his hand and put him out on my lawn!"

Continuing onto K Street, Sierra recalled the second ride their thumbs had hooked. The Jeep Cherokee of a UVA senior named Luke traveling with his roommates Matthew and Mark brought them from Charlottesville to DC. The driver announced the single condition for securing a ride: "First time either of you cracks an apostle joke, you're out."

When the girls at last arrived at Gilly's parents' friends' home, they did an elegant verbal tap dance to explain why their 'bus' was four hours late. Then at their hosts' urging, they each enjoyed a long hot shower, ate delicious lasagna and crashed in the king-sized guestroom bed. After a blessed seven hours of sleep, they slipped out at sunrise.

Now, moving with the crowd up K Street, they could see the crowning point of the Washington Monument looming in the not-too-distant sky.

"Oh my God, isn't this fantabulous?"

Through the gloved hands jammed deep into the pockets of his wool pea coat, Zayd felt the richly appreciated heat from the battery-operated hand warmers he'd purchased on Mass Ave. Considering he'd lost all feeling in his nose and feet, it seemed like an undeniably good idea to get a steaming adrenaline jolt from a Venti black coffee at the nearest Starbucks. What Zayd hadn't anticipated was a line that went out the door and halfway down the block. On this particular morning in the nation's seat of power, the only way to get in out of the cold was to stand in a slow-moving queue with a like-minded legion of caffeine deprived patriots.

Zayd departed the bus station just after 2:00 a.m. and wandered to the Capitol to witness the final bits of preparation. Myriad security checkpoints surrounded kiosks of souvenirs at every turn. They were selling bootleg DVDs of "The Historic Road to the White House," T-shirts, commemorative coins and bobble-headed Baracks. Taking in the sights and smells surrounding him, Zayd kept moving to stay awake.

Now a little after 7:00 a.m., he found himself in a thick throng of people stopped dead. In the distance behind him he could see the phallic Washington Monument. Ahead was the Capitol where the swearing in would take place.

"What is happening?" he asked the pair of brown eyes beside him. Zayd wondered if the rest of this woman was as attractive as her luminous eyes. With the plaid scarf covering the bottom half of the girl's face and the Sherpa hat enveloping her head and ears, she looked like a mobile mummy.

"No clue," came the muffled reply. "Probably another security checkpoint. They're everywhere today."

Looking ahead, Zayd eyed the unyielding backs of people of every size, shape, color and age, all trying to get to the same place at the same time; nobody was moving. "I cannot believe the crowd is already this enormous. How many you would estimate?"

"It's gonna be more than a million today," the muffled girl said.

"That is amazing to me. By the way, I am called Zayd."

The girl inched her scarf to her chin and returned the smile. "Sierra. And this is Gilly. I love your accent; where're y'all from?"

"Iraq."

"Awesome. Saadam Hussein, right? Didn't know he let you guys out."

"I am on a student visa. They are paying for my education in exchange for my pledge to return home to accept state employment when I am finished."

"Wow, so they basically took out a mortgage on ya, huh? No bueno."

Confused, Zayd shrugged. "I came to New York City to visit my uncle eight years past and knew then I very much wanted to return for university."

"Well, Zayd-from-Iraq, please allow me and Gilly to be your US Ambassadors today; it'll be our personal mission to see that you have a kick-ass time in DC!"

Unclipping the Obama/Wegemer pin from the collar of her knee-length down coat, Sierra turned to Zayd. "May I?" He nodded; she pinned on the campaign button to his lapel. "Welcome to Washington."

Stopped at a security checkpoint far back from where her coveted purple tickets permitted her to be, Gina could feel her temper flaring. "We can't get down there? What's the point of having tickets if they don't mean anything?" To accent her point, she waved the paper pair in the policeman's face.

"I appreciate your frustration, ma'am, but crowds are larger than anticipated; there's a huge human traffic jam up ahead. We're being told it's not safe to let anyone else move forward at the present time."

"I've worked for the FBI for more than twenty years. Believe me, I'm perfectly capable of handling myself in a mob."

"I'm sure you are, but I still can't let you through."

Feeling Gina's surging ire, Russell put a calming hand on her shoulder. "It's cool. No matter where we are we'll be able to catch the action on the monitors. For real, it's fine; in show biz, adaptability is the only way to survive. Whatever I get will be golden."

The officer told Gina it would behoove her to listen to her son. Gina held her tongue but she wanted to tell him she wasn't *nearly* old enough to be Russell's mother – and, besides, what gave him the right to use the word "behoove?"

"Perfect," Russell declared looking through his viewfinder as they stood amid a throng waiting for the ceremony to start. "Probably better than being up front." Gina thought he was only saying that to make her feel better but Russell went on, "No, from a filmmaking standpoint, this'll be easier to match. Considering my budget, we lucked out."

On the giant monitors mounted every couple hundred yards from the Capitol steps to the Lincoln Memorial, the cameras picked up shots of dignitaries and celebrities moving to their seats on the Inaugural platform. Russell shifted his Red camera from his left shoulder to his right, taking great care not to knock out the girl in the plaid scarf beside him.

"Is that awful?" Gina asked. "Having to lug that around all day? I don't know the first thing about movie making but the whole process looks like a nightmare."

"It is," Russell agreed, "but it beats the hell out of working for a living."

"Believe me, I feel the same way about the FBI."

"Hold up," said the plaid scarf girl. "I promise I didn't mean to eavesdrop, but… you work for the FBI? That's SO rad. How many bad guys have you smoked?"

When Gina confessed she'd never killed anyone, the girl looked a little disappointed; a beat later, she extended a hand to Gina. "Oh well. Since it looks like we'll be smushed together all day, I'm Sierra; this is Gilly – we came up from Texas. And that's Zayd – student at Penn, native of Iraq. He has to go back after graduation to work for Saddam; isn't that hectic?"

Following a round of handshakes and greetings, Zayd stomped his feet in a futile attempt to bring feeling back to his near-frozen toes. Gazing at him, Gina smiled. There was a light in his eyes and an open radiance in his face that instantly made her feel safe with him.

"How old are you, Zayd?"

"Eighteen years, Missus."

"How does an eighteen year old Iraqi decide to come to the United States to attend college? Your family's upper-class, I'm assuming…"

"My father is a surgeon, we are hardly aristocrats, but more prosperous than many. My mother and late grandmother held a deep fascination with your country that they passed along to me. As I told these ladies, I was here on holiday eight years prior and became determined to return. My father would have preferred I remain at home to follow him into medicine but he has come to accept my choice; my mother, she is a very persuasive woman."

Gina shared that much of her work at the FBI had been focused on the Middle East. "And I did my semester abroad in Amman as an undergrad. Such a fascinating and complex part of the world." Zayd concurred. Gina turned to Sierra and Gilly. "So what drew you two here today?"

Gilly jumped in, "Ever heard of the guy who kept President Kennedy – John, not Bobby – from being assassinated?" Gina asked if she was talking about the incident in Dallas and Gilly nodded exuberantly. "That was Sierra's granddaddy."

"Wait," said Russell, "I remember hearing something about that…what was the deal?"

"I was only three months old," Gina said, "but my family talked about it often; my Uncle David especially. He was a USC history professor and he'd ruminate about how different the world might be if the assassination hadn't been thwarted. How wild he was your grandfather. Remind me his name?"

"Ed Callahan."

"Of course! Oh my God, wait 'til I tell David I met you."

Sierra turned to Russell and Zayd, "President Kennedy was in Dallas; his parade was passing the Book Depository where my Poppy worked. Poppy went upstairs to look for his lost lighter right when the parade was going by and he saw this man – Oswald something – in the window with a rifle; Poppy knocked him away before he could shoot. After President Kennedy got reelected, he gave Poppy the Medal of Freedom; he and Granny came here to meet JFK and Jackie. It was the first time Granny had been on an airplane, isn't that hilarious? She still has a napkin and an ashtray she got at the White House, plus the medal, duh. She said Mrs. Kennedy was the most elegant lady ever. Anyway, hearing about their trip made me want to do something like it, too. Also, if y'all want the truth, I think Barack is hot." Sierra looked to Gina and Russell. "How do you two know each other?"

"Quite the saga, actually," Gina sighed. "His dad was the doctor who saved my life when I was a child."

"Why, what was wrong with you?" Sierra asked. "If it's not too personal."

"Nothing eight hours of brain surgery and two years of rehab couldn't cure. It was very scary, especially for my poor parents." There was a catch in Gina's throat; she wiped her stinging nose. "Sorry. It's just…my mom's dying of cancer out in LA."

Russell dove into the awkward silence. "You know, if there's anything you want me to bring back to her, I'm happy to pay a visit when I get home."

Sierra smiled. "You're from LA, too? Guess that explains the fancy-ass camera. What's the dealio? Are you making a movie?"

Russell informed her he was there to grab crowd footage to use in the climax of his upcoming feature film.

"So…what…you're, like, the director?" Sierra asked.

"Yup. And the writer…and part-time cameraman…."

When Gilly and Sierra hopped in front of Russell striking a pose, requesting to be in the movie, Russell told them they already were.

On the flickering video screens surrounding them, California's senior senator delivered her welcoming remarks. Each cutaway to images of the attentive crush of humanity served as a vivid reminder of how cold it was. Visible breath, shivering bodies, chattering teeth, thermal blankets, glistening furs…yet not one person was attempting to leave. After each speaker there was gleeful, spontaneous chanting and singing. Many people had tears in their eyes all day.

Moving gingerly, the eighty-year-old Reverend Martin Luther King Jr. stepped up to give the invocation in his rich baritone as a million-and-a-half people stood in awed silence. When the eloquent prayer ended, a blonde pop star with a chillingly powerful voice stepped up to sing "My Country Tis of Thee." By the time she held the last sustained note, the clapping of gloved hands along with the whistles of appreciation created a deafening din.

With the program finally rolling, things were happening swiftly. An elderly female Supreme Court justice administered the oath to the new vice-president, Gail Wegemer as her husband and two grown children stood nearby. "A woman swearing in a woman," Sierra crowed. "Wow. Can't believe it took this long."

As the entertainment resumed, Sierra, Gilly, Zayd, Russell and Gina filled each other in on additional biographical bits, trading anecdotes, connecting over shared cultural touchstones. They realized how narrow and ill informed their assumptions were about Zayd's life in Iraq.

"Don't your mother and sister totally hate having to wear a *burqa*?" Sierra asked.

Zayd laughed, informing her that neither his mother nor his sister had ever been near a *burqa*. Out in public, they wore modest dresses but at home, Zayd told them, his mother was usually in jeans. Gilly wondered how women got along without driving and once again Zayd countered: "In my country, a greater number of women drive automobiles than men. And more women than ever are attending university."

Gina smiled at Gilly, Sierra and Russell, "Amazing how quickly stereotypes get upended when we actually talk to each other."

Shortly after noon, Chief Justice Jonathan David stepped up to the incoming president as Michelle Obama, resplendent in yellow, held the bible used to swear in Abraham Lincoln. The crowd began a swelling chant of "this is it!" Every hair on Russell's exposed forearm stood up.

On the podium, surviving ex-presidents Tanner, Conrad and Rice sat together with RFK's widow Ethel as the Chief Justice swore in Barack Hussein Obama as the forty-fourth president of the United States. Tears freely flowed down the pink faces of Gina, Sierra and Gilly. Russell sniffled but never fully succumbed.

When Obama began his inaugural address, nearly every other one of the million-and-a-half voices was stilled. In the quiet, acutely aware of the wind's sharp sting, Gina had a sudden image of her shriveled mother in her sickbed. Forcing herself back to the unfolding moment, she heard Obama say: "Our economy is badly weakened, a consequence of greed and irresponsibility on the part of some, but also our collective failure to make hard choices and prepare the nation for a new age."

"Good luck with that," Russell snorted. "The rich will keep getting richer because they control the politicians."

"You wait," Sierra protested, "my Barack is gonna change all that."

Russell turned to Gina with a cynical smirk, "Ah, the innocence of youth!"

Gina pressed a finger to her lips and nodded at the podium. The president's voice reverberated through the plethora of speakers surrounding them.

Gina gazed around. To the right, a mesmerized young woman clutched a handmade sign reading, "You may say I'm a dreamer...I'm not the only one." A few feet back, a heavy-set man wore a T-shirt over his parka featuring Obama in boxing gloves and satin shorts looming over a flattened Norman Tanner. Gina couldn't help but be moved by the awed admiration on the multicultural faces surrounding her.

Not dodging the harsh realities of the threats from global terror, the president said, "To the Muslim world, we seek a new way forward, based on mutual interest and mutual respect."

Sierra beamed at Zayd: "Hear that, doodley; he's talking to you."

Zayd smiled and nodded as Obama continued: "Your people will judge you on what you build, not on what you destroy."

Gina shuddered. Russell put a hand on her shoulder, asking if she was okay.

"I'm just..." Gina struggled to maintain composure. "I guess after so many years at the FBI, knowing all the evil that's out there...seeing these hopeful, optimistic faces...I just, I so want to believe a day like today can last."

The rising cadence of the president's words signaled he was nearing the end of his address: "...and with eyes fixed on the horizon, and God's grace upon us, we carried forth the great gift of freedom and delivered it safely to future generations."

A sustained roar of applause and trilling whoops exploded in the frosty air. The president smiled and waved acknowledging every portion of his vast audience. The speech was followed by an awkward poem, a whimsical benediction and the US Navy band's rendition of the National Anthem. And then the program was over.

The presidential party retreated into the warmth of the Capitol. The invited dignitaries began their slow exit. The other million-plus people that had risen before dawn slowly started to drift away, too numb to feel many parts of their bodies.

A giddy Sierra looked to her new friends. "A-mazing! History! Yay us."

Continuing to capture the surrounding sights and sounds through his camera lens, Russell fixed on one of the many blue beach balls being kept aloft by batting hands slapping it skyward. Each ball had Obama's name on one side and a slogan on the other: "Keep Hope Afloat."

"My mom would've loved everything about today," Gina said. "Will you folks excuse me? I want to call to give her the headlines while it's all still fresh."

Gina pulled her phone from the pocket of her big coat and punched the contact tab beside the picture of her gray-haired mom and dad. Glancing over Gina's shoulder, Sierra laughed. "Oh my God, they're so adorable."

When someone picked up on the other end, Gina voice danced in delight. "David – perfect!" Momentarily moving the phone away from her ear she looked to Sierra. "It's my Uncle David, the professor!" Bringing the phone up again, she plugged her other ear with her index finger for the best chance to hear over the rumbling crowd. "You'll never guess who I'm with… Yes! I'm still here, might be for hours…the crowd is – oh right, of course you're watching. No, we never got anywhere near where we were supposed to be. Noah isn't with me; I'm with Russell Scott, Brian's son. Yes, the filmmaker. I'm impressed you remember."

Sierra lurched up to bat one of the beach balls away in order to keep it from landing on the preoccupied Gina's head. "Wait, first let me tell you one quick thing: I met Ed Callahan's granddaughter. She's right here with me… Yes, *that* Ed Callahan! Incredible, isn't it? I told her you'd be thrilled. She and a friend from Dallas are with the sweetest young man from Iraq." She smiled at Zayd. "That's a whole other story. What an amazing day, David. Beyond description."

Hearing David say something she couldn't grasp, Gina felt an electric shockwave zap her heart. Zayd was the first to notice Gina standing frozen with her mouth agape. "I'm sorry…what do you mean? When?" Her voice became a broken whisper. "Oh God. I'm…wait, how's Dad?"

When Gina's call ended, Zayd, Sierra, Gilly and Russell formed a protective circle around her offering muffled condolences. Still absorbing the news, Gina nodded, speechless, as the inauguration spectators continued to ooze away. "I know I'm not the first to say this, but no matter how much you prepare, it's still an absolute shock. How can something so expected be so stunning?"

Russell took one of Gina's gloved hands as his other hand steadied the camera on his shoulder. "My dad always said your mom was a great lady. He wished all his patients had an advocate as ferocious as her when you had your brain thing."

With the tide of red-white-and-blue inaugural attendees inching past, Sierra gazed at Gina with an empathetic smile. "When Poppy Ed died, I was only thirteen; I'd never been to a funeral and was totally freaked out. The biggest shock was how much everybody laughed that day. I mean, people were sad for sure, but he was such a great guy and there were so many great stories; that's what everybody focused on. I bet that's how it'll be with your mom, too."

As the group commiserated, a young man a few feet ahead in the dispersing throng unwittingly captured Zayd's attention. He was tall and thin and so pale he looked like a phantom. Despite the biting cold, the fur-lined hood of his olive parka was down and his ears were peppermint pink against his white-blonde hair. He set his stuffed backpack at his feet as he addressed a young mother toting her year-old baby in a carrier strapped to her chest. The baby wore a canary-colored snowsuit with a matching yellow-and-white knit hat covering her ears. When the crowd made a sudden forward surge, the skinny kid pushed ahead absently leaving his backpack behind, preoccupied as he bid goodbye to the baby's attractive mother.

Zayd jogged forward and snatched the abandoned bag from the ground. He called out to its oblivious owner: "Excuse me, friend! You have forgotten your bag!"

Turning toward Zayd, the white-blonde's face filled with panic. Spying the hoisted backpack, the kid whirled forward and broke into a desperate run. Furiously shoving people out of his way, he was sculpting a path where there wasn't one. Pulling a phone from his pocket, the ghost fumbled to punch the keypad. In his frenzied determination to keep moving, the phone got knocked from his grasp. The chaos he was creating ignited a backlash of people jostling him in resistance. He made a dive for the phone but before he could retrieve it, it was crushed under the heel of a rushing Rhode Island reveler.

Sierra and Gilly turned to a bewildered Zayd clutching the orphaned backpack. Gilly urged him to see what was in it; when Zayd resisted, Sierra tugged at the bag's zipper. Up ahead, its owner disappeared, leaving a wave of agitated humanity in his wake.

Peering into the bag Zayd was confused. The satchel contained some sort of slow-cook device like the Crockpot his beloved *BB* Rima kept on her counter in Baghdad. Eying the backpack's contents, Sierra felt no such uncertainty. With a shrill shriek she cried out, "Oh my god, it's a bomb!"

Madness flared in a flash. Spying Zayd and the bag, a man shouted, "Terrorist! Get him!"

The young mother, afraid of her baby being crushed in the ensuing stampede, simply froze. Caught in her own paralyzing panic, Sierra couldn't process how rapidly everything escalated. Two men dove on Zayd and yanked him to the ground. A guy with his face painted like the American flag grabbed the bag, tugged out the device and began to recklessly rip out wires, spilling nails and other bits of would-be shrapnel. Russell passed his weighty camera to Gilly, ordering her to keep it aimed at the melee as he dove in to rescue Zayd. To Gina, still reeling from news of her mother's death, nothing was computing.

The infuriated man sat on Zayd's chest repeatedly slamming his fists into the Iraqi's face while his buddy in an army surplus jacket kicked Zayd's ribs. Russell tugged on Infuriated Man's collar, attempting to get him to cease the brutal beating. Sierra burst into tears.

"He didn't do anything," Russell bellowed. "It's not his backpack!"

Scores of people were screaming, reeling, shoving; the deafening din encircled all of them. Most folks were doing anything possible to escape. There was no sense to be made, no peace to be negotiated. The area was swallowed by wholesale panic. Parents grabbed kids too big to be carried, clutching them to their chests. One man thundered by with a child under each arm like a determined quarterback pushing downfield.

A swarm of DC policemen with guns drawn charged into the center of the insanity pointing their weapons at Zayd's bloody head. Regaining her voice, Gina screeched above the cacophonous roar with thundering authority. "Stop! Everybody stop! He didn't do anything!"

Miraculously, for a split second there was silence. Infuriated Man quit punching. Army Jacket stopped kicking. Russell ceased tugging. The police, with arms outstretched and fingers wrapped tightly around their triggers, kept their guns trained on Zayd's face. That unexpected beat of tense quiet lasted for a holy eternity.

Damming up the powerful swell of emotion threatening to strangle her, Gina breathlessly huffed out one word between each desperate breath, "The...person...who left...this device... escaped. They're...attacking...an innocent man."

Two policemen pulled Infuriated Man to his feet. Another officer subdued Army Jacket. A third cop reached under Zayd's armpits, ordering him to not make any sudden moves. Zayd couldn't summon the words to tell them he was barely capable of moving at all. Russell stepped in to steady Zayd but a federal marshal eased Russell aside, assuring him he and his men would handle things. Two cops barked questions in Zayd's face; Russell answered for him. "Look, a skinny blonde guy left that backpack and took off. Zayd only wanted to return it to him; he had no idea what was in it. None of us did."

Zayd looked to the cop propping him up. "Please, sir, I must be seated." Zayd's eyes were nearly swollen shut; blood was leaking from one ear. Deep cuts ran down each cheek like fissured earthquake faults. Guided by the officer, flanked by Young Mother and Russell, Zayd was slowly lowered onto a cold iron bench on the Capitol walkway. A tumbling Keep Hope Afloat beach ball passed overhead and got lost in the white-streaked sky.

Gathered in a makeshift holding area under a canopy that began the day as a security checkpoint, a team of DC Metropolitan policemen and FBI agents took statements. Sierra, Gilly, Russell, Army Jacket, Infuriated Man, Flag Face and Young Mother huddled with their interrogators. Zayd sat on a gurney nearby as a paramedic tended to his multiple wounds. Gina remained outside the assembly speaking in hushed tones to one of her FBI cohorts. "I know nothing's official until all evidence has been collected and corroborated, but it seems eminently clear that the trampled cellphone was intended to be the device's detonator. I never got a sufficient look at the young man — as you may have heard, I'd just received word my mother passed away this afternoon in Los Angeles—"

The tall agent offered his condolences.

"Thank you; I've yet to even process it. I mean, after twenty years at the bureau, this is hardly my first tough day."

Scanning Gina's face, the agent issued a soft chuckle of recognition. "Hold on, you're the agent Dan Motolla screwed over when he grabbed the credit for your work in thwarting the 2001 planned hit on the Trade Center, am I right?"

Gina demurred, "I suppose, but if we can focus – "

The FBI man clapped a warm hand on Gina's bicep. "If it's any consolation, anybody who really matters knows exactly what you did."

"Thank you. But again: today. You need to be clear that Zayd Ahmed was an innocent bystander simply attempting to do a good deed."

The January sun was sinking out of sight when the law enforcement personnel released Army Jacket, Flag Face and Infuriated Man. Unlike Humpty Dumpty, Zayd had been put back together again. The only thing he required now was time to heal.

Russell allowed the authorities to make a copy of the footage he'd shot that day in the hope that they might find a clear image of the would-be backpack bomber somewhere in the prolific crowd shots.

Sierra, Gilly, Gina, Russell and Zayd clustered together, forever bonded by the incredible highs and shocking lows of this infinite day. Their voices were leaden, hushed, thoroughly spent. Rubbing the back of her neck, Sierra realized her drooping eyelids felt incredibly heavy.

Sierra and Gilly made Russell promise they'd be invited to his film's premiere. Russell asked Gina to notify him once they finalized plans for her mother's funeral in LA; he knew his father would want to be there. Gina offered Zayd an open door if he ever wanted to return to DC; it would be her honor to escort him on a much less traumatic tour of the capital. She handed him her FBI business card. Zayd carefully bended his battered fingers to slip it into his coat pocket.

As the group was saying their final goodbyes, Young Mother appeared from the cove she'd created to nurse her infant. She shyly stepped up to Zayd, tears gleaming in her bloodshot eyes. Through the swollen slits of his own dark eyes, Zayd fixed on the child swaddled in a blissful afterglow lit by her belly full of mother's milk.

"If it wasn't for you, we would have both been killed. My daughter and I were right next to that guy for the longest time. His backpack was only inches behind me." Young Mother choked on her emotion. "My daughter would have been blown to bits."

Gina stepped up to wrap a protective arm over Young Mother's shoulder. "But you're fine. You're both beautiful and fine." Gina trained her gaze on Zayd as she continued to address the woman. "Thanks to this remarkable young man, we all get to go home to our loved ones."

After a long beat studying the baby's serene face, Gina reached out to gently stroke the child's cheek stained red by the day's chafing wind. "I can tell you're a special one. I can't wait to see who you'll grow up to be."

ACKNOWLEDGEMENTS

Great Gratitude to the Book Building Construction Crew:

My diligent UC Riverside CWPA MFA research assistants, Victor Zamora and Eric Montgomery.

My medical consultant, Dr. Carol Zaher

My Vietnam consultant, R. Miles Hyland

My 2009 Inauguration consultants, Tod Goldberg and Marc Sandalow

Our Washington, D.C. four-star hosts, Tom & Dr. Ellie Hamburger

My smart & generous Middle East consultant, Yasser Shahin

My mentor and the man responsible for my joyful journey into academia, Lawrence Turman

And for the fabulous book cover design, thank you Joe Chang

To my colleagues in the UC Riverside Department of Theatre, Film & Digital Production: thank you for teaching me daily that an old dog really can learn new tricks.

Profound Thanks to the "Bringing the book to life" crew:

Enormous appreciation to the stellar Publishizer team, Lee Constantine, Guy Vincent and Ylva Monsen. A million thanks for finding me and supporting me through the process.

Lauren Hughes, my assessment editor. I so appreciate all you had to say.

The Artful Editor team: Naomi Eagelson Long and Jonathan Starke. Thank you, Jonathan, for your insights, intelligence and the amazing line notes.

And to the folks at Harvard Square Editions. Eternal gratitude!

More books from Harvard Square Editions